'So, you're better.' Thpletely by surprise. She
ing the rug around her t

Kemp was standing in
hand, his eyes alight with
and clinging to his body.

'Why did you move my gown?' she asked breathlessly.
'You have no right . . .'

'I had every right.' He took a step nearer her. Her pulse
began to race as his eyes travelled over her body. 'I have
thrown a lot more overboard than an expensive gown,
Elaine. I threw your lands and title, your inheritance, your
wealth and your wedding ring.' His eyes gleamed as she
held up her hand where her finger was bare of its gold band.
'From now on you are a pirate's woman!'

Kate Buchan was born in Nottingham and educated in Hertfordshire and at Edinburgh University, where she read history. She then worked for various publishers before becoming a freelance editor. During this period she began writing short stories and articles, and in due course she gave up editing to write full time.

Buccaneer Bride is her fifth Masquerade Historical Romance, and was written while living—with her husband, two sons and seven cats—in a rambling, pink-washed Tudor farmhouse not far from the lovely old town of Woodbridge and the beautiful Suffolk marshes, which are the setting for this story.

BUCCANEER BRIDE

Kate Buchan

MILLS & BOON LIMITED
15–16 BROOK'S MEWS
LONDON W1A 1DR

First published in Great Britain 1986 by Mills & Boon Limited

© Kate Buchan 1986

Australian copyright 1986 Philippine copyright 1986 This edition 1986 ISBN 0 263 75479 0

Set in 9½ on 10 pt Linotron Times 04–0886–88,600

Photoset by Rowland Phototypesetting Limited, Bury St Edmunds, Suffolk Made and printed in Great Britain by Cox and Wyman Limited, Reading

PROLOGUE

THE TIDE had turned. Already little eddies of mud were appearing at the edge of the salt grass and the wind was veering. Elaine Howard felt it on her cheek as she stood, swathed in a dark cloak, at the river's edge watching the ship drop her lines and begin to ease her way out into the main current of the deserted river. It would soon be nightfall.

On deck Elaine could see the silent men standing by the ratlines and clinging high in the rigging as the dark sails dropped soundlessly from the yardarms and bellied before the wind, giving the vessel steerage on the tide. No pennant or flag flew from the raked masts, and no name showed on the blackened planking of her hull.

A lone figure stood erect on the quarterdeck, his face like carved stone as he turned his ship down-river towards the sea. Elaine ran a few steps along the bank, her shoes slipping on the grass, still straining her eyes for Tom, but even now there was no sign of him, and she blinked back her tears, her gaze drawn inexorably to that single figure. Tall and broad-shouldered, he radiated sinister power, his eyes coolly surveying the darkening river ahead. Abruptly his gaze shifted towards the shore and for an instant she felt it rest on her. Then he turned his head away as the ship moved silently off into the dark.

In the shadow of the trees, a second figure had been watching the vessel leave. As he stepped forward, impatiently parting the fronds of willow to see better, he stopped, catching sight of Elaine for the first time. At once he drew back so that she should not notice him, and studied her. At that distance he could see nothing but the dark green cloak, the soft hood pulled well up over her hair and held fast with one hand as she raised the other to her eyes, trying to focus on the dark shape as it vanished into the night. Only the slap of water against the ship's prow as she gathered speed betrayed her presence in the distance.

He moved forward stealthily, his soft leather boots making no sound on the dew-wet grass, his hand on the hilt of his sword as he stopped about five feet from her. The cloak still concealed everything about her save her stature, which was slight.

'Mistress! A word with you, if you please!' His voice was harsh in the silence.

Elaine spun round. He had an impression of huge amber-coloured eyes in a small oval face and long silken hair the shade of ripe wheat as her hood slipped back. The slim figure wore a servant's plain dress and apron, and he had a swift impression of skin as fine and pale as that on any woman he had ever seen. Momentarily stunned by this unexpected vision of beauty, he did not move. And in that second she whirled out of his reach and fled up the bank.

As he gathered his wits and turned to follow her, the sound of a horse's hooves echoed over the dry ground. He glimpsed a fleeting shadow as a horse leapt away through the trees, and she was gone.

He did not bother to chase her. He would never catch her now; his own horse was liveried at an inn in Woodbridge and he had left it when he strolled down the River Deben from the bustling quays and boatyards, curious to follow up the rumour about the ship anchored below Kingston Point.

Sir Edward Brandon, pirate-catcher to his grace King Henry VIII, turned back thoughtfully to where the vessel had slipped out of sight. If, as he suspected, this was the pirate ship, maybe that young woman had a friend or a lover on board. He smiled softly to himself. It would not be hard to find her again in Woodbridge; hers was a face he would not forget, and once he had her, his job would be easy. It only took one lead, one member of the crew or their family to betray the others. And it was a very exceptional man—or woman—who could resist the methods of persuasion available to him in the dungeons of the King's castles as he travelled round the coasts of England.

He smiled as he began to walk thoughtfully back towards the lights of Woodbridge. Tomorrow he would introduce himself to the rich merchants who had begged the King for help and begin to buy in supplies of wool, cloth and grain, spices and rich silks and wines for the royal storehouses— the reason he always gave to explain his presence in the ports of the realm. Tomorrow his hunt for the pirates who haunted this particular shore would begin. But this time his quest would be a little different from the usual, for it was on his own doorstep, in Suffolk, and in addition to the duty he performed for the King was another—far more pleasurable—for himself. Tomorrow he would meet the woman who had topped his list of possible brides; the daughter of one of the richest merchants in Suffolk; the woman he had chosen to be his wife.

CHAPTER
ONE

ELAINE HAD been woken that late May morning by the rattle of wooden rings as the heavy tapestry curtains were thrown back and the clear dawn light flooded into the room. For a moment she lay still beneath the embroidered tester, still dazed with sleep, then she sat up abruptly, clutching the bedclothes to her near-naked shoulders as she saw a figure standing at the window, pushing back the shutters.

'Tom? Is that you? What are you doing here?'

'Sssh!' At the sound of her voice, her brother turned and put his finger to his lips, conscious of her maid asleep in the ante-room. He left the window and came to perch on the edge of her bed.

'I had to talk to you, Elaine. Listen, sweetheart! I want you to do something for me.' Tom's handsome face was unusually troubled as he looked at his sister propped against the feather pillows, her ash-blonde hair spilt in tangled curls across the sheets.

'What is it? You sound so solemn!' Staring at him, she felt a sudden tremor of fear, thinking automatically of the person dearest to them both. 'Is it something to do with Father?'

He shook his head with a rueful smile. 'Not unless Papa has taken to breaking the King's peace in his old age.' He raised his hand to stop her speaking. 'No, I'm the felon in the family, I'm afraid, and I need your help.' He paused as she stared at him, puzzled by his words. 'I never wanted to tell you all this, sweetheart,' he went on, 'but I think I must.' He frowned, picking at the silk counterpane on her bed. 'Just in case something happens to me, someone here ought to know the truth of where I am, and you are the only person I can tell.'

Her fear deepened as she watched her brother's anxiety,

and pulling her shawl from the bedpost where she had thrown it the night before, she drew it round her shoulders and half knelt up beneath the bedclothes like a child, reaching out her hand to his in her uncertainty.

He gave a tight smile. 'Did you ever hear of the raid on *Santa Maria*?'

'Cousin Richard's ship? Of course I heard. She was attacked by pirates in the North Sea, and he lost everything. I remember him coming to tell Papa about it. He was so angry that I thought he would have apoplexy . . .' Her voice tailed away as she studied her brother's face. 'Why do you ask?'

'I was on the ship which carried out that raid, Elaine. In fact she is half mine. It was I who planned where to strike, and when.'

Elaine went white. 'No, I don't believe you. Dear God, Tom, men died on that ship! Tell me it isn't true!' She slumped back on her heels as she studied her brother's face.

'I'm afraid it is true, sweetheart.' His strong hands gripped hers suddenly. 'I wouldn't have had you find out for worlds, but there are reasons you must know. No, you must listen to me!' His hold on her hand began to hurt as she tried to pull free. 'I go on another raid this evening. It may take me away for longer than I intended, so there are two services you must perform for me.'

'No, Tom!' Elaine dragged her hands free at last and threw herself from the bed. 'I won't listen! I don't want to hear any more. If what you say is true, then it's despicable! How could you betray your own family! Oh, Tom, why? And who else? Have you done it to our friends? For all I know, you have robbed Papa's own ships!' As the full horror of his admission sank in, she began to shake uncontrollably. That her beloved brother, whom she had adored all her life, should admit so calmly to being no more than a brutal pirate and a murderer filled her with terror and loathing. It was as if in the space of a few short minutes he had become a stranger to her.

'Elaine, listen . . .

'No!' She raised her hands to her ears and tried to shut

out the sound of his voice. 'No, Tom. Please! Just go away!'

He had followed her across the room. 'Sweet Elaine! Please just try and understand a little. You want to know why I did it? I'll tell you. For excitement; for danger; to relieve these fat, rich men of a small part of their wealth, and with it to buy freedom! Freedom to feel the ship beneath my feet! To travel; to learn to steer by the stars and to ride the wind! To be my own master, not my father's lackey.' He shook her gently. 'Do you know where my future lies? It lies in that counting-house and in the ware-house down by the Deben, collecting money while other men have the adventure. I have begged Papa a thousand times to let me go with the ships to learn my trade, but no, never! "Why go?" he says. "Stay here, Tom, and learn the business end; I need you with me, Tom. One day it will all be yours, Tom." One day! But even while I am at his side learning the trade, I can see he still thinks of me as a child in short coats. Well, on *Black Witch* I am the master, and I make men like my father jump through hoops at my command!'

Elaine looked at him, frozen with horror, seeing for the first time the reckless colour in his cheeks and the wildness in his eyes.

'You sound as if you hate Papa!' she whispered.

Tom shook his head slowly. 'No, that's the strange part. I don't hate him. I would never hurt him if I could help it; you must never think that, Elaine. It is his way of life I hate, and what he has come to stand for.'

'Supposing you are caught?' Her lips had gone dry.

He grinned. 'I won't be.' He saw the softening of her expression, and stooped and kissed her gently on the fore-head. 'I knew you'd understand,' he said softly.

'No, Tom!' She shook her head violently. 'It means that men have died at your hand.' She shuddered. 'You cannot justify murder—and robbery—just . . .' she hesitated, fumbling over the words in her anguish, 'just for excitement and adventure! Oh, Tom, for pity's sake stop it now. Don't go, I beg you.' She clutched at his arms.

'I have to, sweetheart.' He removed her hands gently. 'I'm too much involved. It's my plan; she's half my ship;

my partner needs me and I don't intend to let him down. Now, are you going to help me?'

'Help you?' Elaine stared at him in real horror. 'No, I won't help you! Never! You disgust me!' Tears filled her eyes. 'What would Mama have said if she had known?'

'Mama is long since dead, Elaine,' Tom said harshly. 'And all I am asking is for you to pass a packet of letters to a friend of mine; not so great a burden, surely? It will not involve setting foot outside this house, I assure you, so your pretty conscience will not be in danger.' He tightened his lips with a stubbornness she recognised well.

'And if I refuse?' The set of her own chin matched his as she angrily blinked away the tears.

'You won't refuse.' He reached into his doublet and produced the packet, which he threw down on the bed. 'Her name is Jane Lockesley. Keep them safe, under lock and key. The chances are I shall return before she comes to claim them, but in case anything happens'—a shadow crossed his face for a moment—'I want to be sure she gets them.' He smiled at her pleadingly. 'Please do this for me.'

Elaine stared at him, the anger in her eyes mixed with fear. 'Don't go, Tom. Stay and give them to her yourself. *Please*!'

'I can't, Elaine.'

'You mean you want to go,' she burst out. 'You want to be in danger! You don't care about us! You're being irresponsible and stupid and stubborn! Think about Papa. If he found out, it would kill him. You know it would!'

Tom frowned. 'He must never find out, Elaine. Perhaps I am being irresponsible—all the things you say, but that's the way I am.' He shrugged. 'And, anyway, I'm going on only two more trips, and then I'll sell out my share of *Black Witch* to Guy and come home and be a dutiful son. Does that please you?'

She shook her head. 'Why two more trips, Tom? Why?'

'Because these particular schemes are mine; without my information, we wouldn't be able to go for such big prizes.'

She gasped. 'You mean you use knowledge from Papa; information he's trusted you with?'

'Of course I do. I'm perfectly placed here. I hear everything, not only from Papa and his colleagues, but his rivals too.'

Elaine was white with anger. 'I think you're despicable. I hope you're caught!'

Tom grinned. 'Thank you, sister dear. I'd best be on my way, then. *Witch* lies at Kingston Point. We sail on tonight's tide.' He strode to the door, and paused. 'Just in case you need to find me, the landlord at the King's Head usually knows Guy Kemp's plans.'

'I won't need to find you, Tom!' She turned away from him, trying to hold back her tears.

'And you won't at least wish me God speed?'

'God would not bless a trip such as yours,' she whispered in anguish.

Her brother made no reply. She heard the door open and close softly.

It was too late to call him back, even if she had wanted to; too late to unsay her angry words. With tears in her eyes she ran to the window, watching as Tom let himself out of the small door in the wall below. He strode quickly out of sight without looking back.

Bitterly she turned to the packet he had left lying on her bed. Picking it up, she turned it over in her hands. The back of the vellum was sealed; the front bore only the simple inscription: 'To: Mistress Jane Lockesley.' For a moment she was tempted to break it open and see what was so important that she had had to be let into Tom's secrets to ensure its safe delivery; more than a love letter, surely? Then, suddenly, she was afraid. Whatever it was, she did not want to know. She dropped the packet into the small jewel chest on the table by her bed and locked it, then she hid the tiny key in the knot-hole of one of the beams of her bedroom ceiling. 'Oh, Tom,' she whispered, 'please come back safely. Please!'

For a long time after Tom had gone, she stood at the stone mullioned window of her room, watching the sun rise above the yew hedges which surrounded the ornamental gardens of King's Brook Manor, and slowly, as she calmed, she began to think about what Tom had told her. She could never condone what he had done, but perhaps she could understand. It was, after all, the same rebellion she had tried so hard to hide in herself; the same resentment against their father's obsession with business. Because Tom was a man, he had been able to act, while all she had managed to do was to refuse the succession of rich, stout, merchants' sons who had been paraded before her as potential husbands, until her exasperated father claimed that she seemed determined to die an old maid.

She sighed deeply. Even if Tom had admitted that he was engaged in piracy, she still loved him—nothing could change that—and her grief was touched with terrible fear as she thought of the danger he must have faced in the past and which he must face again, and soon.

The day passed in a miserable dream as she went about her chores, supervising the huge household, and working in the still-room and the herb gardens, and by evening she knew that she had to go to Kingston Point to see Tom before his ship sailed. She had to tell him that she did wish him well. She could not let him leave thinking she did not care.

Climbing the stairs to her room, she sent for her maid. 'Mab, do you know when the tide is high at the town quay?' She was sitting at her carved oak writing-table, a quill in her hand, a memorandum open before her.

Mab was a plump, dark-haired girl with a happy wide mouth which displayed a gap between her two front teeth. 'Why, mistress, you're never working for your father?' Automatically the girl bent to pick up a fallen shift. 'I heard it was three hours before midnight or thereabouts. But the *Bonaventure* doesn't sail for days yet . . .'

'I know that!' *Bonaventure* was her father's flagship. Impatiently Elaine stood up and threw down her pen, abandoning all pretence of writing. 'I want to borrow one of your gowns, Mab.'

'You want to . . .' The girl gaped at her, her hands on her ample hips. 'Now why on earth should you do that, mistress, with all your lovely things?'

Elaine sighed. 'Use your head, Mab. Because I don't want to be seen in lovely things! I want to go out secretly!'

'To meet a young man?' Mab's eyes sparkled suddenly.

'Of course! You can have my Sunday gown. It's clean, and it's plain enough.' Already she was running to the door.

Elaine picked up her hand-mirror when the girl had gone and stared at her face. Her eyes were unnaturally bright, her pale skin flushed. Yes, perhaps she did look as though she were going to an assignation. She drew a deep breath, put down the mirror and went to look out of the window. If only that were true! It must be wonderful to have a lover.

The shadows were lengthening across the grass, painting deeper colours across the formal beds. Birdsong filled the air, and the scent of early honeysuckle and roses drifted up to her window.

Mab's dress made them both laugh. Two of Elaine could have fitted into the ample waist, even with the lacings tight as they would go. But with the aid of a long, plaited girdle and a tightly-tied apron they managed the transformation. Mab brushed out Elaine's hair and knotted it beneath a snowy cap, and she was ready. Taking her darkest cloak, Elaine tiptoed down the staircase and fled towards the stables.

The grooms were idling over a game of loggats, lazily pitching sticks at a stake they had stuck into the dry ground, and showed little interest in her change of costume. Grumbling quietly, old Ned Potten detached himself from the game, saddled Elaine's black mare Cressid, and led the animal out to her.

'You see she don't put a foot in a rabbit-hole; that light is going fast,' he said grumpily, as he tossed her up into the saddle. Then, to her relief, he turned back to his game without suggesting that one of them accompany her.

It was quite dark in the grassy lanes which led from King's Brook towards the coast. Hedges of oak and foaming hawthorn met above her head, cutting out the bright evening light as Elaine skirted round to the south of Woodbridge, not wanting to ride through the steep, narrow, noisy streets of the town or along the quayside with its attendant lounging sailors.

She rode slowly, glimpsing the water through the trees. Pale bands of silver streaked the surface with carmine and gold reflections from the sky, while the wind stirred in the heavy canopy of leaves as she slipped from the high saddle.

Tethering Cressid, she gathered up her skirts and walked towards the edge of the trees to look down a small sandy cliff into the creek. Sure enough, a ship lay there in the lee of the woods, her spars in black silhouette against the gilded water.

There was no sign of life on deck. Elaine drew back slightly behind a huge old Scots pine and contemplated the scene, uncertain what to do next.

Her courage was failing her fast. The thought of boarding the graceful caravel, deserted though she looked, to seek Tom among cut-throats and thieves suddenly lost its appeal. She glanced up and down the beach, praying she would see Tom approaching, her heart aching with misery at the thought of missing him after she had come so far, as, cautiously, she crept to the very edge of the low cliff, clutching a branch to steady herself.

She was leaning out as far as she dared, when, without warning, the sand beneath her feet gave way and with a scream of terror she fell into space.

Desperately she flung out her arms, trying to save herself, her full skirts tangling between her legs as she scrabbled for a foothold, but her fist closed on air as her fingers missed their grasp and the branches of the trees swung out of reach.

Then a man's hand was there, clamped on her wrist, and another round her waist, and even as she began to fall she was swung back from the cliff edge, sobbing with fear.

'You mustn't throw yourself away like that, my pretty,' a rough voice whispered in her ear. 'That would be an awful waste, that would. Now, what are you spying on so quietly, I wonder?'

And she found herself being pulled round violently to face her rescuer.

Elaine struggled to free herself, but she was held fast, and she stared up at the man who had saved her, unable to move. He was a man in his middle years, dressed in a stained leather doublet and breeches, his hands and face as tanned and scarred as the hide he wore. A naked cutless was thrust through his belt.

'Fancy your chances with the sailor boys, do you, my pretty?' He grinned at her, not slackening his grip.

She shook her head, too shocked for a moment to speak.

'Then what?' His eyes, deep set in the harsh face, were shrewd and not unkind as they scanned her. 'You don't look like a tavern wench.'

At last she found her tongue. 'My brother is down there on the ship,' she stammered. 'I wanted to say farewell to him, that's all.'

'Your brother?' He threw back his head and laughed. 'That's a new one! And who might your brother be?'

She was too frightened to lie. 'Tom. Tom Howard. Please will you tell him I'm here. I must speak to him!' She broke off, gazing pleadingly into his eyes.

He nodded slowly. 'Maybe you are speaking the truth. I can see a look of him in you. So you came to see *Black Witch* off and catch a glimpse of your brother's cronies, did you?'

'I must see him. Please?' She stopped, as a faint whistle sounded from the ship, echoing up through the trees on the still air. As if obedient to it, a faint ripple stirred on the water and she felt the wind touch her cheek once more. He turned and glanced down. 'It's too late, missie. That's "All hands aboard." We catch the tide, and the ship will be moving any minute. You wave your goodbyes to your brother from here, if you must, but don't let Kemp see you. He doesn't care for fond farewells!'

'Please,' she grabbed his arm. 'I must. Tom and I quarrelled and I didn't wish him luck. Please!' She paused as the man looked at her white face, and she knew it was useless to plead. 'At least tell him I'm sorry,' she whispered. 'Tell him I didn't mean it, and that I do wish him well.'

He nodded soberly. 'I dare say I'll manage that.' And, with a wink, he turned and began to climb down the cliff.

Elaine leant against the tree, defeated, watching as two more figures detached themselves from the undergrowth and made their way aboard. The ship had not been as deserted as she looked; dozens of silent figures had appeared at the foot of the masts, and running nimbly up into the rigging as the gangplank was hauled inboard, but there was still no sign of Tom.

Disappointed, she turned away and began to walk along the point towards the river, following the cliff edge. In places, the sandy soil had partially collapsed, and she began carefully to climb down the crumbling escarpment, sliding, and clinging to torn roots and branches, the loose sand filling her shoes.

Near the bottom, she lost her footing and tumbled to the soft jumble of soil and sand. Bruised, she rose to her feet slowly, glancing round to make sure she had not been observed. She gasped. *Black Witch*, drifting silently with the tide towards the mouth of the creek, held fore and aft by warps to the shore, had come level with her. As she looked up towards the towering deck, a line of grinning faces peered at her from the bulwarks. Then the high sterncastle of the ship was abreast of her, and she could make out the features of the sailor who had accosted her at the top of the cliff, and another. Almost irresistibly her eyes were drawn to the second man, and she knew instinctively that this must be Guy Kemp, Tom's partner, the captain of the ship.

The tanned, handsome features, long straight nose and square jaw were framed by the wild tangle of flame-gold hair and beard. She stared at him, shivering, unable to drag her eyes away. Never had she seen so attractive a man—or one who looked so cruel.

His gaze raked her as his ship drifted silently past. For a moment their eyes met, and she felt his sardonic glance hold hers. She could not breathe, and her mouth went dry. Then his white teeth flashed as he began to laugh, and she knew that he, like all his crew, must have seen her fall. Mockingly, he raised his hand in salute before turning away.

She fled up the beach, careless now of who saw her, ducking beneath the willow and aspen to cut across to the main river and the footpath. Her cheeks were burning with indignation, and her breath caught in her throat as she rounded the corner and lost sight of the ship. Only then could she try to calm herself and straighten her cloak. It would be full dusk before *Black Witch* dropped her towing-warps and turned out into the main river. Then she could look for one last time unobserved at the ship which carried Tom away and at the man whose eyes had caused such a strange turbulence in her breast.

When the tall figure in black accosted Elaine on the river bank, she nearly died of fright. She had time only to see that he was broad-shouldered and dark, and that his doublet was trimmed with silver lace, before she ducked away from him and ran. Behind her, she heard him hesitate for an instant, and in that time she had gained the trees and found Cressid. She threw herself on to the horse and allowed it to pick its way along the rutted path through the trees.

She did not draw rein until she was a couple of miles away, slowing to a standstill on the edge of the heath. When she held her breath and listened, there was no sound of pursuit.

Trying to steady herself as she set the mare towards King's Brook at a sedate walk, she felt nothing but sharp bitterness and misery. Far behind her, Tom was well on his way without her ever having caught a single glimpse of him, while instead she had been seen and ridiculed by the entire crew of *Black Witch*, including her captain. At the sudden thought of Guy Kemp's mocking gaze, the blood began to drum once more in her temples, eclipsing completely the fear she had felt when the stranger challenged her. It was as if she could feel again the strange power of Kemp's glance. Furious at her own foolishness, she tried to change the drift of her thoughts as she urged Cressid on. She would look forward, she comforted herself, to telling Tom exactly what she thought of his Captain Kemp!

She was home and already half undressed when the door of her bedroom opened and Mab slipped into the room.

'Why, Mistress Elaine!' The girl started visibly. 'I didn't know you were back. Why are you in here with only one candle? Look at you!' Scolding, she bustled about fetching fresh candles for the sconces, closing the heavy shutters against the moonrise, and taking an embroidered gown from the press.

'No, Mab. Not my clothes. I just want to go to bed,' Elaine protested. 'It's late.'

'I know, my love.' Mab had instantly noticed her mistress's pale face. 'Near midnight, I'd guess. But I'm afraid you must go downstairs to your father. He's been asking for you since supper.' She picked up the discarded dress and apron, not commenting on the sand-stains as she folded them. Briskly she helped Elaine to dress, not giving her time to argue, and pushed her out of the room.

Elaine ran. Her father was sitting in his library, poring over a map spread on the table. He looked up as she let herself into the room and dropped a deep curtsy in the doorway.

'Papa dearest? I'm sorry. I didn't know you wanted me. I was in the still-room earlier, and then I was so tired I went straight up to bed.' She adapted the truth a little, not liking to lie to her father.

His hard face relaxed into a smile. 'It is Thomas I want, daughter.' He straightened and walked to the fireplace, where a log was burning in spite of the warmth of the night. 'I guessed you might know where he was. No one else seems to.'

Elaine went white. She looked away quickly, unable to meet her father's eye. 'I haven't seen him since last night, Papa.' To admit that he had come to her room at dawn would have been as good as confessing that she knew his secret.

Robert Howard squinted at her shrewdly, and sniffed. 'You are quite sure you don't know?'

'Quite sure.'

He sighed testily. 'Off wenching with his cronies again, I suppose! I only hope he returns by tomorrow. We have an important visitor whom I want him to meet and work with. Sir Edward Brandon.' He eyed her thoughtfully, gnawing his knuckle. 'I particularly want you to meet him, my dear. He is unmarried, and, I hear, looking for a bride.'

Elaine gasped, all thought of Tom forgotten. 'Papa, you promised I need not marry unless I chose the man myself!'

'True, child. But you are too slow in choosing. You will soon be past the age when you should be married.' He walked stiffly to the table and poured a glass of wine. 'What are you? Twenty? Your poor mother had borne and lost two children already at your age. But there, I have said I'll not force you, and I don't wish to, but you begin to try my patience.' He shook his head sadly. 'I blame myself for not marrying again when your mother died, Elaine. Tom and you should have had more brothers and sisters, and another mother to raise you; to keep order and to bring some light and joy to this house.'

There was a moment's silence.

Elaine saw her father's tears, and knew that he was thinking of the tomb in the church across the garden with the stone effigy of her mother and the five small figures beside her of her own brothers and sisters, none of whom had survived infancy.

Taking a deep draught of wine, Robert Howard walked with deliberate steps back to the fireplace. 'I met Sir Edward in London, although he lives only some twenty miles from here at Aldebourne,' he said thoughtfully. 'Ostensibly he is here to buy stores for the King.'

'Ostensibly?' Elaine had seated herself nervously on the high-backed settle near the fire.

He gave a tight smile. 'He has to have a reason for being in Woodbridge that would give him access to all the warehouses and ships round here. At my request, Sir Edward has the King's commission to seek out and exterminate these pirates who have been preying on our ships over the past eighteen months. Things cannot go on as they have been. It is quite obvious that these rogues are based somewhere near here, and I mean to have their heads nailed to the town gates!'

He had not noticed Elaine's stillness, or the pallor of her skin as she stared, horrified, at him. 'Papa . . .' she spoke at last, her voice husky with terror. 'Surely the merchants of Woodbridge can guard their own ships? They have no need of an outsider.'

'I told you, girl, he is not an outsider. He's Suffolk born like ourselves, and is experienced in these matters; he's acted as pirate-catcher to the King before, rooting out nests of the varmints down in Cornwall and Dorset. No, he's the man we need.' He rubbed his thin hands together and held them out to the smouldering logs. 'Good-looking, too.' He gave her a sly glance. 'You'll like him, daughter.'

Elaine did not hear the last comment. Her mind was spinning as she thought of Tom, Sir Edward's possible designs on herself momentarily forgotten. Somehow she had to warn him. She got to her feet, making towards the door, still reeling with the shock of what he had said. 'Papa, if you will forgive me, it is late and I'm tired.'

'Of course, child.' He grinned to himself. Mention a handsome man, and the girl skittered off like a frightened filly.

Elaine closed the door behind her and walked, dazed, towards the staircase, her father's words echoing in her ears. He meant to have the pirates' heads nailed to the town gates. And one of those pirates was Tom!

Letting herself into her bedroom, she leaned against the oak panelling and took a deep breath, numb with fear. She had to get word to Tom. Sitting at her table, she cudgelled her brain to remember the name of the tavern Tom had mentioned where they would know about the whereabouts of *Black Witch*. She had to help Tom; then he, in his turn, would help her to be rid of yet another unwelcome suitor.

She frowned at the thought, wishing to convince herself that there was nothing to fear and that this man, Sir Edward Brandon, would be rebuffed as easily as the others, but she could no longer be entirely certain.

Silently Mab let herself into the room, carrying a pitcher of warm water. She looked sympathetically at Elaine, guessing some of what had been said in the library. The linenfold panelling on the door was thin, and the ears of the steward, David Churchman, had been long as he passed down the passage outside. It had not taken him long to relay to the kitchens what he had heard.

'Shall I help you to undress, mistress?' Her voice was unusually gentle.

Elaine turned with a start. 'I never heard you come in! Yes, Mab, I am tired.' She stood still as the maid unfastened the lacings at the back of her gown.

'I reckoned you'd want to go straight to bed now,' the girl went on, pulling expertly at the stiffened fabric until it fell rustling around Elaine's knees.

She looked up wearily. Mab was right. The only thing to do now was to go to bed and sleep. Tom would be far out to sea. Perhaps tomorrow, when the sun was high and her wits were about her, she would be better able to decide what to do when he returned.

In spite of the lateness of the hour she lay awake for a long time, however, tossing and turning feverishly on the deep feather bed, haunted by her fears of this unknown man whom Robert Howard had unwittingly hired to ensnare his own son. But when at last she drifted into an uneasy sleep, it was not Tom's face she saw in her dreams, nor that of her suitor, his unknown prosecutor. It was the face which had stared down at her from the ship that had carried her brother into the darkness; the cruel, handsome, haunted face of the man who had laughed when she fell almost at his feet in the sand—the face of the pirate captain, Kemp.

The great hall, the main room in the large, lavishly furnished house, was used as a dining-hall now only for very special occasions. But next day Robert Howard had invited the leading merchants and landowners in the area to meet his guest, and the tables were being set out early. Elaine did not see Sir Edward arrive. Mab was brushing her hair and coiling it beneath the elaborate head-dress that complemented her stiff pale blue gown and heavily embroidered kirtle when he rode up to the front of the house, and she could see nothing from her windows. Mab, however, was a mine of information.

'He's tall, and ever so dark, and really quite handsome; but he's not come to stay. His traps are at a tavern in Stone Street, so Hal says. He hasn't even brought a boy with him.'

Elaine breathed a sigh of relief. To have him as a guest

under their very roof would have proved too great a strain
for her. She was calmer and more rational this morning.
Was Sir Edward, after all, so great a threat? He had no
way of knowing that Tom was involved; he had come to
King's Brook not because he suspected Tom, but because
her father had asked him to. The son of the house would be
the last person on earth he would suspect. The knowledge
made her almost cheerful as she watched her reflection in
the mirror while Mab fastened a jewelled pendant round
her neck. And as for the threat of his being forced on her
as a husband—her father had never insisted yet, and she
was confident she could persuade him, once more, that she
was more useful to him at home than ever she would be as
another man's wife.

'You look quite lovely, mistress,' Mab said, when at last
she was ready. 'I should think every man there will fall in
love with you.'

Elaine smiled. So Mab knew that their guest was unmarried and in the market for a wife. She wondered whether
there was anything at all that the servants in the house did
not know, and she raised her eyes to meet Mab's innocent
blue ones. How many of them knew that Tom sailed on
Black Witch?

She could hear the rumble of male voices before she
reached the turn of the stair which led down into the great
hall, and paused to summon up her courage before she
began to descend the last flight, conscious of some dozen
faces raised towards her as she walked slowly down. Her
father held out his hands, as he made his way towards her.
'Here she is at last, my lovely Elaine. Sweetheart, you
know Thomas Seckford, Ned Wolsey, Cousin Richard—
in fact I think you know everyone except our special guest.
Come, meet Sir Edward Brandon. Sir, this is my daughter
Elaine.'

Overcome suddenly with nervousness, Elaine took the
outstretched hand and curtsied to the ground as the conversation resumed around her and a burst of laughter floated
over her head. Only as she rose gracefully once more did
she look up at the face of the man who still held her fingers
so lightly in his.

The silver lace trimming to the doublet was the same; only, this time, the doublet was midnight blue, not black. She was intensely aware of her father standing expectantly at Sir Edward's elbow, watching, as she finally met his gaze. It was the man who had tried to catch her the night before on the shores of the Deben: the stranger who had been observing *Black Witch* sail.

CHAPTER TWO

THERE WAS no sign of recognition, however, in the deep-set brown eyes as, smiling, Sir Edward raised her hand to his lips. 'Mistress Elaine, this is indeed an honour.'

With a silent prayer of thanks that he had obviously not seen her clearly in the dark at Kingston Point, she murmured a few quiet words of welcome, drawing her hand away as soon as she could. Under cover of the general conversation, she studied him. He was tall and well built; in his early thirties, she guessed. His features were even, strongly drawn beneath dark brown hair, but he was not handsome; striking, perhaps, but his eyes were too calculating, his mouth too hard. She felt a strange revulsion.

As their guests crowded close to him, impressed with the competence with which he discussed the King's trading policies, a matter of passionate interest to them, Elaine quietly withdrew to the window embrasure, trying to compose her thoughts. It could have been no coincidence that Edward Brandon had been at Kingston watching *Black Witch* sail. He had been in Woodbridge for only a few hours, and already he had pinpointed the ship. She bit her lip in an agony of anguish before glancing back towards their guests, all soberly dressed in furs and silks; all important figures who would stop at nothing to see that their trade was unhindered. And, at their centre, this tall, observant man who was the King's pirate-catcher.

Her eyes went automatically to his face, and she met his speculative gaze, which had followed her to the window. Colouring sharply, she looked away, but not before she had seen his stern features relax into the suspicion of a triumphant smile.

She was seated between Sir Edward and her father at dinner, saying very little as the conversation sparked back

and forth. There was talk of trade and wool and war, of
the likelihood of a good harvest, of politics, and of the
court of King Henry and his Spanish queen, Katherine,
and then of more trade as the courses of the meal came
and went: broths and stews, pies and fishes, cockerels,
peacocks, lamb, quince pie and custards and marchpane.

As she sipped slowly from the delicate Venetian glass
into which the wine had been served on this special
occasion, she longed for the meal to be over.

'I'd have wished my son to be here,' her father said
suddenly to their guest of honour, 'to meet you straight
away and give you his help, but these young blades are all
the same. Take your eyes off them for a minute, and they
are off wenching or bear-baiting or losing good money at
the dice!'

Elaine swallowed a little gasp, and then prayed that Sir
Edward had not heard her. If he had, he gave no sign. 'I'll
meet your son soon enough, I dare say,' he reassured his
host affably. 'And I'll work him hard then, have no fear!
Let him enjoy himself while he can.' He glanced at her
with a smile.

At the sight of her white face, his eyes lingered thoughtfully on her. A moment before, he had imagined her at
last beginning to relax in his company, but now she was as
tense as ever. He frowned. There was much to intrigue him
about Elaine Howard. Inwardly he gave a grim chuckle. He
had not expected to find the girl from Kingston Point so
easily. That she should be the daughter of one of the richest
of the pirate's victims had taken him aback for a moment
or two when he met her, but he had not betrayed the fact
that he recognised her and he had seen her fear and
embarrassment slowly subside; already one or two of the
pieces in the puzzle were falling into place. Elaine would
be in a position to pass on the information about cargoes
and sailing dates; he wondered whether she was really the
innocent victim of an unscrupulous man, not even knowing
what his true trade was.

The girl was quite beautiful. Her ash-blonde hair and
clear skin gave her a sense of fragile loveliness which
caused his breath to catch. He thought for an instant of

the list of rich heiresses he had drawn up in an idle moment
in his room at the King's palace at Greenwich: potential
wives, every one. How strange that Elaine Howard, whose
name topped that list, should be mixed up somehow with
the very piracy he had come to eradicate. But it did not
matter; probably she was being used. If it were more than
that, if she had a lover among the pirate crew, all the more
reason to track them down and ensure that every one of
them paid the full penalty of the law. He smiled quietly to
himself. Watching her lover swing would add spice to his
wooing.

When at last the meal was over, Elaine excused herself
as soon as she could and left the great hall where her father
would continue to entertain his guests for the best part of
the afternoon.

Her mind was fixed on one thing: she had to find the
tavern and warn Tom that *Black Witch* was under suspicion. Snatching her cloak, she let herself quietly out of
a side door of the house and ran. When she glanced over
her shoulder towards the house, there was no sign of life.

Under the hot afternoon sky, the gardens were deserted
except for one of the weeding-women bent over the beds
of hyssop and roses. Through the stable arch she could
hear the bees in the clover of the paddocks behind the
stables. Cressid was fresh, jibbing at the bit, her hooves
dancing sideways through clouds of bluebells, but Elaine
hardly saw the beauty of the afternoon around her. Her
mind was fixed on her task.

She left the horse at Goody Cattermole's house in New
Street, and headed towards the market place, holding her
skirts clear of the filthy cobbles. The town was full of
jostling crowds and the rattle of wheels as laden wagons
swayed up the narrow streets between the jettied houses.

Her brain was whirling as she stared at the shops and
taverns, searching for the King's Head. Then she saw it;
the carved sign was half hidden behind the tailgate of an
abandoned wagon. Without giving herself time to think,
she opened the door. Inside, some half-dozen men were
seated round a table, staring at a sheaf of lading-bills. They
looked up as she entered.

Elaine looked at the man nearest her, judging by his filthy apron and the tray beneath his arm that he must be the host. She cleared her throat, forgetting to be cautious; all she wanted was to be gone. 'Please, can you help me? I'm seeking news of a ship called *Black Witch*. Do you know when she will return?'

The man stared at her with blank, insolent eyes. 'Never heard of her, my pretty. Whose vessel would she be?' Slowly he put down his tray, and took a step towards her. 'Stopped away too long, has he, my dear? Maybe we can supply you with what's missing from your life . . .'

'No!' Elaine backed away from him towards the door. 'You don't understand! The ship belongs to my brother. He gave me this address and said I could ask here.'

'And what is your brother's name, lady?' Another man looked up, bored, from the documents.

She hesitated, not wanting to use Tom's name. But whose could she give? She felt increasingly panic-stricken as all six faces now grinned insolently up at her.

'Kemp,' she said desperately. 'It's Kemp's ship.'

The atmosphere in the shadowy room became suddenly tense. The standing man moved another step towards her threateningly.

'What do you know of Guy Kemp, lady?' he whispered hoarsely. 'With your fine clothes and your dainty complexion.' He pulled at her cloak contemptuously. 'You're no sister to Guy, lady!'

Behind him, one of his companions sniggered. 'They're all sisters under their clothes, Wilf.'

Elaine looked from one to the other, her cheeks flaming. 'No, you don't understand! I'm *Tom's* sister. I only want to know when the ship will berth. Please!' She had her back to the door.

'I see. You are Tom's sister!' The seated man lunged towards her and grabbed her wrist. 'Well, I reckon it doesn't matter whose sister you are. There's time enough for you to pleasure us a bit before *Black Witch* returns and still be ready for your Tom when he gets back.'

Struggling frantically to free herself from him, Elaine kicked out at the man's ankles in a panic as a quiet voice from the table cut through the general laughter.

'Let her go, Tad. Whatever she is to the men on *Black Witch*, you'll not want to tangle with Kemp when he returns. He's more likely to put a dagger in your gizzard and ask questions after if you mess about with one of his women!'

Tad dropped her wrist as if it had burnt him, and Elaine staggered back trying to restrain her tears. At the table, the man who had spoken last stared at her thoughtfully. 'Don't come here again, ever, Tom's sister. Do you understand? And don't go anywhere else to ask about *Black Witch*. This town keeps its secrets close.' He gave a grim smile. 'For what it's worth, they might come in on the night tide tomorrow, but then again they might not. That's all we know.'

Not stopping to thank him, she opened the door and dived back into the blinding sunshine of the street. From within, she heard a gale of coarse laughter. Trembling with relief and humiliation, she began to return down the hill to reclaim her horse, and only a tall shadow that fell directly across her path made her stop.

Sir Edward Brandon was standing in front of her. 'Mistress Howard! How strange that I should meet you here.' He bowed, his eyes searching her face. 'I had thought you to say you were going to rest after dinner.'

She felt her colour heighten even more, as anger surged through her. 'I changed my mind, Sir Edward. I was not aware that you wanted to know my whereabouts!'

He gave a tight smile. 'It hardly seems proper that Robert Howard's daughter should be running about the streets of Woodbridge in full view of half the town without so much as a maid to attend her,' he said coolly. 'I cannot believe that your father would approve of such conduct, mistress.'

Her amber eyes were blazing. 'Whether or not my father approves of my conduct, sir, is hardly your business! Now, if you will excuse me, I wish to pass.'

She took a step towards him, but he did not move. 'May I ask what business you had in that tavern?' he demanded suddenly. She could feel his eyes on her face.

'What tavern?' She had to bluff her way out of his trap. 'I visit no taverns, sir, I assure you! I have been to see a friend; her name is no concern of yours.' Anger and indignation gave her courage as she stared at him. 'Did you follow me from home?'

To her immense satisfaction, he began to look slightly disconcerted. 'It appears that I must have,' he said coldly.

'Then I am sorry you should have had so boring a journey!' This time, as she moved forward, he stood aside to let her pass. Her eyes had deepened to the colour of topaz, and her pale cheeks were alive with the touch of blood beneath her skin. Had she but known it, the face which glared so furiously at Edward Brandon as she swept past him was one of passionate beauty.

She walked swiftly down the hill, and only when she reached the gate of the stable where Cressid waited did she glance around. Sir Edward had not followed her.

There was no sign of Sir Edward that evening, to her immense relief, when Elaine joined her father for their evening meal in the small supper-room beside his library. The two of them were alone.

Robert Howard was ill at ease and cross, but he had already forgotten his daughter's over-hasty departure from the great hall after dinner, and was once more thinking irritably about his son. 'It is too bad of Thomas! I need him here with me.' He coughed, his hand pressed against his side dramatically. 'I want someone to represent me at the warehouse tomorrow when Brandon begins his ordering.'

'But, Papa!' Elaine stared at him. 'I thought that was a pretence. He is here as a spy, not to purchase goods for the King!'

Robert looked at her sharply. 'A spy! That is a strange word to use. Whatever his purpose here, Elaine, he does mean to buy for the King, and I'm not strong enough to go down to the town to supervise. Not yet.'

'But your cough is better, Papa.' Elaine smiled coaxingly. 'And Tom will soon return. Wherever he is, he will be back before long. I'm sure of it.'

Robert nodded wearily, pushing his plate away. 'I'm sure you're right. But, anyway, things will be easier from tomorrow. I have told Sir Edward to pack his chests and come here as our guest. He said at the start that he wanted to stay in the town with his ear to the ground, but now he feels he can do just as well from King's Brook. I think he has found an attraction here he had not dared to expect,' he chuckled.

'Not me, Papa, I hope?'

'Of course you, you silly child! It's certainly not Mabbet! Sir Edward is showing great interest in you and you should be glad of it. A fine-looking man like that!'

Elaine blushed violently. 'Papa, I have told you. I have no wish to consider any man yet.'

'Pish!' He banged the tankard down. 'I'll not allow much more of this childish modesty. You think about him, and think about him well, my girl. And, for once, Tom will agree with me. It is time you were married!'

As she lay in bed that night, her father's words streamed through Elaine's head, filling her with foreboding. The dark, unpleasant presence of Sir Edward Brandon was beginning to haunt her. Just how much did he know of Tom's ship and her crew, and why had he followed her that afternoon to the tavern in the square? Could he have recognised her as the girl he had seen at Kingston Point? Surely he would have shown some sign?

Sir Edward arrived early the next morning, accompanied by two servants and a pack-horse. He was shown to the finest guest-room in the west wing before joining Master Robert for refreshment in his library. Elaine refused to leave her room.

'Tell Papa I am not well,' she instructed Mab. It was almost true. After her sleepless night, her eyes were heavy and her head throbbed painfully as she lay on the bed. She wanted the day to pass as quickly as possible; at nightfall she was going to slip out once more and ride to Kingston Hill to await the return of *Black Witch*.

The day passed interminably. Mab reported that Robert Howard had had himself carried into Woodbridge in a litter so that he could supervise the choice of goods on Sir Edward's list, and the two, obviously fast becoming friends, had returned only in time for the evening meal. Her presence had been sorely missed, Mab added darkly, and Elaine smiled a little, thinking of her father's fury that she was not there to flirt with their visitor.

At noon she had finally fallen asleep and slept for several hours. When she awoke, her head was clear. Restored by a tray of bread and meat and a posset of milk curdled in sweet wine, she began to feel almost cheerful. Mab giggled on hearing that her mistress was about to make another mysterious visit to the town, but was greatly relieved that she did not once more claim her Sunday gown. Instead Elaine selected one of her own, a full-skirted high-waisted dress of deep burgundy silk worn over a cream kirtle. She reached for the key to her jewel chest and threw back the lid. Tom's packet of letters lay there on top, and gently she touched his scrawled, almost illegible writing with her fingertip before pushing it aside and selecting a heavy ruby necklace. She clipped it round her throat, then, closing the casket, turned away to wrap herself in her green velvet cloak. Briefly she wondered why she should be dressing so carefully for her dangerous lonely ride to Kingston, but deep down she knew it might have more than a little to do with the thought of confronting Tom beneath the sardonic gaze of the captain of *Black Witch*.

Mab waited with her in her room until the house had fallen silent. The three-quarter moon had floated clear of the yew hedge and Elaine could see across the garden as though it were daylight. Drawing the bed-curtains to deceive anyone glancing through the door, she picked up a candle and beckoned Mab to follow her. The two girls crept through into the empty bedroom beyond Elaine's, which lay at the very end of the house, where beneath a tapestry wall-hanging, a small door led to a forgotten narrow stair that she and Tom had used since childhood to escape their nurses. Tom still used it when he wished to leave the house unobserved. Elaine led the way, the candle held high before her, and at the bottom, she paused before the small door in the outside wall of the house. It was heavily bolted. Mab was close behind her, her eyes huge in the candlelight. 'Take the candle, Mab, while I open it.' Her hands were trembling as she forced back the bolts and dragged the door ajar, peering out into the moonlight through the curtain of ivy which hung across it. Looking back at Mab, she put her finger to her lips.

'Don't lock it behind me,' she breathed. 'Go back, and go to bed. I'll see you in the morning.'

Tiptoeing over the grass, she headed for the stables. She did not notice Sir Edward Brandon sitting on the low moss-covered wall until she was a few feet from him. He had risen as he saw her, and walked swiftly to intercept her.

'Well met, sweetheart! I am glad to see you have recovered from your megrims,' he said quietly. His fingers on her forearm were tight enough to prevent her from pulling away from him.

'Sir Edward! You startled me!'

He looked down into the wide eyes, taking in the velvet cloak and the glowing gems at her throat. So, the little trollop was off to another meeting with her pirate lover. He smiled grimly; his information too had been that *Black Witch* would return that night.

'You seem bound for an assignation, my dear,' he went on softly. His fingers had not relinquished their hold on her arm. 'I wonder who the lucky man can be?' His voice was smooth.

Her mouth had gone dry, and her mind, stunned for a moment by the shock of meeting him, began to race. She tried to make herself relax beneath his grasp, looking at him as warmly as she could. 'Indeed, Sir Edward, I only hoped for an assignation. And I think I have found it.' Her lips were stiff as she forced herself to smile.

She felt his fingers loosen slightly on her arm. 'I hope you don't think me too forward! I was looking out at the moonlight from my window up there, and I saw you . . .' She looked down, unable to go on with the lie.

The house lay in darkness, and somewhere near by a peacock screamed, disturbed by their presence. Elaine gasped at the sound, stepping involuntarily backward with a shiver. Sir Edward caught hold of her once more. 'Not so fast, my dear! I have something to say to you.'

She looked up at him, suddenly afraid again. 'I must go back, Sir Edward. I should not have come out here . . .'

'Yet you did. You came to see me.' Both hands were on her arms now. He was drawing her to him, enjoying the fear and anger he saw as his mouth drew near hers.

At the touch of his lips, she dragged herself away from him, shuddering with revulsion. 'Sir Edward! You forget yourself!'

He was laughing at her now, standing, arms folded, as he watched her.

'I doubt if my father would find it amusing, sir, if I told him that a guest under his roof had forced himself on me.'

'Oh come, Elaine,' he sneered. 'I didn't force you. You can't pretend that was the first time you have been kissed. I doubt your moonlit tryst had anything to do with me at all. A groom, was it? Or a farm boy? Rumour has it that your tastes run very low!'

Stung to silence by his sarcasm, she stared at him. Colour flared in her cheeks for an instant, and then she felt herself grow pale. 'How dare you!'

He had seated himself on the wall now, and his face was insolent with amusement. 'You were going to the stables, weren't you? To see a groom? Or was it just to fetch a horse, perhaps—to ride to your lover?'

'No!'

'Then you really were coming out to meet me?'

'No!' She took a few steps away from him. 'No, I was not. I merely wished for some air.'

'Some air?' He echoed her mockingly. 'And, for some air, you dress in silks and put on your finest jewellery.' He gestured contemptuously at her necklace. 'You honour the moon, perhaps? Or the nightingale, with your best clothes? Come, Elaine, why not tell me who he is?'

Elaine stared at him for a moment, then, all thoughts of going to Tom banished from her mind, she began to run back towards the house, intent only on reaching safety before Sir Edward laid hands on her again. She ran past the little hidden door, instinctively not wanting him to see it, slipping round the corner to the front of the house.

Sir Edward had not moved. He watched the flying shadow of the girl in her dark cloak as she sped out of sight. Beauty, spirit and money. Oh yes, he would enjoy making Elaine Howard his wife, once he had disposed of the crew of *Black Witch*.

CHAPTER
THREE

THE FRONT door was unlocked; Sir Edward must have let himself out by it to go into the garden. With relief Elaine pushed it open, her hands shaking in her haste as she fumbled with the heavy iron latch, and slipped into the great hall. She crept through deserted bedrooms until she reached the small one next to her own where Mab slept. Straining her eyes in the darkness of the shuttered room, she looked towards her recumbent form. Mab was obviously fast asleep.

In her own room there was enough moonlight to see, just. She felt about for her tinder-box, nearly dropping the flint in her agitation as she groped to light a candle, her heart still pounding with fear and anger. Sir Edward had insulted her and taken liberties with her, and worse than either of these, he had stopped her going to Tom. With a sigh of relief she had the candle lit at last, and she ran to the window and cautiously peered out between the shutters. The garden was still as bright as day. Below, on the grass, Sir Edward was pacing slowly up and down between the beds. He appeared to be deep in thought. With an exclamation of anger, she left the window. It was as though he suspected her, as though he deliberately intended to stop her leaving the house. She sat down on the end of the bed. Had he, after all, seen her at Kingston Point? Did that explain his insulting remark about her fondness for low company? In spite of her anger, an irresistible urge to giggle bubbled up in her throat. So, he imagined that she had a lover on the ship!

She rose and went back to the window, her amusement gone as soon as it had come. Whatever his reasons for being there, he was keeping her from Tom. From the shelter of the shutters, she watched the figure pacing the

gardens, still seething with resentment as she saw him
methodically walk towards the stables and back.

There was only one entrance to the stable-yard, and
without using it, she could not reach Cressid. Briefly she
debated trying to catch one of the horses out in the distant
paddocks, but she dismissed the idea almost at once. The
harness was all in the stables, and she doubted if she could
catch one unaided at night.

Frustrated, she paced the room, glancing out each time
she approached the window. But each time he was still
there, and the last time she looked, he was standing
immediately below her window, staring up. She moved
quickly out of sight, and furiously sat down on her bed
once more, determined to wait.

She did not realise that she had fallen asleep until she
woke with a jerk to find herself perched uncomfortably at
the end of her bed. Puzzled by the sudden darkness outside,
she saw that the moon had risen further and was now
soaring behind the tall, twisted chimneys of the house.
Wearily she rose and stretched her arms above her head.
The tide must have long ago been full; had *Black Witch*
come tonight, she would already have berthed and her
crew dispersed. It was too late to intercept Tom now.

With a heavy heart she reached up to unfasten the heavy
jewels from her throat and dropped them on the table by
the candle, then slowly she began to loosen the laces that
fastened her gown. Stepping out of the deep red silk, she
picked the dress up and threw it over a stool. Dressed in
nothing but her fine white shift she went once more, almost
from habit, to the window and peered out one last time.
The gardens were still bright, the shadows foreshortened,
but there was no sign of the patrolling figure now that it
was too late for her to go to Tom. Sadly she turned to the
bed, her eyes heavy with misery and exhaustion. In only
seconds, she was once more asleep.

A sharp click in the next room woke her. It was a sudden
awakening—one minute she was deeply asleep, the next
wide awake, her heart pounding with fright. She sat up,
her ears straining in the silence. She could just see the
window faintly, the small leaded panes dimly silhouetted

against the starry sky. Beside her bed, the candle guttered and smoked in a sudden draught as the door slowly opened. Holding her breath, she stared as a figure materialised out of the shadows and closed the door silently. In a second she was out of bed, running in her thin shift towards him.

'Tom? Oh, Tom, thank God! He didn't see you, did he? He's been waiting out there for hours, patrolling the stable, watching my window. It's almost as if he knew . . .'

Her voice sank to an uncertain whisper as she reached out her hand towards the figure. 'Tom? It is you?'

'No, mistress, it is not Tom.' The quiet voice that answered her was deep and vibrant; the voice of a stranger. 'Please make no sound.'

Her gasp of surprise and fear was cut off as he stepped towards her. In two strides he was past her and had reached the candle. She caught a glimpse of the arrogant nose, the burnished hair and beard, the watchful steel-blue eyes, before he snuffed the dying flame and plunged the room into total darkness. It was Guy Kemp.

Elaine backed away from him, her mouth suddenly dry with fear as she heard the scrape of his heel on the boards. He had turned to face her.

'You must keep silent, Mistress Howard. I have no wish to cross swords with your watcher outside, whoever he may be,' he said quietly. He went to the window and looked out through the half-open shutters. Elaine could see him now in the faint starlight as her eyes accustomed themselves to the darkness. His mouth was set in a grim line.

'How did you get in?' she stammered at last.

She saw his lips relax slightly into a sombre smile as he turned towards her. 'Through the door. Tom told me about your secret entrance beneath the ivy. How lucky it was unbolted!' He glanced again at the window, stepping back out of the faint starlight into the darkness of the shadows. 'Now, please light a new candle so that we can talk. I shall close the shutters.'

Elaine ran to the table. With shaking hands she lifted the still-warm candle-stump from its pricket and found a new one to jam in its place. As the pale light flared and

steadied, she turned to look at her visitor. When he had
fastened the shutters and drawn the heavy curtains, he
came towards her, dressed in a rich deep-blue doublet and
soft shirt. There was a cutlass at his waist. Vibrant power
seemed to emanate from his body, and she began to shiver
in spite of the warmth of the room.

He in his turn was scrutinising her in the candlelight, his
eyes straying from her loosened hair and pale face to the
fine gossamer shift which clung to her body. He bowed
slightly. 'Perhaps I should introduce myself. I am Guy
Kemp, master of *Black Witch*.'

She did not move. 'I know. I saw you the evening I came
looking for Tom.'

His eyes became strangely enigmatic. 'Ah yes. You were
lying on the sand; a veritable stranded mermaid.' He smiled
gently. 'My crew were all in favour of rescuing you from
your uncomfortable fate and carrying you out to sea with
us.'

Elaine's cheeks coloured violently. 'The vulgar opinions
of your crew don't interest me, sir,' she retorted, trying to
counter the strange excitement which coursed through her.
'You have no business here. Where's Tom?'

He looked away from her abruptly. When he met her
gaze again, the mocking humour was gone. His eyes were
suddenly full of intense compassion.

A whisper of fear touched her. 'What is it?' she breathed.
'What has happened? Why are you here?'

For a moment he did not speak. She stared at him
pleadingly, then rushed on, crying softly into the silence,
'It's Tom, isn't it? Something has happened to Tom!'

'He is dead, Elaine.' The deep voice was gentle.

'Dead?' she echoed, not understanding, not wanting to
believe him.

But his expression told her the truth. She could not
breathe. The room began to spin and sway, and she reached
out to steady herself as her eyes filled with tears, blindly
stepping towards the grim-faced man who stood before
her, too overwhelmed with grief to know what she was
doing.

His strong arms gathered her to him and he held her

close, her face pressed against his shirt, his fingers gently stroking her hair, comforting her, as if it were the most natural thing in the world for him to be standing there in her bedroom holding a half-naked girl in the candlelight.

There was the smell of the ship on him: the tar and the salt and the night sea air still clinging to his clothes; and, disquietingly, she could feel the iron-hard muscles of his chest and the strong beating of his heart beneath her cheek as her tears fell. 'How did he die? Why? What happened?' Her voice was muffled with sobs.

'We were alongside a Flemish galleon. We'd put a boarding-party on her. There seemed to be no resistance, then someone on the Fleming turned a mortar on us. Tom was wounded.' He hesitated, not wanting to tell her the truth—the blood and the agony as the young man's chest was blasted away, and the long minutes it had taken Tom to die in his arms. 'His last words were of you and your father. Then he said he loved you both.' He looked down at her sternly. 'He said, "Tell Elaine not to tell Papa how I died. Ever."'

She looked away from him, brushing her arm across her face and pushing her knuckles into her eyes in a vain attempt to stem the tears. Then suddenly she turned, her misery and despair overflowing into anger. 'How could you let it happen? How could you? With your cursed ship and your raids and your robbery! Tom would never hurt anyone! He had so much to live for . . .' She could not go on. Overwhelmed by a fresh torrent of sobbing, she flew at him, pounding his chest with her fists, wanting him to suffer as Tom had suffered, wanting to kill him with her bare hands.

Taken by surprise, it was a moment before he reacted. Then he caught her wrists with an oath and held her at arm's length. 'By Our Lady! Tom said you were a spitfire! I risk my life to tell you what happened because Tom asked me to come personally, and you attack me!' His hands on her wrists had the strength of steel. 'You are right,' he went on grimly. 'As the captain of my ship, I am responsible for the life of every man on her. I make no excuses. As to the profession we follow, Tom knew, as well as anyone, the risks as well as the rewards, and he enjoyed the danger!'

'*Enjoyed* it?' she exploded. 'How can you say that?'

'He came with us for the danger and the excitement, Elaine.' He gave a rueful scowl. 'It certainly wasn't for the money. He needed none of that, though he got his share, the same as every other man.'

He released her wrists abruptly. 'I loved him as a brother, too, so, when I say I am sorry for what has happened, I mean it. And I have no wish to cause you and your family more unhappiness than is necessary.' He swung away from her and stood staring down at the candle. 'Obviously you would wish his body brought home?'

'Yes.' Her choked whisper was barely audible.

'Then I shall have it done tomorrow. My men will be instructed to say he was attacked by footpads while on his way back here from a visit to London. It happens often enough.'

'Yes.'

'May I suggest that you tell your father yourself before they arrive? It would be kinder.'

'Kinder!' Her voice broke. 'Do you care how my father reacts, Master Kemp?'

'Tom cared.' His voice became suddenly forbidding. 'He cared a great deal for your father, and he told me that his health was precarious. If you care for him as much, you will try and prepare him for the shock. You may tell him that a servant of Tom's escaped and ran here to tell you what had happened.'

Elaine raised her hand, pressing it against her aching head. 'I don't understand. You are prepared to murder and rob, and yet you care about my father's health. It makes no sense!'

'Perhaps it would make more sense to you if I said I wanted your father alive for my own purposes,' he said harshly. 'You would believe that, I have no doubt.'

'Yes,' she said wearily after a moment. 'I would believe that of you, sir.'

'Then my next request will not surprise you.' He turned away so that his face was invisible again. 'For there is something further I have to discuss. I would not have mentioned it now, while you are still newly grieving for your brother, but it is urgent, and it may prove hard for me to speak to you alone again.'

Elaine stared at his silhouette, her indignation returning. 'I hope it will prove impossible for you to speak to me again, sir. Ever!'

He gave a quiet chuckle. 'Have you taken me in such dislike, then? Perhaps that is understandable. And there is no need, I assure you, for us to be friends; but colleagues we must be for a short while.'

'What do you mean?' She was beginning to tremble again. The restraint had gone from his voice, and she heard a new harshness there.

'I mean that there is something you have to do for me: a duty Tom was to have undertaken. As he can no longer help me, you must.'

He turned to her. 'I am sure you would wish to honour your brother's promises.' There was an undertone of menace in his voice now that frightened her, but she was determined not to show it.

'I think Tom has more than paid his debts to you, Master Kemp,' she retorted with as much spirit as she could muster, 'and paid dearly.'

'Perhaps he did,' he said harshly. 'Nevertheless, you must take his place, Mistress Elaine.'

'Take his place?' she echoed, her heart beating wildly.

'That is what I said. My plans are set; they depended on a meeting between Tom and a colleague of your father to reassure him that he can return safely without waiting for an escort, and to discuss the date of his return to be set at my convenience.' He laughed grimly. 'Although our friend will no doubt be surprised to find a lady carrying the authority of the merchants of Woodbridge, I am sure he would not query the Howard seal and your name.'

'No!' Cold horror flooded through her at his words. 'No! How would you even suggest such a thing? With Tom's body not even cold, you think only of your pocket! You are . . . vile. *Vile*! I shall never help you. And Tom wouldn't have, either, I'm sure of it! Not against my father's friends . . .' But even as she spoke, she was remembering

Tom's words to her in that very room only two days before, 'I'm perfectly placed here. I hear everything . . .'

'I assure you he did.' Kemp's voice was very quiet.

'I won't believe you,' Elaine said, her voice trembling. 'I can't.' Turning from him, she groped her way towards the bed, blinded by her tears. 'Go away! Go now, or I shall call the servants.'

'And have your father find out the truth about Tom?' The words hung for a moment in the silence. He had come to stand only a few feet from her.

She froze. The threat was unmistakable. 'You would not tell Papa!' Overwhelmed with grief and fear, she was unable to hold back the tears any longer.

'As long as you do as I say, Tom's secret is safe.' His hands were on her shoulders, and he turned her unresistingly towards him. 'Defy me, and Tom's body will hang in chains till his bones turn to dust.'

She shrank from his hands, but he held her firmly. 'The shame would kill your father, Elaine.'

He saw fear, anger and defiance chase one another across her pale, tear-stained features and then the spark of fury that showed briefly in her amber eyes. For a long time they remained staring at each other, and she felt the shock of his determination like a blow. Defeated, she looked down, her long lashes veiling her expression.

'You are a cruel man, Master Kemp,' she whispered.

He gave a harsh laugh. 'Only when it is necessary. I am the soul of courtesy to those who give me their loyalty, I assure you.'

'And that is what you expect of me?' Her eyes blazed up at him again. 'Loyalty?'

He met her gaze levelly. 'I think I shall expect much more than loyalty from you,' he said after a pause. 'Much more.' Releasing her shoulders, he raised his hand almost absent-mindedly to brush a tear from her cheek with his fingertip.

Then he turned from her, looking down at the table beside her bed. There with the candle and a small vellum-bound Book of Hours lay the ruby necklace she had carelessly tossed aside only an hour or two earlier—a heap of sparkling stones the colour of fire. Picking them up thoughtfully, he weighed them in his hand.

She gave a bitter little laugh. 'Oh yes, they're valuable! They're worth a king's ransom, I believe. Take them; Master Kemp. Theft is your proud trade, after all, is it not? Why not take all my jewels? They lie there, in the casket. It is not even locked . . .'

She broke off with an exclamation of fear at the expression which crossed his face as he turned back to her. Throwing down the necklace, he seized her wrist and dragged her hard against him. She could feel the steel muscles of his chest, and then his hand was forcing her to look up at him. To her amazement, he was smiling. 'A spitfire indeed! No, my pretty, I shall leave you your king's ransom. The prize I seek is of far greater value. And I'm not so sunk in villainy that I would take a bauble like this from a child.' He released her and scooped the necklace into his palm once more. He smiled enigmatically. 'It would please me, however, to see it properly. Put it on.'

'No!' She stepped away from him hurriedly as he held out his hand. 'Why should you wish to see that? Leave me alone.'

'Put it on.' His tone had not changed, but there was determination in his eyes. They were hard as sapphires in the candlelight.

'I will not,' she whispered.

'Then I must do it for you.' He advanced and caught her wrist again, backing her against the high bed so that she had either to stop and submit to him or to fall back. Her heart beat frantically as she stood still, her head held proudly high while he reached up and fastened the necklace, lifting her hair carefully out of the way. Elaine held her breath as the strong square-tipped fingers gently stroked the stones. Then his hand was moving downwards, lightly touching the soft swell of her breast beneath her shift.

Acting so swiftly she did not know she had done it, she broke away from him, and struck him across the face as hard as she could. Then she ran for the door to the ante-room.

'Mab!' she screamed. 'Mab!'

But he was behind her; before she could utter another sound, his palm was clamped across her lips. She tasted bitter salt briefly as he lifted her off her feet, then he threw her face down on the bed.

'Another sound, sweetheart, and Tom's sister or no, I'll slit your tongue,' he breathed. 'Do you hear?' Without waiting for a sign that she had understood, he pulled her over to face him. There was a tight knot of panic in her stomach, but she could not fight him. She lay still, held by the warm light of his eyes, feeling his strength and his will as a tangible web that bound her.

He inclined his face slowly, and she submitted without a murmur as his lips claimed hers in a powerful kiss which left her trembling, every nerve quivering. He stared at her, the blue of his eyes deepening. 'So,' he said in a husky whisper. 'You do not find a pirate's kiss altogether distasteful.' He ran his finger lightly across her lips. Then, tracing a path down her throat, his hand moved towards the rubies, then on, light as a feather, towards the neckline of her shift, where he slipped his hand gently under the fine lawn to cup her breast. A pulse pounded in her throat. Every instinct told her to struggle and scream, yet still she could not move, held by his eyes as once more he lowered his lips to hers, his tongue probing gently till her mouth opened obediently beneath his, and she returned his kiss.

Abruptly he stopped, and sat up. The warmth faded from his eyes as she stared blindly at him, scarcely knowing what was happening to her.

In his face now was only the calculating hardness she had seen before. It brought a fresh stab of terror to her heart. He smiled coldly. 'I think we begin to understand each other, Tom's sister.' Pushing himself from the bed, he stood and looked down at her. 'Silence is all I ask of you for now. Tomorrow two of my men will bring your brother home. Tell your father whatever story you please, but remember,' he paused significantly, 'Tom's secret is in your hands.' He strode across the room and opened the door, then turned. 'I shall return soon. When I do, I shall expect your help.' He allowed himself a brief cynical smile.

'I trust you will be ready to give it wholeheartedly.'

Closing the door softly behind him, he disappeared into the darkness beyond.

For a moment, Elaine did not move. Then she turned over on the bed, and burying her head in the pillow, began to sob as though her heart would break. But not for long. In sudden terror that he might come back, she dragged herself up and ran over to the door, fumbling desperately with the key.

Then, slowly, she crossed to the window, and dashing the tears from her eyes, she stared out. The gardens were still deserted. Somewhere a barn owl screeched sharply, and she saw the pale shape of it drift by level with the window. Below, she heard the grating sound of the door being eased open in the ivy-covered wall, and Kemp emerged cautiously into the moonlight, his hand on the hilt of his cutlass. For a moment he stood to check, then he turned and looked up at her window. She drew back quickly, but he had seen her. He bowed low in her direction, sweeping the air with his free hand in a mocking salute, then sprinted towards the corner of the house.

Behind him, a shout echoed from the bushes near the wall. She saw Kemp whirl round, his cutlass in his hand. He stood still, staring into the darkness, before he ran towards the trees and was out of sight. After an instant, Sir Edward Brandon, the starlight glinting on the naked blade in his hand, burst out of the cover of the yew hedge and plunged after him in pursuit.

CHAPTER
FOUR

ELAINE GASPED, shrinking back from the window. If Sir Edward caught him, Kemp would betray Tom. Of that she had no doubt at all. The man was completely unscrupulous, and he had no reason to want to preserve the Howard name. No reason except one: to force her to help him with his evil plans. 'Tom,' she whispered out loud in anguish. 'Oh, Tom!' Hot tears welled up in her eyes once more, and falling on her knees beside the bed, she cried until she could cry no more.

It was a long time before she dragged herself to her feet, aching with misery. The last feeble flickers of candle-light had burned themselves out, and she was shivering violently.

'Mab!' she called. She wanted suddenly to have the reassurance of a fire in the empty hearth, the comfort of another person to hold her in her arms. 'Mab, where are you?' Her voice broke into a sob.

She ran to the door which led into the small ante-chamber. Mab's truckle bed was empty, as she had known in her heart it must be. Retreating, she latched the door of her own room miserably and made her way back to the window. The garden was completely silent. There was nothing to tell her whether Kemp had made good his escape.

All she could do was to creep back into her bed. She pulled the covers over her and huddled in one corner, staring at the window as the dawn began to dim the stars; somewhere above the meadow beyond the yew walk the first lark began to sing.

It was broad daylight when she awoke, cramped and stiff. Mab was on her knees, folding clean linen into a chest in the corner, humming quietly to herself. Elaine raised herself on her elbow and tried to call out, but no sound came. Frightened, she wondered if she were dreaming, if the whole terrible night had been a dream.

'Mab?' she tried again. The call came out as a whisper, but the girl heard her.

'Mistress? Oh my Lord, child, your face!' Scrambling to her feet, Mab ran to the bed and took Elaine into her arms. 'What in the world have you been doing, my duck, your face is that swollen!'

'Where were you, Mab? Where were you when I needed you?' Elaine put her hands on the girl's shoulders and shook her gently.

Mab went white. 'I was asleep . . .' she stammered.

'You weren't there!' Elaine repeated, almost hysterically. 'You weren't there when I called!'

Mab blushed crimson, and looked down at her hands. 'It was after you'd gone out. I thought there'd be no harm . . .' she faltered. 'I went out to see my young man; I didn't think it was wrong if you were doing it, too.' She looked stubborn suddenly.

'If I were doing it, too . . . Oh, dear God!' Elaine pressed her hands to her face, feeling the tears well up once more.

'What is it?' Mab held her close. 'Aren't you well? Come, sit down again and tell me.'

'It's Tom!' Elaine cried almost hysterically. 'Tom is dead.'

'Dead?' Hastily Mab crossed herself. 'That can't be!'

'It can be.' Elaine stared at her wretchedly. 'And I have to tell Papa.'

While her maid was downstairs fetching a restorative drink, Elaine went over to her mirror. As Mab had said, her eyes were red and swollen from weeping. And there was a small cut on her lip. The sight of it brought a vivid tide of colour to her cheeks. She pressed her fingers to her mouth in anger and shame as she thought of Guy Kemp and his importunate kisses, his insolence and his threats. The ruby necklace was still clasped round her throat, a gaudy reminder of her visitor in the night. Her hands shaking with humiliation and fury, she unfastened it, throwing it down on the table as if the stones had burned her.

If anyone came to inquire where she was that morning, Mab must have sent them away, for she was not disturbed. It was late before she heard the horses of her father's guest being brought out and round to the front of the house, but only when the last hoofbeat had died away did she begin to dress, knowing that she could put off the hour no longer.

The house was completely silent, as though it knew already of the tragedy that had hit the family, as she made her way through the empty rooms and down the broad staircase. Her father would be, she knew, in his library. Taking a deep breath, she opened the door and went in, giving herself no time to think.

'Papa, there is something I must tell you.' Looking up, her eyes swimming with tears, she realised too late that he was not alone. Sir Edward lay sprawled in a chair by the window, a ledger open across his knees. Both men rose as they saw her, their faces registering concern.

Sir Edward reached her first. 'Mistress Elaine! What is it?' His hands outstretched for hers, his brown eyes full of anxiety, but she brushed past him, their previous night's unpleasant encounter almost forgotten as she threw herself into her father's waiting arms.

'It's Tom, Papa. Tom!' she cried in anguish, her carefully prepared words of gentleness and sympathy flying out of her head as her father's embrace encirled her. 'There's been an accident. He's dead!'

Her father stared down at her for a long moment, his face blank with shock. Before her eyes he appeared to crumple, his face becoming that of an old, old man as his arms fell away from her.

Quietly Sir Edward moved to his side, and Robert Howard clutched at his arm. But only for a moment. He straightened almost at once, and raised his chin with a determination she had not realised he possessed.

'Pour me a goblet of wine, there's a good fellow,' he murmured to Sir Edward as he groped behind him for a chair. He collapsed on to it, his face grey with fatigue. Quietly Sir Edward moved away to fill one of the silver cups standing on the sideboard, and returned to give it to his host. Then he filled another, and brought it to Elaine.

'May I suggest you sit down too,' he said gently. 'And drink this. It will give you strength.'

She took the goblet from him automatically, not even noticing the light touch of his fingers on hers as he pressed it into her hand.

'How did you hear about Tom?' She was conscious suddenly that Sir Edward was staring at her, and she looked at the floor. 'One of his servants came to me this morning.'

'Early this morning?' His eyes had become hard and probing. 'When your father's servants tried to reach you this morning, they were not admitted to your room.'

Too late, she saw the trap. She looked away from him defiantly, her fingers clutched white around the cold metal of the goblet. 'It must have been very early,' she said softly. 'Before dawn, I suppose. I don't remember clearly. Afterwards I told my maid to let no one in. I was too upset. I could not face Papa . . .' Tears poured down her cheeks. 'I loved my brother, sir,' she cried wildly. 'Why question me like this? All I know is that he is dead!'

He bowed slightly. 'And I am deeply grieved at your loss,' he said. But there was still suspicion in his voice.

They brought Tom's body home on a litter just before midday. He was escorted by four men, all soberly dressed. One of them, Elaine recognised with a sharp pang of fear, was the pirate who had accosted her at Kingston Point. He bowed to her gravely, as she stood looking down with frozen stillness at the pall, and drew her a little to one side.

'I thought you would want to know, mistress, that I gave him your message,' he said quietly. 'He knew that you had regretted your quarrel, and that you loved him and wished him well.'

She stared at him for a moment, then tears blinded her eyes and she fell to her knees beside the figure beneath the scarlet embroidered cloth.

Tom's body lay in state in the old church across the garden from the house, surrounded by incense and candles in the soft light of the medieval stained glass. After the

requiem, he was laid to rest with his mother and his
brothers and sisters in the Howard vault beneath the
church, while the two remaining members of his family
tried desperately to come to terms with life without him.
Slowly the pattern of life resumed. The pile of silken palls,
gifts from Tom's mourners, were folded away in the church,
the sprigs of rosemary lying on his tomb dried and
crumbled, and Elaine, dressed in a black gown and kirtle,
and sombre hood, went about her duties as before.

Sir Edward had never again mentioned the visitor in the
midnight garden, and if he pursued his enquiries about the
pirates on his daily rides to the quay and the warehouses
at Woodbridge, he did not speak of them in her presence.
And if she remembered Guy Kemp at all, it was firmly to
put any memories of him aside, shamefully conscious that
even the thought of the man and the hands that had roamed
so freely over her body for those few moments brought a
feeling of disquiet which had nothing to do with the terrible
news he had brought.

It was Mab who told her that *Black Witch* had gone.
They were in the still-room, making rose-water, when
she glanced shyly at Elaine, checking nervously over her
shoulder that they were alone. Then she reached into her
apron and produced a sealed letter.

'This is for you, mistress. I was given it in Woodbridge
and told to pass it to you in secret.'

All unsuspecting, Elaine took the letter and examined
the seal. It bore the imprint of a flying gull. She broke
it open and studied the scrawled message inside. Mab,
watching with interest, saw her face grow pale as death as
she read. Then, angrily, Elaine crumpled the letter up and
threw it into the still-room fire. 'Some stupid joke,' she
said, shrugging, as Mab stared at her, and she ran from
the room.

Elaine pressed her hands to her burning cheeks, trying
to calm herself as she ran through the house towards the
great staircase. The letter had been from Kemp. The
memory of his threats and his insolence, which had faded
to nothing compared with her grief for Tom, now returned
in full. She could see his tall figure as though it stood before

her, with his savage blue eyes and his arrogant strength, and she remembered that, but for him, Tom would still be alive!

She stopped by the virginal in the great hall and ran her finger violently over the keys. 'No, Master Kemp,' she breathed. 'I shall not remember our pact when you return to Woodbridge. I shall never help you!'

'Mistress Elaine?' The strong masculine voice behind her made her jump. 'I'm sorry. I didn't mean to startle you, but I thought you addressed me.' Sir Edward Brandon was looking at her from the far side of the room, an expression of cruel amusement crossing his face as the colour rose and faded in her cheeks. 'I have just come from your father's room. He wishes to speak to you.' He smiled, and she was aware suddenly of a new light in his eyes as he looked at her—a new confidence, and possibly something more.

Puzzled, she stared at him for a moment. Then she forced herself to return his smile, putting Guy Kemp for the moment to the back of her mind.

'I shall go to him at once,' she said, as graciously as she could. For the past weeks she had had no cause to complain of Sir Edward's manner, and her dislike of him had lessened now that she no longer feared for Tom. Nevertheless, as she let herself out of the door, she saw him watching her with a look of open triumphant glee.

Robert Howard was pottering about his library, but looked up as Elaine came in, and she noticed again how frail he had become since Tom's death. She kissed him warmly, however, and squeezed his arm.

'Not reorganising your library again, Papa?'

He shook her off gently. 'Why not, pray? It's one of the few things I can do which I enjoy, and which doesn't exhaust me.' He coughed fretfully. 'Now, girl, sit down, sit down. I want to talk to you, and I am too tired to argue, do you understand?'

He sat down heavily on the oak settle, and she saw with alarm that he was pressing his hand to his side as though in pain.

'Papa!'

'No, girl, sit down.' He shook her off testily and, chastened, she obeyed him, gathering her skirts round her and sinking on to a stool at his feet.

He looked down at her thoughtfully, and at last she saw his tired face break into a smile. 'Sweet child, I wonder, has it crossed your mind that, since your brother's death, you have become my only heir?' She saw the wave of unhappiness cross his face at the mention of Tom, but in a second it had passed and he was resolute once more. 'You will one day inherit my houses and farms, my ships, my business, my wealth—everything.'

Elaine swallowed. 'But, Papa, you may yet marry again. You're quite young; you could have other sons . . .' Her heart cried out against the thought of there ever being someone else to take Tom's place, but her father's unhappiness was more than she could bear.

He shook his head. 'No, child. It is too late. There will be no more sons.' He reached out and touched her cheek. 'I have been pondering about how to ensure that your inheritance is safeguarded. There will scarcely be a man in the kingdom who will not wish to marry you, and I may have very little time to see that you are safely disposed of.'

Elaine stared up at his face, full of a sudden terrible misgiving, 'Papa?'

'No, child. Be silent. We have discussed your marriage on numerous occasions'—he gave a rueful smile—'and always you have talked me out of any alliance I might have considered. But I had to reach a decision. And it is made.' Stiffly he stood up and walked to the window. Elaine stared after him, numb with apprehension. For a moment she could not speak as the silence stretched out between them. At last he turned.

'I have agreed to your betrothal to Sir Edward Brandon.'

'No!' With a cry, she caught at her father's hand. 'No, Papa! I will not marry him!'

His eyes were full of sorrow as he gently disengaged his hand. 'I have already signed the preliminary agreements with him,' he said softly. 'My mind is made up.'

'I won't marry him, Papa. You cannot make me!' Scarcely knowing what she did, Elaine slipped to her knees at her father's feet. 'Please, Papa! You cannot insist!'

'Sit down here, child.' He pulled her down beside him on the settle. His face had paled to the colour of old parchment and his breath was coming in harsh gasps.

'Edward is a fine young man—and he is handsome, which I believe counts much with you ladies.' He attempted a smile. 'He knows much of my business already and has handled it with skill these past weeks since Tom's death. I trust him, Elaine. And I trust very few men.' He looked at her pleadingly. 'He also has another great recommendation, one which I confess I did not know before. It helped me finally to make up my mind when he asked me for your hand. You know it has always grieved me that, for all our wealth, our family has never been ennobled. True, we are distantly connected to the Norfolk Howards, but I had wished one day to please the King enough to win a title of my own.' He sighed. 'It is too late for me, Elaine, but Sir Edward is related to the Duke of Suffolk and, more important still, will be successor to his cousin the Earl of Thetford, who has no wife.' There was a feverish sparkle in his eyes as he scanned her face.

Elaine was pale as milk. 'And that won you to his cause, Papa?' she said through dry lips.

He nodded. 'That convinced me. My property will be secure, and my daughter will be a countess and welcomed at court. I shall be able to die in peace.' He broke into a paroxysm of coughing.

She stared at him in sudden terror as he gasped and spluttered, then jumped up and ran for the wine. 'Papa, don't . . . Please don't be upset. You're not going to die yet. Not for years, Papa!' With a shaking hand she held the cup to his lips. But after a sip or two he calmed a little, and a smudge of colour returned to his face.

'Obey me quietly in this, Elaine,' he breathed. 'I have no wish to force you, but force you I will if I have to.' His voice was gaining in strength. 'And I may not live long. I half have it in mind that I would rather be with your mother and Tom now, in the church.' He sighed. 'Do I have your promise that you will obey me?'

For a moment she could not answer. The room spun and

rocked until she thought she was going to faint, then it steadied, and she saw her father's taut, anxious face and she knew she could not do anything to put his health any more at risk. She forced herself to give a little smile.

'You have my promise, Papa.'

Sir Edward was waiting for her in the great hall. She shrank back with dislike as she saw him, but already he was coming towards her, a thin smile on his lips.

'I can see by the look on your face that your father has told you of our agreement. I hope it is not too displeasing to you?' He caught her hands and drew her to him.

She tried to pull away. 'I am afraid you must give me some time to grow used to the idea, Sir Edward,' she said coldly. She struggled to free herself, but in a moment he had an arm round her waist, pulling her hard against him.

'Such maidenly modesty is hardly necessary,' he whispered harshly, as his lips sought hers. 'You need not pretend with me, sweetheart. I am a man of the world.'

'Pretend?' Struggling harder now, Elaine tried to tear her wrists free. 'Please let me go . . .' But her words were stifled as his mouth claimed hers with triumphant possession. Closing her mind as best she could, she froze, submitting to his embraces with stony immobility. Almost at once he released her, as if his desire had gone once she stopped fighting him.

'That's better, though hardly the warm greeting I would expect from my betrothed,' he said unpleasantly. 'Don't tell me your indifference means that you had hoped to marry your pirate lover!'

'What do you mean?' Her heart was hammering furiously as she looked at the gloating face of the man who stood before her.

He smiled coldly. 'I mean the man whom you wave to on the deck of a caravel that slips out of Woodbridge in the night; I mean the man you visit in a bawdy tavern where no lady should be seen; I mean the man who creeps up to your bed by way of a secret stair in the moonlight.' His voice had sunk to a whisper as he shot out his hand and seized her arm once again. 'Oh, do not fear, my Elaine!

I shall not tell your doting father that the daughter he offers me is not a virgin. I shall not tell him she consorts with the very men who rob him. That would break his heart, would it not?' He pulled her close until her face was only inches from his. 'I can keep silent, my dear . . . if I want to.' He released her so suddenly that she staggered. 'I will not even ask you—yet—the name of your lover.' He smiled thoughtfully. 'Once we are married and your allegiance is totally mine, then I shall make you tell me everything about him. Or, perhaps, by then I shall have taken him, and you shall watch me put him to the question at my leisure before I hang him.'

Elaine flinched, afraid that she was going to faint. 'You're wrong,' she cried. 'You are quite wrong! I have no lover, and I have never consorted with the pirates.'

'No?' His eyes were like gimlets. 'Then who was it you waved to with such emotion on the deck of that ship? Who was it who saluted you at your window? A stranger, perhaps? Your dead brother's servant?'

Her retort froze on her lips. 'Yes.' She grasped at the lead he had unwittingly given her. 'At my window it was Tom's servant.' Her voice faded away, as his eyes held hers, mocking. She was remembering the night Guy Kemp came to her room, and the way he had comforted her after he had given her the news. How strange that, overwhelmed by her memories of his insolence and his threats, she had forgotten that one sweet moment of tenderness.

Edward seemed to be trying to read her mind. An unpleasant sneer curled his lip. 'No matter, sweetheart, who it was. I'll have little time for you, virgin or not, you'll be glad to hear. I have a lady at home who keeps me more than satisfied.' He laughed at the blush which mantled her cheeks. 'She'll not be pleased to see you. I suspect she'll flay me alive when I take you back to Aldebourne. But when she hears of the wealth you bring with you, she may change her mind.' He laughed again.

'Do you so blatantly covet my money, Sir Edward?' Elaine was shivering, in spite of the warmth of the afternoon.

'Why not? Your father understands. Our agreement is

clear. Your wealth, for the title I shall one day inherit. A bargain, don't you think? But don't fret. I'll have some time for you; enough to ensure that you are an obedient and fruitful wife.' He raised her face to look at it with insolent attention. 'Oh yes, Elaine, I shall have a little time for you. But now I have other things to do, if you will excuse me.' He bowed.

She watched him walk the length of the room and disappear through the door before she sank on the nearest chair, her heart pounding with anger and fear.

Time and time again over the next few days Elaine pleaded with her father to release her from her promise before the formal betrothal was made, but he would not listen. Deaf to her pleas and her tears, he called his lawyers to meet Sir Edward to talk of jointures and portions and estates and farms, and the final binding betrothal was made, and the date of the wedding fixed. It was to be Midsummer Day.

Robert Howard's two unmarried sisters descended on the house with a retinue of maids and dressmakers, and Elaine was forced to endure hours of fittings as her wedding gowns were made. Room after room vanished beneath clouds of silks and damasks, velvets and brocades, and Mab grew almost hysterical with excitement as she ordered the visiting servants about and gloried in her position as Elaine's personal maid.

Amid all the noise, Elaine herself grew more silent. A cold chain of misery seemed to be bound about her heart as she moved in a dream, trailing from room to room at her aunts' beck and call. To her relief she scarcely saw Sir Edward at all, and when she did, there was no sign of the savage triumph he had displayed the day their marriage had been agreed. It was as if now that he was sure of her, he had lost interest in her. For several days he disappeared, riding to his great house at Aldebourne to warn his servants there to make ready for a new mistress, and Elaine breathed again. But then he returned, attended by several young men and servants, and as he bowed and kissed her hand in greeting, she saw again the cruelty which lurked in his eyes.

Each night she would dutifully sip the possets that Mab produced for her, then sink into her bed and lie awake, as the hours slipped by, trying to force her mind to merciful blankness. When sleep eventually came, it was the deep blackness of total exhaustion.

Two weeks before her wedding, Kemp reappeared. He was waiting for her with three of his men as she rode back across the heath with Mab after visiting her godmother's house at Bromeswell. They were walking their horses slowly over the rabbit-cropped turf, several paces ahead of the two escorting grooms, when without warning the four men rose from the undergrowth.

Mab gave a little scream, but it was bitten off short as she found herself staring at the glinting blade of a dagger. In a moment, she and the two grooms had been led away and Elaine was alone, looking down into Kemp's face as he took a firm hold of her horse's bridle. Her fear was followed by a sharp sense of shock as she realised that it was the first time she had seen him clearly in daylight. His teeth were brilliant white in his deeply tanned face as he sketched a low bow. 'Mistress Elaine, I trust you have not forgotten our tryst.' His eyes were the colour of the sky arching high above.

She swallowed nervously, her gloved hands clutching at the scarlet reins. 'I could not believe you meant it, Master Kemp,' she managed to retort.

The heath was deserted. A shimmering heat-haze hung over the low bushes, and the silence was broken only by the clink of the horse's bridle as it shook its head, annoyed by the weight of the man's hand on its bit. The air was full of the bitter-sweet scent of gorse.

'You could not believe I meant it?' he repeated. 'Then I must convince you, it seems.' His tone was pleasant, but she heard the slight hint of a threat behind it and shivered in spite of the warmth of the afternoon.

She stared down at him. He was tall, as she had found out that night in her bedroom, and broad shouldered, and the salt-stained leather jerkin did little to hide his muscular physique. In his belt, besides the vicious cutlass, was a

small carved dagger. There was something violent and
frightening about him, but at the same time something
alarmingly attractive, and suddenly, in spite of her fear
and anger, she saw what it was that must have drawn Tom
to this man's side and made him his friend, and what it was
that had made her respond so wantonly to his kisses,
whilst those of her betrothed left her cold and afraid. The
compelling charm of the man was reaching out to her
once more now, and she could not help reacting automatically with a quickening of the breath and a little nervous
smile.

'How did you know I would be riding here?' she asked
after a moment.

His eyes narrowed a little. 'I have my spies.'

'And what makes you think that my servants will remain
quiet about our meeting?'

He grinned. 'That will be for you to ensure! I know you
will find a way of persuading them that it would be in your
father's best interests not to alarm him unduly.'

She bit her lip in quick anger. 'You seem to have outma-
noeuvred me, sir. And what is it that you wish to say to
me, now that you have so cleverly managed to arrange our
tryst, as you call it?' She tried to hide her nervousness by
patting the horse's neck.

'The time has come for you to help me,' he said swiftly,
lowering his voice. 'There are two things you must
find out; then tomorrow evening you must be prepared
to come aboard *Black Witch*. You will be away for
three days at most if the wind holds. Bring as little as
you can. A small coffer is all I allow. And you will come
alone.'

She gasped in disbelief. 'I cannot come with you!'

'You must.' His hand came down on both of hers,
pressing them against the high pommel of the saddle.
'Nothing I ask of you is too hard, Elaine. I wish to know
the date your father expects to receive his shipments. And
I want you to bring with you your father's seal of authority.
Do you understand?'

'No!' Her eyes were suddenly blazing with anger. Pulling
her hands free of his, she raised her whip. 'Let go of my

horse, sir! I shall have nothing to do with your plans. Nothing!'

Desperately trying to wrench the mare's head from his grasp, she kicked the black flanks, lashing at Kemp's head and hands. Cressid leaped forward and reared with a whistling scream of panic, but in a second Kemp's hand had closed over Elaine's, twisting the whip out of her grasp before he pulled her headlong from the saddle. She fell heavily on the sandy ground, and lay, too stunned to move or speak. Behind her, she was conscious that he had retained his hold on the horse to calm it, and was tethering it to a fallen tree. Only then did he turn his attention back to her.

'I trust you are not hurt,' he said curtly as he pulled her to her feet.

Speechless with anger, she shrank away from him.

'How dare you lay hands on me?' she cried. 'My father will have you flogged when he catches up with you.'

He smiled at her, his blue eyes dancing suddenly. 'Me? Flogged? I think not, mistress.' Then the humour had gone as swiftly as it had come. 'He would not flog Tom's partner in crime, his son's dearest friend, would he? I think you forget that it was Tom's last wish that you hide his connection with me from your father.'

Elaine glared at him unhappily. Was there any way in which she could fight this man, knowing he would always be able to defeat her by cynically manipulating her love for her father? Trembling, she turned from him, and realised nervously that her horse's sudden terrified cavorting had carried them out of sight of the others. She and Guy Kemp were alone.

She swallowed hard, trying to recover some vestige of courage. 'You know I will do anything to save Papa from that knowledge,' she said at last.

'Then you will do as I ask. A date, a seal, and three days from your life. That is all I ask, mistress,' he said, more gently this time. 'You won't find me constantly returning to demand your help. This one piece of business in Tom's memory, and then you will never see me again.'

She turned to face him, 'There is something you should

know: why I cannot go with you tomorrow, even if I wished it.' She looked up at him wearily. 'I am to marry Sir Edward Brandon on Midsummer Day.'

A conflict of emotions played over his face, and his eyes darkened enigmatically. 'Are you, indeed? The man who dares to think he can capture *Black Witch* by spreading his gold and his spies around the taverns and ale houses.' He laughed bitterly. 'So, he has been wooing my little Elaine as well.' He face became harsh. 'And does it please you, this marriage?' His eyes held hers, and she could feel the colour mounting in her cheeks.

'It pleases me very much,' she managed to retort. 'As it will when he catches you and hangs you.'

He frowned. 'So, you intend to confide in him, do you, this new husband of yours? You'll tell him of your pirate friend, and beg him to keep your secret while he hunts me down? You have already told him about Tom's activities, of course . . .'

'Well, no . . .' She hung her head. 'I couldn't tell him about Tom . . .'

His eyes narrowed. 'But I would, sweetheart. One thing you should know. When they bring a man of my calling to trial, they torture him first, to make him tell the names of his colleagues. I'm a brave man, I think, but I doubt if under torture even I would shield a dead man's name.'

She stared at him, aghast. 'Torture?' she whispered through stiff lips.

'Of course. King Henry wishes to discourage piracy, as he does other crime. In particular, successful crime.'

'And you are, of course, successful?' She managed a small smile.

He bowed. 'And intend to remain so. With your help.'

She shook her head slowly. 'I can't help you.'

'You can, Elaine. You have no choice, unless you want your father's illusions destroyed. Tomorrow evening my lieutenant will come for you. You may tell your father that you are staying with Mistress Ashley, your godmother, for three days, while she instructs you in some basic wifely skills.' Again the flash of humour showed in his eyes. 'She and I are old friends, and she will not give you away.'

'I don't believe you,' Elaine whispered. 'Aunt Margaret would never be a friend to someone like you!'

He grinned. 'You will have to ask her that yourself, sometime. It would surprise you, I think, to learn the names of some of my friends. Now, before Sam Fletcher comes for you tomorrow, make sure you have the seal. Your father will understand, I am sure, that in your nervous state you picked it up and dropped it into your pocket by mistake. Your maid will accompany you as far as Bromeswell. Then she will stay with Mistress Ashley out of sight until you return.'

'Why can't she come with me?' There was something like panic in Elaine's voice.

'Because one woman on a ship is like to prove an encumbrance,' he replied brutally. 'Two would be a disaster. And make sure she knows how to hold her tongue, for your father's sake.'

He fell silent, looking down at her. Then, as though only half realising what he did, he raised his hand to touch the lock of hair that had escaped her headdress and was curling loose on her shoulder. 'I hope you know what you are doing, Tom's sister, marrying Ned Brandon.'

Her eyes widened, and she felt the colour rising to her cheeks once more. 'You speak as though you know him.'

He grinned bitterly. 'I do indeed. We were neighbours once, he and I. I think it would please him immensely if he were to learn the name of the man he is trying to hang.'

'You were enemies then?'

He laughed. 'My brother and he were friends, put it that way. But my story is not one I tell, even to you, sweetheart. Come, you did not answer my question. Do you know what you are about, marrying him?'

'It is arranged. My father is satisfied, and I do not find Sir Edward unattractive.' It seemed very important somehow that he should not guess how much she had come to hate her betrothed.

'But do you love him?' His eyes held hers.

'I like him very much, Master Kemp. More than I have ever liked anyone else,' she replied with spirit. 'But I fail to see that how I feel is any business of yours.'

She started towards her horse. 'I will help you tomorrow because it seems that I must. But beyond that, I see no reason for us to speak again. If you will move out of my way, I shall go to find my servants.'

He did not stir. Hands on hips he grinned down at her, effectively barring the path. 'It would be churlish to leave without saying goodbye, mistress,' he said.

'I feel churlish, sir! Do you think my brother would have allowed you to be so familiar with me if he were here?'

'I think the answer to that would surprise you, Elaine,' he said softly. 'He spoke of you often and with much affection, and he told me of the processions of eager suitors you had turned away and the need one day for you to be furnished with a husband who would be capable of ruling you.' He paused thoughtfully. 'I only regret that the one you have chosen is Ned Brandon. However, chosen him you have, and it will give me enormous pleasure to know I have stolen a further kiss from his bride!'

His strong arms had enfolded her before she knew what he was about, and his lips, seeking hers, were demanding and powerful. She started to pull away, but then, hardly realising that they did so, her lips parted eagerly beneath his kisses, and she stood helpless in his embrace, feeling a delicious languor creep over her limbs. The hot sky spun into a dome of gold as her arms slipped treacherously about his neck.

It was a long time before he released her and looked down at her, his eyes enigmatic. 'I look forward to our next meeting, mistress. It promises well,' he said softly.

She was horrified, her cheeks burning with shame, but already he had turned away. Stooping, he released the rein of her horse, and almost before she knew it, his hands were on her slim waist and she was in the saddle.

'Until tomorrow, Tom's sister,' he said with a chuckle, and sweeping his cap from his head, sketched an elaborate bow. Then he turned, and with a shrill whistle to his henchmen, he vanished into the tangle of gorse and brambles.

CHAPTER
FIVE

MOMENTS LATER, Mab and the two servants appeared, leading their horses at the run. At the sight of her mistress, Mab burst into tears. 'Oh my love, I thought you'd been killed!'

Shakily Elaine steadied Cressid. She was frantically trying to think of something to say to the three anxious people which would reassure them and at the same time ensure that they understood her need for complete secrecy. Then her problem was abruptly solved for her. The elder of her two escorts, John Palmer, who had been her brother's man, smiled knowingly, his eyes gleaming in the sunlight.

'We'll tell no one of this incident, Mistress Elaine. I know he was Master Tom's friend,' he said quietly.

'You know?' she echoed in disbelief. She had not seen any sign of recognition pass between the two men.

He nodded. 'Will and Mabbet will stay silent, too, if that is your wish, you may depend on it.' He was watching her face closely.

'Yes.' She was still trying to compose herself. 'Yes, that is my wish. No one must know that we met him here.' She could feel herself becoming agitated again, in spite of his reassuring manner.

'No one will ever find out from us.' He snapped his fingers at Mab and Will. 'Mount up,' he commanded. 'We are late, and Mistress Elaine must not be missed.' Releasing her bridle, he swung himself on to his own horse and fell in next to her on the track which led towards home.

For the rest of the ride, Elaine retreated into her own anxieties, trying to think of a way to accomplish the tasks Guy Kemp had set her, and long after she was once more at King's Brook she had still not been able to see her father alone. Sir Edward had been at his side the whole time since his return from his estates, and this day seemed to be no exception. Tired and depressed, she retired to her room.

Her father had two seals. A large official one, which was carried by one of his clerks in a leather pouch, and a smaller signet which he wore on the forefinger of his left hand. Both were as inaccessible as a piece of the rainbow.

Increasingly panic-stricken, she went down to supper, only to find that one of her problems was being solved for her. The men were discussing the very shipment that Kemp had asked her about, talking with easy familiarity across the top of her head as if she were not there at all. Her father could not conceal his excitement.

'The ships have been delayed for months by storms and sickness on their voyage back from Venice.' He reached for his wine, colour showing in his cheeks. 'But they are now on the last lap of their journey, and wait only for the next fair wind to bring them home.'

'How many ships are there, Papa?' Elaine asked, her eyes almost unwillingly straying to the signet on his finger.

Her father looked at her, surprised at this sudden interest after her long rebellious silences at meals. Then he smiled with a pleased shrug. 'Four galleons left Woodbridge. One was mine, the others belonged to three other merchants. *Star*, James Carpenter's ship, foundered, but the three others return.' He rubbed his hands together.

Elaine noticed then that Sir Edward was watching her, with his lip curled cynically.

'Why this curiosity I wonder, about the number of ships,' he asked softly. 'Does it reflect your new-found interest in the sea?'

She could feel herself colouring under his gaze, and looked away quickly. 'I have no interest in the sea, Sir Edward,' she retorted. 'Only in my father's welfare. What interests him, interests me.'

'And you don't wish to know how the galleons are armed or the numbers of their crew?' His eyes were merciless as they bored into hers.

'I should very much like to know both, of course,' she

said defiantly. 'And every detail with which you can furnish me!'

Her anger, fuelled by the knowledge that, this time, she really was the spy he suspected her to be, exploded in her eyes, and for a moment he looked taken aback. Then he smiled.

'They are well armed, Elaine,' he said smoothly. 'More than well. They have fought pirates off Spain and Algiers and in the bay of Syracuse to bring their cargoes home, and their crews are unscathed.'

· Behind her, her father shook his head sadly. 'No, my boy, you are wrong. They have been very unlucky. The letter my messenger brought from Antwerp says that the ships are sadly undermanned. Sickness has taken many of the men and many have deserted. Had they been attacked, they would have stood little chance.'

Elaine felt a little treacherous surge of triumph as she turned back to her betrothed and saw the anger on his face. She forced herself to laugh lightly. 'Had I been what you suspected, Sir Edward, I should have been glad to have that information,' she murmured, so that her father could not hear.

By the time she had bidden her father good night and returned to her room with Mab, she was still no nearer to thinking of a way to obtain her father's seal. The more she racked her brains to try to produce some plan, the more worried she became. Kemp's face kept appearing in her mind; with the implacable coldness of his eyes that replaced so swiftly the far-away look as he kissed her, and the cruel twist of his lips when he threatened to expose Tom, haunting her.

Long after she had gone to bed she lay awake, listening to Mab's steady breathing on the truckle bed in the corner. She had insisted that her maid sleep with her every night since Kemp's visit to her room, terrified that he might reappear although the door beneath the ivy was now securely bolted.

The thought of Kemp made Elaine blush violently, and her mind returned to their encounter on the heath. It did not seem possible that a man of such unscrupulous cruelty would also be the one who had with his insolent caresses turned her body to fire and melted her resentment and anger to helpless delight. She could not understand herself; her body had seemed to react quite independently of her feelings, and the realisation filled her with shame. She shuddered, and dragged her mind back to the seal, not allowing herself to remember even for an instant that one of the ships they had been discussing that evening belonged to her father. The anguish he would suffer at the loss of his cargo was still a thousand times less than anything that he would suffer if he were to find out about Tom. She was trapped, and she could do nothing but obey Kemp's instructions. And, to do that, she had to obtain the seal.

Only one course of action seemed possible. To creep down to the library now, while the household was asleep, and see if she could find it. She sat up reluctantly, half hoping that Mab would wake, but with a little snort and a mutter, Mab threw out her arm and turned over, then lay quietly again and her breathing steadied. Cautiously Elaine slid out of bed, wrapped her cloak round her and tiptoed towards the door. The heavy latch stuck briefly, and then came free with a rattle. She held her breath, but Mab did not stir again.

Trembling with anxiety, she let herself into the next bedroom. Her Aunt Mary was fast asleep, snoring in the high bed, the curtains tightly pulled. On a low bed in the corner a maid lay, mouth open in the faint moonlight. Leaving the door ajar, she tiptoed on through the successive bedrooms. No one heard her. Only in the great hall below did the dogs stir and raise their heads. Breathing more freely now, she thrust a taper into the embers of the fire to light a candle before she moved on towards her father's library. The faint circle of candlelight showed the big table covered with books and manuscripts, and a carved chair, also piled high—but no seal.

Beyond the library was a small room used by Robert Howard's clerks and transcribers as an office. She held the candle at arm's length and peered in. It was barely furnished with two stools, a shelf piled high with documents, the chequer table on which the clerks did their accounts, and the high desk with its ink-pots and quills, an abacus and rolls of unused parchment. And there, on the corner, lay the bag. Elaine caught it up, her heart beating as she prayed the seal would be there and not locked away. But her fingers found its hard shape at once and she extracted it carefully, then replaced the bag on the desk, glancing as she did so at the black, unshuttered windows, each pane of glass reflecting accusingly the bright flame of her candle. Shamed, she blew it out, and made her way back.

It seemed to her that she did not breathe again until she had regained her bedroom. She thrust the seal deep under her feather pillows and jumped into bed. In the corner, Mab had never stirred.

Next morning, while the maid was downstairs fetching her hot water, Elaine snatched the seal from the pillow. She had to leave it somewhere secure because there would certainly be an outcry as soon as its loss was discovered, and it was more than likely that her father would have the whole house searched. Fumbling in her haste, she found the key to her jewel chest in its usual hiding-place in the beam above her head. She unlocked it and threw back the lid. A pile of jewels sparkled up at her, on the top of them the ruby necklace, but the packet of letters Tom had given her had gone. She stared down at the casket in horror, then she emptied it on the bed. Silver and gold chains, an ivory rosary, enamelled brooches, pearls, rings and pendants spilled out, but no letters. She looked round the room, half expecting to see the packet lying on the table or on the floor, but there was no sign of it, and she knew that she had locked it away safely.

Putting everything back, she dropped the seal into the casket with the jewellery, locked it and looked at the small key in her hand. 'Was it you, Mab?' She turned furiously on the maid as she staggered in with a pitcher of fast-cooling water. 'Did you take Tom's letters?' The look of blank incomprehension on Mab's face answered the question for her before the girl could open her mouth.

With a shiver of fear, Elaine glanced back at the little chest as she went downstairs, the key safely knotted this time to the end of her long silk girdle. Until that morning she had barely given a thought to Tom's packet of letters and the mysterious Mistress Lockesley who would come to claim them, but now, without quite knowing why, the loss of the letters filled her with foreboding.

The expected uproar about the loss of the seal never came. Robert Howard, in a high good mood, had decided to dispatch his two clerks on an errand to Norwich as soon as they had broken their fast, and himself prepared to go down to Woodbridge with Sir Edward. The door of the little office behind the library remained closed.

Elaine watched her father leave with an overwhelming feeling of sadness. By the time he returned, she would have gone, and he would never know how much she was risking for his sake. She tried to close her mind to the thought of what the evening would bring, but the knowledge that she was trapped as surely as if Kemp held her under lock and key kept coming back to her. She had to go to her fate willingly and agree to anything he had arranged for her to do. The thought was not a pleasant one.

The day passed slowly, as she followed Aunt Mary and Aunt Jane through the hollow tasks of preparing for her wedding as the tension inside her built up and in the courtyard the shadow inexorably moved round the sundial. She asked Mab to pack them both small trunks with a change of clothes, telling her that they would be away for a few days with Mistress Ashley. In the end, it was almost with relief that she heard her whisper late in the afternoon. 'Mistress Elaine, the steward from your godmother's farm is here to escort us to Bromeswell.'

Elaine looked up from her stitching, her stomach knotting with fear. But she rose calmly, kissing each of her aunts on the cheek, explaining that a visit to Mistress Ashley had been arranged; then she made her way with every show of outward confidence towards her room.

The small trunks with a change of clothes were ready, and her cloak laid on the bed. Bidding the girl take the boxes down, Elaine waited for her to disappear, then, her fingers clumsy with haste, she unlocked the casket and retrieved her father's seal.

Two men were waiting with four horses openly on the carriageway in front of the house. She recognised neither of them as they bowed to her. Mab was already seated on one of the horses, the trunks strapped behind the men's saddles.

The elder introduced himself as Sam Fletcher, then he helped Elaine to mount. He was elegantly if soberly dressed, but the clothes could not disguise the deep rich tan of his skin which could have come only from the sea, or the serviceable sword and brace of daggers thrust into his belt.

Determined not to let him see her fear, Elaine sat proudly erect as she gathered her reins. Neither man had spoken as they set off up the drive, and the oppressive silence was somehow more frightening than any speech would have been. Even Mab had grown quiet, glancing in puzzlement at her mistress as they rode.

They rode towards Woodbridge along tracks, avoiding the roads until they reached the village of Melton, where they halted.

At last Fletcher spoke. He reached forward and took the rein of Mab's horse. 'Get up behind the lad there,' he commanded curtly. 'He'll take you to Mistress Ashley at Bromeswell.' He turned to Elaine. 'Have you told the girl to hold her tongue?' Elaine shook her head miserably. 'Then do so now. You know the risk if she doesn't.'

She looked at Mab pleadingly. 'You must go on to Mistress Ashley alone, Mab, and stay there until I return,' she said quietly. 'If anyone asks for me, you must say I am ill and can see no one.' She swallowed desperately. 'Please, Mab. Tell no one at all that I have gone.'

'You're going to him?' Mab said incredulously. 'To Kemp! He's your lover?'

Elaine gulped. 'No! He's not my lover.'

But Mab's face had blossomed into happy smiles. 'Oh, my love, I'll not tell a soul. They won't drag it out of me with wild horses!'

Elaine shuddered, glancing at the impassive face of her escort. But she knew it was sensible to let Mab go on thinking she was going to an assignation with her lover.

That was a secret the girl would know how to keep.

Then Mab was gone, jolting behind the younger man on the back of his horse, and Elaine and her guide were alone.

Almost at once he plunged back into the woods, leading the horse which carried her box at a brisk trot, gesturing her to follow. The track he took was almost imperceptible, winding steeply down towards the river through the fresh green bracken. They rode north, following the curving banks of the river where it narrowed dramatically to meander through soft meadows bordered with reed-beds. Only when they were across it did they turn eastward, splashing the horses through the sandy shallows, keeping up a steady fast pace.

'Where are we going?' Elaine could bear his silence no longer. She felt sick with fear, and tired after her sleepless night and the long day of tension.

Fletcher reined back slightly to ride beside her. 'Not far now. The *Witch* is anchored out in the tideway a bit further down the river.'

With a shudder, Elaine glanced beyond him to where the water was widening rapidly now as they rode towards the sea, the grey tide running in strongly. A cluster of boats were anchored in the centre of the water, their bows pointing towards the sea, but there was no sign of the raked masts of the caravel. The wind off the land carried the smell of pines and bracken. There was no hint in the air of the open sea half a dozen miles away. The sun was low now as it fell towards a bank of purple storm-cloud. The tide would soon be high.

They had been riding for some time in the deepening twilight when they rounded a corner and Elaine saw *Black Witch* anchored in the tideway, the three masts almost invisible against the dark trees of the opposite side of the hidden bay. She tightened her grip on the horse, resisting the urge to turn and gallop in the opposite direction. As if sensing her terror, her escort reined back beside her and reached across to take her bridle.

'We'll leave the horses here,' he said abruptly. 'A boy will come by and by to take them to the farm.'

Helping her to dismount, he untied her small trunk and

hefting it on to his shoulder led the way down a rabbit-track in the direction of the water. The wind had freshened, and her cloak was blowing behind her as she hurried after him. Almost imperceptibly, the tide had turned.

A small boat was drawn up on the beach. Two sailors were sitting near it, idly tossing dice.

'Hurry it up, lads!' The voice beside her was peremptory. 'The captain is waiting for his guest.'

The men scurried to the boat, and ran it down the sand until it floated. One held its bow, up to his knees in the darkening water, while the other returned for Elaine's trunk. Elaine stared at the water in horror. There were perhaps ten feet of black ripples between the sand and the waiting boat.

The man beside her grinned at her suddenly. 'No, mistress. You'll not get your skirts wet. Captain likes his guests dry!' And, without a by your leave, he swung her high as he strode into the water, heedless of his own boots and hose.

Breathless and frightened, she was seated in the bow, clutching the little boat's sides as the three men climbed on board with her, rocking it violently. Then they were being paddled swiftly out towards the ship.

The men sat in silence, keeping their eyes averted from her until they came alongside *Black Witch*. Elaine could feel her terror mounting. The ship rose black above her, blotting out the fading red of the sunset, her timbers creaking gently as she rode the tide. High up on the deck was the outline of a figure. Without being told, she knew it was Kemp, and she felt another tremor. A small seat was lowered into the boat on the end of a piece of rope, and she stared at it in incomprehension.

Her guide laughed out loud. 'You sit in it, mistress,' he instructed patiently, 'unless you can shin up a rope.' Behind him, one of the sailors was doing just that, pulling himself up hand over hand until he disappeared over the bulwarks.

She shrank back, but there was no escape. Almost fainting with fright, she allowed Fletcher to fit the rope over her shoulders until she was sitting on the seat as if it were a child's swing. Then she was whisked up into the air. Her eyes were still tight shut long after she had landed on the gently moving deck of the ship and was safely on her feet.

There was a low chuckle at her side. 'You may open your eyes now, Mistress Howard.' Kemp's voice was quietly triumphant. 'Welcome aboard *Black Witch*.'

Elaine then saw that he was watching her, a sardonic smile on his face. The last crimson segment of the sun was sliding into gold-rimmed blackness. She shivered violently, feeling the cold river wind brush her face.

'Do you wish to hide yourself straight away in the cabin, Mistress Howard,' he went on softly, 'or are you going to stand with me on deck?' There was open challenge in his voice.

Raising her chin a fraction, she met his gaze squarely. 'I should like to stand with you,' she said as firmly as she could, and was rewarded by a glimmer of admiration in his eyes.

She followed him aft to the steep steps which led up to the high poop deck, as the ship came to life and, in practised silence, the crew made ready for sea. Some were already swinging aloft in the rigging, their bare feet clinging to the ropes as they inched along the yards, lowering the sails, while others manned the capstan, bringing the anchor slowly swinging clear of the water, its flukes laden with wrack. Within minutes, *Black Witch* had begun to move, the water slapping her sides as she headed majestically down river.

The huge dark sails bellied strongly in the wind, and, with a little gasp, Elaine felt the vessel heel slightly beneath her feet. Kemp was staring ahead of them, eyes narrowed. Sam Fletcher had joined them, resplendent now in a dark red shirt. His feet were bare, like those of most of the crew.

'Take over, Sam, if you please.' Kemp stood back from the rail. 'You know where we're bound,' and he winked at his lieutenant, who grinned broadly in return.

Elaine was clutching a wooden stanchion as the angle of the planking beneath her feet increased slightly. 'Where are we bound?' Her voice sounded slightly breathless even to her own ears.

Kemp had come to stand beside her, balancing effortlessly on the moving deck. 'South-east.' His arm brushed hers, but he did not appear to notice. 'We make our rendezvous tomorrow if the wind holds.'

The ship righted herself as they rounded a bend in the river and the sails spilled wind, flapping in the lee of a hill. The speed dropped, until they were being carried only by the tide. To any watcher on shore, the ship must have looked like a black ghost drifting on the gleaming water.

Beside her, Kemp smiled. 'Frightened, Mistress Howard?'

'Not at all. Why? Is there something to fear?'

'There is always something to fear at sea.' His voice was taunting. 'The wind, the tides, the deep water; shifting sands, enemy craft coming out of the mist; serpents which coil round your ship in the darkness and draw her down to the depths below.'

Elaine could not hold back her gasp of horror as she looked down at the river sliding past them.

Kemp laughed. 'Not here. Out beyond the bar. That is where the sea is mistress.' His eyes gleamed. 'Here, the dangers lie on the land. Most of the river folk here are our allies, but there are spies. Men who would sell us to the King's justice.'

His hand clamped on her wrist so suddenly that she let out a little cry of fright, struggling to free herself as he swung her to face him. 'I wonder. Did you resist the temptation to tell your betrothed about me?' He shot the question at her. 'Did he charm you into forgetting your promise to your brother?'

Elaine blazed with anger. 'If I had told him, Master Kemp, you would be in chains already, and your crew with you,' she retorted. 'I should have told him. I wanted to tell him. If it wasn't for Papa, I would have!'

Kemp chuckled. 'So you are good at keeping secrets. You are indeed an exceptional woman.' He turned, as a sailor padded up to stand near them. 'What is it, Walt?'

'Cook's compliments, master, and dinner is served!' the man recited. He was grinning widely, his disfigured teeth gleaming. 'He says you're to eat now, in the river, before the storm sets, or your lady'll not have the stomach for food and it will all be wasted!'

'Does he now!' Kemp roared with laughter. 'You hear him, Mistress Howard? Our cook seems to have made a special effort on your behalf. Come, let me show you to our dining-hall.'

Elaine followed him unhappily, feeling the eyes of all the crew on her as she climbed awkwardly down the steep steps, but she could not escape from him as he ushered her through the low door into the cabin. It was like a small room, the large square windows which overlooked the stern shuttered now against the night. Two lanterns swung gently from the bulkhead, lighting up the furnishings. A broad bunk against the wall, furnished with woollen covers and rugs of soft fur, some chairs, a couple of sea-chests, brass bound and padlocked and an oak table nailed to the floor, covered by a rich red carpet, were the main contents of Guy Kemp's home.

He watched her as she gazed round, trying to accustom her eyes to the light. 'This will be your cabin while you are on board,' he said quietly. He unbuckled his sword-belt and laid his weapon on the bunk. 'I hope you will be comfortable. Come and sit down, you must be hungry.'

Elaine sat gingerly in one of the chairs, her cloak still round her shoulders. Was she to share the cabin, she wondered suddenly, with its rightful owner? At the thought, she felt her cheeks colour sharply.

His hands touched lightly on her shoulders. 'May I take your cloak?' His voice was very quiet. 'You will need it if you go on deck later. The sea air is cold.'

Unresisting, she let him have it, and he laid it next to his sword.

To her surprise, she was hungry. Two of Kemp's men entered carrying heavy trays, and they served her a thick spicy broth, while on a platter near her was bread, butter and creamy cheese.

She was astonished by the food. 'I thought sailors ate hard biscuits?' she said with a little smile.

'They do usually.' He carved at the loaf with his knife and tossed her a wedge of bread. 'Ship's biscuits, salt fish, dried peas, oatmeal. But ours would be a sorry ship if we could not feed you properly barely an hour from our anchorage.' His face was gleaming with laughter.

She was acutely conscious suddenly of his presence near her, seated so closely across the table that their hands could touch. The cabin seemed very small, and she did not dare to meet his gaze, as the very air between them seemed to crackle with danger.

'How do they manage to cook like this?' she asked without looking at him. It seemed important somehow to keep talking in this polite vein; but her hand as she picked up her spoon was shaking.

'There is a charcoal cooking-box on deck,' he replied gravely. 'You may see it later, if you wish. I'm glad to see you feel a housewifely interest in the running of the *Witch*.'

She glanced up at him, trapped by his teasing tone. 'Not at all. I just wondered how they managed, that's all . . .'

In the lantern light, she was unable to read his expression, so she looked instead at the bowls and plates upon the wetted cloth which covered the table. They gleamed softly in the swinging light.

His eyes were still on her, reading her own thoughts as though she had spoken out loud. 'I would be a poor follower of my profession if I could not eat off silver,' he murmured.

She bit her lip. For a while almost, with the novelty of being on the ship and in his presence, she had forgotten the nature of his calling.

Hastily she groped for a change of subject, once more anxious to avoid a dangerous silence. 'Will there really be a storm?' The thought brought a tremor to her voice.

'Didn't you see it coming in the west? Storm and wind. They'll hit us before midnight. I'm sorry your first trip with us is likely to be a rough one.'

'My first and my last!' she said vehemently. 'I trust you are not going to forget your promise. You assured me you would not keep coming back with more demands.'

He grinned, ignoring the taunt. 'Just the one raid, to be sure. And, who knows, this one may prove so rich a haul that I can retire, in which case it will be my last adventure, too. Which reminds me that I have yet to ask you whether you have brought the seal.' His eyes hardened suddenly. 'I trust you weren't so foolish as to come without it?'

The edge in his voice made the hair prickle on the back of her neck. The charming host was gone; in his place was the ruthless schemer.

'What would you do if I had?' Elaine asked defiantly before the last of her courage trickled away.

'Throw you overboard,' he replied without hesitation. 'The *Witch* does not carry useless passengers.'

'You would really do that?' she whispered.

'Of course.' Hiding a smile, he put out his hand lazily. 'Perhaps you had better let me have it, in case my worst instincts get the better of me!'

'You shall have it, sir, when the moment comes,' she said as sternly as possible, and for a moment she quailed before the anger in his eyes.

Then, unexpectedly, he laughed. 'You are afraid that I will throw you over once I have the seal? There would be all the time in the world for that on the voyage back. No, I'm afraid, my sweet Elaine, that you will have to trust me. I'll have it now, if you please.'

She swallowed, and reluctantly got to her feet, looking at him defiantly. 'I must ask you to turn your back, Master Kemp,' she said at last. 'I have the seal tied in my petticoat.'

He stood up gravely. 'An enviable place to hide.'

Blushing scarlet, she turned from him as she drew up the front of her heavy black skirt and fumbled for the kerchief in which she had wrapped the seal. It came free at last, and smoothing down the layers of silk and linen, she turned back to him.

He was leaning against the table, arms folded, watching her with interest. 'I did not agree to turn my back,' he said with a grin. 'I'm afraid my small supply of polite behaviour does not extend to turning my back on beautiful women. On the sea, such an action is considered the height of bad manners. Besides, I've seen you in your chemise before.'

Her cheeks flamed again, and angrily she held out the seal. 'Take it, sir. I trust it will ensure your admission to everlasting perdition!'

He gave her a mocking look. 'A fitting end to my career, no doubt.'

In the distance, there was a faint rumble of thunder. Elaine caught her breath. Once more the ship was heeling, and the lanterns were swinging crazily beneath the low beams of the cabin.

Kemp strode towards one of the chests in the corner and threw back the lid. Withdrawing a small coffer, he set it on the table, sweeping aside the remains of their meal. 'The seal will be safe enough here,' he commented tersely. 'But first we shall use it on a document I want you to sign.' He rummaged through a pile of charts and almanacs and then fished out a piece of parchment and unfolded it before he read it through carefully. Then he produced a pen and ink-horn, and held out the pen to her. 'You will sign here, if you please.'

Elaine drew back. 'What is it?'

'Your brother bequeathed certain items on this ship to you as he was dying. This is a receipt to say that you acknowledge that they are now yours.'

She stared at the lines of cramped black writing suspiciously. With the uneasy motion of the ship and the pale swinging lantern-light, she knew she would not be able to read it. There was a faint buzzing somewhere behind her eyes, and she put her hand to her head. 'I have received nothing of my brother's, Master Kemp. Nothing at all.'

He nodded. 'This other sea-chest was Tom's. There are some clothes. Also books, charts, and a certain amount of booty.' He smiled at her. 'You are free to inspect it whenever you wish. I shall have the chest transported back to King's Brook for you when we return.'

Tears suddenly pricked Elaine's eyes, and she sat down and took the pen from him. Without looking at the document, she scrawled her signature at the bottom of the page, the quill stuttering drops of the soot-black ink, then she threw it down and watched dully as he warmed wax and appended her father's seal.

He surveyed her for a moment. 'Do you feel ill?' he asked curtly.

The motion of the ship was stronger now, but she shook her head resolutely, holding to the edge of the table. The buzzing in her head was worse and she felt a little odd, that was true, but she would not be sick. Not in front of this man! She clenched her fists tightly, feeling her hands wet with icy perspiration.

'Perhaps some air. It is rather hot in here,' she said desperately.

He was folding the document she had signed, and put it away in the coffer with the pen and ink and the seal. In a moment it was locked. Then he turned towards the bunk and scooped up her cloak.

'Come. It is time I was on deck anyway. We have reached the sea.' Dousing the lanterns, he pulled open the cabin door and ushered her out on to the deck. They were travelling fast now, under a full head of sail. The two men stood braced at the helm while Sam Fletcher remained on watch, his face faintly visible in the half light of the moon. The silver segment was cut and sliced by straggling, rushing cloud. From somewhere behind them came another rumble of thunder.

Suddenly Kemp's arm was round her, holding her close against him. With a violent shock she felt the warmth of his body against hers, and his breath on her cheek.

'Stand over here,' he spoke directly into her ear, 'out of the wind.' He was pushing her against the wall of the cabin. He grinned, and she saw the gleam of his teeth in the dark. 'Are you sure you are not afraid?'

She shook her head and knew suddenly that it was true. Now that they were out of the cabin, her head had cleared. The wind and the fresh cold smell of salt and sea filled her lungs, exhilarating; as was the power of the huge sails straining above her. She stared up at them, seeing the long pennants streaming before the wind, bearing the insignia of the flying gull, and below them, the yards and rigging a spiderweb of strength against the stars, and her spirits soared, her fear and exhaustion eclipsed by the sheer force of the elements around her. She caught her breath in awe. In the lightning she had seen the sea, radiant and lonely, surrounding them. There was no sight of land.

'I do believe you're enjoying it!' The quiet voice beside her was gently mocking.

She turned to him, catching the wisps of trailing hair out of her eyes where they had escaped her hood, unaware that her amber eyes had been brilliant with excitement. 'But—it's beautiful!' she cried. 'I never guessed!'

He caught her hand. 'Come aft. You'll see better from up there.'

The full force of the wind caught her, and she staggered against him as they climbed the steep steps, a peal of thunder reverberating over the water as lightning stabbed the waves, turning the air an eldritch green.

He laughed out loud. 'I think we're kindred spirits, you and I, Elaine.' Turning slightly, she looked up into his face. It was remote, full of hidden excitement, once again the cruel face she had seen when the *Witch* cast off from Kingston Point the first time she had seen him. Rain was blowing in her face as their eyes met, and neither looked away, steel blue meeting fiery amber in the blaze of light. For a brief instant it was as if their very souls had reached out and touched. Then the moment was past. Elaine was shivering violently, glad that the thunder and the roar of the wind prevented them from speaking.

The storm lasted several hours, and long before it was over, she had gone, exhausted, back to the cabin, thankful to be out of the wind and the rain. It was stuffy in the darkness, but she was too tired to care. Feeling her way towards the bunk, she slipped off her sodden cloak and then kicked off her shoes. Her queasiness had shown no sign of returning.

Hours before, Kemp had left her side to supervise the ship, ignoring Sam Fletcher's advice to reduce sail, revelling still in the mad thrash across the wave-tops. Elaine, turning to watch him descend the steps to the waist of the ship, saw Fletcher staring aloft, worried, gesturing at the straining rigging, and she had seen Kemp throw back his head and laugh, stretching out to touch the taut halyards as though testing the very nerves and flesh of the vessel, and she knew he had forgotten her existence.

Wearily she sat down on the bunk, wishing there was

some light, feeling the shuddering of the ship's timbers all round her as she reached up to loosen the heavy braids which held her hair.

Within a few moments, the cabin door opened and a flash of lightning revealed Kemp silhouetted against the storm. He grinned. 'I wanted to make sure you were still on board,' he said. 'One minute you were there, watching us like a figurehead against the sky, and the next you had gone. Get some sleep if you can. Do you have all you need?' He braced himself easily, balancing as the deck swayed beneath his feet. 'As I said, the cabin is yours. I shall remain on watch.'

Elaine clutched a rug closely round her shoulders, acutely conscious that his presence in the confines of the cabin made her pulses beat faster, terrified of the sudden longing which overwhelmed her. It was wicked and wanton of her even to consider the thoughts which flitted, taunting, through her mind.

'Thank you, I need nothing,' she said as calmly as she could. 'Please leave me to sleep.'

He laughed softly. 'You'll have to take off those wet clothes first. Do you wish me to help to unlace you?' As he stepped towards her, the wind caught the door and flung it shut, cutting out the worst scream of the storm, enclosing them in pitch darkness. Elaine shrank back against the wall. Only six steps would bring him to her across the cabin floor.

'Leave me, Master Kemp, I need no help.' She tried to keep a firm note of command in her voice. 'I prefer to be alone.' Holding her breath, she heard him laugh softly. He was very near her now.

'Do you indeed?' His finger ran lightly down her wet sleeve.

'No!' she breathed. 'Please . . .'

She clenched her fists, trying to still the frantic beating of her heart. 'Leave me, Master Kemp,' she whispered desperately. 'Leave me now.'

'Or?' His tone was conversational as he caught a tress of her hair and weighed it experimentally in his hand. 'If I don't leave you, what will happen? Your tone implies a threat, Elaine. If I decide to exercise the rights I have as captain of this ship to do as I please with every member of my crew, and use you in the only way a beautiful woman should be used, what will you do?'

'But I am not a member of your crew,' she cried, her heart hammering with fright as his fingertips explored the warm angle of her neck behind her ears beneath her loosened hair.

'And I carry no passengers. Can you have forgotten so soon?' His voice was smooth as velvet.

She stared up at him in the darkness. 'You need me, remember?' She was summoning the last vestiges of her courage. 'You need me to help you convince your—friend —that I am your messenger from Woodbridge.'

He laughed. 'I need your father's seal, Elaine. To have you as well is a bonus, I admit, but one I could forgo if I had to.' He drew her against him slowly. Fear battled with longing as she felt his lips on her brow, moving down to kiss her eyes and then her cheeks. 'Do you still want me to leave you?' His voice was husky.

Desperately she pushed him away from her with all her strength. 'Please, you must go!' Her agonised whisper was cut short by an ear-splitting crack from outside the cabin door, followed by a crescendo of cries and thrashing canvas.

'God's blood! What's that?' Thrusting her aside, Kemp leapt for the door, pushing it open against the force of the wind.

'The mizzen-yard has gone!'

The words of one of the sailors was snatched from his lips and tossed away on the wind as Kemp vanished into the night, slamming the door behind him.

Trembling, she could not move. She listened, frightened by the thundering of the split canvas and the howl of the wind. Then, with a sob of fear, wrapping herself tightly in one of the fur rugs, she lay down and buried her head beneath the pillow.

When Elaine woke, the cabin was full of pale shadows from the sunlight seeping through the shutters on the stern windows. The motion of the ship had steadied, and she could hear water creaming past the oak planking. Unsteadily she sat up, remembering the events of the night before with a little shiver of unease. Stiffly she pulled herself upright and tiptoed to the shutters, trying to see out, but to no avail. Even if she could, she did not doubt she would see nothing but an eternity of waves. She shivered, and suddenly felt very hungry, but she dared not open the cabin door. She had no wish to see Kemp a moment sooner than she had to.

It was some time later that the door opened and a man came in with a tray. He grinned at her amiably. 'Ship's biscuit, mistress,' he said, sliding the tray on to the table. 'Captain said you were to eat as one of the crew.' Then he left her alone. Elaine felt her face colouring slightly as she stared at the unappetising fare. Had Kemp won a point against her? She sniffed cautiously at the jug which accompanied the plate of hard biscuit. It smelled of rough ale. She picked up the biscuit and began very carefully to try and nibble the corner of it as the door opened once more and Kemp appeared. He looked her up and down critically.

'You look as though you slept in that dress after all, mistress,' he said softly. 'I trust you brought a fresh one with you to impress the guests at our meeting.'

Her cheeks flamed. To her fury, he looked calm and tidy as usual, with no hint in his appearance to show he had been up all night wrestling with his wounded ship in the storm.

'I'm sorry,' she said, as haughtily as she could. 'If you will find my trunk, I shall try and improve my appearance.'

'Your trunk is there.' He pointed to a dark corner of the cabin. It had been there all along. 'Sam! Send someone to take down the shutters!' he called over his shoulder. Then he grinned. 'Are the ship's rations not to your liking?'

She had thrown down the biscuit in disgust. 'I cannot even bite it!' she replied in anger.

'You're supposed to soften it first,' he explained mockingly. 'Dip it in your ale.'

She looked at him in horror. 'Don't you have anything else?'

'It's what the crew eat.' His voice was soft.

She shuddered in spite of herself. 'And I am no passenger. I remember,' she said.

'Perhaps we can make an exception for ladies in the crew. Harry! When you've done the shutters, bring our guest some porage.'

The sailor who was unfastening the bars on the shutters nodded acknowledgement.

'When you've eaten and changed, come out on deck,' Kemp told her as he strode towards the door. 'We are nearly at our destination.'

The second tray contained a porage sweetened with cinnamon and honey, and a jug of wine. Refreshed and changed into the thin deep blue silk gown which had travelled rolled up in her trunk, Elaine suddenly found herself gazing down at Tom's sea-chest. She hesitated, then tiptoed forward and pulled up the heavy brass-bound lid. The top half was packed with clothes. She began to lift them out, then, overcome with misery, pushed them back. She could not face the memories they revived. As she was pulling the lid back into place, something caught at the back of the chest, stopping it from shutting. Feeling round to clear it, she found a small dagger in a hard leather sheath. After hesitating for a moment, she quickly tucked it into the bosom of her gown, then let herself out of the door.

There was no sign of the damage of the night before. The sails all seemed set and pulling. To her amazement, there was a low hazy coastline ahead of the ship.

Kemp grinned at her as she appeared beside him. 'Look, there is the ship we are to meet. She will have been watching for us since dawn.' A stately galleon was drawing near them, sails set. Elaine felt a tremor of fear, half expecting him to order an attack, but nothing happened. The two ships approached one another with deliberation and then hove to some distance apart; a longboat appeared from the galleon's stern, rowing quickly towards them, three passengers on board between the oarsmen. Only then did she realise that the long pennants with their flying gulls had disappeared from the *Witch*'s mastheads. Instead, they carried the ensign of the merchants of Woodbridge.

Elaine jumped as Kemp seized her wrist suddenly and swung her to face him.

'Now, mistress, you remember the part you are to play.' His eyes as he looked into hers were those of a stranger again, iced flame in the rock-hard face.

She swallowed. 'What am I to say to them?'

'You smile. You look gracious. You confirm the news as your father told it to you, and you assure them,' he pulled her towards him suddenly, 'that there is no danger in these seas. Why else would Robert Howard allow his daughter here to greet them? The rumour of a pirate vessel is quite untrue, and there is no need to wait for an escort home. You understand?'

Elaine's eyes hardened with disdain. 'So I am to lure him into your trap.' She struggled to free her wrist, conscious of the interested faces of Kemp's crew turned towards her.

'Exactly.' The menace in his voice was real.

'And if I don't, you'll throw me overboard?' She met his gaze defiantly. 'But you'll have lost your prize cargo.'

He smiled, and the sight of it sent a shiver up her spine. 'No, I won't throw you overboard. At least, not until you've seen your father's reaction to the news that Tom was my partner and that both Robert Howard's children planned to rob him.' He put his hand beneath her chin contemptuously and raised her face towards his. 'Don't try and trick me, Elaine.'

Beside them, the trickling grains in the sandglass by the helm ran out, and impassively Sam Fletcher reached forward to turn it. There was a gentle bump as the longboat came alongside the ladder which had been lowered to meet it. In moments the three men were on deck.

Elaine swallowed, watching Kemp as he greeted the newcomers and led the way into his cabin. Sam Fletcher gave her a gentle push, and there was nothing for it but to follow them.

The interview took exactly ten minutes. Elaine's presence, it seemed, once their first astonishment at seeing

her had worn off, completely reassured the men. Her
miserable lies uttered through stiff unwilling lips must have
sounded convincing to their foreign ears. They bowed, and
kissed her hand and pocketed the document she signed,
sealed with her father's seal. They drank a toast in best
burgundy, and then they were once more in the longboat,
heading back to their ship. Elaine's part in the betrayal
was complete.

She followed Kemp slowly to the side as he raised his
hand to the parting guests and looked down, blinking back
tears of anger and remorse. Beside her, he was laughing.
He caught her hands and raised them to his lips. 'You
played your part well, sweetheart.'

'Leave me alone!' She pulled away from him and turned
towards the cabin, wanting to be alone with her shame,
conscious as always that the crewmen nearest her—mocking no doubt, as their captain was—were watching her with
open curiosity and enjoyment.

Defiantly she raised her eyes to the sailor who stood
ready by the helm, his eyes fixed on her face.

Then she stood rooted to her spot. It was one of the men
who had returned with Sir Edward Brandon from his house
at Aldebourne. And she knew, without a shadow of doubt,
that he had recognised her.

CHAPTER
SIX

ELAINE SLAMMED the cabin door after her, her heart hammering with dread. At Kemp's curt command, the ship once more got under way, the sails filling as the *Witch* heeled over, coming round to set course back for the mouth of the Deben.

The door opened and closed softly, and she knew that Kemp had come in after her.

'Who is he?' His voice was cold.

'What do you mean?' She was standing at the window, staring down unseeing at the foaming wake with its attendance of dancing gulls.

'The sailor at the helm, Robert Wood. You recognised him.'

'No.' Her fingers were clenched tightly on the oak frame of the window.

'I think you did, Elaine.' Seizing her arms, he spun her round towards him. 'I ask you just once more. Who is he?'

'Don't you know?' She raised her chin defiantly, determined not to show him how afraid she was. 'He is in your crew, isn't he, one of your chosen men?'

'Yes, he is in my crew.' His tone was repressive. 'And he came recommended as trustworthy, but this is his first trip. He's from Aldeburgh way.' Thoughtfully his blue eyes scanned her face.

She dropped her gaze miserably. 'I know nothing about him.'

'Sam!' Without releasing her, Kemp yelled over his shoulder.

Fletcher was in the cabin in seconds, his hand on his cutlass.

'Take two men, Sam. Bring Wood here.'

'Sir.' Fletcher disappeared, and then there was the sound

of a scuffle on deck. Elaine swallowed. Her arms were hurting in Kemp's grasp, but he held her easily.

When the four men entered, Kemp dragged her away from the window, propelling her to stand before Wood, whose arms were held behind him.

'Now, look again, mistress,' Kemp hissed through clenched teeth. 'And look well. Who is he?'

She raised her eyes, meeting a stare which regarded her with blank hostility. 'I don't know him,' she said miserably.

Kemp's grip on her arms tightened, and she clenched her teeth desperately to stop herself crying out with pain. 'Is he one of Brandon's men?' he demanded furiously. 'Is he?' He shook her till a small sob escaped her lips. Abruptly he let her go, so that she staggered away from him. 'I repeat,' he said. 'Is he one of Brandon's men?' His eyes were holding hers, his will forcing her to obey him. Almost without realising she had done it, she gave an almost imperceptible nod.

Kemp straightened, and turned to Fletcher. 'You know what to do.'

Wood had turned chalk white. Spitting obscenities, he began to struggle frantically, but it was no use. He was dragged from the cabin and the door banged shut behind them. Within a few seconds there was a strangled scream, then a resounding splash.

Elaine stared at Kemp in disbelief, her eyes huge and shadowed in her pale face. 'They've thrown him overboard!' she whispered. Her lips were stiff with horror.

She flung open the door and ran out on deck. The three men were still standing, looking over the side. She forced herself to go and look down at the spot they were watching. Wood's body floated face-down in the water, a cloud of blood drifting away from the vicious wound across his throat.

Fletcher put his hand on her shoulders. 'Come away, mistress,' he said gently. 'There's no call for you to see.'

But she did not hear him. She pushed him aside and whirled to face Kemp as he came out of the cabin. 'You killed him! You had him murdered in cold blood! What kind of man are you?'

He looked at her impassively. 'I thought you knew that, Elaine. Death is the universal punishment for spies and traitors. Wood realised what would happen if he were caught.'

'But if I hadn't recognised him, he wouldn't have been caught!' she said brokenly.

'Then we all owe you a debt of gratitude.' He bowed. 'Don't blame yourself. We would have discovered him in the end. You should thank your stars that he was found out before he had a chance to betray us all.'

'Betrayal, murder, robbery, blackmail!' Elaine turned away to hide the tears she could not suppress. 'You must be very proud of your calling, Master Kemp.' She was shaking. 'First Tom, now Wood. Who else has to die on this ship so that you can gratify your lust for wealth?'

Kemp glanced past her, scanning the hazy horizons. Then he turned to the helmsman. 'Set course for the Deben,' he ordered. 'The wind has come round a few points in our favour. You'll be home by tomorrow evening, mistress,' he said coldly.

'You mean you're not going to throw me over, too, now that I've served my purpose?' Elaine flung at him. She was too distraught to be cautious.

He face was closed. 'There is always that chance. We have yet to discover whether you knew Brandon was sending a man to watch over you; whether it was you, after all, who betrayed me.'

She stared up at him, the blood draining from her face as the implications of what he had said sank in. 'But I didn't . . .' She groped for a handhold to support her. 'I never said a word to him!'

Kemp stepped towards her. 'He suspects *Black Witch*. He contrived to join my crew. He chose the very trip on which you were coming, and you expect me to believe you did not betray me?' The expression on his face was grim.

All round, the sea glittered as the ship heeled further before the wind. Elaine felt more alone than she had ever felt before. Little bubbles of panic rose in her throat, half choking her as she saw the fierce faces around her. 'I didn't betray you,' she whispered again. 'I swear it. You must believe me!' She spun away from him, diving between two of his men, running for the sanctuary of his cabin, slamming the door behind her and groping for the latch before standing, her shoulders braced against it, as though her puny strength could hold Kemp and his crew at bay.

It was only seconds before the splintered wood gave way and the door caved in. She ran to the far side of the table, putting the width of it between her and the man who had appeared in the doorway. Her fear was so great that she had lost all sense of reason as she groped for Tom's dagger and pulled it out.

Kemp's voice reached her through a haze of fear. 'Put that dagger down, you foolish girl. You've nothing to be afraid of.'

'Don't come near me!' Her hands were trembling as she stared at him, and behind him, where Fletcher and the other men were going about their duties on deck as though nothing had occurred. Another sob bubbled up inside her as she moved round the table, keeping it between her and Kemp.

His face was dark with anger. 'You are acting as though you are guilty,' he breathed. He dodged towards her suddenly, and in one movement seized her wrist, twisting the dagger from her grasp.

She screamed, raking his face with her fingernails, the only weapons left to her, but to no avail. He caught her other wrist, too, twisting her arms behind her, holding her immobile. 'Now, we will have the truth.'

She struggled feebly, conscious that her hood had been dislodged in the struggle and that her hair was cascading about her shoulders.

'I have told you the truth,' she cried. 'I told Sir Edward nothing about you!'

'But he knows you are acquainted with me.' He held her in front of him, her back towards him, her arms still twisted. She could feel his breath warm on the back of her neck.

Colour flooded her face as she thought miserably of Edward Brandon's taunts about her pirate lover.

'He has guessed something,' she admitted at last. 'After all, he saw you leaving the house the night you came to

tell me about Tom.' Her voice wavered. 'But he didn't
recognise you, I'm sure of that. He would have said something. I admitted nothing except that you were Tom's
servant, and he hasn't questioned me further.'

'Tom's servant!' He laughed out loud. 'Tom would have
appreciated that! And he has asked you nothing at all?'

'He and I seldom speak.'

He stared down at her grimly. 'Unusual . . . for lovers.'

She raised her chin slightly. 'He is a busy man, Master
Kemp.'

'That I believe.' He laughed coldly, still holding her. 'So
why did you not tell me that he suspected the *Witch*?'

'Because I didn't know. He never mentioned her; he
never did anything other than taunt me about my pirate
lover . . '

She bit off the words too late as his low chuckle sounded
in her ear.

'So, I am your lover, am I? Does that idea please you,
Elaine?' Kemp turned her round to face him, and slowly
raised his hand to the silk curtain of her hair which had
fallen across her pale face. 'I'm surprised Ned Brandon
would tolerate for one moment the idea of a rival to his
betrothed's affections.' He stared down into her eyes, his
expression deep and unfathomable. 'But I'm not averse to
the role he's given me.'

Elaine gazed at him, uncertain of his mood, knowing
only that the very touch of his hand on her hair quickened
her pulses and made her breath come in tight little gasps
which had nothing to do with fear. She turned her head
away from him, trying to hide her tears, but she was too
late. His hand caught her chin, and gently he tilted her
face to his.

'I've frightened and shocked you, Tom's sister,' he said
quietly. 'Forgive me. You are right. My calling is un-
savoury, and sometimes it makes me forget how vulnerable and innocent a child you are.' He gave a grim smile,
his eyes sad. 'It was not my choice to live by piracy. One
day, perhaps, I shall tell you the reason I have no choice
but to follow the sea; until then, you must accept me as I
am. But you have nothing to fear from me. I know you

told Ned nothing. He's no fool. He's found out about the *Witch* from the spies he's been plying so lavishly with his gold.'

His hands slid up her arms and he drew her gently against him until she rested her head against his shoulder and his face was lost in the golden haze of her hair.

'You don't really intend to marry Ned, do you?' he murmured. 'You don't love him; I doubt if you even like him. You cannot throw yourself away on a man like that. Doesn't your father know what kind of man he is?' His hands were caressing her gently.

'He is the kind of man my father wants for me; one who will know how to run the property I bring him,' she said miserably. 'It is foolish to talk of love. People don't marry for love!' She was unaware of the poignant sadness in her eyes as she tried to push him away.

With a muffled curse, Kemp drew her closer. 'Ned Brandon is a vicious libertine, Elaine. You can't go to him.'

'I have no choice.' Suddenly she was angry. More than anything, she wanted now to surrender herself to his arms, to raise her mouth to his. But he must never know it. She pushed against his chest with pummelling fists.

'Don't you see . . . I have to marry him! I have to obey my father. To hurt Papa would be to kill him.' Tears filled her eyes as her voice rose passionately. 'It is my choice to marry Edward Brandon, and none of your business!'

'And you would throw your life away; your hopes, your freedom—for your father.' His eyes held her remorselessly.

'It is my duty,' she whispered. 'Besides, I love Papa. I could never do anything to hurt him.'

'So, the trap that holds you to Brandon is the same one that brought you so obediently here to me,' he said thoughtfully.

Slowly he raised his hand. Almost absent-mindedly he touched her throat, running gentle fingers down over the pale skin towards the neckline of her gown.

'You don't have to go back, Elaine,' he breathed. 'You could stay with me.'

She looked at him, dazed by the hope which suddenly overwhelmed her. 'I don't understand.'

'It is your life, Elaine. If you go to Brandon, he will take you away from your father.' His eyes, a moment before soft as a zephyr's breath, showed steel beneath the long lashes. 'He will not tolerate you giving any loyalty to another man, even if it is your own father.'

She shook her head stubbornly. 'No. He has promised. We shall live most of the time at King's Brook.' Again she tried to pull herself free of his hands, but he would not let her go. 'Please!' she cried. 'I have to marry Edward. It is all decided. I want to marry Edward.'

'Then why do your lips lie?' He stared at her mercilessly.

She drew back. 'I don't know what you mean.'

'I think you do.' He raised his finger to her mouth and laid it gently over her lips. 'These tell me that you love another; that you dread your marriage to Ned. That you are sacrificing your entire future to please a father who may not even live long enough to watch the results of his arrangements bring his daughter to bitter unhappiness and ruin.'

Elaine's cheeks paled. 'Of course Papa will live!'

'He is an old, sick man. You are young.' The implacable anger in his face frightened her. 'He thinks only of himself.'

'No!' She stared at him defiantly. 'He loves me. He wishes to do what is best for me.'

Her words faltered as she stared pleadingly up at him, her hands still captive in his.

'Stay with me, Elaine,' he repeated. 'I would marry you myself. And, God knows, I would run your property as well as Ned—if that is what worries you.'

'No!' At last she succeeded in twisting herself free of him. Her eyes blazing, she backed further from him. 'I could never marry you!'

Bitter disappointment flooded her mind. For one exhilarating moment she had thought he wanted her, thought that his concern and tenderness sprang from love, but the moment he had mentioned her property, she knew the truth. She forced herself to smile, turning away from him quickly so that he could not see the tears in her eyes.

'I would never marry a pirate,' she said, keeping her voice proudly steady. 'Never!'

With a muffled oath, he pulled her against him again. 'I'll make you gainsay those words, sweetheart,' he said softly.

She could feel her heart thudding tumultuously as he held her so tightly to his chest that she was afraid she would never breathe again. Almost unconsciously she had raised her mouth towards his once more, unable to fight her own longing, and as she did so she caught sight of the expression in his narrowed eyes. The desire she saw there brought such a response from her own body that it was like an icy shock surging through her veins.

'Take back that remark, Elaine,' he repeated softly, his lips on hers. 'Or do I have to make you?' His kisses were fierce and demanding, sending shivers of ecstasy coursing through her, until her knees grew weak with the longing to surrender to him utterly.

He slid his hands up her body, cupping her breasts for an instant before winding his fists into the spun gold of her hair, drawing her head back so that she had to look at him. 'You will not marry Ned Brandon, Elaine. Do you hear me?' Then came a tentative knock on the splintered wood of the cabin door. 'What is it?'

'Lookout has reported two King's ships, sir!' Fletcher looked in, his face impassive as he stared at Elaine.

Kemp cursed. Slowly he released her, giving her cheek a little regretful caress with one finger as he did so. Then he was gone.

For a moment Elaine could not move, then she threw herself on his bed, her face buried, her whole body trembling. For a long time she lay still, waiting for the tumult of her heart to subside, trying to rid herself of the memory of his hands, so practised in their mastery as they roamed across her body; trying not to think of the offer he had so cruelly made.

With a groan she moved uneasily, trying to find a cool spot on the burning pillow, and as she did so she became aware of something crackling beneath her elbow. She pushed herself up and thrust her hand into the crack between the edge of the bunk and the bulkhead, and drew out a folded piece of parchment. As she was about to throw it down, the writing caught her eye. Scrawled across the back of the fold, bold and black and flowery, impossible not to read, it said: ' 'Til very soon, my heart and love, from Yr devoted mistress and friend, Jane Lockesley.'

Suddenly Elaine's hands were shaking and her eyes were blind with tears. So, all her suspicions had been right! However much her treacherous body betrayed her into wanting to believe Kemp loved her, the accusations she had thrown at him were true. Just as Brandon bragged of having a mistress while he taunted her that he wanted her for her money alone, Guy Kemp, too, loved another, but could not resist her because of her wealth.

It was a moment before she realised that Kemp had returned to the cabin and was standing before her, his face a careful blank as he held out his hand. 'I'll have that letter, if you please.'

Obediently she gave it to him, still too stunned to react. Then abruptly she stood up, her eyes brilliant with tears.

'You were mocking me all the time! You pretended to make love to me. You talked of marriage, and asked me to stay here with you, while all the time you loved another. This . . . This Jane!' She kept out of his reach. 'Did you really hope to win my money and lands with your offer, Master Kemp? Did you really hope to make yourself the richest man in Suffolk by marrying me? Well, I'm sorry to disappoint you, but my father would disinherit me rather than let a single farthing go to anyone but Sir Edward. And I have further news for you. I despise you! I would not marry you if you were the last man alive in England! I love Edward. I intend to marry him next Sunday, and after you have taken me back to the land, I never wish to set eyes on you again!'

In a flurry of silk skirts she crossed to the window. The sea had changed from amethyst to emerald under the hazy sky, with streaks of warm sand-coloured water that echoed the gathering cloud.

Kemp was scrutinising the letter as though he had not

seen it before. Then he went over to drop it in his sea-chest, before turning to her and bowing.

'You make yourself very clear, Mistress Elaine,' he said curtly, surveying her with cold disdain. 'Once you are Ned Brandon's bride, I doubt if I should wish to see you again, either. There is, however, one fact which links us now. You are half owner of this ship.'

Elaine swung round. 'That's not possible!'

'You inherited your brother's share of *Black Witch* with the contents of his sea-chest,' Kemp said. He paused, and then went on, a strange gleam in his eye. 'You signed confirmation of your ownership last night and sealed it with your father's seal.'

She gasped. 'I don't believe you! You tricked me! I don't want it . . .' The expression on his face frightened her more than his anger had done. 'Why? You needn't have told me. The ship would have been yours entirely. I would never have known . . .'

He stared at her thoughtfully for a moment. 'And there would have been no reason for you to hold your tongue about me should your father die.'

Stunned, she found herself swallowing back fresh tears. 'But Papa isn't going to die!'

'Let us hope not. Nevertheless, I feel more comfortable knowing that your silence protects your own neck as well as mine. You are my partner, and my partner you shall remain until I choose to buy your share of *Black Witch*. And you are, Elaine, as much a pirate, now, as I.' He bowed grimly. 'Now I have matters to see to on deck. I shall not impose my presence on you further as it has become suddenly so abhorrent.' He turned on his heel and left her alone.

Elaine did not see him again until the anchor once more hurtled into the opaque green water of the Deben, and the *Witch* swung slowly to lie to it beneath a stand of gnarled Scots pine. The shore was deserted. Wearily she rose from the bunk, smoothed her gown as best she could, and neat-ened her hair beneath the linen head-dress and hood. Although she was composed, her face was pale and her eyes were red from weeping.

When Kemp appeared at last, her hands clenched in her skirts as she tried to control the longing and misery that the sight of him caused in her. She straightened her shoulders. 'Is Master Fletcher to take me home?'

He nodded. 'He'll take you to your Godmother Ashley's at Bromeswell. From there, your maid can escort you back to King's Brook. I shall have Tom's chest taken there direct.' He took a step towards her.

She did not move. Her whole body ached for his touch, but her pride had returned to her. He would never know how closely she had come to surrendering herself to him or how agonising the last long hours of the voyage had been, contemplating her approaching wedding and the brief hope of an escape which might have been hers and which now would never happen. She stared at him frostily. 'Don't let me keep you from your duties.'

He was standing, arms folded, watching her. 'My duty at present is to see my passenger safely disembarked from my ship.'

'But I am not a passenger,' she retorted. 'And, as I recall, it is half my ship.'

His eyes gleamed maliciously. 'A ship, Elaine, is a she, not an it,' he said softly. 'From the very first days that man sailed across the sea, he realised that so temperamental and so devious and so beautiful a creation could only be feminine in her soul.' He paused, eyeing her, his mouth twitching with sudden grim humour. 'Do I gather you have felt the power of ownership and would like to try your hand at the helm? If so, the *Witch* is yours to command on our next voyage.'

Elaine blushed. 'I have no desire to set foot on this boat again, as you well know.'

He bowed. 'As you wish. But should you change your mind . . .'

'I won't! Now, may I go?' She was almost choking with misery.

'I shall call Sam.' For a moment she thought he was going to say something else to her, but he remained silent, and then turned away. As he was about to duck out of the cabin door, he stopped and glanced back.

'I'll come and dance at your wedding, Elaine,' he said softly. 'My salute to the marriage of a pirate bride to Ned Brandon. It would be fitting, don't you think?'

Before she could reply, he had gone.

CHAPTER
SEVEN

THE SMALL boat drew away swiftly from the brooding silhouette of *Black Witch*, the men's oars drawing gold-rimmed circles in the still water. Sitting in the bow with her back to the shore, Elaine raised her eyes to the high decks, where a figure was looking out. He did not raise his hand in farewell, and neither did she.

Sam helped her ashore, and beckoned forward the boy who had brought the three horses to meet them, and she waited as her small trunk was strapped to the saddle, clutching the gunwale of the boat where it had been beached on the sand. As she stepped on to the ground, it had seemed to lurch beneath her feet, and she staggered a few steps in frightened surprise.

Sam's face wrinkled kindly as he caught sight of her. 'You have grown used to the motion of the ship, mistress,' he said. 'You'll find the earth will steady soon enough.'

He helped her to mount, then stood for a moment before he reached into the deep pocket inside his doublet. 'Your seal is here.' He handed it to her, wrapped in a kerchief. 'Kemp asked me to give it to you.'

She took it with a tight little smile, unable to read the expression on his face as he turned away. Only then did she turn and glance once more at the ship. The enigmatic figure of her captain had gone.

It was a glorious evening, warm and honeyed beneath a westering sun, as they turned at last into the yard in front of the low rambling farmhouse at Bromeswell with its half-timbered walls and ochre plasterwork pargetted into intricate whorls and designs beneath the golden thatch. Elaine slid from her horse, her legs still unsteady as she tried to stand, looking round at the peaceful scene. It was only a moment before her godmother appeared, beaming, in the doorway, wiping her hands on her apron as she called out a greeting.

Elaine's fingers had been wound in the horse's mane for support, but then she threw down the reins and ran into Mistress Ashley's arms.

'Aunt Margaret! Oh, Aunt Margaret! It's so good to see you!' She burst into tears, her face buried in her godmother's ample bosom.

Margaret Ashley's smile of welcome faded on her lips. She glanced at Sam, and then down at the weeping girl in her arms.

'I knew no good would come of it!' she exclaimed as she drew Elaine to her. 'Go on, Samuel! Put those horses in the barn and take a sup of ale before you go back to the *Witch*. Mabbet!' she called over her shoulder, and then led Elaine into the cool interior of the house and pushed her into a low chair.

'I couldn't believe my ears when the message came that Guy had taken you on the *Witch*,' she said. 'How dared he! I'll give him a piece of my mind when I see him next, so I will!'

'So, you really do know him?' Elaine said with a rueful little smile. 'I couldn't believe it when he told me.'

'Of course I know him. I've known him since he was a boy.' Margaret pursed her lips. 'And I blessed his friendship with Tom.' She looked sad for a moment. 'But that does not mean I'd bless a friendship with you—indeed it doesn't! And I'll tell him so!'

Elaine felt herself blushing through her tears, and was unable to meet Margaret's eye. 'Do you know why he wanted me on the *Witch*?' she whispered at last.

Margaret grimaced. 'I have an idea there were two reasons, and I don't want to know either. I don't approve of Guy's way of life. How could I? But I do know the reason he chose it.'

'What was it?' Elaine looked up suddenly, her eyes golden behind her tears.

'Did he not tell you?' Margaret studied her soberly for a moment, then she shook her head. 'No, how could he, with you about to marry Edward Brandon.' She stood up and walked across the room, her full skirts stirring the soft hay and dried woodruff which strewed the floor. 'And for that reason I can't tell you either. But are you still displeased with your father's choice of a husband for you?' She turned, and eyed Elaine closely.

She looked away with an expressive shiver. There was no need for her to speak.

Margaret laughed wryly. 'So you still can't abide the man. Why? Is he ugly? Or old? Is he the kind to beat his wife? Are his teeth rotten? Does his breath stink? What is so wrong with him?'

In spite of herself, Elaine giggled through her tears. 'Oh, Aunt Margaret, I do love you! You know the answer to all those things. He's quite handsome and fairly young and his teeth are fine, as far as I know. It's just . . .' She shook her head miserably. 'I have no wish to marry him.'

'Is there someone else, then?' Her godmother's shrewd hazel eyes scanned her face. 'I thought before perhaps there might be.'

'No! No one,' Elaine said violently.

'You're not attracted to Guy, I hope,' Margaret went on quietly. She was still watching Elaine, and saw a stillness descend over her body. She frowned. 'He's attractive, I grant,' she went on gently. 'But Kemp's not for you, Elaine, and never can be.'

Elaine raised her chin a fraction. 'I had not even contemplated it!'

'Good!' Margaret patted her hand. 'Love will come between you and Sir Edward, you'll see. I felt the same as you when my William first approached my father for me, but I grew to love him.'

'So, you are to scold me for being silly and send me home to my fate?' Elaine said with a wistful shake of her head, trying to control the sob in her voice.

'That's right, child.' Margaret reached for the apron she had left hanging over the back of the settle. 'But not before you've eaten supper with us and put some colour back in those pale cheeks. We can't have your husband complaining he's married a girl with green sickness, can we?'

*   *   *

Sir Edward was waiting for Elaine in the great hall at King's Brook, lounging on the settle before a chessboard on which five pieces remained. There was no sign of Robert Howard. As she walked in, he rose to his feet.

'So you are back. I am glad to see that your megrims have at last left you,' he said sarcastically. 'They appear to trouble you rather frequently.'

He walked forward and took her hand in his, scrutinising her clothes as he lifted her fingers to his lips. She was at once conscious of the streaked salt stains on her gown and tried to move back into the shadows, but he reached out and touched her face lightly with his fingertips. 'On each occasion, your illness leaves a flush of gold on your face, my dear. Had I not known it to be impossible, I would have wondered if you had been spending the last few days travelling the country as a gipsy, not lying in a darkened bedroom at Bromeswell. Your maid looks more convincingly sick than you do.'

Elaine's eyes flashed rebelliously. 'Had I been travelling the countryside, Sir Edward, I doubt if I would have returned. Now, if you will excuse me, I shall go to my room and lie down. The ride has exhausted me, and my headache is coming back. Please give my greetings to my father. I shall see him tomorrow when I am better.' Without waiting for his response, she ran past him and up the stairs towards her room.

It was a long time before the house was silent and Mab fast asleep on her truckle bed in the corner. Elaine rose cautiously, and pulling a shawl round her to cover her fine shift, she tiptoed to the door. The house was more crowded now than she had ever known it. Each bedroom, except the small end one beyond hers where her bridesmaids were to sleep, had its occupants, and even the great hall now, as in her grandfather's time, was full of sleepers on their pallets: Sir Edward's men, her aunts' attendants, her father's apprentices.

With her ear to the panelling, she listened intently. There was no sound in the room beyond. Holding her breath, she drew her father's seal from under her pillow, and

concealing it beneath her shawl, quietly pulled the door
open. She knew she must make the risky journey through
the house to replace it. In daylight there might never be
an opportunity to return it to the office without being
observed, and every second that it remained in her possession she grew more afraid of being discovered.

With her heart in her mouth, she crept through the dark,
sleeping house, thankful for the occasional taper burning
on a table in a corner as she stole from room to room
and down the stairs to pass through the great hall which
reverberated with snores from one of the sleeping men.
She opened the library door, and crossed the room before
entering the tiny office and groping her way towards the
high desk. Sighing with relief, she dropped on her knees
before it, and reaching down as far as she could, pushed
the seal under it, into a distant corner where it slid and
disappeared among some old strewing-herbs. With luck,
when it was found, her father would think it had been there
all along.

Climbing to her feet, Elaine turned back towards the
door, much happier now that she had got rid of the seal,
hands outstretched to feel her way. She was silently
retracing her steps to the doorway when a slight sound
from the library made her stop, her heart pounding with
sudden fear. Someone was standing in the darkness near
her. She froze, her fingers clutching the panelled wood of
the door as she heard the chink of flint on metal and saw
the tiny spark from a tinderbox in the room in front of her.

Now knowing what to do, in a panic she ran for the far
door. If she reached it before whoever it was had succeeded
in making a light, she would be into the hall and up the
stairs before he had time to turn and recognise her. Cursing
the dry rustle of the rushes beneath her bare feet, she flew
past the intruder, but with an exclamation he dropped the
tinderbox. A hand closed over her shoulder, and she was
flung violently to the floor.

'Lights!' Sir Edward's voice filled the room. 'Bring lights,
someone!'

With a cry of terror, she rolled away from him, desperately trying to regain her feet as shouts echoed in the

passage outside, and the door was flung open. Two sleepy servants appeared with flares which filled the room with light, throwing dancing shadows on the pale vellum bindings and the rolls of manuscript stacked on the long shelves.

Sir Edward's silhouette towered over Elaine, and she saw the gleam in his eyes. There was no surprise there as he looked at her, and as she rose slowly to her knees, she knew with bitter certainty that he had expected to see her. Perhaps he had even been waiting for her. She met his glare as coolly as she could, as she stood up clutching the shawl tightly round her to conceal the thinness of her chemise from the servants' eyes. Her betrothed, she noticed suddenly, was fully dressed.

'So you were not as tired as you thought,' he said coldly. 'Or were you sleep-walking, mistress?'

Elaine stared at him, recognising with a shock something like open dislike in his voice. She swallowed hard. 'I was not sleep-walking, Sir Edward,' she said evenly. 'I thought you were an intruder. I blew out my candle when I heard a noise out here. I was not expecting to see anyone in my father's rooms at this hour.'

'Indeed?' His voice was heavy with suspicion. 'And what, pray, were you doing in here, Mistress Elaine?'

She breathed a silent little prayer of thanks that the seal was already safely disposed of and that he could not possibly find out what she had been doing. Taking courage from the thought, she raised her eyebrows haughtily. 'That is hardly your concern, Sir Edward. But, if you must know, I came down to visit the still-room. An electuary is kept there which helps my head. As I came back, I thought I saw the light of a candle. I assumed that Papa was working late and I came in to see him. I see I was wrong. It must have been your light that I saw.' She held his eye defiantly.

His expression was hard to read in the leaping shadows. 'Could your maid not have fetched your medicine for you?' he said softly.

'I always keep the keys myself,' Elaine replied.

'I see.' Sir Edward's smile was knife-edged. 'And where is this potion you went to fetch?'

Elaine bit her lip. 'I took it in the still-room,' she said quickly. 'And now I wish to sleep; so, if you will excuse me . . .'

She made to pass him, but he did not move. Instead, he caught her hand and raised it, stroking it with light fingers. 'Was it not foolish not to bring a further dose with you, Elaine, in case you continued to feel unwell?' he murmured. 'Come, let me have your keys. You and I shall return to the still-room and procure some more for you. Boy, give me your torch, and then you can go to bed.' He reached for the flare and stepped towards the doorway. 'Come, Elaine.'

She hung back. 'I need no more. All I want to do now is sleep.'

His voice was very smooth. 'I think we shall get some, all the same,' he said, and she knew it would be no use to argue. She shivered. Why had she not said she was on her way to the still-room instead of coming from it? Cursing herself under her breath, knowing that he had guessed she was lying, she had to turn to walk in front of him into the passage, feeling the heat of the torch on her back.

In the great hall, she was conscious at once of a dozen pairs of eyes watching them from the pallets as they walked towards the doorway, then they were outside again, and she and Sir Edward were alone.

Setting her jaw determinedly, she made for the still-room and throwing open the door, stopped on the threshold. It was several days since she had been in there, and the room smelt of the heat of the sun which had blazed through the windows, and of the drying herbs which hung from the rafters. Jars and bottles, labelled with her meticulous writing, stood in rows on the shelves, glinting in the sudden flaring light as Edward followed her in and thrust the torch into a wall-bracket.

'Your keys, if you please.' He held out his hand.

She drew herself upright. 'I have no keys.' There was only the faintest hesitation in her voice. Her eyes held his, tawny in the flickering light.

He smiled. 'I thought not. Are you going to tell me the truth?' He turned to close the door and leaned against it as she backed away from him, her knuckles white as they clutched the embroidered shawl.

'I have no desire to tell you anything, Sir Edward,' she said with weary defiance. 'All I want is to return to my bed.'

His smile deepened. 'Soon, even your bed will be no refuge from me.' His voice was a silken purr. 'And, once we are married, you will learn that lies and defiance are most unwise. I would advise you to start learning obedience before it is too late.' He stepped towards her, his hands outstretched, and snatched her shawl from her clasp, eyeing her body slowly up and down, dwelling possessively on the swell of her breasts beneath the low-cut neck of her shift. Elaine closed her eyes, unable to watch the triumphant leer with which he studied her. Exasperated, he snapped his fingers in her face. 'Look at me, woman!' he barked.

Her eyes flew open, and she found his face only inches from her own. He was sneering as he reached out and touched her throat with his finger. 'Look at you! Sunburned like a farm wench! You will make a most unfashionable bride, my love.' His hand slid down to touch her breast, and she recoiled violently. 'Not squeamish about a man's hand, sweetheart, surely!' he snapped.

She moved as far from him as the small room would allow. 'On Sunday, Sir Edward, I become your wife,' she said with as much pride as she could summon to her aid. 'Then you may do with me what you will, for so the law commands. Until then, I am my own mistress.' With dignity she scooped up her shawl and wrapped it round her shoulders. Then she stepped past him towards the door. Her mouth was dry with fear, and at every pace she expected to feel his hand on her arm, but he made no move as she pulled open the door and walked alone into the darkness.

He did not follow her.

Mab was still asleep when Elaine regained her room. Trembling with relief at having reached it safely, she climbed into the high bed and sat among the tumbled bedclothes, staring dry-eyed into the dark. She had cried on Aunt Margaret's shoulder, but she would not cry again.

'Kemp's not for you, Elaine, and never can be.' Her
godmother's words rang with a mournful echo in her brain.
Angrily she shook her head. Why should the thought of
Guy Kemp spring into her mind now? What was the point?
What had happened to her that the very thought of him
awakened in her such longings? Why did her treacherous
soul respond to him with fire and surrender, while to the
man she must marry she remained cold and unresponsive?
She bit her lip miserably. No, she was not merely unresponsive to Edward Brandon. What she felt for him was a deep
and violent loathing. Sunburned, indeed! Only the tip of
her nose was slightly pink. She shuddered. She must not
allow herself to think of Guy's sea-blue eyes narrowing
with desire as his mouth sought hers, or of the living bronze
curls of his hair beneath her touch, or his hands roaming
her body with such delicious insolence, or the very scent
of him which made her tremble with longing. She dug
her knuckles into her eyes. If only she could have stayed
with him! If only she could have lived at his side, on
the *Witch*, turning her back on Edward Brandon and King's
Brook and her father's constant recriminations and selfish
demands.

What was it Tom had said to her—freedom to feel the
ship beneath my feet . . . freedom to ride the wind . . .
She knew what he meant now, only she had fallen in love,
not with the sea, but with the master of *Black Witch*.

Suddenly an answer to her problem came to her. There
was one way to avoid marriage—to become a nun! In the
morning she would tell her father. Even he could not forbid
her from entering a convent, and if that were the only
alternative to life with Edward Brandon, she would gladly
take it.

When she went downstairs next morning, her father was
already deep in conversation with Sir Edward, and she
could not contrive to see him on his own. At every turn,
or so it seemed to her, Sir Edward thwarted her, his thin
lips curling with faint amusement as though he knew exactly
what it was she wanted.

Finally, in desperation, she sought her father in his

bedchamber the following night, ignoring the protestations of his servants. Robert Howard was not yet undressed, and he turned in some astonishment as Elaine came in.

'Papa, please, I have to speak to you,' she whispered. 'Please, please, don't make me go through with this marriage.' The tears she had held back all day spilled on to her cheeks as she caught his hand.

He frowned. 'Edward warned me this would happen,' he said testily. 'Leave me alone, girl! All women are frightened before marriage. It's natural. All is decided. You will learn as others have before you that your father and your husband know what is best for you. Edward is a good man. He will rule you well. Now go away!' He dragged his thin hand out of hers and turned towards the bed.

'Then let me go to a nunnery, Papa, I beg you!' For all her efforts to control it, her voice wavered. 'I wish to become a nun.'

'Out of the question!' He turned on her furiously. 'Do you think I would stand by and allow the church to lay its hands on my money?' His face darkened. 'I have told you, Elaine, that all is decided. You marry Edward on Sunday. The arrangements are made.' He raised his voice suddenly. 'John!'

His manservant appeared at the door, 'Take my daughter to her chamber and lock her in. I will not be hounded by her any more!'

She went white. 'Papa!'

'No more, girl! I am tired of the whole subject. You will stay in your room until you are married. Then Edward can have the controlling of you.' He turned his back on her. 'You try my health too much, Elaine,' he went on, his voice suddenly feeble. 'It is very unfair of you. You know I am not strong.'

Elaine stared from him to the servant and back in disbelief. John's face was sympathetic. Like every member of the household, he knew that Elaine, like Master Tom before her, had fallen under Kemp's spell—but where Tom could come and go as he pleased, and indulge in his taste for excitement without anyone finding out, for a woman it was different. The man shrugged apologetically and started to take her arm.

'Best come with me, mistress.'

'*No*!' Elaine dragged herself free. 'Papa, you must listen!' She caught her father's robe desperately. 'Please?'

Behind her, John hesitated, but her father whirled round. With surprising strength he pushed her away from him. 'Take her away, John,' he said furiously. 'Lock her up and bring me the key!'

Elaine stood completely still. For a moment she stared at her father, then she walked from the room. John followed her uncomfortably as she made her way in silence, threading a path through the crowded rooms unseeing, unaware of the speculative glances and whispers as she held her head high, her face like frozen marble. When she reached her bedchamber, she went straight to the window and sat down on the seat, staring out at the garden as the door was pulled shut behind her and she heard the key turn in the lock.

No one came, not even Mab. The garden grew hazy with mist as darkness fell, and the room grew dark and cold.

Rising shakily to her feet, she groped her way to the bedside table and felt for the flint. Then, as the candle-stump flared, she found that the room was in disarray. Mab had not come to tidy her clothes after she had changed for supper, and there were no new candles, only the burned-down stumps in the brackets and candlesticks.

She stared at the flame. Her father did not care. He had shown that he did not love her. Like every child of her time she had been taught to show unquestioning love and absolute obedience to her father. To disobey him was unthinkable, yet . . .

Shaking her head angrily, she tried to dispel the image that still so persistently returned of the man with the tawny hair, the strong muscular arms, the mouth which could be so tender and so cruel. Guy had not wanted her to marry Edward Brandon – from the very beginning he had tried to warn her. If only she had listened! If only, while she was free, she had taken the chance he offered her.

But Guy Kemp had been thinking of her inheritance.

Was he no better than Brandon, coveting her wealth? She straightened suddenly. Whatever his motives for wanting her, surely the man she now knew she loved was better than a man she hated and feared? In seconds, her mind was made up. She would swallow her pride and go to Kemp and beg him to take her on board *Black Witch* to save her from Edward Brandon.

Her fingers were clumsy as she lifted the lid of her clothes coffer and pulled out her salt-stained black gown. She pulled it on, fumbling with the laces, and bundled her hair into a linen cap as the candle burned low. Throwing her warm wrap about her shoulders, she picked up the candle-stick and slipped through into the end chamber. To open the door beneath the arras, she had to set it on the floor. The flame guttered dangerously in the pool of melted beeswax as she dragged the door open and peered down the dark narrow stair. Praying the light would last till she reached the misty garden, she began to run down the dusty flight. At the bottom, the flame reflected with a dull gleam on the bolts and hinges as she set the candle down and listened. There was absolute silence around her. Taking a deep breath, she reached for the top bolt and dragged it back. The noise seemed deafening, and she glanced desperately up the stairs behind her, hoping no one had heard. Then she crouched to pull back the bottom bolt.

The latch was stiff. With both hands she lifted it and pulled at the door. It did not move. In a panic she tried again, rattling the latch up and down in its socket, but still the door did not open. Her hands shaking, she picked up the candle-end and held it tight, looking at the ornate lock with its empty keyhole. With a soft hiss the flame died slowly to a blue point and flickered out, leaving her in the darkness. But not before she had seen the dull gleam of the lock, tongued into the doorframe. Her father had, after all, remembered the little door beneath the ivy and sent someone to fasten it from the outside.

She sank to her knees and allowed her tears to fall at last. There was to be no escape.

CHAPTER
EIGHT

THE ROOM was full of birdsong. Forcing open her eyes, Elaine stared at the thin crack of daylight between the shutters and then around the familiar walls of her chamber, where hung warm, brilliantly-coloured tapestries with their scenes of knights and ladies hunting unicorns and leaping pards. The tracks of the enchanted forest shone gold in the thin dawn light. It was Midsummer Day.

Her wedding day.

Her stomach muscles clenched with terror as the realisation returned after the blissful short oblivion of sleep, like a sword cleaving through her fuddled mind. There was to be no rescue for her, like the ladies in stories of old, no turning back, no knight on a horse to carry her off and save her from her fate. She clutched at her embroidered covers, drawing them up to her chin, and closed her eyes tightly against the dawn.

Sleep would not return, however, and she dragged herself shivering out of her bed—the last time, she supposed, she would ever sleep in it—and went to open the shutters. A soft mist lay over the garden, and the cool walks and hedges reverberated with the song of the birds. It was going to be a beautiful day.

She drew her feet up on the seat and hugged her knees miserably, thinking again about Edward Brandon. She had seen no one but Mab since her incarceration. Mab had brought her trays of food, with whispered, hasty reports on what was going on in the household—the guests arriving, the gifts, the dozens of pairs of gloves, and scissors for the bride, the last-minute extra supplies of food and wine for the banquet which would follow the ceremony, the fittings for the gowns of her bridesmaids—not now lodged in the room next to her, but somewhere else in the maze of attics. But of Edward there had been no sign, and no word, and for that she was grateful. Her last encounter with him alone had frightened her more than she cared to admit. For the first time he had openly threatened her, and she was terrified of what would happen to her once she was his wife. Was he the kind of man to beat his wife? Aunt Margaret had asked her that question. Elaine had the feeling that he was.

She heard the key turn in the lock, and her heart contracted sharply. Closing her eyes, she took a deep breath as the soft knock which followed the rattle of the key announced Mab and the serving-wenches with ewers of hot water and scented towels.

The day was beginning.

In a daze, she allowed herself to be prepared. Her hair was brushed until it shone like spun silver, then, instead of the usual braids beneath the stiff head-dress, it was combed out loosely on her shoulders, hanging nearly to her waist and crowned with a diadem of gold, interlaced with real rosebuds and gilded wheat. Her gown, made from eleven ells of silver damask embroidered with coloured silks and stitched with tiny pearls and knots of ribbons, was put on over a stiffened kirtle of flame brocade and several petticoats of silk. Fine stockings, gartered with blue ribbons, and white velvet slippers—and she was dressed. She was ready to be escorted by young men and maidens down the newly-raked carriageway towards the church.

Dazed and defeated, she gave Sir Edward Brandon her hand in the church porch and listened to the words which would bind them together for the rest of their lives. She felt the weight of his heavy gold ring on her finger and then his arm was round her and the hot wet pressure of his lips on hers before her father and all their friends, a kiss that reeked of possession and triumph and told her that the deed was done and that there would be no escape until death.

Throughout the nuptial mass in the old church, so near to Tom's grave, she stood, still dazed, her mind a blank as the old-age prayers tightened the bonds which held her. Then it was over, and she was walking back down the aisle on Edward's arm, and there was laughter among the guests as the pair emerged into the sunlight. Edward handed her up into the open carriage covered in flowers, which was pulled, not by horses but by the men from the estate, and the air was full of cheering and laughter and music as it was dragged back towards the house. And still Edward was beside her, resplendent in velvets and silks, his hand raised in acknowledgment to the crowds who followed them.

He did not look at her as they walked into the great hall, hand in hand, and took their places at the high table for their bridal feast, and thankful to be left alone with her thoughts even in the midst of such tumult, Elaine withdrew into herself, her throat aching with the effort of trying not to cry. She ate nothing of the banquet, turning away course after course of peacock, swan and quail, tarts and sweetmeats, and drank only a few sips of the wine, listening as the musicians serenaded her on lute and fiddle and pipe with ballads of days gone by and the latest popular tunes from court.

Then it was time for dancing. Edward turned to her at last, his eyes burning as he looked at her and she quailed at the possessive lust she saw in his face.

'Come, my Lady Brandon, we must dance for our guests!' His hands as they took hers were hot and sweating, and their fingers slipped as they touched. Reluctantly she stepped with her husband off the dais as the musicians struck up a spirited galliard. The dancing went on for hours. First one, then another partner claimed her, and Elaine danced with them all, the rich and distinguished, the tenant farmers from the estate, and the apprentices—everyone and anyone rather than be held again in her husband's arms.

The great hall grew hot. It stank of wine and sweat and crushed herbs, and still the music played. When one player grew exhausted, another took his place as the guests whirled and strutted. Elaine barely knew what was happening around her. Her head was light from hunger and the heat of the thousand candles which sputtered wax on the heads of the guests, in spite of the brightness of the day outside. Her mind was shuttered against the horror of what was to come when the night brought a lull in the first day of the festivities.

One dance ended, and she found herself seated amid a throng of chattering neighbours, a silver goblet in her hand. She raised it to her lips, sipping the scented wine, her eyes straying listlessly across the sea of laughing, animated faces which filled the room and overflowed out of the open doors into the gardens. And then she saw Kemp.

He was standing half turned away from her, talking to her godmother. Elaine caught her breath in astonishment. For a moment, every other person in the room ceased to exist as she stared at him, her heart aching with misery and longing, watching as he touched Margaret Ashley's arm and threw back his head and laughed. Then he turned. As though he had felt her eyes on him, he looked straight at her and the smile died on his lips. She gazed at him as he moved swiftly, dressed in a doublet of the finest velvet trimmed with lace, his hair and beard neat and gleaming as he threaded his way towards her, his face grim. Then he had her hands in his, and had raised her from her seat. 'I promised I would dance at your wedding,' he said huskily. 'I always keep my promises. May I kiss the bride?'

His eyes were like lapis, infinitely deep and unfathomable as he looked down into her face; then his lips brushed hers, so lightly that she barely felt them.

'Edward will see you,' she whispered in agony. 'You must not stay!'

He smiled as a fiddler struck up a new tune, and at once his hand slipped round her waist. 'First I must dance with Lady Brandon. Then I'll leave.'

'You are mad!' She trembled as he pulled her close and spun her into the wild country dance. 'If Edward sees you, he will kill you!'

'Why? Does he know who I am?'

She shook her head. 'I have told him nothing.'

'Then I am but an unwelcome neighbour who dares to salute his wife.' He smiled again, turning her faster in time to the music as around them hands began to clap and feet to stamp out the beat as they spun down the floor, further and further from the spot where Robert Howard and his new son-in-law stood deep in conversation, towards the huge front doors which stood open on to the garden. Elaine could feel her hair flying out, a curtain of spun gold, as she clung to him breathlessly, trying to keep her feet, her face raised to his as they moved faster still in time to the muscic. Then his mouth was on hers once more, his lips burning this time as they crushed hers hungrily for a moment, hidden in the curtain of her flying hair. They were once more in the thick of the guests. There was laughter, and hands reached out to touch her, to pull the knots of coloured ribbon from her skirt for luck. One moment his arm was there, round her waist, strong and possessive, and the next it had gone. Another hand was on hers, another face was near her. Bewildered, she stared round, reaching after him, but he had gone. The crowd of guests had closed their ranks and swallowed him as if he had never been there at all.

'Elaine!' Edward was beside her again, his eyes greedily sliding over her slim body, almost ethereally pale in the silver gown. He smiled and took her hand. 'Come, meet some friends of mine, then we shall dance again.'

Elaine followed him, her heart still beating tumultuously. Had he seen her wild dance with Guy, and that burning kiss? It seemed that everyone in the room must have seen, yet no one had given any sign. She curtsied dutifully to a row of waiting guests, lowering her eyes bashfully before their crude banter, and followed Edward down the hall.

Abruptly he stopped as a woman pushed her way through the guests towards him. Elaine did not recognise her, but noted the flaming red hair looped with jewels, the slanting green eyes reflected in the exotic green silk of her gown, and the kirtle of indigo beneath it, stitched with silver. She was elegant and tall for a woman, as tall as Edward, with the same straight nose and deep forehead, but where on him they looked coldly forbidding, on her they gave her the symmetry of cool beauty.

Elaine smiled uncertainly, glancing at her husband. His face had become a deep red. 'What in the name of all the saints in heaven are you doing here, madam?' he hissed at the woman.

She smiled tauntingly. 'I came to see you married, Ned. And to meet your wife. Come, are you not going to introduce me to her?'

Elaine looked from one to the other, puzzled by their obvious hostility, as Edward stepped forward and locked his jewelled fingers once more round her wrist.

'My dear,' he said, 'it appears that I have no choice but to make the introduction. May I present my sister, Mistress Jane Lockesley.'

Elaine gasped as she saw the sea-green gaze regarding her with cool amusement. She felt her cheeks burn. So, Guy had brought his mistress! He had brought his mistress to dance at her wedding, to mock and tease her, and she was none other than Edward Brandon's sister. Yet how was it possible she could be Guy's mistress, and Edward not know?

'Why, Ned, I do believe you never mentioned me to Elaine at all.' Jane's voice was deep and melodious as she gently disengaged Elaine's hand from her husband's grasp. 'Tell me now, my dear, did he?'

Elaine swallowed, trying to compose herself. What did it matter, after all, whom Guy loved? What did anything matter now? She forced herself to smile. 'He did mention a sister who looks after the house at Aldebourne,' she said quietly.

'Oh, fiddle! That is our elder sister, Olivia,' Jane replied with an infectious laugh. 'The longer you avoid meeting that harridan, the better.' She tucked Elaine's arm through her elbow. 'Come. I want to know you better, and I shall never manage that with brother Ned scowling over you like a possessive cock on a midden! Let us withdraw to rest for a while from the dancing.' Ignoring Edward's furious glance, Jane led Elaine up to a deserted bedchamber. Jane closed the door and leant against it.

'Thank our sweet Saviour to be out of that noise!' she exclaimed. 'We won't have very long to ourselves, and there is much we must discuss.' Her voice changed to a brisk undertone. 'Tom's letters; do you have them safe?'

Elaine stared at her, all her anguish and rage returning. This woman dared to ask for Tom's letters, and she had not even said she was sorry that Tom was dead! Her mind raced as she stood in the centre of the room, unable to speak or to think clearly.

Jane was waiting impatiently. 'Well? Where are they?'

Abruptly Elaine sat down on the edge of the bed. 'They are gone.'

'Gone? Gone where?'

'Stolen. They were locked in my jewel casket, and some-one took them.'

'Sweet Jesus!' Jane spun away from her, her green skirts swirling with a rustle of taffeta petticoats. 'When? Have you any idea who took them?'

'None at all,' Elaine answered listlessly. 'Tom had told me to keep them safe, so I locked them up—no one knew they were there. Then, one day, they had gone.'

Jane came back and sat beside her. She put her hand over Elaine's. 'Do you think Ned has them?'

Elaine shivered, drawing her hands away. 'I hope not!'

'Why?' The cat's eyes narrowed. 'Have you read them? Do you know what was in them?'

'No, of course not!' Elaine blushed. 'I just meant . . . Why would Sir Edward want to take letters from my room?'

'Why, indeed?' Jane pursed her lips. She stood, and went to stand with her hand on the door latch. 'Did Tom tell you anything about me?' she asked.

Elaine shook her head. She was picking at the seed pearls sewn into her skirt, wishing that this woman with the beautiful face whom Guy loved would go and leave her alone.

Jane was watching her in silence, her brow puckered, when the latch flicked up beneath her fingers and the door swung open, nearly knocking her off her feet. Sir Edward stood there, glowering.

'So, it's as I thought!' He swung his head from side to side like an angry bull. 'You are at work already, Jane, trying to poison my wife against me!'

Elaine had leapt to her feet as he appeared, nervously

fingering her skirts, but his anger was directed against his sister.

He stood back, holding the door for her. 'Out, you hussy!'

Jane drew herself up to her full height. 'You make yourself ridiculous, Ned,' she said softly.

'No, Mistress Lockesley,' his voice was an acid purr. 'That is your prerogative entirely. First you marry a pauper who hasn't even the wit to stay alive, then you consort with gaol-bait. It is you, sweet sister, who are ridiculous.'

Without another word she swept past him, not even glancing at Elaine, and they heard the rustle of her skirts as she ran down the broad staircase, back to the dancing.

Edward slammed the door and stood breathing heavily, staring at Elaine.

'So, wife, did she tell her story well?' His eyes had narrowed to cruel slits.

Elaine stood without moving, paralysed by his gaze. Her skin had the pallor of death as she stared at him, framed in the silver gilt of her hair and the radiance of her gown. In spite of himself, Edward caught his breath. She was a creature of another world as she stood there before him, as unreal and untouchable as the moon herself.

He shook himself and took two steps towards her. 'Well, woman? I asked you a question.'

Elaine raised her eyes to his, their amber brilliance veiled by fear. 'She told me nothing, Sir Edward. She merely welcomed me as her sister.'

He snorted. 'I was in time to prevent a tarradiddle of lies, then. Good!' He smiled suddenly. 'I had no wish to have my wedding spoiled by her presence. She should have had the good sense to stay away like Olivia.' He reached forward and touched her hair, almost gently. 'My God, you are beautiful today. I've a good mind to advance our bedding, sweetheart, and take you here and now. What do you say? Shall we bolt the door and miss the rest of the celebrations?'

Elaine stepped away from him at once. 'No! Indeed no, we can't . . .' She dodged past him, fumbling at the latch. 'What would our guests think, and Papa?' She dragged the door open, slipped through it, and was down the stairs before he could react. By the time he had followed her, she had lost herself in the thickest part of the noisy throng.

Her flight could only postpone the inevitable, however. It was still early in the evening when the dancing guests surrounded her and Edward, and began to suggest with much laughter and crude joking that it was time for bed. White and shaking, Elaine found herself being escorted up the stairs, garlanded with chains of flowers, her arms imprisoned, to the huge newly-furnished bedchamber which had been made ready for the young couple. The deep feather bed was covered in rose-petals and the tester and hangings were hung with greenery.

The pins were meticulously moved from her hair and clothes and thrown away for luck, her gown removed and her white skin bathed and anointed with fragrant oils. A chemise of the finest transparent fabric, soft as a spider's web, was put over her head and she was led, still prisoner, to the huge bed.

Then Edward appeared, captive in his turn, clad only in a nightshirt to hide his nakedness from Elaine's attendants, and amid much bawdy laughter he was tucked into bed beside her. The laughter, the jokes, the flowers, and even the music now from one of the minstrels who had followed the crowd of guests filled the room, and jugs of posset made from hot wine, with milk and eggs, sugar and spices were passed round.

Elaine was past fear. She sat beside her husband, propped against the pillows, feeling his thigh burning against her bare leg, a fixed smile on her face, as the guests drank and joked and threw her stockings about the room.

Then suddenly Jane Lockesley was in front of her, her green eyes vivid as she approached. She held a posy, which she tossed on to the covers on Elaine's lap. 'Good luck, sweet sister,' she breathed. 'You'll need it!' She leaned across to her brother and kissed him on the forehead. 'Good night, Ned!' She bent closer, a conspiratorial smile on her lips. 'Tell me, does Lady Rosalind bless this union of yours?'

Edward's face had turned almost purple. 'Get out!' he

shouted. 'You termagant! Get out, get out all of you! Now!' He picked up the flowers and hurled them at his sister. 'Get out, every one of you!'

Laughter turned to mock panic as he pushed back the covers and began to get out of bed; the guests scattered, running for the door, taking Jane with them. In moments, the chamber was empty. He closed the door and shot the heavy bolt triumphantly.

Elaine watched in numb terror as Edward went over to the table and reached for a jug of posset. He poured himself a goblet full and drank it down, then slowly he turned towards her, hurling the empty goblet to the floor, where it rolled across the richly woven carpet—Robert Howard's priceless gift to the couple—and came to rest against the wainscot.

His eyes were burning as he sat down on the high bed and looked at her, leaning forward to pull off the covers. Rose-petals fluttered in all directions, but he ignored them, his face twisted with drunken lust. 'So, the beautiful, rich Lady Brandon, meek at last, awaits her husband's pleasure,' he murmured softly. 'Tell me, do you look so cold and disdainful when your pirate lover wants to bed you?'

His eyes were intent on her face and the deep blush which mantled her cheeks. He laughed harshly. 'I thought not! You obviously greet him more passionately than you do your husband.' He hooked his finger disdainfully into the neckline of her chemise. 'It's strange, but I had hoped to take a maidenhead on my wedding night. It seems that I must make do with secondhand goods.'

He pushed her back against the pillows, and catching her chin between cruel fingers turned her head from side to side as though inspecting his property for the first time. She could feel herself beginning to shudder deep inside, but with the fear there came, slowly, a faint spark of anger.

He had what he wanted, now—her dowry, her mother's inheritance, the promise of her father's fortune one day— what right had he to disparage her like this? As his wife, she had to submit to him, but his scorn and disdain were more than she could bear.

As he put his hand once more to her chemise, obviously intending to rip it from her, her hands came up, catching his wrist and forcing it away. Caught by surprise by her sudden movement, he was pushed off balance and released her. In a second she was out of the bed, the torn garment clinging to the curves of her body as she moved.

He laughed. Instead of following her, he turned back to the posset and helped himself to the other goblet on the tray, filling it and draining it swiftly, following it with another. 'So, you have spirit, at least,' he murmured. 'And you intend to disobey your vows already, do you? So be it. It may add some spice to the wooing if I have to force you. I never did care for milksop women.'

Draining the last dregs in the goblet, he tossed it over his shoulder after the first, then he moved towards her.

She had nowhere to run. He had her immediately cornered against the wall, his face alight with supercilious amusement as she stood before him, proudly refusing to let herself shrink from his touch. His hands on her shoulders, he lowered his head, his lips greedily seeking hers as she tried to turn away. His breath stank of wine, and there were red stains from it all down the front of his nightshirt.

When she closed her eyes in trepidation, Sir Edward laughed. 'So I begin to frighten you, my lady? And not before time.' He licked his lips greedily.

Then his arm was round her, pulling her off balance, and he had thrown her on the bed. With a grunt he pulled at the frail chemise and tore it from her body before throwing himself across her.

After her first frantic struggle, Elaine lay still, winded by the overwhelming weight of the man, then as she turned her head away, desperately trying to avoid his probing tongue, she caught sight of Jane Lockesley's nosegay lying on the floor and Jane's words came back to her like a magic charm: 'Does Lady Rosalind bless this union?'

Was Rosalind the woman who lived with Edward? The mistress with whom he had taunted her? Her amber eyes were clear as glass as she looked into the sweating face so close above her own and asked, 'Who is the Lady Rosalind?' For a moment, she thought he would kill her.

His face went white and then puce, and his grip tightened on her wrists until she felt her bones begin to crack. Then he released her. The pulsing urgency beneath his nightshift died and he sat up slowly, blazing with anger. 'Lady Rosalind, madam, is the woman I love. Worth a hundred milk-and-water wenches like you.'

With some dignity he drew away from her and sat on the edge of the bed, sweating profusely. Then he stood, and crossing the floor unsteadily, picked up a fallen goblet. Refilling it with the last dregs from the jug, he drank deeply.

'God's curse on Jane Lockesley,' he muttered darkly. 'She came to my wedding to make trouble, the cold-hearted bitch.' Stumbling to the door, he dragged back the bolt. Then he turned to Elaine, his eyes full of hate. 'Tomorrow, my lady, you and I will leave this house. At Aldebourne you will learn the meaning of the vows you took today, and you will come to know how to be meek and obedient in bed and at board as you swore at the church—if I have to use a whip to make you!'

Elaine lay still for a long time after he had gone, not daring to move. This time the merciful release of sleep would not come, and she lay and waited for the dark.

Much, much later there was a small tap at the door, and Mab appeared with a lit candle, and an embroidered bed-gown over her arm. She crept towards her mistress.

Word had flown among the servants at King's Brook that Kemp had danced at the wedding. They had seen the few brief moments when their young mistress had looked as radiant as a bride should look on her wedding day, as she whirled in the arms of the pirate captain, and they had seen the radiance die as her husband claimed her once more; tacitly they had closed ranks against the Brandon followers, seeing that Kemp could slip away as silently as he had come.

Mab had half expected to find Elaine in tears, but she was lying in the dark, still as a carved stone. Only when the girl whispered her name, did she stir.

'I've brought a gown against the cold, my lady,' Mab

whispered, hesitating for a moment over her mistress's new title. 'I knew it was safe, as Sir Edward is asleep in the great hall.' She did not add that all could hear his stentorious snoring beneath the huge oak refectory table.

Elaine sat up slowly. 'He means to take me away tomorrow,' she whispered brokenly.

'I know, my lady. He gave orders when he came downstairs.' She hesitated. 'He said that there was to be no more music tonight or tomorrow outside your window, and no more celebrations, and that everything was to be ready so you could leave for Aldebourne at dawn. I doubt if he will be himself, though.' She smiled pertly.

'Does my father know?' Elaine pulled the soft robe round her. Then, seeing Mab's eyes on her bruised wrists, she hid them quickly beneath the bedcovers.

Mab shook her head. 'He went to bed hours ago, my lady. The excitement and all, it tired him out.'

'And Mistress Lockesley? Is she still here?' Suddenly it seemed terribly important to know where Kemp's beautiful mistress was. Had she gone back to *Black Witch* with him? Was she even now lying in Kemp's arms in the bunk where he might have made love to Elaine if she had let him? She turned her head away to hide her tears.

'She left just before dark, my lady,' said Mab, without looking up.

So she had gone to him.

It was long after dawn when Elaine finally closed her aching eyelids and slept. There was no sound of preparation in the courtyard, and no one came to wake her, so she slept on, exhausted, until mid-morning when Mab arrived to open the shutters before she shook her roughly by the shoulder.

'What is it?' Elaine struggled up against the pillows, pushing her hair out of her eyes.

'It's your father and Sir Edward, my lady.' Mab looked frightened. 'Please come! They are quarrelling so, and Master Robert looks that ill . . .'

In terror, Elaine dragged her weary body from the bed. Pulling the bed-gown round her, she ran down the stairs and across the crowded hall, oblivious of the dozens of eyes that watched her, towards the library, whence the sound of raised voices echoed round the house.

Her appearance in the doorway, undressed and with her hair hanging tangled around her shoulders, caused both men to stop their shouting at once. Sir Edward's face darkened. 'What do you mean, appearing downstairs dressed like that?'

'I came to see why you were making so much noise!' Elaine's fear evaporated into anger as she saw her father's piteous white face and heard his laboured breathing.

'He means to take you from me, Elaine,' Robert moaned. He sat down abruptly on the settle. 'He promised you would stay here . . . He promised.' His voice rose pathetically as he reached for her hand.

Elaine bit her lip. 'But this is what you arranged,' she wanted to cry out. 'It is all your fault: I begged you not to make me marry him!' But what could be the use? Her soft heart was breaking at the sight of her father's unhappiness, and in her compassion for him she almost forgot her own misery.

She had seen at once the flash of stubborn anger on Sir Edward's face, and knew she could not fight him. By law, she was her husband's chattel now, and she had to obey him. She had to try to pacify her father, and make peace between the two men.

'Papa!' She dropped on her knees by the settle. 'Please try to understand. It is natural for my—husband . . .' she stumbled over the word, scarcely able to bring herself to say it, 'to want to be alone with me for a while, and I wish to visit my new home.' His face clouded. 'This will always be home to me, Papa, but Edward's house must be my home as well now. Very soon, we shall come back . . .'

She knew it was the truth. Her inheritance was too important for Edward to dare to oppose her father for long.

Robert leaned against the ornately carved back of the settle. 'Are you sure, child?' He patted her hand with his white bony one.

'I'm sure, Papa,' she said, and turned to Sir Edward. The effects of the wine still showed in his flushed cheeks and red-rimmed eyes, but her quiet acquiescence had taken him by surprise and placated him. With an effort, he smiled at his father-in-law. 'Of course we shall. You must allow me to present Elaine to my household and to my sister. Some time alone . . .' he could not restrain himself from shooting her a vicious look, 'is all we need. Then, if all has gone well, we shall come back and see you.'

The message in his words was clear. If Elaine did not submit meekly to him, she would not be allowed to return to King's Brook to see her father.

It was early afternoon when they set out at last for Aldebourne with an escort of Brandon retainers, but not before Elaine had been forced to concede a further victory to her husband. As the riders mounted, and the loaded wagons began to move off towards the gatehouse, Sir Edward, sitting astride a huge stallion, swung his horse back and raised an accusing finger. 'That strumpet does not come.' He was pointing to Mab, who was ready to mount Cressid, Elaine's black mare.

In spite of her resolution to remain docile, Elaine gave a cry of protest.

'Mab is my personal maid! And she is my friend!'

'You have no need of friends, my lady.' His eyes were like daggers beneath his black velvet hat with its sweeping plume. 'You have a husband now. That woman remains here.'

No amount of pleading would change his mind. Elaine begged and wept but he remained adamant, his cold scorn visible to the whole entourage as he berated her while she sat numbly on the beautiful grey palfrey which had been one of her wedding gifts. In the end she had to accept defeat and ride away at her husband's side, leaving behind an openly weeping Mab holding her mare in the deserted courtyard beside the desolate figure of her father, as the last of the servants and guests wiped their own tears surreptitiously from their eyes and returned to the house.

They arrived at Aldebourne in the early evening, riding up a long tree-lined avenue towards the house several hundred yards ahead of the dust-cloud which enveloped their escort and the baggage wagons. The long hours of their ride had been passed in silence, even when they stopped for refreshment and to water the horses, Sir Edward's only words being curt commands over his shoulder to his followers to dismount or remount to continue the journey. With every succeeding mile Elaine grew more miserable, but now, as the house came into view, she felt a new stirring of interest in spite of her apprehension as to what the end of the journey would bring. Built half of mellow brick and half of timbered plaster-work, it nestled in a pocket on the top of a low hill. A cordon of rugged Scots pines obscured whatever view lay beyond, while around it stretched green orchards. It was a beautiful house, its south-facing windows glittering in the slanting evening light.

Behind her, Edward had reined in his horse, his expression unreadable as he stared round. Then he suddenly spurred the tired animal into a canter, leaving Elaine standing, as he disappeared up the drive.

Not wanting to wait alone for the rest of the escort, she kicked the palfrey into a trot and rode after him, glad of the veil she wore against the dust, which would also serve to hide her face when she met Olivia Brandon for the first time. Edward's sister was waiting at the door. There was no sign of Edward, and Elaine had to rein in before her, completely alone. She had no strength to move as they exchanged long appraising glances.

Olivia Brandon was at least forty, her face drawn and severe beneath a head-dress some twenty years out of date. Her dress of rusty black carried no adornment other than the stark crucifix and rosary at her girdle. Her expression was anything but welcoming. Elaine sat still, not wanting to dismount unaided before those critical eyes, but when no one appeared to help her, she had to slip to the ground and walk towards Olivia on her own. Nervously she pulled her veil closer round her face, appreciating the illusion of privacy it gave her.

'You must be Olivia?' She summoned up her courage, reminding herself that as Lady Brandon she took precedence over this formidable-looking female.

There was no answering smile.

'Edward has told me not to give you the keys,' the cold voice said. 'He feels you are as yet too young and untrained to become mistress of his house.'

Elaine felt her cheeks grow warm. She clenched her fists on her riding-whip. 'Where is Edward?' She tried to steady her voice. 'He rode ahead of me.'

'He has gone to greet someone.' Olivia's expression was mocking. 'Someone important to him.'

Raising her chin a fraction, Elaine met Olivia's gaze unflinchingly from behind her veil. If he meant to insult her by visiting his mistress before he had even welcomed his wife to his house, his aim had fallen short of its mark. Her only feeling was one of profound thankfulness that he obviously had no intention of forcing her immediately to fulfil her wifely duty.

'Does the Lady Rosalind live in this house?' She managed to keep her voice disinterested, and was rewarded by a glimpse of the unguarded surprise in the other woman's eyes.

'You know about Rosalind Berkeley?' Olivia asked slowly.

'Of course.' Elaine began to draw off her gloves, hoping the action would hide the shaking of her hands.

Olivia shrugged. 'She lives in the Dower House on the other side of the estate. Even Edward would not have her here in my house!' The haughty sniff conveyed, as no words could, Olivia's feelings, and Elaine felt a little surge of triumph. Olivia might be her enemy, but at least she was no friend to Rosalind either.

Slowly she followed her sister-in-law into the house. The front door led directly into the large hall, just as it did at King's Brook, but here a huge new brick chimney had been built where once the hearth had stood. The fireplace now was empty. Rich furniture and tapestries adorned the room and the floor was paved with black and white tiles. There were no servants to be seen, and the escort who had accompanied them had not yet appeared. The place seemed deserted.

The bedchamber to which Elaine was shown was small. It did not take her long to guess that this was not one of the main rooms of the house, and certainly not the one in which Edward slept. Relief flooded through her.

Olivia's face gleamed with triumph. 'Edward said you were to have this room,' she said smugly, anticipating Elaine's protest.

Elaine smiled at her. 'It is lovely,' she said, and meant it. The view from the mullioned window was exquisite. It looked across a thin strip of orchard towards the marshes. The soft green beds of whispering reeds, interspersed with shining mud creeks, stretched almost to the horizon, and in the distance was the faint line of the sea. She had not realised how much in the last few days she had come to regard the sea as something very special to her. Above it, a deep haze rose into the sky, with banks of clouds so faint and distant they they were almost invisible.

Slowly she turned to Olivia, unpinning her veil, and with an enormous effort, she smiled. 'Would you ask for my trunks to be brought up to me?' she said gently. 'And I shall need a maid.'

Olivia's mouth tightened into a thin line. 'You brought no maid of your own?' Her tone implied that Elaine had committed an appalling solecism.

Elaine could not help colouring. 'For some reason, Sir Edward saw fit to forbid my maid to accompany me,' she replied.

Olivia raised an eyebrow as she put her hand to the door latch. 'Lord knows where I'll find someone for you! I suppose you'll want water as well,' she said ungraciously. 'There are so few staff here. Up until now, Edward has had little money to spare for Aldebourne. All has gone to his other houses, or on that strumpet . . .' She did not finish the sentence. With a sniff and a shake of the head, she swung out of the room and disappeared towards the staircase, leaving the door open.

Elaine closed her eyes and took a deep breath. Then she shut the door, noting with a pang of fear there was no bolt on the inside to give her any privacy. For a moment she stood still, looking at the heavy studs and dull plaster-work which made up the walls of the room—no hangings here

to give warmth or comfort—then the first scalding tears
spilled on to her pale cheeks.

She did not see Edward that night. The surly wench who
brought her a pail of cold water to wash in informed her
that the house had already supped. If she wanted food,
something could be brought to her. Although she was no
longer hungry, some spark of defiance made her demand
both food and wine, and once again her coffers and chests,
some of which finally did appear, humped up the stairs by
an unwilling manservant. But there her nerve failed her.
Shutting the door behind him, she searched for her combs,
and undressing quickly in the gloom, she slipped beneath
the covers of the narrow bed without resummoning the
maid.

When Elaine woke, the rising sun was blazing through the
unshuttered window, and she jumped to her feet and
looked out. The marsh was breathtaking in its beauty. The
shimmering reeds were silvered with dew, while the creeks
brimmed with the high tide, sapphire ribbons winding in
from the sea.

It was still very early. She dressed herself in haste in a
simple gown of pale blue watered silk over a kirtle of
parchment-coloured taffeta, and twisted up her heavy hair
beneath a white linen hood, then paused for a moment in
the doorway. Running back to the table, she dragged off
the heavy wedding ring and threw it down, before she crept
down the stairs.

Her caution was not needed. There were no signs of the
servants inside or out as she let herself out of the door.
The air smelt like heaven: the sweetness of high summer
mixed with a sharper tang which tantalised and seduced her
senses. She began to run—through the orchard, through a
small wicket gate and up to a high grassy bank. The wind
caught her hood, blowing the long flaps back and cooling
the heaviness of her eyes after a tearful night. Suddenly
daring, she pulled it off and shook her hair loose. Then
she jumped from the bank down to a narrow muddy path.

She walked for quite a while, heading determinedly
towards the bank of rose-coloured mist that shrouded the

sea, following the narrow creeks, watching the water as it began to ebb, leaving glistening mud in its wake. She scrambled at last up a high bank of shingle decorated with trails of purple sea pea and clumps of lavender, and stood with her face to the sea.

A ship appeared, following a course up the coast, her dark sails glowing mahogany in the golden light. Her heart seemed to miss a beat. Could she be *Black Witch*, even now in pursuit of some new prey? She stood transfixed, her pulses racing, her fingers laced together in anxiety.

Guy, oh Guy . . . Without realising it, her lips had framed the name that had haunted her dreams the night before—the name of the man in whose arms she would have longed to lie on her wedding night, instead of frightened and alone . . . The dark sails altered course, and the ship, sailing hull down in the mist, headed for the horizon. Elaine shook her head, and turned back to the land.

She was once more half-way towards the house, when the sound of galloping hooves stopped her in her tracks. Her heart in her mouth, she shaded her eyes against the glitter off the still pools of marsh water. Edward Brandon was riding towards her at a gallop. He reined his horse in to a rearing halt and looked down at her, white with anger.

'What in God's name do you think you are doing out here?' he shouted. 'Get back to the house, my lady, and never—never—let me see you outside looking like that again! Do you want the whole countryside to know you are a gipsy?'

He stared at her hard. God damn it, but she looked beautiful with that wheat-coloured hair blowing round her head in a cloud and her simple unstiffened silk gown pulled against her slim figure by the wind! Her cheeks, white as porcelain now as she confronted him, had been, before she recognised him, alight with the honey glow of the sun and the sea, and he had sensed the wild spirit of the woman as she moved in that world of light and air which bounded the edge of his estates.

He wrenched his horse's head round viciously. If he had not spent so violent a night with Rosalind, if he did not still ache in his loins from her attentions—by God's wounds, he'd have his wife now, on the mud beneath the burning sky!

His smile made Elaine, still staring up at him, speechless with fear, and shrink even further back. He had not meant to spend the night with Rosalind. He had meant to drag Elaine from the chaste discomfort of her servant's room and carry her to his own huge canopied bed and subdue her there, but Rosalind had delayed him with her warm generous mouth and her expert supple limbs.

'You won't sleep with her, Ned,' she had said, her mouth hovering over his. 'I won't let you. Take her money and her land, but if you touch her, I'll know it.' Her eyes narrowed as he felt her muscles begin to tighten. 'And I'll punish you for it!'

He smiled again. You'll know it, will you, madam? Not from a hundred miles away when Queen Katherine recalls you to court, as she surely will when she receives my letter!

With his mistress gone, Elaine would be his sole amusement for the weeks he would be forced to remain in Suffolk. He would have plenty of time to take her once Rosalind had departed, and until then, he would let her wait. Let her fear build, and then she would be ready to obey and open those sweet limbs to him! He would enjoy her for just as long as it took for her to betray her lover, so that he could sink *Black Witch* and hang her crew in chains.

CHAPTER
NINE

OLIVIA WAS waiting for Elaine in the hall, seated primly on a carved oak chair. At the sight of Elaine's wind-tangled hair and the mud-stains on her gown, her lips pursed in disapproval, and finding Edward in the doorway behind her sister-in-law did nothing to temper her expression.

'So,' she said coldly. 'You have returned.' It was not clear which of them she was addressing.

'Good morning,' Elaine said as calmly as she could, conscious of Edward behind her. 'If you would summon the girl who waited on me last night, I shall dress for breakfast. And, please, ask her to see that the water is hot this time.'

Aware of the fury in Olivia's face, she began to walk swiftly towards the door, trying to conserve her courage as Olivia stood up, bustling with irritation. Her anger, however, was directed not at Elaine, but at Edward.

'Why could you not have seen to it that your wife brought servants with her, brother?' she complained. 'I am hard pushed to run this house as it is on the pitiful allowance you make me, without having to spare women from their jobs to run after her.' She nodded at Elaine, who had paused in the doorway. 'I have no time to train a new maid.'

Edward frowned. 'I didn't like the look of the maid she wanted to bring. An impudent baggage.' His frown deepened to a scowl. 'The servants at King's Brook are an idle, ill-trained bunch.' He ignored Elaine's gasp of indignation.

'Nevertheless, they are no doubt used to this . . .' Olivia sniffed '. . . this lady, and her strange ways.' Again she eyed Elaine's hair.

'My lady is going to change her ways.' Edward's voice

was silky with venom. 'But, as you say, it will be easier to send for the girl than to get a new one.'

Elaine attempted to hide her delight. Mab would help to ease her loneliness; Mab would be a friend, when she needed one so desperately.

That night, Elaine withdrew after the evening meal to her small room hoping she would once more be allowed to spend the night alone. But almost at once the door crashed open all of a sudden, and Edward strode into the room. Ignoring her cry of alarm, he grabbed both her hands and held them out before him.

'I thought not,' he said at last. 'Your wedding ring. Where is it?'

Elaine froze. The ring still lay on the table where she had thrown it that morning. Following her gaze, he saw it gleaming softly on the polished oak surface. Pushing her away, he picked it up, holding it for a moment in his palm. Then he smiled.

She grew colder at the sight, but straightening her shoulders, she met his gaze. 'I'm sorry, Edward. It was a little loose and I was afraid it might fall off . . . I'll put it on now.'

She put her hand out to claim it, but once more he caught her wrist. With deliberate roughness he forced the ring back on to her finger. 'Never, never take it off again,' he said softly. 'To remove it is to tempt the devil and break your vows, madam, and to bring my curse down on your head.' For a moment he stood still, watching her through narrowed eyes, then let her hand fall and swung out of the room. The heavy ring felt like a shackle on her hand.

To her relief she saw little of Edward during the next few days, and nothing at all of him at night, when he invariably returned to the Dower House; but even without his presence, her situation was irksome. Olivia went out of her way to torment her, following her from room to room as if she were afraid she would steal something if left alone. If Elaine hoped that her constant companionship might turn into a conducted tour, she was sadly disappointed. Her escort followed her in grim silence, except when she used her cold tones to tell her that in no circumstance was she to meddle in the still-room or even visit the kitchens or brewhouse.

It was when she announced her intention of riding round the estate that her first real shock came. 'That will not be possible,' Olivia stated firmly.

'Why not?'

'There is no horse suitable for you to ride.' Olivia had the grace to look uncomfortable.

'But my beautiful grey, my wedding present . . .' She broke off, feeling suddenly cold. 'What happened to him?'

'Edward gave the horse to Rosalind.' Olivia clicked her beads furiously.

Elaine swallowed hard, but she would not show Olivia how much she cared. With an effort, she smiled. 'Tell me why Edward did not marry the Lady Rosalind when he had the chance?'

Olivia snorted. 'Because she is married already. Her husband is in Lincolnshire. She had to leave court when the scandal of her affair with my brother broke, but I hear the Queen has decided to forgive her. She'll be called back soon as one of the Queen's ladies.'

'I see. I would still like to go for a ride, though. Perhaps another horse could be found?'

'No.' Olivia closed her mouth with a snap. 'Edward does not wish you to leave the house.'

'You mean I am a prisoner?'

'I mean that Edward would rather you stayed in the house. Your servants have not arrived yet from King's Brook, and there is no one to escort you. I have no time.'

Elaine gave a wry smile. As yet, she had seen Olivia do nothing at all except follow her about. The house was run by Edward's very efficient steward, James Catchpole. 'Then please tell me about the estate,' she said gently, hoping to win at least a little unbending from this hostile woman. 'How big is it?'

Olivia had seated herself on a high-backed chair, and gave a little shrug. 'Edward is lord of dozens of small farms, two villages, the orchards, I don't know how much. The sea is on the eastern boundary. On the other side, running along the river, is the old Kemp estate.'

'Whose estate?' Elaine sat bolt upright.

For a moment, Olivia surveyed her with suspicion. 'Old Lord Kemp's place. He died three years ago, and his son Henry inherited the lands. He spends all his time at court and the place is ruinous now, so I've heard. The tenants are insolent and withhold their tithes; ruffians haunt the place. It's a disgrace.'

Elaine could feel her breath coming in small quick jerks. 'I heard once from my brother of a Guy Kemp,' she said cautiously, hugging to herself the joy of saying his name, just once, out loud. 'Would he be one of that family?'

Olivia said, 'He died three years ago. He was a thief and a murderer. He broke his father's heart and tried to steal his brother's inheritance. It was a great relief to the whole country when he came to the bad end we all expected. It was only sad that his behaviour hastened the old man's death.'

Elaine stared at her in disbelief, then asked softly, 'How did Guy Kemp die?'

Olivia shrugged. 'He drowned, I believe. He was fleeing abroad when his ship foundered.'

And so Kemp lived and sailed and robbed his neighbours, and was so confident of his position that he had not even bothered to change his name. Elaine felt stunned. This was his story, the reason for his silence about his past. It was not the romantic tale of misunderstandings she had hoped, which would excuse the trade he followed. It merely confirmed the fact that he was a rogue and a murderer . . .

She noticed Olivia's speculative gaze on her face, and hastily changed the subject. 'Tell me about your sister Jane?' she said. 'I met her at our wedding.'

Olivia's face turned bright pink. 'Edward never told me that she was there! You may as well understand now that, as far as I am concerned, we have no sister.' She strode in agitation up and down the floor. 'I suppose you'll have to know. You'll only hear it from servants' gossip otherwise. Jane was bad from the day she was born. Our mother always swore she must have been a changeling. She was Geoffrey Kemp's goddaughter, too! She married Colin

Lockesley, who was a tutor at Framlingham castle, a penniless, callow young man who died within the year, leaving her nothing but debts which she had the temerity to ask Edward to settle. Then her godfather gave her some money, and she decided to go and live by herself. And now I believe she has taken a lover somewhere near Woodbridge.' Olivia curled her lip. 'An unpleasant package, my sister!'

A lover near Woodbridge! Elaine stared out of the window towards the orchards. So the story came full circle. Kemp and Jane, brought up as neighbours—both outcasts, both alone. What more natural than that they should comfort one another in their adversity?

Lady Rosalind Berkeley was summoned to Queen Katherine's court by Queen's Messenger the day Mab arrived. Olivia could not restrain herself from smiling as she gave Elaine the news. 'She leaves tomorrow, bag and baggage, and then Edward will have time to give you his undivided attention,' she said solicitously. 'You must have been so unhappy to know he was spending so much time over at the Dower House.' Her tone was heavy with sarcasm.

Elaine went white. She had become used to her little room, and she had even grown less afraid as the hot July days passed and Edward showed no further interest in her. Little bits of gossip had reached her from the maidservants and retainers, and they had all reassured her. Sir Edward Brandon was, according to them, a slave to his mistress's will. How else had she been able to talk her way into the Brandon Dower House? And why else, they asked themselves with significant glances in her direction, would he be ignoring the young and beautiful Lady Brandon? The sick fear which rose in her stomach must have shown on her face, for she saw the triumph in Olivia's eyes. She knew that, this time, there would be no escape.

Her despair was so great that she failed to take in the arrival of the party from King's Brook. Only when Mab and her two companions were actually inside the hall, curtsying and bowing to Olivia, did it dawn on her that they were really here at last. With a cry of joy she ran to

Mab and the two girls embraced beneath Olivia's scandalised gaze.

With Mab was Tom's man, Will, and Snook, one of her father's young clerks, both bowing deeply first to Olivia and then to her. When she was able to speak at last for her tears, Mab caught Elaine's hand. 'My lady, you must return to King's Brook! Your father is so ill. He needs you desperately.'

'What's wrong with him?' Elaine cried. 'Oh, Mab! I'll come home at once, of course I will.' Sudden fear shot through her as she looked at Mab's face. 'He's not dying, is he? Tell me the truth!'

Mab shook her head. 'He's very weak, my lady, and he coughs all the time, but he would pick up, I reckon, if you were there. We tried to get him to take your hyssop medicine, but he won't. He just lies there, shaking his head and calling for you.' She hesitated, her voice falling to a whisper. 'And for Master Tom, as if he's still alive.'

Elaine shivered, and shot a glance at Olivia, remembering for the first time that she was at her elbow, listening to the exchange. 'As you hear,' she said with a sad smile, 'I must go to my father. Where is Edward? I shall tell him what I intend to do.' She tried to keep her voice firm.

Olivia expression turned to one of deep scorn. 'My brother is no doubt trying to calm Rosalind's ravings. She won't be pleased she's wanted at Richmond, and even less so if she ever finds out that it was Edward who reminded the Queen it was Rosalind's time to wait on her.' She laughed harshly. 'I find it hard to imagine that Edward could spare your presence just now, my dear.'

Although Elaine quailed inwardly, she looked her sister-in-law in the eye. 'I am sure he will when he understands how important it is,' she said. 'Would you send someone for him, please? Tell him we must go back at once.'

'*Must*?' Olivia echoed, darting her face forward, like snake about to strike. 'Perhaps, my lady, now that you have them, you might like to send one of your servants. They can tell him that he *must* come.' She emphasised the word.

Elaine bit her lip, then turned to Will. 'You'll find Sir Edward at the Dower House,' she said firmly. 'It is, I believe, at the eastern end of the estate. Please ask him to return here at once. Explain the reason.'

Will bowed, and in a moment he was trotting up the winding drive and out of sight.

Avoiding Olivia's eyes, Elaine turned to her maid. 'Come upstairs and help me pack a coffer, Mab, while Harold finds someone to saddle fresh horses to take us back.' Already she was running towards the stairs. In her bedroom, she caught Mab's hands. 'Is Papa really so bad?' she asked softly.

Mab was staring round the small room, unable to believe what she saw. 'He's bad, my lady. He's not ill so much as very weak, and with his cough and all, he cannot rise from his bed. Is this really your chamber?'

Elaine saw it suddenly through Mab's eyes. The lack of furnishings to make it comfortable, the narrow bed, much like the one Mab slept on in the ante-room at King's Brook, the table and the few small coffers. She laughed bitterly. 'My husband thinks to bring me to heel by denying me feather mattresses and my trunks of clothes and jewels and forbidding me to leave the house. He'll find it harder than that to tame me!' Her eyes flashed rebelliously.

Mab looked embarrassed. 'My lady, you must take care. Sir Edward is a cruel man.'

'I know.' The words came out in a whisper. 'Mab, I cannot . . . I will not give in to him.'

The pinkness heightened in Mab's cheeks. 'You mean that you still haven't lain with him?' There was open admiration in her eyes.

'Only because his mistress forbids him to consort with his wife!' She laughed again. 'I drink to her health and prosperity and her rule over him every single night! But now . . .'

'But now?' Mab was scrutinising her closely.

'Lady Rosalind is to go to court tomorrow, and nothing will come between my husband and me any longer.' Elaine swallowed.

'Unless we ride straight back to King's Brook.' Mab

clapped her hand over her mouth. 'But he'll never let you go, my lady, will he?'

'No.' Elaine sat down suddenly on the edge of the bed.

'Unless you go without asking him?' Mab's eyes sparkled suddenly.

For a moment Elaine allowed herself to feel hope, then she smiled ruefully. 'He would follow and bring me back,' she sighed. 'My only chance is to appeal to his kindness, and his respect for my father.' It was a slim hope.

It was two hours before Edward arrived back from the Dower House, but when he did, he was in a towering rage.

Elaine was waiting in the hall in a fever of impatience beside the box that Mab had packed, as he strode into the room. He faced her at once.

'You are not going, so don't bother to ask. I forbid you to leave this house!'

She gasped. 'But Papa is ill!'

'Your father is an old fraud. In my opinion there is nothing wrong with him. And if there is, there is a houseful of servants to take care of him without you fussing over him as well. I need you here.'

He swung round to Mab. 'Now you're here, make yourself useful. Take that coffer upstairs and unpack it!'

He turned back to Elaine, who was standing white-faced beside Olivia. 'I have sent the two manservants back to King's Brook. You have no need of them here. They carry a message of greeting to your father and your regrets that you are too busy to see him at the moment. Olivia!' As he addressed his sister, she jumped visibly. 'I have decided to ride south today with Lady Rosalind to see her on her way to Richmond. I am relying on you to see that my wife is waiting for me when I return.' He pursed his lips, and then, without another word, ran from the house.

Elaine looked at Olivia in despair. 'He doesn't believe my father is ill,' she whispered brokenly. 'Yet how can he deny it, when he saw the state he was in when we left?'

Olivia stood up. 'In these matters a husband always knows best,' she said pompously. 'It is for you to learn to obey him quietly.'

'Obey!' Elaine burst out. 'How can you say that! My

father trusts Edward. He liked him. He chose him because he thought Edward would be good to me!'

'He chose him because he knew Edward was a kinsman to the Duke of Suffolk and cousin of an earl and close to the King,' Olivia retorted succinctly. 'Your father was not as idealistic as you thought. Perhaps it would have been better if he had been, so that you need not have been doubly disappointed in your marriage.' She looked positively gleeful. 'I believe Edward forgot to tell him that our cousin, the old earl, remarried a year ago, and his wife was brought to bed of a son at Easter.

'Easter?' Elaine echoed, the colour draining from her face. 'You mean, Edward knew months ago that he was no longer the heir? He lied to Papa!'

'He wanted your money, Elaine.' Olivia's voice was harsh. 'Besides, it was but a small lie. He is still next in line, and the baby might sicken and die, who knows.' She shrugged.

For a moment Elaine was speechless with humiliation, thinking of her father's disappointment, then, gathering her last threads of dignity, she turned towards the stairs without another word.

Mab was waiting in her chamber, and stared at her mistress warily as she sat down on the bed. 'What are you going to do, my lady?' she whispered. 'Your father is expecting you to come back.'

'Sir Edward has sent Will and Harold back with a message saying I'm too busy,' Elaine replied, her voice almost too faint to hear.

Then suddenly she straightened, her eyes alight with rebellion. 'But I am not going to let Edward keep me from Papa.' She jumped to her feet. 'I shall go anyway, Mab. Olivia can't stop me . . .'

She broke off as the sound of shouting and the barking of dogs floated up to them from the hall.

'That is Olivia's voice,' she said apprehensively. Hesitatingly, with Mab close on her heels, she began to go down the staircase once again. In the doorway to the hall she stopped, with Mab peering over her shoulder.

Olivia, her face waxen with anger, was hurling abuse at

another woman who was standing there, half-hidden by the settle, while half a dozen servants were standing round open-mouthed, listening unashamedly. For a moment Elaine hesitated before stepping into the room. As she did so, she recognised the unexpected visitor. It was Jane Lockesley.

In a break in Olivia's stream of invective, Jane's cool voice was suddenly audible. 'I defy you to try and make anyone in this house throw me out, sister, especially as Ned is not here to take your part—I passed him in the drive with his paramour.' She gave a malicious smile, then suddenly caught sight of Elaine. Her smile broadened.

'So, the latest member of the Brandon family is here! I'm glad, for it was you I came to see. I'm sorry you had to hear that display of family affection.' She pressed her warm cheek against Elaine's cold one. 'But no doubt you have already witnessed Olivia's generosity to the full!' She laughed as she took Elaine's arm through hers. 'By pure chance I arrived as Ned was leaving, and my sister thinks I am sneaking in to wreak havoc in his absence.' She stared balefully at Olivia. But she suddenly faced Elaine once more. 'Come, I like my new sister better than the old,' she went on cheerfully. 'We'll go to my mother's solar and talk. It is still kept as she liked it, I suppose?' She turned back to Olivia who, defeated, had sunk on to a stool.

The room they entered was a beautiful, small, tapestry-hung chamber on the first floor. As in Elaine's bedroom, the main windows looked out across the marshes, but here there were other windows in the opposite wall that flooded the room with light and warmth. It was the prettiest place Elaine had ever seen.

Jane pushed her gently towards the window seat. 'It is obvious you haven't been in here before,' she said, after a pause. 'I had assumed that Olivia would have given it to you for your own.'

Elaine smiled ruefully. In spite of the ache of jealous misery when she thought of her in Guy's arms, she could not help liking Jane Lockesley. She sensed in her an ally against Olivia and Edward. 'I didn't know there was any-where nice in this house,' she said with painful honesty.

Jane's mouth dropped open. 'But your bedchamber?'

'Is small and dark. Your brother has preferred to spend his nights at the Dower House,' she said defiantly.

Jane still stared at Elaine, before coming to sit beside her. 'Do you mind very much?'

Elaine shook her head violently. 'I'm glad!'

'Has he ever bedded with you?' The candid green gaze held hers steadily. 'No, I can see he hasn't. That virago, Rosalind Berkeley, has forbidden him to touch you, no doubt. Otherwise he would not have resisted so pretty a face.'

Elaine blushed. 'He married me for my money,' she murmured. 'He does not love me. Everything I do displeases him, and now Papa is ill and he has forbidden me to go to him. He lied to Papa,' she rushed on suddenly. 'He said he would live at King's Brook.' She knew she was talking too freely, but could not stop herself. 'Your friend Master Kemp was right. He told me that Edward would not honour his word and that he would take me away from Papa—and he did, the day after our wedding.' She was glad that now at least Guy Kemp's name was out in the open between them.

'You don't love Ned at all, do you?' Jane said softly. 'It is someone else who has captured your heart, I think.' There was a long silence. 'I think you should know that Guy mentioned some of what passed between you both on the *Witch*,' she went on at last.

Elaine's humiliation was complete. So he had not even been gentleman enough to keep the secret of her craven kisses from his paramour! Defiantly she raised her eyes to Jane's. 'He told you I made a fool of myself, no doubt!'

Jane smiled again. 'I don't believe he mentioned that fact, no. He said you were beautiful and spirited; he also said you were stubborn and blind, and that you deserved everything that happened to you at Ned's hands. That was before he got disgustingly drunk at the thought of you in bed with my brother.'

Elaine clutched her shaking hands together. 'He said all that?' she stammered.

Jane nodded emphatically. 'He talked about you endlessly until he drank himself into a stupor and Sam put him to bed.' She stepped forward and caught Elaine's hands impetuously. 'He'll be pleased to know Ned hasn't touched you. You are in love with Guy, aren't you?'

Elaine was frozen by the directness of the question, unaware of the wistful longing which showed so clearly in her eyes.

Jane smiled impishly. 'You didn't really believe that Guy and I were lovers, did you?'

Mutely, Elaine shrugged.

'And Tom never told you anything about me?' Jane's voice was very gentle suddenly.

'No.'

With a deep sigh, Jane released her hands. 'The letter you found on *Black Witch* was not addressed to Guy, Elaine. It belonged to the other occupant of that cabin. It was your brother and I who were lovers. Not for very long —we had only just found each other. I think he might have wed me if we'd been given time.' There was a long silence.

Elaine recognised the slow sad dawning of the truth. 'Tom never so much as hinted,' she whispered at last.

'No. That was so like Tom, wasn't it?' Jane's features were under control again. 'Don't be sad for me. I'm not one to dwell on past sorrows, and Tom wouldn't have wanted it.' She was almost calm again. 'Guy asked you to marry him, didn't he?'

Elaine felt her cheeks colouring as she looked down. 'I told him I could never marry a pirate,' she said softly.

'Why?'

'Why? Because he's a murderer and a thief, and I thought he loved you. I thought he was interested in me only for my money, like Edward!'

'Of one thing I can assure you,' Jane said. 'He has no need of your money! He has fortunes of his own—albeit ill-gotten!' She grinned. 'He knew that if he married you, your father would disinherit you. If he mentioned money, it was to tease you, nothing more.'

'Whatever it was for . . .' Elaine turned away, her heart like lead. 'It is too late. I am married to your brother, and nothing can change that.'

In the silence that followed her words a board creaked in the next room, but neither of them noticed.

'But you're not really married to him!' Jane's face was triumphant. 'Don't you see? Your marriage has not been consummated, so in the eyes of the church it is not valid and can be annulled! We must get you away from here! Ned is weak and a fool, but once Rosalind is away with the Queen, he won't hesitate to defy her. By the time he gets back, you must be out of his reach!'

Elaine felt a piercing ray of hope. 'You mean I would be free of Edward? Is it possible? But what about Olivia? She will keep me here . . .'

'Fie on Olivia! You leave her to me. Tell me. If you were free, would you go to Guy now? Do you love him enough?' She gripped Elaine by the shoulders. 'Love— real love—means you'll give up everything for a man. I know. I did it. Everything, Elaine. Your wealth, your security, life itself, if it is asked of you. Would you do that for him?'

Elaine hesitated. She was thinking of those bright blue eyes, so harsh in their anger as they looked at her last on board *Black Witch*. Then she remembered again the dance at her wedding; the fleeting touch of his lips as he pulled her to him, and the anguished longing he roused in her as he left her and vanished into the crowd.

'I love him enough,' she whispered.

Jane released her, smiling. 'Then we must take you to him. He'll know what you must do to obtain the annulment. If only Tom were here. If only those letters had not disappeared!'

Elaine looked puzzled. 'What was so important about them?'

'Of course, you don't know.' She sat down on the window seat. 'The reason Guy fled to the sea and took up his way of life was because he was accused of attempting to murder his younger brother, Henry. God knows, no one would have blamed him if he had! Henry Kemp is a dissolute rogue, as unlike his brother as I am unlike Olivia! But it wasn't true, and Tom was sure there would be someone, somewhere, who knew the real story, and he set out to find them. A couple of weeks before he died,' she hesitated briefly over the words, 'he sent me a message saying he had found witnesses. Then, the day before he sailed, John Palmer came to tell me that Tom had letters which would clear Guy's name completely, and that he was leaving them with you.' She sighed. 'They really were stolen? You didn't just say that to pay me back for being Guy's paramour?' Her face was lightened by a small twinkle.

Elaine shook her head sadly. 'They disappeared from my jewel casket.'

'And no one else knew they were there?'

'No one. Only Mab, my maid, perhaps.' Elaine frowned. 'But I asked her, and she swore she had not touched them.'

'Is she here?' Jane's voice was suddenly intense with excitement.

'She arrived today.'

'Then let us question her again. She might have seen someone in your room. It is worth a try, surely?'

Neither young woman noticed, as they crossed to the door, another creak of the floorboards in the next room, nor saw the flurry of black skirts as a shadow slipped ahead of them out of sight.

Mab was sitting on a stool in Elaine's room, mending a tear in one of her gowns. She rose and bobbed a curtsy as the two young women came in.

'Mab.' Elaine glanced at the door as Jane shut it. 'I want to ask you something. It is about the letters that vanished from my casket. Is there any way someone could have gone into my room at King's Brook and taken them? Anyone at all?' She held out her hands. 'They are so important.'

Mab blushed scarlet, her eyes darting from Jane to her mistress and back.

'I don't know,' she stammered.

'Are you sure?' Elaine insisted. 'Please, Mab, try and think.'

Jane was watching her. 'You took them, didn't you!' she said softly.

Mab shook her head, but Jane persisted.

'I think you did, girl. No one else could have guessed they were there.'

'Please, Mab, if it was you, tell me?' Elaine cried.

Mab burst into tears. 'It was for you, mistress. I didn't know what to do for the best!'

'Where are they?' Elaine's gentle voice interrupted her, trembling with excitement. 'I'm not angry, but I do need them.'

'They're with my clothes, my lady,' Mab sniffed. 'Sewn into the hem. What could I do? Sir Edward . . . He said he wanted to search your room. He asked for your keys. I knew the letters were special—' she glanced at Jane suspiciously '—so I thought I'd hide them where he'd never find them'.

'Edward searched my room?' Elaine sounded horror-stricken.

'Oh yes, my lady. When you were out riding one day. He had two of his men go over it. They even split the mattresses open, and he tipped out your jewel casket himself. Then he put everything back and locked it and gave me the keys again.'

'But why didn't you tell me?' Elaine's fists were clenched tightly.

'He said he'd kill me if I told.' Mab lowered her eyes. 'And I believed him.' She shivered. 'I couldn't think what to do, and as he hadn't found anything . . .' She looked up again, pleading. 'I'm very sorry, my lady . . .'

Elaine swallowed hard.

Jane had gone white. 'But what was he looking for? Surely he didn't know about the letters?'

'He suspects me of being in league with the pirates,' Elaine confessed. 'He caught sight of Guy coming from my room when he came to tell me about Tom . . . No, not close enough to recognise him, but he saw him. And he saw me once, watching *Black Witch* leave Woodbridge.' She looked down, her cheeks colouring slightly. 'He suspects that I have a lover on the *Witch*.'

Jane's face was very grave. 'If he found out for certain!'

'He has already told me what he will do to the crew of the *Witch* if he catches them. I don't think it will make any difference to him if he knows it's Guy,' Elaine said bitterly. 'With me, he has to be a little more circumspect. After all, if I were hanged, my fortune would be forfeit to the King. Edward would not like that at all.' She turned to Mab. 'Fetch the letters quickly!' Her voice was full of hope once more. 'Who knows, they may contain enough to win Guy's pardon from the King!'

CHAPTER
TEN

It took Mab a few minutes to return, clutching a bundle of clothes wrapped in a woollen shawl. She unrolled it on the floor and picked out a grey woollen dress. With a tiny pair of scissors, she began to rip at the hem until three separate letters fell out.

Jane pounced on them. 'Have you read them, girl?' she asked, examining the seals carefully.

Mab shook her head indignantly. 'I don't know how, mistress.'

'Then you don't know what is in them?'

'I thought they were love letters,' Mab confessed.

Jane laughed sadly. 'If only they were!' Her hands trembled slightly as she broke the seal on the first.

Elaine and Mab watched in silence while she read the three documents, both turning away in silent sympathy as slow tears began to run down Jane's cheeks when she read the third. Without a word, she passed all three to Elaine.

She turned to the first one with curiosity. It was a scrappy piece of parchment, written in an unlettered hand: 'I, Steven Darcy, did see my master, Henry Kemp, set upon by thieves, among them Roger of Leiston and William Compton. They beat him about the head and left him for dead. When he recovered, he and his friends, John Farrier and Ned Brandon'—Elaine raised shocked eyes to meet those of her sister-in-law—'planned to set the blame for the attack on Henry's brother, Guy. Guy, now discredited and hiding from the King's justice, was taken in secret to a ship where he was to be killed and his body thrown into the sea. This was all done so that Henry, the youngest son, could have the lands of Kempsmere and the old lord's title when he died.'

The second was shorter, and obviously written by an

amanuensis: 'I, Will Compton, being about to die of a creeping consumption, and wishing to settle my affairs before God and man, do admit that I attempted to kill Henry Kemp for his gold. His brother was not of our band and did not know of our intention.'

Elaine hesitated, not wanting to open the other letter, but Jane said huskily, 'Read it—please.'

The sight of Tom's writing brought tears to her eyes, too, but Elaine read the hasty scrawl, and then read it again.

Sweetheart,

I sail with Guy tonight and in case anything should happen to me I leave these with my sister Elaine. She knows nothing of our business and I pray she need not, until Guy's name is clear, as I am sure it will be when you give them to the King. Then perhaps at last I can introduce Elaine to Guy. As I told you, I think he is the man to tame my sister and make her happy.

Take care of yourself, my darling Jane. Once this is over and my days on *Black Witch* are complete, perhaps you and I will find our futures lie together.

My love, always, Tom.

'Oh, Jane . . .' Elaine's voice trembled. 'Oh, why did he have to die?'

Jane shook her head slowly. 'It was God's will,' she whispered. Then she stood up. 'But now my way is clear. As Tom can't do it, I have to take these letters to King Henry without delay.' She caught Elaine's hands. 'And you must leave with me, now, before Ned comes back.'

Elaine nodded, still numb.

'You do want to go to Guy?' Jane's eyes were gentle. 'As you see, even Tom knew you were made for each other.'

'Does he really want me?' Elaine's hands were shaking with excitement as she folded the letters.

Jane laughed, bravely thrusting her own sad memories aside. 'He wants you.'

Elaine's eyes lit with joy. 'Then I want to go to him! But

you must ride straight to the King—you mustn't wait to help me.' Suddenly she was feverish with impatience and fear lest something happen to the precious documents.

'I intend to leave this minute,' Jane said, 'and you must come too. Now. There's no time even to pack some clothes.' She glanced at Mab. 'Your maid is trustworthy, of course. She must ride with you. I'll accompany you both for a little of the way so that I can show you where you can hide till Guy comes for you. Then I shall go south to find the King.' She laughed grimly. 'If I'd known sooner, I could have offered to keep the Lady Rosalind company on her way to court!'

The letters tucked firmly into her bosom, Jane opened the door and listened. Elaine looked once round the room which had been her home for the few unhappy days of her stay at Aldebourne. She caught up her wrap, but made no attempt to take anything else. Neither did Mab. Leaving the maid's clothes scattered on the floor, they followed Jane on tiptoe towards the stairs.

To Elaine's relief there was no sign of Olivia; the hall was deserted as Jane motioned them through it and into a passage where they could wait unseen. Then she summoned her own servants.

'Saddle the horses once more. I dislike the welcome I received here,' she said haughtily as they appeared. 'We'll ride back to Framlingham without delay.' Cautiously she drew her groom to one side. 'We need two extra horses. See if you can find anything in my brother's stable capable of galloping.' He nodded and winked at her, then disappeared.

In the damp, closed part of the house Elaine and Mab waited anxiously for Jane's signal. It did not seem possible that they would be able to ride off openly in full daylight without Olivia's knowledge, but Elaine was content to leave the planning to Jane. She was on fire with hope and excitement. At one stroke, all the impenetrable barriers to her happiness had gone. She would escape from Edward; her marriage would be declared invalid; Guy would be pardoned by the King; and her father . . . She sighed. Had she really forgotten him in her new-found happiness and hope? She whispered a little prayer that he would get well and understand, and that he would come to love Guy—who had been Tom's friend.

'There's the signal!' Mab's taut whisper roused her. Gathering their skirts up lest they rustle on the flagstones, the two girls ran to the deserted yard where Jane and her three servants waited with their mounts, and with them two extra horses.

'They're slugs, I'm afraid, but at least they're sound,' Jane said caustically. 'Ned still keeps his good animals in the south, I see. Mount quickly.' She looked nervously over her shoulder as her groom helped Mab and Elaine into the saddle.

Near the northern boundary of the estate, Elaine turned to glance back the way they had come, frowning in the glare. Suddenly her stomach lurched with fear. Several horsemen had appeared in the distance, throwing up clouds of dust.

'They're after us!' Her cry was barely audible, but the others heard it. As one they set off at the gallop across the heath.

Jane cried to Elaine, 'If we become separated, head for the river. There's a shack about three miles down towards the sea—on Barton's Beach. You'll know it by the blue gull on the door. Wait there for Guy . . .' Already the two horses Mab and Elaine were riding were slowing. Elaine closed her eyes and urged her horse on, but to no avail. The animal's stride was shortening.

Again Jane was shouting. 'Those horses are blown, Elaine. I'm going to lead them away from you. Give me your wrap.' Reining back her own horse, she leaned across and grabbed it from Elaine's shoulders.

'No!' Elaine cried in anguish. 'You'll be caught! You must get to the King with the letters.'

'I'll get to him, never fear!' Jane's face was alight with excitement. 'We'll have to split now—as we reach that stand of trees. You head east and hide in the forest till they've gone. I'll lead them south. Good luck!'

Her horse lengthened its stride beneath her whip, and she tore off down the track, her servants after her.

Grimly Elaine and Mab headed for the trees. But first they had to cross another hundred yards of coarse heather, its wiry stems hampering the horses' already meagre speed. Behind them there was a shout, but Elaine did not dare to look back. She prayed that their pursuers had followed the blue wrap and the arrogantly waving Jane. She pressed her mount on.

'It's no good, my lady!' Mab's shout reached her over the whistling breath of the horse. 'They've not even hesitated. They're following us!'

The sick chill of fear gripped Elaine more tightly, but still she could not bring herself to look back. If only they could reach the trees and lose themselves in their shadows, they would be safe.

But it was no use. She could hear the hoofbeats now, and she knew her horse was failing, even as she tried to push it on. Slowly, she began to rein in, obeying the ancient instinct to turn at bay.

'Stop, Mab! It's no use,' she called. Her voice was strangely calm as she pulled up her mount and turned it to face her pursuers, patting it gently as she waited, head held proudly high, for the horsemen to surround her. She recognised them at once: Olivia's steward James Catchpole, the groom from the stables, and two men from the estate. Catchpole touched his cap as he approached, spurring his horse through the others until he could lean and catch her rein.

'I'm sorry, my lady, you must return with us.' Another rider closed on her other side, and her horse was forced to walk between them as they turned back towards Aldebourne.

Elaine did not argue. She sat erect as they led her back, a prisoner, with Mab trailing disconsolately behind. Her only comfort was that her captors had shown no interest whatever in following Jane.

Olivia was waiting in the hall when Elaine, still escorted by Catchpole, was brought into the house. She had changed from her habitual black to a gown of scarlet fustian, and suddenly appeared very threatening as she surveyed the two dishevelled young women.

'Daniel—take the maid to work in the wash-house,' Olivia instructed one of the men who had followed her in. 'If she gives trouble, have her beaten.'

Her eyes did not stray from Elaine for a second as, with a whimper of protest, Mab was dragged away.

'I knew when my sister came here that she would try and make trouble,' she said slowly. 'I should have known you would allow yourself to be influenced by her. So you think you can cast off my brother and marry Guy Kemp!' Her face twisted into a mocking sneer.

Elaine felt herself grow cold. She said to Olivia in disbelief, 'You were listening?'

'Of course I was listening! Do you think I would allow Jane to carry you off for a cosy chat in private and not be there to hear her calumny!' She laughed. 'And just as well! Ned will be so interested in all I have to tell him this time!'

'But you mustn't!' Elaine cried. 'Oh, please, don't tell him.' She was shaking with fear. Olivia was watching her with interest, her arms folded, and it was the sight of the open enjoyment on her face that gave Elaine the strength to summon back her courage. With an enormous effort, she face Olivia, her eyes blazing. 'You have no right to bring me back here!' she cried. 'How dare you treat me like this! Do you think that Sir Edward will want the whole world to know his private affairs?'

To her satisfaction, Olivia took a step back in surprise, seeming to see for the first time the crowd of servants standing in the doorway and around Elaine. But her discomfort was short lived. Within seconds she was smiling again. An unpleasant smile.

'The servants should know,' Olivia said clearly, 'what kind of woman their master has taken for a wife. They will rejoice the more when you are brought to heel, as you will be when Edward returns. Don't think the Lady Rosalind has any power over him that can save you now that she is no longer here. He merely did not wish to offend her. But he will deal with you as you should be dealt with. And I intend to see to it that you are here to receive him when he returns. James, take Lady Brandon to the store-room beneath the old kitchens, and lock her in.'

Catchpole stepped forward slowly, a frown on his face. 'But, Mistress Olivia . . .'

'Do it, James!' Olivia hissed. 'And put a guard on the door. She'll not make a fool of my brother again.'

Reluctantly the man put his hand on Elaine's arm. 'This way, my lady.'

Elaine drew herself up to her full height as he led her out. She did not look at Olivia again.

Catchpole, followed by two of the other menservants, took her into the old part of the house, through deserted rooms thick with dust, until they came to the old kitchens. There, a short flight of steps led down to a stout door. The bolts that held it were bound with matted spiders' webs.

Elaine had no more courage left. 'Please,' she pleaded in a whisper. 'Don't put me down there!'

Catchpole looked uncomfortable. 'I'm sorry, my lady, but there's none here who would disobey Mistress Olivia.' He walked down the steps ahead of her and pulled back the bolts with some difficulty. She was numb with terror as he pushed open the heavy door. Behind it there was darkness. A heavy musty smell drifted out. Standing aside, he allowed her to pass, stumbling, into the fetid gloom. Then he pulled the door shut behind her and the bolts grated home.

For a long time Elaine was too afraid to move. She forced her knuckles into her mouth to stop herself from screaming as her ears strained to pick out a distant rustling noise which seemed to echo off the cold stone walls. Then, as her eyes grew used to the darkness, she saw that it was not so intense. Somewhere ahead of her there was a definite but faint source of light, and cautiously she began to grope across the rough earthen floor towards it.

She located a pile of old crates against the wall, and pulling at them frantically, found an unglazed, barred window that had been hidden behind them. Standing on tiptoe to see out, her face was level with the ground outside. The faint rustling she had heard was from the trees in the orchard. Eagerly she took several deep breaths of the clean, sweet air, then turned to survey her prison by the light now filtering in between the curtains of grass that

veiled the window. The small room was empty, save for
the crates which now lay scattered around her feet.

Miserably she sat down on one of them, and put her
head in her hands. No one came. Slowly the sunlight faded,
and the light at the window grew dim. She began to shiver
more violently as the air grew damp and sharp.

It was almost dark when she heard a quiet voice at the
window. At first she was too frightened to move, then, her
heart alive with hope, she leapt to her feet and ran to peer
out. 'Who is it?' she whispered.

'It's me—Mab,' the voice replied. Mab plumped down
on her knees and her face appeared at the bars. With her
was a small basket. 'One of the washerwomen told me
where to find you, my lady. I've brought some bread and
cheese. Then I'm going to find Master Kemp.'

'Mab!' Elaine's heart leapt with excitement. 'Oh, Mab!
He is the only person who can save me. Unless . . .' She
clutched at the girl's hand through the bars. 'You could
release me. There are bolts, but . . .'

The girl shook her head. 'There's someone on guard in
the old kitchen, and likely to be all night. That old witch
Mistress Olivia says so. She really hates you, my lady.'
Mab's eyes were dark with sympathy. 'So I'll go and find
the hut like Mistress Lockesley said, and wait there. But
I'll need something from you.' She fished in the basket and
produced a crumpled scrap of parchment and a piece of
charcoal. 'You write for him to come, my lady. He'll not
believe me otherwise. He'll think it's a trap.'

Slowly Elaine took the writing materials. It was too dark
to see what she was doing properly as she smoothed the
parchment over one of the crates and laboriously began to
write: 'Guy—please come and save me. Mab will show
you where I am. Hurry. Your partner and friend, Elaine
Howard.' She could not bring herself to use her new, hated,
name. She thrust the message through the bars. 'Take it
quickly, Mab. And God go with you.'

The girl passed her bread and cheese from the basket,
and a mug half full of ale. Then, with a frightened grin,
barely to be seen in the gloom, she vanished. Elaine
strained her ears for the sound of footsteps and the rustling

of her skirts in the grass. After a moment they grew faint and disappeared, and she was alone again.

She ate the food Mab had brought her and drank the ale, then once more settled herself to wait, shivering with cold as she leaned back against the clammy brick wall, overcome with weariness. The night was very silent. There were no owls; no companionable songs of the nightingale.

Eventually she must have dozed, for when she woke with a start the daylight had returned and her bones were stiff and aching.

She would not let herself think of Mab, alone in unfamiliar countryside in the dark, perhaps lost, perhaps overcome with fear; or of what would happen if Guy did not come—or if he did not believe Mab's story. The message after all could as easily have been written by anyone. She had signed her name for him once, but she did not know if he had even noticed what her writing looked like—what he had wanted after all was her father's seal on the deeds of *Black Witch*. Hot tears welled up in her eyes, and she impatiently rubbed them away with the back of her hand. If there was to be no rescue in time, and Sir Edward returned to claim her as his wife, he was not going to find her tearful and defeated.

Some time later she heard the footsteps outside the door. Fighting down her panic, she got to her feet, struggling to appear calm as the door swung back and James Catchpole entered. He was carrying a tray, which he carefully set down on the floor. A tallow candle wavered on it in a pewter candlestick, with a mug, and a plate covered with a linen napkin. 'There's food and a bit of light, my lady,' he said in an undertone. 'There'll be no need to mention to Mistress Olivia that I came. I'll try and bring some more later, if Sir Edward is not home.' He glanced at her for the first time. 'Are you all right, my lady?' He was amazed to see her dry-eyed and quiet.

Elaine smiled warily. 'I'm very cold. If you could find me a blanket, perhaps,' she said, her low voice sounding husky even to her own ears.

'I'll try and find something, my lady.'

Elaine sat down again, glad of the warmth and light of

the feeble candle flame as she began dispiritedly to eat,
her thoughts flying once more to Mab. Even supposing
Mab had found him, and he had read the note and knew
her writing, she still could not be sure Guy would come.
She had only Jane Lockesley's word for it that Guy cared
for her. What if Jane were wrong? Perhaps it was her
money he had coveted? Now he knew there would be no
money, would he risk his life to remove her from her lawful
husband? She dashed away the fresh tears. All she could
do was to hope and pray.

It was several hours before she saw Catchpole once
more, and the candle had long ago burned to nothing. With
him this time he brought, not the comfort of a blanket, but
Olivia, who lifted her skirts fastidiously as she followed
him down the steps. She stared at Elaine, showing a gleam
of satisfaction as she saw by the light of Catchpole's lantern
the dirt and mildew on her sister-in-law's gown, and the
smears of dust on her pale face.

'You are still here!' she said, with undisguised malice.
'You will be glad to hear that your husband has returned
home, and wishes to see you.' She turned to Catchpole,
who was watching her with eyes kept carefully blank of
expression. 'Bring her!' Then she turned and swept back
up the steps.

Elaine followed them, feeling Catchpole's steadying
hand beneath her elbow as she stumbled in the sudden
bright daylight of the kitchen. She was numb. All hope of
rescue had died as she saw Olivia's triumphant face in the
doorway.

She was led through the hall into the smaller room
beyond it which Edward used as his own. He was there,
sprawled in a chair before the table, his clothes still dusty
from his ride. As she came into the room, he looked her
up and down, taking in every detail of her dishevelled gown
and the tear-stains on her face. Then, without speaking,
he looked back to the desk where he had been studying
something when she came in. Following his gaze, she saw
a piece of torn parchment lying before him. One glance
told her it was her message to Kemp, and that Edward was
watching her with a self-satisfied smile.

'So, now we have the truth at last,' he said softly. 'You are condemned by your own hand, my lady. That letter, and Olivia's information, tell me all I need to know about your lover.' He picked up the note and flicked it with his nail. 'Guy Kemp,' he said reflectively. 'I should have guessed he wasn't dead.' He laughed. 'And my wife is his lover. There is a certain irony in that.' He threw the note down on the table again. 'Your messenger was intercepted last night, and I have her under lock and key. I shall probably have her hanged for helping a pirate. I am greatly tempted, my lady, to do the same for you.' His voice cut suddenly like a whiplash. 'Have you any idea of the seriousness of your crimes?' He sat forward suddenly and grabbed her wrist. 'Only your marriage to me saves you from the consequences of what you have done. A marriage you are eager to dissolve, it seems. I think we should put an end, now, to your hopes of an annulment, but first, you will be pleased to hear that I am sending your message, as you intended, to your lover.'

He smiled. 'Here, James. Have this taken to the shack at Barton's Beach, and nail it to the door.' He handed the note to his steward. 'Of course, it won't be you who waits for him when he arrives, Elaine,' he went on conversationally. 'It will be I with a strong party of the King's men. You will be where you belong, in my bedchamber.' He stood up suddenly. 'And that is where we are going now. James, you know the message you must take to Woodbridge. I shall want a detachment of men here by dawn at the latest. Ride yourself, with my authority, now.' He tossed a second sealed document to the man.

Then, dragging Elaine after him, he strode out of the room past Olivia, who had been standing in the doorway. Elaine had a glimpse of the greedy joy in the woman's face, as, sick with horror, she stumbled after her husband, then he was pulling her up the stairs and towards his chamber.

It was huge and sumptuous, dominated by a four-poster bed hung with scarlet and gold damask. He closed the door and pushed her on to the bed, before beginning to remove his doublet. The expression on his face was murderous as he grabbed her and threw her back against the pillows. For a moment he stared at her without a word, then, with a single violent movement, he tore her gown and kirtle from her body, ripping the silk and velvet and the delicate chemise beneath. He snatched off her head-dress and ran his fingers roughly through her hair to loosen the braids, until her hair was a curtain of pale rippling gold.

'Now,' he breathed, throwing himself over her struggling body. 'Now, we will have the consummation!'

As his lips ground into hers, the door on the far side of the room was flung open without ceremony and Catchpole appeared, too agitated even to notice what his master was doing. His face was the colour of alabaster.

'Sir Edward,' he cried. 'It's too late to summon help! Too late for anything! *Black Witch* is already in the river!'

Sir Edward stared at the naked body of the beautiful woman beneath him for a moment, and then gave an ugly laugh.

'So,' he whispered. 'Your lover did not wait for his summons after all. No matter. We shall take him anyway!' He raised himself on his elbow. 'His lust for my wife has signed his death-warrant. Ride, James! To Woodbridge, and fetch those reinforcements as fast as you can!' He slowly climbed to his feet and began to reach for his clothes. 'They can be here before dark. Cover yourself, madam!' he added curtly, and threw a sheet across her as Catchpole's round eyes focused on her. 'I will attend to you, later. It will be all the more enjoyable once my task is complete. Who knows! Perhaps Master Kemp would like to watch our mating!' He smiled as he took hold of his sword and buckled it into place. Then he turned and left her.

CHAPTER
ELEVEN

THE DOOR was fastened on the outside. Desperately Elaine pulled at it, then she ran to the window, peering out at the placid river. There was no sign of a ship. Clutching a bed cover to her, she knelt and resting her head on her arms on the wooden seat in front of the huge window, she wept.

There was no sound in the house, until somewhere she heard running footsteps and the quick clash of steel. She scrambled to her feet, her mouth dry with fear, and ran to the door, listening. But there was no noise now, just the cool rustle of the reeds as the wind changed.

Suddenly she could bear it no longer. 'Please, help me! Let me out! Please!' she cried, and beat with her fists on the thick panels of the door. For a few moments nothing happened and she thought no one had heard, then there was a sound of steps, and, out of the silence, she heard her name.

'Lady Brandon?' The mocking voice was unmistakable. 'Can it be you?'

With a gasp she rattled the latch desperately. 'I'm here!' she called. 'Please let me out.'

A key was turned in the lock, and then the door swung open. Guy Kemp stood in the doorway, a naked cutlass in his hand. 'Your husband, Lady Brandon. Where is he?' His voice was cold now.

She stepped back abruptly, stunned by his tone, her joy and relief fading as she realised with a shock that he knew nothing of the circumstances of her marriage, nor even of the note she had tried to send him. He thought her allied for ever to his enemy. You're wrong! she wanted to cry out. It's you I love, not Edward . . . but the words would not come. The scorn in his eyes froze them on her lips.

'He . . . He went out when the report came that your

ship had been seen in the river,' she said, her voice shaking.
She was intensely conscious of her nakedness beneath the
embroidered coverlet.

He went to the window and looked out. Then his gaze
went to the disordered bed, and then slowly back to her.

'I see I interrupted the knight and his lady at an awkward
moment. I regret the intrusion, my lady. I appear to have
missed him, unless . . . Perhaps he is here, after all? I
wonder, are you hiding him as a dutiful wife should?' He
raised the cutlass and slashed at the bed-hangings until
swathes of red damask fell across the linen sheets like pools
of blood.

Elaine drew back, terrified by his violence. Had she
really been ready to beg this man to come and save her?
Had she really believed Jane when she said that Guy loved
her? There was no love in his face as he sliced through the
hangings with the flashing blade. He was, as she had always
known deep down, no more than a cut-throat; a vicious,
handsome thief.

A tiny moan escaped her lips. Immediately he swung
round. 'Did you say something, my lady?'

She looked up at him. 'Why did you come?' she murmured through stiff lips.

'I have a score to settle,' he replied under his breath.
'And I always pay my debts. You haven't told me where
he is.'

'I told you . . . He went out to lie in wait for you. Your
ship was sighted. He had planned to lure you here with a
note from me, but you arrived too soon. He wasn't ready
. . .' She did not dare to lift her eyes from the coverlet.

'You wrote me a note?' His tone was mocking again.
'And what did it say, this note?'

Elaine drew back as far as she could. Then she raised
her eyes to his again. 'It doesn't matter, now, what it
said.'

He smiled grimly. 'So, a note to lure me to my death!
How sorry I am that it did not reach me, Lady Brandon.'

'Don't call me that!' She stamped her foot. 'You called
me Elaine before.' In spite of the tears, there was anger in
her voice.

'That was when you were a sea sprite,' he said, 'on the deck of my ship, as much of a pirate as I was, with the wind in your hair and the devil in your eyes.' He chuckled softly. 'Now you are a respectable married lady. It was your choice, *Lady Brandon*.' Suddenly he released her. 'Now, there are things I must attend to.' He strode towards the door. As he reached it, he turned. 'I suggest that you, in your turn, find an intact garment, and dress . . .' She blushed. 'Tell me something,' he went on relentlessly. 'Why does Ned Brandon need to keep his wife locked in his bedroom?'

Elaine held her head high. 'Perhaps you had better ask him that,' she said proudly.

He looked at her thoughtfully for a moment, then said, 'I believe I shall.'

She gave herself no time to think. As soon as he had left her, she flew to her own small room at the far end of the house. Throwing down the coverlet, she pulled a chemise over her head, and over it her gown of scarlet brocade. Her heavy hair she bundled into a net sewn with pearls. Then, thrusting her feet into soft slippers, she whirled out on to the landing and down the stairs. She had to find Mab, then together they must escape. The house was silent again; whatever fighting there had been, had ceased. She stood uncertainly in the hall, looking round, then she ran towards the old kitchens.

At the doorway she stopped short at the sight of a man, a drawn cutlass in his hand. He grinned when he saw her, obviously recognising her.

'Kemp is out in the yard, mistress, and your maid is with him,' he said gruffly. 'My orders are to stand guard here.' He jerked his thumb over his shoulder at the door behind which she had been so recently imprisoned. It was once more bolted.

Elaine shuddered. Who, she wondered, was shut in there now? She did not wait to ask, but ran out into the cobbled yard. Kemp was there with some of his followers, and with them was Mab. As Elaine appeared, they all turned towards her.

Kemp stepped forward. His expression was quizzical.

'Your husband appears to have fled, my lady,' he said. 'Do you wish to follow him?'

Elaine clenched her fists. 'I wish only to leave here. Please release my maid, and she and I can go on our way.'

'Ah, yes, your maid.' Kemp looked thoughtfully at Mab. 'Is your maid given to lying, Lady Brandon?'

'She is not!' Elaine's angry denial echoed Mab's gasp of indignation.

Kemp moved towards her. 'When . . .' he said softly, 'when she tells me that you love me, and had written to beg me to come and rescue you from Ned, she was telling the truth?'

Elaine's cheeks coloured vividly, and she looked down, unable to meet his eye as he took her hands.

'Tell me the truth, Elaine,' he murmured.

She nodded, unable to speak.

'And you do not wish me to send you back to Ned?'

'No!' Her voice slid up in panic. 'I shall never go back to him! He is not my husband.' She looked up at Kemp. 'He didn't . . . That is, we are not properly man and wife.'

She could not read the expression on his face. His eyes were unfathomable.

'So,' he said at last. 'You are still a sea sprite.' He touched her hair lightly. 'And I thought we had lost you.'

'You haven't lost me,' she whispered.

For a moment he did not move; then, with a muttered oath, he pulled her against him, his lips claiming hers in a hungry, savage kiss. Stunned, she stood quite still, her eyes closed, her arms slipping round his neck to hold him closer still, until she remembered suddenly where they were and tried to free herself. The spectators raised a ragged cheer as he lifted his face from hers.

Kemp grinned, pulling her close again. 'Come, friends. We must go, or Ned will be back to corner us.' He lifted Elaine to the saddle of his horse and swung himself up behind her. Arranging her comfortably in the circle of his arms, held close against his chest, he looked around. Behind them, one of his men had taken Mab up. They were ready. At his signal, they set off out of the yard at a canter.

'Where are you taking me?' Elaine managed to ask eventually.

He smiled down at her. 'To the Kemp family seat, where I take all my prizes.' His eyes gleamed. 'It should have been mine, but because of a long and distressing story, which I do not intend to relate now, it is my brother's. He ignores it totally, preferring the fleshpots of court life, so to all intents and purposes it is again mine. My refuge, anyway, though he milks it of its rents and tithes.' The lines of bitterness on either side of his mouth deepened. 'It is the perfect place to bring *Black Witch* for her careening. The creeks and rivers are hidden from everyone in the woods and marshes, and the people there are all mine. You will be safe there. The Brandons are not welcome.'

Elaine stared at his hand, so brown and strong, holding his horse's rein loosely. 'But I am a Brandon,' she whispered. 'I hate him. And Olivia.'

He laughed. 'Never!' he said. 'You could never be of the same family as Ned or Olivia.'

'Or Jane?' she asked with a little smile. 'How is it possible that she could be their sister?'

Guy Kemp laughed again. 'She was born under a different star. You've met Jane at last, have you?' Amusement still flickered in his eyes.

'Tom found witnesses to the attempted murder of your brother,' she said. 'He left their letters with me for Jane. She has taken them to the King.'

He stiffened, his whole body taut with excitement for a moment, then he shook his head, kicking the cob into a canter once more. 'A royal pardon would be pleasant, and I'd dearly like to see those rogues get their deserts. But, sweetheart, you forget. I am a pirate now; a man of the sea. I have a string of crimes to my account which the King would never pardon.'

She felt a sudden sick pang of disappointment and fear. 'But the King doesn't know it's you on *Black Witch* . . .'

'Ned knows.' He gave her a wry smile. 'Every man, woman and child for miles around knows. So I expect the King is acquainted with my name by now.'

She hung her head. 'And it's my fault. If Edward had

not seen my note to you; if Olivia had not heard Jane
talking . . .' She was struck by a sudden thought. 'What
happened to Olivia when you came to the house? I didn't
see her there.'

He chuckled. 'One of the servants, your servants, Lady
Brandon, told us that she had had you locked in a dungeon,
so I felt it was only fair to put her there in her turn. No
doubt Ned will hear her shouts when he returns from
scouring the countryside for me! Though, if he's any sense,
he'll leave her there!'

Elaine was smiling, too. She found the thought of
Olivia's discomfort somehow immensely pleasing.

'You will get a royal pardon somehow,' she said softly.
'I'm sure of it. Jane will manage it. She was so confident
that those letters would work.'

Kemp dropped a kiss on the top of her head. 'Jane is
always confident, my dear. It is her way. Part of her charm.'

'Why did you let me think she was your mistress?' She
looked away as she spoke, feeling the heat flooding into
her cheeks.

'Why did you,' he replied, his voice gently teasing, 'tell
me once that you loved Ned Brandon?'

The horses covered the miles with easy strides, until they
were on a winding overgrown track which led through the
woods towards the river. Just before the marshes, it bent
sharply towards the west, and Elaine saw that they were
approaching a long, low, timber-framed house, almost
completely overgrown with ivy and festooned with dog-
roses. There was an air of decay and sadness over the
whole beautiful place.

As Guy reined in the horse, Elaine caught her breath.
'Is this your home?' she whispered.

'Yes, but no one lives in the house now. My activities
are usually carried out nearer the river.' He nudged the
horse forward again. In the distance was the gleam of
silver, where a cool arm of the river formed an elbow round
the house on its northern side. Near it was a range of old
outbuildings and stables, also now deserted, and several
sheds in much better repair, their doors shut. Jutting into

the river below them was a wooden landing-stage. But there was no sign of *Black Witch*.

They all dismounted. The horses were led into the stable, as the door of one of the sheds opened and several men appeared.

Guy turned and chucked Mab under the chin. 'You help Walt with his cooking, girl, and keep an eye on Sam, while I show your mistress the estate,' he said, and winked at her as he caught Elaine's hand. 'Come. We'll talk to the men, then I'll take you to the house so that you can see what is left of my inheritance.'

Elaine followed him, and Mab disappeared towards a cooking-fire that was burning merrily near the river's edge. 'Where is the *Witch*?' she asked. 'I thought she would be here.'

'She's gone back to sea. I wouldn't let her sail up here into a possible trap. She'll come back for us, don't fret.' He grinned. 'Now wait while I give the men their orders.' He nodded back at the outbuildings near the jetty. 'Those sheds must be emptied without delay. Some of the stuff is going by pack-horse and some by river, but every single thing must be spirited away before your husband arrives.' At the shiver of fear that passed over her, he pulled her close. 'Don't worry, my darling. Ned won't come until he has his reinforcements; he doesn't know how many men are with me. And, by the time he comes, the buildings will be once more empty except for the dust on the floor, and the house will be locked and deserted. We shall all be far away.' He paused. 'There's still time to change your mind and go back to him if you wish.'

'No,' she replied. 'I shall never change my mind.'

'You are quite sure?' For a moment he looked down at her, his eyes narrowed in the slanting evening sunlight, then he put his finger gently on her lips. 'Wait here while I speak to the men.'

He strode towards the sheds, directing the groups of waiting men in different directions. There were two or three dozen of them now, she noticed uneasily, all of them armed. She could feel her heart beating faster as he came back to her, and nervously she clenched her fists.

'They should be finished by dusk,' he said. 'Then we'll make our way down-river in the dark. Let us take that walk while your maid and Walt prepare us some food.'

In a daze she followed him along the river bank and up through what had once been a rose garden. As they stepped on to the terrace, he stopped and caught her hand, raising it gently to his lips. 'You said I hadn't lost you,' he murmured. 'Did you mean it?'

For a moment she hesitated, her eyes dreamy as they met his, then slowly she nodded. 'I meant it.'

Her mouth was dry and her pulses racing as he led her towards the door of the house. Producing a huge ornate key from under the creepers, he unlocked it and pushed it open, ducking under a curtain of honeysuckle as he pulled her inside, and shut it after them.

The next instant, he had taken her into his arms. His lips sought hers as she stood on tiptoe to reach him, her eyes closed, her tender mouth opening willingly beneath his. Half fainting with longing, she began to slip down into his arms, unable to resist the overwhelming urge which was spreading over her to submit utterly to this man who so enflamed and enslaved her, and it was only after several minutes that he raised his head and looked at her, drowning willingly in the depths of her gaze.

'Enough, mermaid! Do you want me to lose my senses here on the very threshold?' His voice was husky with emotion.

She drew back, trying to regain control of her spinning wits, as he took her hand and began to move slowly through the darkening rooms, leading her through shadows smelling of warm resinous wood and the flat dampness of the flags beneath their feet. Eventually they came to the creaking oak stair and slowly they climbed it, not speaking, their hands still clasped.

The end bedroom was the only room in the house that was furnished. In the centre of the floor stood a large canopied bed. The hangings, suspended by cords from the roof beams, had rotted, but they showed still the rich blue web of colour that had once graced the main chamber of the house. The mattresses had been torn and shredded by mice, and the coverlet, of royal blue and gold, was now but a fragile film of lace. Staring down at it, Elaine felt herself shiver strangely as Guy slowly closed the door.

He walked across to the window and slid the heavy shutter back so that the horizontal evening light poured into the room, and with it the cool smell of the river. Then he turned towards her and gently released her hair from its net, his hands barely touching her as he allowed the heavy locks to fall loose. She scarcely breathed. She could not have moved if she had wanted to, mesmerised by the strange preoccupied look in his eyes as he put his hands lightly on the neckline of her gown, gently pushing the sleeves down until her shoulders were bare and the heavy red material slipped to the floor. His eyes were deep and thoughtful as again he raised his hands to her unresisting body and loosened the kirtle, letting it rustle round her ankles, and after it he began to unfasten the ribbons that held the loose bodice of her chemise, until it, too, lay in the dust and she stood before him naked, her pale skin touched by the golden light that poured over the floor. Then, gently, he picked her up and laid her on the bed. She lay in a new-found calm as he removed his shirt and came and stood for a moment, looking down at her.

His lips were everywhere. On her face, her neck, her ears. On her breasts, touching her nipples with a tongue like fire until she was gasping with pleasure, and then he moved on, concentrating his attention on her stomach and her thighs, forcing her to lie still as she tried for one brief moment to resist. Slowly he turned once more to her mouth, his lips hungry as they forced hers first to surrender, then to return kiss for kiss, as her body took fire and her passion grew to match his.

'So, my sea sprite, you have decided to yield,' he breathed, his eyes like slits of quicksilver. He did not allow her to answer. Already she was drowning in his kisses again, feeling the strength and urgency of his body on hers grow as the desire which coursed through her made her pliant and yielding to his touch.

The quick pain as he took her made her gasp, involuntarily tearing at his shoulders with her nails, but behind the pain came quivering pleasure such as she had never known possible. Clinging to him, she felt her body move as one with his as a little sob of ecstasy escaped her lips. Then he lay still at last, covering her face with quick light kisses, imprisoning her hands as he held her still. He was smiling. 'It seems you spoke the truth,' he said softly. 'I have stolen more than a kiss from Ned Brandon this time. What kind of man is he who allows his wife to keep her maidenhood so long after his wedding?'

She tried to turn her face away, tears spilling down her cheeks, but he held her, gently kissing them away, his eyes soft. 'Don't cry, sweetheart. You are mine, now! And I shall find a way to keep you.'

As she lay looking up at him, trying to gather her scattered senses, she still trembled from the violence of the passion that had been between them. She did not want to remember the awful reality of her marriage to Edward Brandon.

'Jane said it was possible for me to get our marriage annulled,' she whispered at last, 'because Edward never lay with me. It was his mistress who would not allow him to touch his wife.' She gave a faint smile. 'Olivia heard us discussing that, too. That is why she had me locked up.'

'To make sure you would still be there when your lord and master returned—a sacrificial virgin?' His eyes gleamed with anger. 'I think there is a better way of putting an end to your marriage, my lady, and a more final one, and that is with my sword.'

Elaine bit her lip. She feared and hated Edward, and she wanted to be free for ever—but to kill him . . . She shuddered as she raised her hand and stared at the heavy gold ring on her finger. Quickly she thrust it back beneath the threadbare covers, her gaze returning to the man she loved.

Guy said, 'We must leave here soon; but first, some food. Are you hungry?' As he reached for his clothes, Elaine made to sit up but he stopped her, pressing her gently back on the bed. 'Lie still, love. I'll bring food for us up here. That will give us a short while longer together.'

Elaine lay back in a dream after he had gone, her body languid, her mind drifting with happy exhaustion as her eyes closed involuntarily. Within minutes, she was fast asleep. She woke to find herself lying again in Guy's arms, his lips once more seeking hers. Her whimper of protest died before it was born, as her body responded to his gentle caresses. The room was nearly pitch dark.

'I've brought food and wine, sweetheart,' he murmured, his hands roaming her sleepy body. 'Then we must go. The loading is nearly completed, most of the men are gone, and I want to be away before midnight with the rest.' Slipping reluctantly from the bed, he fetched a flagon of wine and two pewter mugs and the large trencher full of bread, cheese and roast meat that he had left on the floor by the door.

'I must get some clothes.' Sitting up slowly, she looked about uncertainly for something to wrap round her, suddenly embarrassed by her own nakedness.

Guy grinned. 'Why do you need clothes? You aren't cold, are you?' he looked at her innocently.

She blushed. 'No.' Indeed, the room was warm and fragrant beneath the old thatch, almost airless now as night fell.

'Then eat. I like to see you naked. You have a beautiful body.' He gently touched her breast, his hand dark against the luminosity of her skin.

Reluctantly she took the wine from him, and then she ate. She was ravenous, for she had not eaten since dawn. 'How will we find the *Witch*?' she asked after a minute.

'She's gone down the coast to lie in the Deben. She'll come back, never fear.' He grinned. 'Word has come that my prey is on the last leg of its journey at last. Have you the stomach to act the pirate's part and go on a raid with me?'

She frowned, not wanting to think about his plans. 'You are asking me to rob my own father?'

'Your father owes me one ship, Elaine.' His voice was sober. 'Tom knew my motives when we planned this raid. It is all I shall take from Robert Howard for his part in the plot against me. One ship. The others belong to other landowners round here who were Brandon's friends.'

'They are my father's friends, too . . .'

'If so, I'm sorry. I shall not change my mind. You can come, or you can go back to your father's house to wait. It is up to you.' He tore a lump of bread from the loaf and began to eat it absent-mindedly. 'I am a fair man, in my way. I rob only from those that robbed me. Call it primitive justice if you will, but it is the code I live by. I respect loyalty and I despise traitors, whether to their king or to their friends.' He poured more wine into her cup. 'But I'll understand, Elaine, if you don't want to be involved with me.'

She shook her head, desperately swallowing tears. 'I want to be with you.'

'And your father?' His voice was gentle.

'One day, perhaps, he'll understand.'

He took the mug from her, and leaned over to put the empty trencher on the floor. Then, pressing her back again, he leaned over her.

'You'll love the sea,' he murmured between kisses. 'I saw the brightness of your eyes as you stood on the *Witch*'s deck. You were born to the sea—you'll love the movement of the ship, the brilliant stars wheeling across the sky at night, the wind which can carry you to the edge of the world and back, the canvas that can scream hate in a gale or lull you to sleep with a love song on a summer zephyr, the warm timber breathing beneath your feet, riding each wave like a living creature, there at your command.' His voice was hypnotic as his kisses strayed to her eyelids, her temples and the tip of her nose, then down to the hollows of her throat.

With a little moan she reached up and wrapped her arms round him, drawing him closer, feeling the warm power of his body covering her. With instinctive coquetry she ran her fingers down his shoulders and round down the front of his shirt, drawing it open so that she could touch his chest, and reaching up, ran her tongue along his collarbones and down towards his nipples. Groaning, he forced her head back, his mouth possessing hers with a violence which was half frightening and half intoxicating.

It was with difficulty that he made himself release her at last, his hands pinioning her wrists so that she could no longer touch him. 'Enough, woman,' he breathed. 'I am beginning to think you are trying to bewitch me out of my senses. We have to leave.'

'Please, not yet?' Her mouth sought his again. 'Just a little longer.' His grip had slackened involuntarily, and gently freeing her wrists, she tried to pull his face down to hers once more. 'Make love to me again.'

She was barely aware of what she was saying, conscious only that she did not want him to leave her.

'We must go soon, my sprite,' he murmured. 'My men are waiting.'

Her mouth trembled over his eyelids, and down towards his lips. 'Could we not stay here till dawn?'

She thought, briefly, that he was going to refuse. He got to his feet, standing for a moment without moving as though making up his mind. Then she heard a soft chuckle. 'Why not? It would be churlish to refuse a plea like that. I'll go down to the men who are left and tell them to leave the last of the loading till dawn. Then I'll come back to you.' His hand rested for a moment on her shoulder, vibrant, possessive, then he strode towards the door.

In only minutes he was back, dragging off his clothes. 'Come, let us make the most of this feather bed! It may be the last for a long time. If you remember, there are no such luxuries on *Black Witch*. There you must share the captain's narrow bunk, with the sea to rock us in her arms. Just a few short hours till dawn, my love,' he whispered. 'But, for those hours, you are mine alone.'

Before first light, they rose and dressed, and tiptoed hand in hand through the empty house to let themselves out into the cold, dew-wet dawn. Most of the men had gone the night before. Those that were left were already hard at work loading the last small boats.

Mab and Walt were handing out a breakfast of meat and bread and ale as they appeared, and Guy took some, handing a pasty to Elaine with a wink. Suddenly she was embarrassed, knowing the men must be fully aware of how she and their captain had spent their night. As he went over to the landing-stage, she sat down in the shelter of a shed doorway to concentrate on her pasty. She looked up, as Mab appeared at last and knelt beside her. The girl smiled.

'Shall I braid your hair, my lady?' Apart from the paleness of her face, she seemed to have recovered from the ordeal of the day before. Elaine blushed, realising that her hair was still hanging in heavy ringlets about her shoulders.

'Thank you, Mab. You know we are going with them, on *Black Witch*?'

Mab nodded. 'It's best.' She shuddered. 'I never want to go to Aldebourne again. Not as long as I live.'

'Nor I.' Elaine smiled grimly. 'Nor shall we. My future lies with Kemp.'

Mab beamed. 'I'm glad. I never liked that Sir Edward!'

She began methodically to unknot the tangles in Elaine's hair and plait it into two heavy braids, tearing a piece of trimming from her own ragged skirt to tie the hair into place. Then she smiled. 'All this galloping around in the sun is putting colour in your cheeks, my lady. You must be careful.'

Elaine laughed. Suddenly she was overwhelmed with happiness. 'I don't care. I'm not interested any longer in being a lady of fashion! After all, I'm going to follow the sea. I shall go barefoot on the ship and burn as brown as a sailor!'

It did not seem to matter any more what Kemp's men thought of her—or what anyone in the world thought. Her future was at the side of the man she loved, and she need never see Edward Brandon or his sour-faced sister again. A warm satisfied glow filled her body, and a quick breath of excitement shot through her each time she caught sight of Guy supervising the last of the loading. His tall figure was everywhere, checking the pack-horses that had been waiting in the stables, seeing that the last heap of goods was piled into two long black boats that the men slid then into the water. Once or twice he came across to her, smiling in greeting, then was gone again, back to the methodical backbreaking work.

The last of the pack-animals plodded out of sight as the sun began to lift clear of the trees. The barn doors were dragged shut and the last box was lowered into the boat from the jetty. The man supervising the loading knelt on the rotting wood to see that it was stacked properly, then he stood, the rope painter in his hand, as his companion in the boat picked up his pole and made ready to set off down the river.

'God speed, Harry!' the sailor said with a grin as he threw down the rope. 'When Edward Brandon finally gets here, he'll find the birds have flown!' He stood, hand on hips, watching the boat move slowly away. Moments later there was a loud crash from the forest behind them. He flung up his arms with a cry as his back was spattered with blood and he pitched forward into the river.

Mab screamed. The remaining men grabbed their cutlasses as the sound of gunfire spluttered again from the trees on every side.

Stunned with shock, Elaine did not move, and behind her Kemp appeared, grim-faced, in the shadow of the barn. 'Our tryst with the dawn has been our undoing, it seems!' he said brusquely. 'God knows how your husband got reinforcements so fast, but he appears to have done it! There are more horses behind the house. Get out of here, both of you. Sam will go with you.' He dragged Elaine to her feet.

'But I'm staying with you!' she cried, clinging to his arm.

'No!' He pushed her from him. 'It's not safe! Go, and go quickly.' He propelled her away from the open ground to the deep shadows. There Sam was waiting, his face white. Kemp prodded her towards his lieutenant. 'God be with you, my sprite,' he whispered. 'I'll come for you, I promise.' Then he was gone.

CHAPTER
TWELVE

SAM LED them at a run round to the front of the house, where half a dozen horses were tethered beside a wall. There was no time for discussion. He almost threw Elaine into the saddle of one of them as Mab managed to scramble, terrified, on to another. Then vaulting on to his own horse, he led the way at a gallop away from the river and towards the trees.

Almost at once a new burst of staccato firing made him veer violently to the west, the two girls riding after him, as a hail of arrows shot out of the trees.

'Dear God, they're all around!' Elaine cried.

'This way!' Sam grabbed at Elaine's rein as though he were afraid she might turn back. He headed for a path overgrown with nettles, which led at right-angles to the drive. A group of men broke out of the forest and ran towards the house, the sun shining on their steel corselets. Each carried a drawn sword. Behind them came others with bows, and hand-guns still smoking from the previous salvo of firing.

Elaine was sick with fear. Guy was surrounded. What chance had he and his remaining few men against these armed hordes? Her mind closed in despair at the thought of what might be happening to the small band by the river.

Sam rode with determination away from Kempsmere and the marshes, heading into the thick of the forest. He did not allow them to slow until they had been riding for some time and the horses were streaked with sweat, then at last he reined in and waited for Mab to catch up with them. All three horses were blowing hard.

'We'll head south,' he said to Elaine grimly. 'Kemp said I was to take you to your father.'

'No!' she cried involuntarily. 'No! I must go back. Back to *Black Witch*!'

He swung round to face her. 'Don't you understand yet, my lady? Kemp is almost alone there with a handful of men. A handful! Against God knows how many! It is no place for women! You'd be in his way.' He beat his hand against the pommel of the saddle. 'Guy should have gone last night! We could have been away by midnight, like the rest. And now I'm wasting time escorting you, when I should be helping him!' There was anguish in his face.

Elaine coloured violently. 'There is no need for you to stay with us, Master Fletcher. Go back to Kemp, please. We'll be all right . . .'

'I would leave you, believe me; but my orders are clear. I'm to take you to your father's house.' Sam gathered up his reins. 'So, the sooner we get there, the sooner I can get back to help! I'd like to know where Brandon got those men so quickly. There must have been at least hundred of them!'

Elaine shuddered, for the first time thinking of her own danger. 'Sir Edward will find me at King's Brook. It is the first place he'll look!' she said desperately.

Sam shrugged. 'Perhaps Kemp reckoned to see to it that your husband wouldn't have the time to go looking for you, my lady. He must have thought you would be safe with your father,' he went on grudgingly, 'or he wouldn't have told me to take you there, not feeling the way he does about you.' Without another word, he dug his heels into his horse's flanks.

It was a long, long ride, and Elaine was distraught. It was her fault that Guy had waited till morning. Without her, he and his men would have been safe by now, far out of reach of Edward. Overcome with guilt and misery, she begged Sam again and again to leave them and return to help Kemp, but stubbornly he refused.

It was dark when the tired animals at last walked up the drive that led to King's Brook. The house was in darkness, but at the sound of hooves, a figure opened a door in one of the stable blocks and came out with a lantern.

'Hal, is that you?' Elaine called as she slid, exhausted, from her horse.

'Mistress Elaine! Why, it's good to see you!' The groom took her bridle, rubbing sleep-filled eyes.

Elaine forced herself to smile at him. 'We have ridden a long way, Hal, to see my father. How is he?' She was astonished to realise that she had given her father not a single thought up until that moment; all her fears had been for Guy. She stared ruefully at the boy, guiltily feeling glad that the excuse of her father's illness made their ill-timed arrival seem less strange.

Hal looked up at her cheerfully. 'He's better, so I hear, Mistress Elaine. But he'll be relieved to see you.'

'Rub them down well, Hal. The horses are hot and tired,' she told him. 'And find a fresh mount for my escort. He must return north at once.'

'You'll be all right now, my lady?' Sam smiled at her at last, but she could see the strain round his eyes by the faint light thrown by the polished horn sides of the lantern.

'I'll be all right, Sam. Thank you for riding with us. Go back to him. Quickly.' Impulsively she kissed the rough leathery cheek. Then she ran towards the house, with Mab following.

The front door was opened by David Churchman, backed by two servants who were nervously clutching drawn swords. The steward smiled broadly when he saw Elaine by the light of the branch of candles he carried.

'I'm sorry, my lady. Welcome! There have been so many robbers about that we take no chances now of nights. Oh, it is good to see you again!' He ushered her and Mab inside and rebolted the door behind them, after glancing out into the dark, obviously puzzled by her lack of escort. 'Sir Edward is not with you, my lady?'

Elaine shivered. 'He was too busy to leave Aldebourne,' she said as firmly as she could, hoping he would not notice the tremor in her voice. 'And I wanted to see Papa at once, when I heard he was ill. We were delayed on the road, or we would have been here hours ago.' She had become aware of how strange it must seem for her to have arrived unescorted and so late at night. 'How is my father?' she rushed on.

'He is much recovered, my lady, I am glad to say,' the old man answered. 'I expect he is asleep, by now. Mistress Jane and Mistress Mary have been physicking him daily with this and that.'

Elaine smiled. 'Then I shall not disturb him. Mab and I shall retire at once, and I can see him tomorrow.'

It was only as she began to undress in the warm friendliness of her old bedroom after tiptoeing past the curtained beds of her sleeping aunts that Elaine realised fully the state she was in—the reason for Churchman's puzzled glances as he escorted her up the stairs. Her gown was stained and torn, and her hair loose. She had no head-dress, no cloak. And Mab was little better, she noticed, as the girl went about her accustomed tasks, humming cheerfully as she rummaged through the chests which had been left behind when they left King's Brook, looking for Elaine's old clothes.

Elaine caught her hand. 'If anything happens, Mab—if Sir Edward should come . . .'

Mab grinned cheerfully. 'He won't come, my lady. You heard what Sam Fletcher said.'

Elaine smiled. 'I know. And I pray he's right. But if he did come, I want you to hide. Do you understand? You must not risk being caught by him again.'

Impulsively Mab leaned over and kissed her. 'He won't come, my duck. We're safe here—I'm sure of it. Now, you get into bed and sleep. I'll be prepared to wager you got little enough last night.' She giggled impudently and turned to blow out the candles.

Elaine lay back on the pillows, her exhausted body stiff and bruised as it sank into the feather mattress. Smiling secretly at Mab's words, she hugged her arms around her chilled body, remembering the touch of the man who owned her heart. Soon Guy would come for her as he had promised. He would come, her marriage would be annulled, and his pardon would somehow arrive from the King. Nothing must spoil their happiness now.

On her left hand she could feel the heavy gold ring that still clasped her finger. With a superstitious shiver, she slid her hand beneath the bedclothes. She must continue to wear the ring until her vows were annulled and her marriage ended. 'Please God, let it be soon,' she whispered into the dark. 'And, please, don't let Edward Brandon come, ever again, to King's Brook!'

Robert Howard was propped up in bed when Elaine visited him next morning. In an old gown of green silk and a deep blue kirtle, and wearing a lace-trimmed head-dress, she was neat and cheerful as she dropped a kiss on his forehead.

'I'm sorry to hear you've not been well again, Papa.'

He scowled peevishly. 'Those silly women have been fussing me. I needed you, Elaine.' He peered past her at the door. 'Where is Edward?'

She clenched her fists firmly to stop a tremor of disgust at the sound of his name. 'At Aldebourne, Papa. He could not come this time.'

He looked at her searchingly, hearing the undisguised bleakness in her voice.

'You are not happy yet, child?'

'No, Papa.' She turned away to hide her tears.

'He has not been unkind to you?' His thin hand groped for hers on the coverlet.

She stared down at it miserably. The blue veins stood out in knotted cords above almost transparent flesh. Then she looked up at him. 'Papa, he did not tell you the truth. He is not what he seems.'

'Rubbish, child! You'll get used to it,' he said irritably. 'He's a good boy, is Edward. Good for King's Brook and for you. When the ships return, I have promised him a share of my profits!'

'So Edward has even more incentive to protect them than before,' she said dully.

He chuckled. 'Good idea, don't you think? And they are nearly home. I have had reports of them. They've been held up by a broken mast, sheltering off Gravesend, but they'll be home any day. And with them, our fortunes are made.' He rubbed his hands together. 'Edward is to escort them with two heavily armed ships, just in case the pirate gets it into his head to attack.' He laughed loudly, his head back against the pillows. 'I almost wish he would, the surprise he would get. He'll be caught like a rat in a trap.' Tears came to his eyes suddenly, as a paroxysm of coughing brought an abrupt halt to his laughter.

Elaine was watching him, white-faced, as he lay back exhausted. Then she bent to kiss his forehead.

'Papa, I have tired you. You must rest now. I'll come back and see you later, after you've had a sleep.'

As she turned to the door, her brain was whirling. If Guy still planned to attack the treasure fleet, he would be sailing straight into a trap! Somehow she had to warn him. She was so preoccupied with her thoughts as she left the bedside that she did not hear the heavy step on the stairs, or the creak of boards in the ante-room, and she had almost reached the door when it was flung back.

Edward Brandon stood in the doorway. He stared coldly at Elaine, then at Robert, who had jerked upright in the bed, his eyes wide and staring.

'Edward, my boy,' he said uncertainly. 'You came after all. I'm glad to see you.'

'And I you, Father.' Edward gave him a perfunctory bow. 'Did your daughter tell you that she disobeyed me in coming here?'

Elaine shrank back, her face white and defiant. 'Papa was ill. I had to see him.'

'I forbade you to come alone, Elaine.' His voice was heavy with threat. 'Your father has plainly recovered, as I told you he would, and I am sure he would not encourage a wife to disobey her husband.'

Robert had pulled the sheet up to his chest, crumpling it nervously between his fingers. 'No, she must obey you, my boy. It was wrong of her to come alone.'

Elaine stared at him in reproachful horror. 'Papa!'

'No, Elaine. Edward is right. Your duty is to him now.' He coughed dramatically. 'I am quite better. I am going down to the town quay tomorrow to make the warehouse ready. And, besides, I have Mary and Jane to look after me. They are going to make their homes here, and devote their lives to me, so really I don't need you.'

Edward looked at Elaine, his eyes icy. Then he stepped

back in the doorway and bowed. 'So, Elaine, your dramatic gesture was quite needless after all,' he said softly. 'Say goodbye to your father. We are riding back to Aldebourne at once.'

'No!' Elaine backed away from him, her eyes blazing. She had not escaped this far to go back meekly with him now. 'I shall never come with you!'

Edward continued to eye her. 'I think you will, wife. Otherwise I shall be forced to tell you father about your brother Tom's spare-time activities.' He laughed quietly. 'Which are yours, too, of course. But whereas I feel your father may not be interested in your behaviour, I am sure that, to hear about Tom . . .'

'No!' Elaine went white, her eyes on her father's face. Whatever he had done to her, however cruel he had been, she could not do that to him.

Robert had leaned forward eagerly. 'Tom? Who talks of Tom?' he cried. 'The boy will come home soon. He's gone to London. He's not dead, you know; that was a cruel rumour.'

Elaine replied, horrified, 'Papa!'

'No. Leave him.' Edward's voice cut through hers like a knife. He turned to Robert, his tone suddenly more gentle. 'We'll leave you now, Father. Sleep. Then we'll talk of Tom later. Come, Elaine.'

Dumb with shock and sorrow, Elaine followed him out of the room. He shut the door and looked round the deserted ante-room in which they were standing.

'You will come with me quietly and obediently now, do you hear me? One word to your father's servants that you do not wish to leave this house, and I shall have to take you by force. But not before I have told him that his son was a cut-throat, a thief and a pirate, who pillaged his own father's vessels.'

Elaine stared at him. 'How did you find out? Who told you about Tom?'

'It was not hard to discover, once I knew it was Guy Kemp I was after.' His eyes narrowed. 'Perhaps it would interest you to know that we killed seven of Guy Kemp's men yesterday after you fled my house and damn near got him as well. I would have, had he not slithered off through the mud like the animal he is. He had moved nearly all his treasure—which apparently he has been storing at Kempsmere—but he'll not use that house again.' He smiled. 'We burned it to the ground, and all the barns and outbuildings.'

Elaine's relief that Guy was definitely alive and had escaped was short lived as she thought of his men and of the beautiful old house where, only a few hours before, she had lain in his arms.

'But his tenants . . .' she protested in horror. 'And his brother! Surely he will have something to say to you for destroying his property?'

'His brother is a drunken sot,' Edward's tone was scathing. 'And the tenants deserve everything that has happened to them for helping him.'

At her gasp of pain, he laughed. 'I really have taken a traitor into my house, haven't I, my lady?' he sneered. 'But, let me tell you, you will not escape me. I need all this.' He waved his arm round the room. 'This house, the money, the property. It comes with you, so I shall have to keep you safe. Very safe.' He seized her wrist. 'I advise you to remember what I have said. One hint, one whisper, in front of your father's servants that all is not well between us, and I shall tell everything I know about Tom.'

Dragging her after him, he began to descend the stairs, and made for the front door, where two horses were waiting, already saddled. An escort of some two dozen men were armed and mounted. As she eyed them in terror, he turned to her with a mocking bow. 'Do you feel rested enough to ride, my lady, or would you prefer a litter?'

Elaine could feel Churchman's eyes on her curiously as he appeared on the steps, and she hoped that Mab would not choose that moment to come downstairs. 'I shall ride, thank you, my husband,' she said haughtily.

She allowed Edward to lift her into her saddle, and sat stiffly, arranging her skirts, as he swung himself up beside her. Then, slowly, they turned and rode away from the house. She did not look back.

*　　*　　*

Aldebourne lay bathed in golden sunshine as the cavalcade turned in at the gateway and rode up to the main courtyard. There, Edward dismounted, and, walking to Elaine's side, lifted her down. 'Welcome home, sweet wife,' he said acidly.

Elaine stepped back, her head held high. 'You won't win, Edward,' she said defiantly. 'Kemp is too clever for you. You may do whatever you please to me, but you will never catch him.'

'I intend doing as I please with you, Elaine. Be sure of that. And I intend to catch Guy Kemp.' He took her arm, his fingers digging brutally into her flesh. 'The trap is already set for him, sweetheart. And set well. Should it fail, we can always set another, with you as bait.'

He strode towards the house, holding her wrist unnecessarily tightly as he pulled her after him through the open door into the hall.

Two women were seated there, sewing. They both rose as Elaine and Edward entered. Elaine looked at Olivia at once; her face was flushed and angry, and her eyes as usual bright with resentment. The other woman, tall and dark, with aquiline features and sloe-black eyes, stood for a moment, then dropping the skein of silk she held in her hand she ran towards Edward, her body exuding a scent of musk and cloves.

He released Elaine's arm abruptly. 'Rosalind! What are you doing here?' For a moment he looked far from pleased as he stared at her. Then his arms closed round the woman's body as she pressed herself against his chest.

'The Queen does not want me after all, Ned,' she crooned in a husky contralto. 'It appears that your sister Jane is at court. She told her grace that I was unwell, so I am not returning to her grace's service until the autumn. Her messenger met me before I reached Chelmsford, so I was able to turn back. That was kind of Jane, was it not?' Her eyes gleamed as she released herself from his embrace. 'When I found you weren't here, I decided to call upon Olivia at last. She has been entertaining me while you went to bring your little wife back home.' She turned for the first time to Elaine, sniffing ostentatiously. 'She really is a

child, is she not?' Unconsciously she ran her hands down
her own figure, dressed in deep blue velvet with a kirtle of
pale blue and silver brocade. 'I trust you intend to beat her
for her disobedience.'

'Indeed I do,' Edward said softly.

Elaine's eyes smouldered. She was suddenly desperately
conscious of her old gown with its unfashionably low neckline and covering of dust from the journey. 'But you are
the one who has been disobedient, Edward,' she said
recklessly. 'I thought that madam, your mistress, said you
were not to lay a finger on me while she was away.' She
smiled archly at Rosalind, blessing Jane silently for seeing
to it that Rosalind returned, and was pleased to see her
study her with renewed interest before Rosalind's anger
flared and she swung round to Edward. 'You and I must
be alone together, Edward,' she said abruptly. 'Walk with
me to the Dower House. This place bores me.' She sent a
venomous look at Olivia, who coloured in response.

Edward looked distinctly uncomfortable. 'I shall follow
you, my love, as soon as I can.'

'Now, Edward.' Rosalind caught his arm. 'We don't
want you to be side-tracked into enjoying the chastisement
of your wife, do we?' She smiled brilliantly at Elaine. 'If
the girl is to be whipped, I suggest you let your sister do
it. She looks as though she would enjoy the sport.'

Olivia gasped, her face puce with anger, but Edward
said casually, 'A good notion, my love. Olivia, I leave it
all to you.' He tucked Rosalind's hand under his elbow.
'Do what you like with her, just so long as I find her
repentant and obedient when I return. And do not let her
escape again.'

Olivia turned frosty eyes on him. 'May I remind you,
brother, that she did not escape when she was in my
custody before.'

Edward and Rosalind walked back into the sunshine,
arm in arm, then Elaine turned to face Olivia. The woman
was still watching her brother as he disappeared across the
courtyard, her eyes full of hatred. Abruptly she clapped
her hands. 'Catchpole,' she shouted.

The man appeared so fast that he must have been waiting

outside the door. 'Take Lady Brandon back to the store-room,' she said.

He bowed. 'If you remember, Mistress Olivia, the door was broken down when we released you,' he said evenly.

Elaine had to suppress a smile in spite of her fury. Determinedly she walked towards the door. 'It will not be necessary for you to take me anywhere, Catchpole,' she said steadily. 'I intend to leave Aldebourne House now.'

For a moment she thought he was going to stand aside and let her pass, but, as he hesitated, she heard Olivia hiss, 'Hold her, you fool! You heard Sir Edward's orders. No doubt you were eavesdropping as usual. She's to be whipped! She must be put somewhere secure.'

Catchpole shot out his hand and caught Elaine's wrist. She was too proud to struggle, and followed him up the broad staircase, stumbling on the hem of her gown, and allowed him to push her into the small ante-room off her husband's great bedchamber. There was no mistaking the sound of the key in the lock as he turned it on her.

In desperation, she ran to the window, but the stone mullions were far too close for her to push even her slim figure between them, had she the strength to smash the heavily leaded glass.

With a little sob, she closed her eyes. Her only comfort in her despair was that Guy was free and that, somehow, he would surely come for her.

After some time, she heard the key in the lock once more. She looked apprehensively at the door, expecting to see Olivia, but Catchpole stood there, his finger to his lips. He beckoned.

'I reckon you'd best get out of here,' he murmured, with a glance over his shoulder. 'I'm off, too. I can't be dealing with Mistress Olivia any more. The old baggage!' He spat on the floor. 'For Sir Edward I've worked for years, and I respect him . . . but that sister!' Words obviously failed him as he looked at Elaine. 'She's out there, finding a whip. She said I was to come and tie you to the bedpost.' He glanced at the huge bed behind him in Edward's room, then shook his head. 'It's a husband's place to beat his wife, if he must, but I reckon she'd half kill you and enjoy doing it. So, get you gone, quick. And don't come back while either of those women are at Aldebourne.' He turned and ran down the stairs and out of sight.

Elaine could not move for a minute or two, then she began to run, flying down the stairs, not giving herself time to think as she dodged through the hall and out into the deserted courtyard. To avoid the stables, she turned sharply towards the orchards, instinctively thinking of the tall reeds in the marsh which would hide her from the house. Gathering up her skirts as she fled, she bobbed under the low apple boughs, seeking the dark shadows out of the blinding sunlight.

She was trying desperately to try and force her whirling thoughts into some kind of order. She had to find Kemp: nothing else mattered now. She knew he was alive—that much at least Edward had told her, and she knew that his beloved home was destroyed, so her only hope of finding him was to make her way to the hut on the beach that Jane Lockesley had mentioned—the shack with the blue gull on the door. If the crew of the *Witch* were not already at sea, someone would find her there and take her to their captain. Racking her brain, she tried to remember what Jane had said about finding the shack. To reach it she must cross the marsh—that much she remembered—and in her flight from the house her instinct had brought her in the right direction.

All round her the sun beat on the water, turning it to blinding silver. Cautiously she walked forward, her feet remaining dry as she picked her way across the banks of rotting reed and sandy grass dotted with willowherb and thrift. But very soon she knew she was lost. There was no shade anywhere, and she was growing uncomfortably warm. She was hungry, too, and thirsty, for she had not eaten since breaking her fast that morning at King's Brook. Where could the river be? The sun was still high, and she could feel the perspiration on her forehead and back and running down between her breats. On impulse, she tore off her head-dress and veil and hid the roll of stiffened fabric in the reeds. She lost all track of time, when, through a break in the reeds, she at last saw the river, curving in from the sea. She almost fell on her knees with relief as she scrambled, slipping and splashing, towards it. All she had to do now was to follow it until she reached the shore.

Wearily she continued, no longer afraid of pursuit; just afraid that her own exhaustion would defeat her before she reached her destination. And then she saw them—a group of fishermen's shacks on the edge of the shingle bank. Cautiously she made her way over. A fishing boat lay upside-down beside them, and wrinkling her nose, she could smell the remains of the last cargo which had been thrown carelessly above the high-tide mark. The shacks were all empty, with nothing to distinguish them, save the last. There, on the bleached timber, someone had scrawled in blue paint a sketchy flying gull.

Feeling a wave of relief, she made her way towards it, her feet painful in her thin wet shoes as she tiptoed over the rattling shingle, and fumbled with the piece of rope that held the door shut. At last it came free from its hasps and swung inwards with an agonised creak. Her throat tightening with fear, she peered into the interior.

The shack seemed to be empty. Holding her breath nervously, she went in and waited until her eyes grew accustomed to the darkness. In one corner was a roll of nets. In another, a box and a couple of leather pails. That was all. She went back to the door and peered out. Apart from a family of swans sailing majestically up the river, there was no sign of life.

Methodically she explored the shacks. They all contained more or less the same equipment. One held a battered lantern and another a set of oars, but nowhere was there anything to eat or drink. When she took one of the buckets down to the river and scooped out some of the cool water, it was heavily salt. In the marsh, it was also brackish. She threw down the bucket. There was nothing for it but to wait now until morning, and to pray that someone would come.

As the light faded and it grew colder, she retired into the shack, pushing the door three-quarters closed behind her, and sat down on the pile of nets, her chin on her knees. Somewhere in the distance, a church bell rang across the lonely water.

CHAPTER
THIRTEEN

It was barely dawn when she awoke. She lay still, listening intently, but the shack was completely silent. She ran towards the river's edge and knelt, shivering, to splash her face and hands. Then, unable to resist it, she kicked off her shoes and walked carefully into the water, feeling the breath-taking cold silkiness of the mud between her toes, and stood for a moment.

'You'll be bitten by a crab if you stand there much longer!' The voice behind her made her jump, loosing her hold on the full skirts she was clutching in her hand. They tumbled into the water and spread round her, sodden, pulling at her till she almost fell.

Guy Kemp was standing a few feet from her, and with a cry of relief she struggled towards him out of the river and threw herself into his arms.

'Guy! Oh, Guy!' She clung to him, half sobbing, half laughing with the joy of seeing him there.

For a moment his arms had closed round her, but almost at once he held her away and looked down at her. Raising her eyes to his, she saw bitter anger reflected there.

She stared at him, puzzled. 'What is it? What's wrong?' Foreboding closed over her heart. This was not the man who had taken her so passionately to his bed. This was once more the cruel, calculating master of *Black Witch*.

'You ask me what is wrong?' His voice was low and threatening. 'Why don't you tell me, Elaine? Why are you here? Is your husband hiding behind that shack? Is there a squadron of the King's soldiers lying out there in the marsh?' He glanced round at the drifting mist behind them. 'Or is the King's navy here, even now on its way in to close the mouth of the river and trap me? How did you know I would be here?'

'I don't understand! Why are you saying this! I came to find you, to be with you . . .'

Kemp gave a grim smile. 'You came to be with me? Good, because I intend to keep you. Your place is on *Black Witch*. I believe we agreed that. You thought, of course, that it was safe to plan to be with me when I raided your father's ships, because you knew you would not be there. You knew the raid would not take place because I would be dead. But, as you see, I am very much alive, and the raid will take place, and you, my little love, as that is obviously your wish, will keep your promise and sail at my side! Only it won't be as a free spirit, but as a hostage.' He gave an ugly laugh.

'Hostage?' she echoed in disbelief.

'That is what I called you, my lady.' He released her so sharply that she stumbled on the stones. 'What else would you be? Do you think you can still claim a place at the helm by my side? Do you think you still hold a place in my heart? You imagine, perhaps, that I still wish to marry you?' His face was like carved flint. 'Your betrayal was too effective for that, my lady. My house is burned to the ground. My servants and tenants and friends are scattered or killed. Some of my treasure is lost, and my ship was almost caught. Almost, but not quite.' He put his hands on his hips and stared at her coldly. 'She will fight a brave last battle if she has to, my *Witch*, and recoup my fortune in one day's work, or I shall die with her.' He ignored her cry of pain. 'And you, too, Elaine. You will be there, on the ship—where your husband can see you. Why he sent you, I cannot begin to guess. But you shall not escape to go back to him with news of my plans.'

'I don't understand!' She raised her arms to him in supplication. 'I haven't betrayed you. Why are you saying all this? Why have you changed?'

'Don't you know? If not, you are either very clever or very stupid, madam. I don't very much care which. Come, it is time we left. Today is going to be busy if the intelligence I gathered before dawn this morning is true, and I doubt if there will be much wind later.'

He began to stride away from her, but Elaine did not move.

'I'm not coming with you,' she said quietly. She was numb. 'I thought you loved me. I gave myself to you . . .' Tears filled her eyes, and angrily she swallowed them back. 'I would have followed you anywhere, even against Papa's ships. But not like this, when your heart is full of hate!' She looked hesitantly down-river, blinded by despair, wondering where she could go, but she had not taken more than one step when his footsteps rattled behind her and he seized her arm.

'You must have misheard, Elaine. You are coming with me,' he said softly. 'I have a boat hidden on the marsh.' This time, he held her arm tightly.

'No!' She was crying now, trying to pull her arm away. 'I don't want to go with you . . . Not like this!'

'You will come, Elaine.'

She glanced up at him, thinking now only of escape. 'Then let me find my shoes first.' She tried to keep her voice steady.

Impatiently, he let her go. 'Get them, then. But hurry.'

She walked painfully across the stones towards the place she had left her shoes and put them on. The thin soft leather had dried stiff, and they chafed her feet. Kemp was no longer watching her. His eyes were on the clouds, his handsome face concentrated as he read the weather signs with a slight frown. Her heart contracted at the sight. If he had ever loved her, he did not do so now. One last glance at the face she had dreamed of ever since she had first seen it, all those weeks ago, then she turned and began to run from him as fast as she could. If she could reach the marshland, she might be able to hide in the misty reeds until he had given up looking for her and gone.

For a moment, she thought she would succeed. Kemp did not move for several seconds as she stumbled on the cascading pebbles; then, as she ran, she heard his pounding footsteps. Panic drove her faster, but she was hampered by her skirts, and her feet were bruised by the stones. In a few long strides he had caught her.

Seizing her arm, he spun her round, his hand closed over

her slim wrist, and he pulled her against his chest. His eyes were like slits. 'Try that again, my lady, and I'll tie your hands and feet and carry you!' he said through his teeth. He glanced over his shoulder, then looked back at her. 'The mist is rising. We must hurry.'

Taking a firm hold of her hand, he began to drag her back the way they had come, past the shacks and towards the marshes she had crossed the evening before. She pulled away, but his grip was like iron and she was forced to run with him, stumbling over her damp skirts. The mist enveloped them in eerie silence, while a skein of duck flew inland against the brilliant blue of the sky. Suddenly Kemp stopped, and looked about, releasing his grip on her wrist. 'The boat is here,' he murmured. He leaped on to a sandy bank, staring round above the mist. Immediately, Elaine turned. She headed straight for the thickest patch in the whiteness, running silently on the sand and mud, praying that she would not blunder into the water as she dived behind a bed of high reeds, panting.

There was no shout to tell her she was being followed. No clue that he had seen her, but there he was behind her, his tall figure looming.

'Sit down!' His command sounded bored and irritated as he stood, barring her way. For a moment she was tempted to defy him once more; then, defeated, she sank on to the bank.

'Take off your shoes.'

After a look of disbelief at him, Elaine obeyed. Stooping, he took the shoes from her, and then straightened to hurl them out into the misty distance. Within a moment, they had sunk out of sight. She was too tired to protest, but his next action brought her struggling back to her feet. He tugged free the thong that laced his doublet, and knelt before her, to knot it round her ankles.

'No, please . . .' she gulped.

'I warned you, my lady.' He pulled the thong firmly, and knotted it again, leaving her hobbled and helpless, then he stood and lifted her up on to the bank. A long, low, black boat lay half drawn up on the mud just beyond them. Tossing her into it, he pushed it off and vaulted in himself, before reaching for the long oar to pole it out into the river.

Elaine struggled to sit up.

'Make one sound, and I'll bind your mouth, too,' he said tersely. The muscles of his arms rippled with the movement of his punting as he drove the boat through the water, feet apart, with sinewy thighs moving gracefully to the rhythm of his strokes.

The mist was evaporating fast, as the first heat of the morning drew the last of the coolness away. A beacon loomed up suddenly on the river bank, and she could see a cluster of several distant houses. Elaine stared miserably towards them, longing to call out for help, but one look at the grim face of the man standing over her convinced her that he would keep his word and gag her if she made a sound.

Round the next bend, they were suddenly in the mouth of the river, and for the first time, Kemp stopped paddling to survey the horizon, his face set. He cursed quietly, letting the boat drift, little ripples slapping gently against the thin wood.

'What is it?' Elaine asked, her low voice shaking.

He looked down at her, as though surprised that she were still there. 'The *Witch* has stood out to sea. I told them not to wait much beyond dawn. They'll hide in the mist-banks.'

Elaine eased her position uncomfortably. The bottom of the boat was hard, and her ankles were beginning to throb. 'Please will you untie me?' she asked in a whisper.

He raised an eyebrow. 'Were you thinking of running off somewhere else?'

She blushed slightly as she shook her head. He was looking at her thoughtfully. Then he shipped the oar and dropped to one knee before her, as he groped for the thong. The knot had pulled tight and swollen with the salt water dripping from her gown and slopping in the bottom of the boat, and with his knife he severed the thong with one quick movement.

The ligature had left deep red weals on her ankles. He looked at them for a moment, then took one of her feet and began to rub it, bringing warmth and feeling back with agonising swiftness. She gasped with pain.

'You should not have tried to run away,' he said, not ungently.

She pushed her hair back, trying to ignore the fact that her naked foot was resting on his thigh.

'You seemed to want to kill me,' she whispered.

'I told you, once, that mine is a violent world. Betrayal has to be punished.'

'But I have not betrayed you!' She tried to get to her knees, rocking the boat wildly, but he maintained his grip on her ankle and pushed her back.

'Then your idea of loyalty, Elaine, is not mine,' he said coldly. 'Perhaps it was my fault to trust you too much.' The long look of appraisal that swept her left her heart pounding; she could not meet his eyes.

He released her, and stood up again, gazing round the horizon. Then he gave a satisfied grunt. A ship had drifted into view out of a distant bank of purple haze. Kemp picked up the paddle and began to drive the little boat out towards the horizon, the oar drawing figures of eight in the glassy water. Once or twice *Black Witch* vanished into the haze again, but not once did he vary the pace of his tireless paddling. Sweat gleamed on his neck and chest, and she felt the sun on her own bare head. What would happen, she wondered, if the *Witch* turned and sailed away without seeing them?

But they reached her safely, and Elaine was swung up, just as she had been before. Then he hauled himself up, hand over hand, to stand once more on the deck of his ship.

Sam Fletcher was there at once. He gave Elaine no greeting as he spoke in a low tone to his captain. His coldness frightened her as much as Kemp's hostility had done. What was this betrayal they thought she had committed? And what were they going to do with her now?

'Wind'll be coming soon.' Sam's voice reached her through her veil of misery. Far away across the water, cats' paws showed on the oiled surface, and then others, rippling towards *Witch*. The air stirred, and Elaine shivered. The deck was, she noticed with a shudder, lined with cannon.

Kemp turned to her at last, taking in the long pale silk of her hair, her beauty almost ghostly in its fragility. Angrily he swallowed back the ache of tenderness that swept over him. Almost, she had captured his heart . . . Tom Howard's sister. He had sensed in her an untamed spirit like his own, held it in his hands, gentled it with her trembling body as he took her and made her his. But she had sold him to her husband, and through her treachery, lost the lives of some of his best men. His face settled into an expression of terrifying grimness.

'Take her to my cabin, Sam,' he commanded. 'And keep her under guard.'

Elaine walked ahead of Sam without a word, holding her head up proudly, aware of the hostile glances around her as she went into the cabin. Almost at once she felt *Black Witch* heel a little as the first wind reached them.

It was a long time before anyone came near her again. Slowly the lulls between the breaths of wind grew shorter until the ship had trembled into life, setting a brisk pace, silent except for the wind in the rigging and the creak of wood and canvas. The crew were subdued. She could hear no shouts or laughter, but sense only the tenseness.

When finally the door was opened, she was lying on Kemp's bunk, her arm across her eyes, trying to blot out the dancing reflections from the water. Sam Fletcher entered the cabin, with a plate and a tankard in his hand. 'You'd best eat,' he said firmly. 'Once the action starts, there'll be no time to wait on you.'

'Action?' She could feel her throat constricting.

'Ay, my lady. Action. An appointment we keep with three galleons bound for Woodbridge.' He grinned. 'We are sailing south now, to intercept them on the last leg of their journey.'

'But you can't!' Elaine flung herself from the bunk and caught at his arm, the memory of her father's gloating words flooding back to her. 'You mustn't try and intercept them. You'll be outnumbered . . .'

'We have a second ship with us today, *Sparrowhawk*, and the galleons are heavy laden and barely armed.' He looked at her with scorn. 'There isn't a sailor on these seas will lay down his life for some other man's cargo when he finds himself confronted with a fast-sailing, heavy-armed beauty like the *Witch*, or her mate out yonder.' He permitted himself a slight smile. 'You'd best hope you bring us luck, Lady Brandon.' He turned towards the door.

'Wait!' Elaine's cry brought him to a halt. 'You don't understand. It won't be only the galleons! Edward knows you intend to go after them. He will be escorting them with king's ships!'

Sam looked at her speculatively. 'I see. Did you tell Brandon of the captain's plans yourself?' The sting in his voice cut like a whiplash. 'And now you're afraid. You realise you are trapped with us on the *Witch*. You think you might be killed, perhaps?' She stepped back, but he went on. 'I'll tell the captain what you have said.'

Elaine was left standing at the door as he shut it behind him. She closed her eyes. So, in her attempt to warn Guy of the odds against him, she would succeed only in convincing him further of her betrayal . . . She had no time to think about it. The door swung open, and Kemp stood before her. He wore only a pair of breeches, like the majority of his men.

Her heart skipped a beat as her gaze travelled over his muscular frame. How was it possible that this man, whom she loved so much, had become her implacable enemy? But one glance at his face showed her that this was so. She tried to meet his eyes bravely. Whatever he did, she must never again let him see how much his rejection of her had hurt.

He folded his arms across his chest. 'You know Sir Edward's plans for me, I hear.'

She swallowed. 'My father told me. He has asked Edward to provide an armed escort for the ships on their journey from Gravesend.'

Kemp's eyes narrowed. 'And you feel that I should call off my attack? After all my planning, after your own assurances to the master of *Santa Anna*, you expect me to go quietly home and forget my raid?'

Elaine shook her head miserably. 'I just wanted to warn you.'

'Perhaps you wished to divert my attention? You are very good at that, after all.' His eyes narrowed. 'Perhaps there is no escort, and you have been sent to distract me, so the ships can safely run for their destination without any intervention from me. Did Ned leave you at the shack to wait for me?' He had not once raised his voice, but she felt that every man on the ship must be listening to his words. 'Let me tell you something, sweetheart. I am not going home. I have no home to go to, thanks to your husband, and I am not going to abandon this enterprise. Whatever Ned told you to say, I happen to know he is at Aldebourne with his mistress. He has been nowhere near Gravesend, and there are no ships in the King's commission in the Deben at the moment. We are going to sail to our rendezvous, Elaine; when those galleons appear tonight or tomorrow, we shall hit them out of this haze and you will be there to watch in your capacity as part owner of the pirate ship, *Black Witch*.'

'It will be five ships against two, then,' she whispered desperately.

'I've faced worse odds than that before.' He frowned. Then suddenly he lunged forward and caught her wrist. Dragging her to the door, he forced her to follow him out on deck. Standing at the foot of the mizzen-mast, he shouted for his crew.

Every man not busy with sailing the ship gathered round. She caught her breath to see so many. The *Witch* carried three times her original crew, and every man was armed to the teeth. She could feel their eyes on her, eyes full of hatred, and in spite of her vow not to show any fear she felt herself quail, drawing a step nearer Kemp as though he would give her protection.

'I have questioned Lady Brandon about her husband's plans for us,' he shouted, his voice carrying easily. 'She believes that he has arranged an armed escort for our treasure ships, and begs me to call off our attack. I say she is mistaken. I think she is here to persuade us to change our minds and creep away with our tails between our legs, while the treasure ships scuttle safely into the Deben without us.' He paused dramatically. 'But you may feel

differently. You may consider that the risk that she speaks
the truth is too great to ignore. It is up to you, men. Shall
we give up our treasure?'

'NO!'

The full-throated roar from the crew rose with frightening ferocity. Someone shook his fist right in her face. 'She's
a spy! A lying spy! Throw her overboard, captain!'

Elaine shrank back with a gasp, and felt Kemp's hand
on her shoulder, forcing her to stand her ground.

'I am not a despot, Elaine,' he said softly. 'My men have
their say in every decision that is made.'

''Tis unlucky to have a woman on a raid, Kemp!' another
voice shouted, carrying over the others from the back of
the crowd. 'She'll bring us no good.'

There was a slow murmur of agreement. One or two of
the sailors stepped forward angrily, and the thought of
being flung overboard paralysed her. Only Kemp stood
between her and the suspicion and superstitious anger of
his men.

He still held her shoulder, and stopped the muttering
around them with a gesture. '*Black Witch* sails against high
odds tomorrow, whether there are three ships or a dozen,
men. This woman is my amulet.' He grinned. 'A mermaid,
to stand at our prow.' She saw the fear deepen in the eyes
around her. Kemp smiled more broadly, and glancing up,
Elaine's blood grew even colder at the sight of it. 'Think,
men. Do you imagine the crew of Robert Howard's ships
will fire at their master's daughter? And do you believe
Ned Brandon would risk the life of his wife, if he does
appear?'

As his ringing tones died away, Elaine saw the men
glancing at one another, muttering between themselves.
One or two nodded, and she felt the tension drop as a
murmur of voices arose, and one or two bursts of laughter
lightened the seriousness of their faces.

'Back to your watches, men!' he called out. 'This ship
must fly like a bird tomorrow. Every rope and sail and
every shackle must be checked and every weapon made
ready. You may leave Lady Brandon to me!'

The throaty suggestive cheer that rang out brought a

mantle of scarlet to her face. He ignored the sound, thrusting her through the cabin door. 'Now you know the feelings of my crew,' he said. 'Your warning has been noted and dismissed. You may comfort yourself, my lady, that you could have done no more, whoever you were. I suggest that you rest now,' he went on curtly. 'You have food and drink. If you need further employment, I suggest you pray.'

Elaine turned to him. 'Thank you for stopping them from throwing me overboard,' she whispered. 'You saved my life.'

'I meant what I said out there, Elaine,' he replied coldly. 'You have caused too many deaths already. If having you on deck saves even one of my men tomorrow, then have you on deck I shall, even if I have to tie you to the mast.'

He looked down at her white face for a moment, then he swung out of the cabin.

CHAPTER
FOURTEEN

IT WAS still dark when Kemp returned, bringing a lantern. She lay on the bunk, not daring to move as he set the light on the table. He glanced towards her, then went to his sea-chest. He brought out his cutlass and a brace of knives before he stripped off his shirt and got out a fresh one.

She must have moved, for he turned and stared at her for a moment, then he came and stood over her. She had closed her eyes tightly, but she felt the thin mattress give as he sat on the edge of it. Gently he pushed the heavy curtain of hair off her face. Still she kept her eyes shut, trying to hold steady the rhythm of her breathing. At the touch of his lips on hers, however, she had to open them, and struggled to push him away. His hands caught hers at once, pinning them above her head as the shadowed blue eyes stared into her furious gold ones.

'So, my amulet is not asleep!' There was a hint of amusement in his voice. 'Tell me, what did Ned say when he found his bride had been bedded by another while his attention was distracted? Was the sacrifice worth it?' His hands had not relaxed on hers. She stared at him defiantly, feeling the familiar sensation of desire sweep over her, even as her body throbbed with shame.

'He does not know,' she said at last.

He raised an eyebrow. 'Oh? What happened when he collected you after your loving reunion at King's Brook? Did he forget?'

Her eyes were smouldering. 'He did not forget. Ours was not a loving reunion, whatever you may think. He forced me to return with him by threatening to tell Papa about Tom unless I went quietly.'

'Ah.' He smiled coldly. 'The secret your father must

never be told. Poor Elaine. Love makes one so vulnerable, does it not?'

She bit her lip. His voice had suddenly become so bitter. She tried to move her hands, but he continued to hold her, his fingers biting into her wrists.

'And you? Did you find that you loved Ned Brandon after all?' he asked.

'I hate him!'

'Then why? Why did you betray me?' His voice was harsh.

'I did not betray you,' she said in an agonised whisper.

'You didn't distract me from finding Ned at Aldebourne? You didn't bewitch me, so that I stayed the night at Kempsmere when I should have been long back to sea?'

She felt cold with horror. 'But none of that was deliberate! I didn't know . . . I didn't!'

'You knew, Elaine, that a troop of the king's men were already stationed at Woodbridge. You knew that Catchpole had been sent to fetch them, and that it would be only a matter of hours before they could reach Aldebourne. So why did you not tell me?'

Her eyes filled with tears. 'I never thought. I didn't realise . . .'

'You didn't realise,' he repeated softly. 'Ned took you back to Aldebourne by force, you say.'

'When we arrived, Lady Rosalind was there. She took Edward away and left me to Olivia.' She forced herself to keep her voice steady. 'Olivia had me locked up. Edward told her to whip me . . .' She turned her head away, indignant at the flash of laughter she had seen in his eyes.

But his mouth sought hers again, his lips caressing. 'And would a whipping have tamed you into a dutiful and obedient wife, Elaine?' he murmured.

She shook her head slowly, helpless beneath the touch of his kisses as he released her at last and brought his hands down over her body, sending fire down every nerve and sinew.

'Now we have the truth!' Between words, his tongue sought out the sensitive little hollows beneath her ears and in her throat. 'You admit that Ned dallies with his mistress at Aldebourne. He has no intention of escorting the galleons. You are tripped up by your own lies.'

She tried to raise herself and push at his chest. 'I am not lying! Papa said there would be an escort, and that Edward would arrange it.' His fingers slid inside the neckline of her gown and caressed her breasts, and she tried to ignore the sensations that flooded through her. 'Please, you must believe me! This time I am warning you. Now I do realise the significance of what Papa said. He said it was a trap.'

'And, this time, I think you are lying, Elaine.' Suddenly his voice was hard, and his caressing stopped. 'I want to believe you, but I can't. Your father's steward is in my pay. He told me you went willingly with your husband back to Aldebourne. The idea to provide an escort was discussed and dropped. The orders are that if there is any trouble, the convoy is to turn and run south for shelter in the Blackwater.'

She stared at him. 'Churchman told you that? He would not betray Papa!'

His eyes narrowed angrily. 'Enough, Elaine. I don't want to hear any more.' He stood. 'On one thing I agree with your husband wholeheartedly at this moment. You do deserve to be whipped. Maybe I'll give myself that pleasure once this enterprise is over.'

He turned from her, pulling his shirt on and buckling his broad belt round his waist. Thrusting his cutlass through it, he strode to the door and opened it.

The first grey light was filtering between the rigging. For a moment he stood, gazing round, then Elaine was left alone with her tears.

'Sail ho!'

The cry of the lookout in the crow's nest brought Elaine to her feet, her heart thumping with fear. She ran to the stern windows, but there was nothing to be seen except the mist, tongued overhead with pink and gold as the rising breeze began to shred it into tatters. The ship was silent, but she felt the angle of the hull steepen as they altered course a few points. The freshening wind was tearing holes in the whiteness, and the sea appeared, dark and cold, below it.

She went to go to the door, pulling at the latch, but it was barred from the outside. With a little sob she turned away, fighting to control the sudden fear that swept her body. The silence lasted a long time. There was nothing to tell her which way they were sailing, or who might be ahead, only the sound of rushing water beneath the stern and the creaming wake behind them.

Then, out of the silence, Kemp's voice rang out in an exultant challenge. 'Heave to, there! We are of the sea, and we demand your ships!'

The wild call was echoed by a roar of voices and suddenly mortar fire crashed out near her as the deck shuddered with the impact. Elaine cowered as a succession of explosions followed the first, and she caught the raw smell of gunpowder.

Only moments later there was an anguished crunch as *Black Witch* jarred against another large vessel, and feet thudded across the deck. Shouting and the clash of steel and two more deafening shots filled the air, kicking the ship as they fired amidships, then once more there was an unearthly silence.

She held her breath, shaking like a leaf as she stared out of the window. At first the sea remained empty, then at last she saw a great galleon drifting astern, her mainmast gone. Alongside her was the *Witch*'s sister ship, and on the deck of the injured vessel, a dozen of Kemp's men lifting the heavy hatches. There was no sign of her original crew. Transfixed by the sight, she waited for the sound of more fighting. But none came.

Then Kemp appeared at the door, grinning. 'Come, Lady Brandon. You are missing all the fun. Join me on deck, if you please.' His shirt was torn and blackened with powder-stains, but he appeared to be unhurt.

She cowered. 'So that you can tie me to the mast and taunt my father's men?'

He laughed. 'It seems that you have been spared that fate, my lady. I require you merely to stand with me and drink a glass of wine, if you will.'

'How many men have you killed?' Elaine demanded in anguish.

He frowned impatiently. 'Not one. They prudently surrendered on all three ships. As I said before, few men will die to protect a cargo which is not their own. Come, we are wasting time.'

She had no option but to follow him, almost blinded by the glare as she stumbled out of the cabin.

Two huge ships lay near them. Only the one she had seen from the windows appeared damaged. The decks of both were quiet. Alongside lay a third, held against the *Witch* by a cat's cradle of ropes and grapples, as sailors swarmed over her decks.

Kemp grinned triumphantly at Elaine. 'Come up to the poop—you can see better from there. I intend to take one of the ships. Sam shall sail her with the main part of the booty to one of our hideouts north of Dunwich. The dismasted one I shall leave to the crews of the three, and the third I shall burn.' His handsome face, tanned by the sun, was alight with satisfaction. 'You see, my dear,' he went on quietly. 'Piracy is not all barbarity. When the crews surrender sensibly, there is no need for bloodshed. How lucky that there were no armed ships to escort them, after all.' His mouth twitched slightly as he suppressed a smile.

Elaine was unable to meet his eyes. 'I'm glad I was wrong,' she said simply.

'So am I.' His voice became grim. Putting his hands on her shoulders, he propelled her towards the after rail. 'That is your father's ship, Elaine. The one with her mast shot away. She's called *Catherine*.'

Elaine nodded miserably. 'I know. I have heard Papa talk of her so often.'

All round them was activity as men systematically emptied their prizes into the second ship, *Santa Anna*. Then, at last, Sam approached with a grin. 'She's got as much as she'll carry now, captain. Permission to take a crew aboard, and I'll sail her home? Jake will bring *Sparrowhawk* to escort us.'

Kemp looked exultant. 'Take care of her, Sam. That

ship contains a king's ransom five times over. If she's fast, we'll keep her. She'll be your command.'

Sam beamed. 'I'll see she's fast, captain! I'll be waiting for you. Don't dally any longer. The mist-banks are lifting, and any minute we might have company. Remember the *Witch*, too, will be heavy laden.'

Kemp smiled. 'The *Witch* is faster than any ship, heavy laden or not.'

Sam touched his forelock. 'I'll be waiting for you, then.' His glance swept across Elaine without recognition, and she looked away, watching as every last case and barrel was brought aboard the *Witch* from the third ship, *Lady Eleanor*.

'As soon as she's empty, we'll fire her,' Kemp said quietly. 'Then we'll be on our way.'

Sam looked at him quizzically. 'What about *Catherine*?'

'I'm in a good mood. We'll leave the men in her hold. She can drift till someone rigs a jury-mast.'

'You want to spare her feelings, I suppose?' Elaine felt Sam's scornful eyes on her.

'Lady Brandon's feelings, Sam, do not concern me.' The harshness of Kemp's voice convinced her that he meant it. 'I have my own reasons for sparing the ship and the men. Now, I suggest that you go. As you say, we have delayed here long enough.'

Kemp watched in silence beside Elaine as Sam led a crew over the side of *Black Witch* and on to *Santa Anna*. They cut her free, and slowly the expanse of water between the two ships began to widen. Within minutes the galleon was showing sail once more, and almost at once she was veering off towards the north, wallowing slightly beneath her increased cargo as she drew away, closely followed by the smaller *Sparrowhawk*.

There was a cheer from *Black Witch*. Kemp smiled. 'Now we must do the same,' he said quietly. 'I hope you are not too shocked by the methods of our calling.' His eyes were teasing her.

He barked a command at the men on deck. The last of the cargo was brought aboard from the longboats and passed down the hatches. At once the sails on the *Witch* were being set again. A barrel of burning tar was loaded into a sling on the deck, and before Elaine's horrified eyes it was fired at close range on to the deserted deck of *Lady Eleanor*. To see so beautiful a ship so quickly hung with fire hurt like a physical pain.

'You are crying,' Kemp said softly.

'Of course I'm crying! You have robbed Papa and his friends. You have condemned that beautiful ship to sink, you have crippled my father's . . .' She turned to see *Catherine*, drifting further from them on the tide, no sign of movement on her decks. 'And, for all I know, you have cut the throats of every man on her.'

He looked at her soberly. 'I might, indeed. But I have a rich haul as a reward. Perhaps a tenth of what Ned Brandon and his friends stole from me when they condemned me to the life of an outlaw so that my brother could inherit my estate.' His voice was bitter. 'And don't tell me that your father was not part of the plan, Elaine. He knew, and he did nothing. That was enough. That was the reason Tom and I planned this raid.'

'Tom was a romantic fool!'

'Maybe.' He took her shoulders. 'But he was my friend. This was the last raid we had planned together. I believe, after it, he was half inclined to give up the sea. Who knows, perhaps I shall also retire now it's over. Once we are safe and the crews dispersed, perhaps I shall buy a farm of my own. What do you say? Do you like the idea of being a farmer's wife?'

Elaine shrugged. 'I am still Edward's wife,' she said, trying to still the sudden hope that flooded her heart.

'Ah, yes. My beautiful traitress—Edward's spy. But not, I think, his true wife, even yet.' The gleam in his eyes sent a hot shiver down her spine. 'Your brother understood two things well, Elaine. One of them was the sea—and the other was women. He said you needed a strong man to master you. Oh, yes.' He held her easily as she struggled to be free of his grip. 'And, by Our Lady, I shall be the one to do it.' There was something like amusement in his gaze. 'You are part of my prize today, Elaine, just as surely as the treasure that lies in the hold. You might have been free, here by my side of your own free will, but you chose to betray me. So you are here instead as my captive. And here you will stay at my pleasure.'

Her shiver of fear was interrupted by a shout.

'Two ships on the larboard quarter!' The lookout's thin cry floated over the sound of the wind and the waves.

With a violent curse, Kemp let her go, and ran to the bulwarks. The horizon was empty, bellying now with cloud, the water topped with spume. Then, as the *Witch* rose to the top of the swell, four small topsails came into view.

Kemp stared at them for a long time, his face grave, then he strode to the poop rail.

'Put on all sail!' he called. 'We'll outrun them, whoever they are!'

His glance swept over Elaine, who still had not moved. 'Perhaps, after all, your escort has materialised,' he said brusquely. 'I'm not taking any risks. We'll lose them before they get any closer.'

Witch heeled over and began to gather speed as the topsails were shaken out from the yards. Kemp made his way back to the larboard rail, his eyes narrowed as the ship threw up sheets of spray. 'We'll outrun them!' he said exultantly. '*Witch* likes a chase!'

'You think they are chasing us, then?' she asked.

'Oh, yes.' His eyes were half shut against the wind. 'They're after us, all right.'

Once or twice, standing beside him, she glanced at him, wondering if he would acknowledge that she had after all told him the truth, hoping that he would relent. But not once was his attention diverted from his ship. Was it her imagination, or were the distant sails larger now? There was tension in Kemp's face as he squinted at the compass and then up at the rigging, searching every detail to make sure it was giving its best.

All too soon it was clear that the other ships were gaining on them. Slowly the lower sails were becoming visible above the horizon, and before long the whole ships were in sight, creaming along under full canvas, their lack of cargo reflected in their speed as the *Witch* wallowed, her belly too full of treasure. There was little they could do. Kemp, expert though he was, could not outrun the faster boats. Inexorably they were gaining ground, the details of their rig and guns plainly visible now.

Elaine quailed as she saw the gunners busy on the distant decks beside the huge cannon.

Kemp saw it, too. Suddenly he seemed to remember she was there. 'Get below,' he ordered. 'And stay there!' He turned and strode towards the helm. 'Run out our guns!' Below them, the men began to pull, sweating, at the cannon. Gradually their pursuers began to draw level, one on either side of the *Witch*, and Kemp cursed again. 'They'll hit us with broadsides,' he muttered, as the ship strained every mast and cable in her fight for speed.

Elaine had not moved. Crouched in a corner of the deck, she clung to the rail, the spray in her hair, as a cannon opened fire on the leading ship and a huge cannonball whistled towards them, falling ahead off the starboard bow. It was followed by another, which tore through the far topsail and fell beyond the *Witch* in a fountain of spray. She screamed as two more explosions heralded further damage, and a hail of lethal splinters from the damaged oak of the ship's sides swept across the deck, cutting down a dozen men. The *Witch* lost way, her wind taken by one of her pursuers as she closed, and in seconds, beneath a shower of arrows, the huge ship had come alongside, barbed grapples flying over to bind the vessels together.

Soldiers poured over the side, wearing surcoats of the Brandon colours over their mail, swords and daggers ready drawn. After them came mariners, waving their cutlasses, while on the deck of the ship they had left, a line of archers stood, their weapons poised for another onslaught of arrows. In seconds there was fighting going on on every side, and Kemp had disappeared.

Elaine shrank back in horror against the rail, as two men fought near her, grunting and swearing, their feet slipping on the spray-wet decks drenched with sticky blood. Then, suddenly an arm was round her and she was dragged out of the fray. It was James Catchpole who pulled her out of the reach of the fighting men. 'Here, my lady,' he gasped. 'Sir Edward said I was to try and find you if you were here!' Like the others, he was wearing a corselet of steel. There was an angry cut down his arm, and the blood stained her gown where he had touched her.

An armed man approached them, his sword raised, his eyes alight with blood-lust as he saw her. Catchpole swept her behind him. 'Lay off, man!' he screamed. 'This is Lady Brandon! Use your eyes, you fool!'

The man lowered his sword and grinned. Then he turned away, furiously defending himself against Walt's determined cutlass.

'So you have a bodyguard to protect you!' Kemp was panting beside her, his cutlass dripping with blood, as he looked at Catchpole. 'I have no need to offer you my services, after all. The final proof that you are the spy I always suspected, my lady.'

'No!' she shouted. 'No, I swear. It's not what you think . . .' The bitter anger in his eyes frightened her as none of the fighting had done. 'I'm not one of them!'

But already he had turned away again, his cutlass slashing as two of Brandon's men descended on him.

'Guy! Oh, Guy!' Elaine's desperate cry was lost in the noise of the fighting as he disappeared again into the mêlée.

She flattened herself against the cabin wall, protected by Catchpole's stout body, watching as a tongue of flame ran up the broken mizzen-mast and licked at its network of shrouds and ratlines.

Minutes later, Walt fell at her feet, his arm half severed. She threw herself on her knees, trying to help him, but Catchpole was behind her at once, pulling her up, pulling her away. After one desperate glance over her shoulder towards the dying man, she was propelled through the thickest of the fighting towards the main deck. Edward was there, by the mainmast, sword in hand. Before him stood Kemp, held fast by three men. Edward was smiling.

The men who were holding Elaine released her at a sign from Edward and turned back into the fray; she saw that her skirts were stained with blood. Kemp struggled to raise his head. On his cheek there was a livid bruise. 'So, my lady,' he said huskily. 'Your husband did come to find you, after all.' He reeled as one of his captors tightened the armlock round his neck.

On all sides, Kemp's crew were being overcome. They were heavily outnumbered, and at the capture of their leader, the heart had gone out of them. Ignoring Elaine, Edward concentrated his full attention on Kemp.

'So, we have you at last,' he said with a twisted smile. 'And a merry dance you led us!' The fire in the sails and rigging was being doused, as the last of Kemp's men was thrown to the deck, bound. 'No, you'll not watch your ship burn yet. Her cargo is too precious,' he went on with a sneer. 'Only when she's empty shall I fire her. You can watch her then, before you hang.'

Elaine groaned, but Kemp had not flinched. He eyed Edward coolly, seeming not to notice the three men who held him so tightly, or the others who appeared, still panting from the fighting, bearing with them heavy shackles which they proceeded to hammer on to his wrists and ankles. Then he was dragged away. Edward watched as he was lowered into the hold of the ship, then finally he turned to Elaine.

For a moment he did not speak, eyeing her torn, stained gown and dishevelled hair, his gaze travelling the length of her body down to her bruised feet. Then he smiled. 'I once promised myself the pleasure of seeing you watch your lover hang,' he said softly. 'And, by Our Lady, I shall do that by dawn tomorrow. After that, I shall decide what your fate will be.'

He turned to one of his men. 'Put her in chains like her lover, and take her to the captain's cabin.'

Before Elaine could shrink back, two burly men were descending on her, forcing iron manacles on to her wrists and hammering them closed. Half fainting with fear and pain, she was pushed to the deck as her ankles were similarly shackled, then she was dragged towards Kemp's cabin and pushed inside.

Already the ship was under way again, turning back towards the shore, gathering speed as her new crew mastered the sails, cutting away the damaged rigging and bending new canvas to the yards. Painfully she went over to the bunk, and sat down in despair. The cabin had been untouched by the struggle. Even the half-empty mug of ale and the remains of the ship's biscuit still lay on the table.

The door crashed open and Edward appeared, his sword in his hand, as she lay back, her eyes closed, her head against the bulkhead. She sat up abruptly when he threw his sword down and looked at her. He smiled to see her chains. 'Expert as you have become at escaping, sweetheart, I think you'll find it impossible this time,' he said. He lowered himself to a stool and pulled the mug of ale towards him. He sniffed it and made a face. 'Catchpole!' he roared. 'Wine, and something to eat, for my lady and me!'

Elaine drew herself up, trying to hide the pain in her bruised wrists and ankles. 'Where are you intending to take us?' she said softly.

'So you haven't lost your tongue! We go to Orford, my lady. They have dungeons there, where we can make you and your friends comfortable. Until the hanging.' His body was flexing with the movement of the ship when Catchpole entered with a tray.

'They're well stocked with supplies.' Catchpole eyed Elaine uncomfortably as he took the wine and two goblets and put them on the table.

Elaine bit her lip. 'Does Sir Edward know it was you who released me from Aldebourne?' she asked suddenly. If she hoped to see him discomforted, she was disappointed. Edward threw back his head and laughed. 'Oh, yes, I know. It was I who told him to let you go! I was not going to let Olivia have the pleasure of whipping you, my dear —that is something I reserve for myself, if I decide to let you live. Besides, I thought your reactions would tell me once and for all if you were the traitor I suspected.'

He poured wine out and pushed a goblet towards her. 'We both see that I was right, Elaine. I'm sure you would like to drink with me to the downfall of the King's enemies.'

She turned away, leaving the wine untouched. 'I'm sure the King knows by now that you plotted against Guy and drove him from his inheritance. That you made him what he is.'

Edward looked at her quizzically. 'Who would believe it?' he said.

'There is proof.'

'Ah, yes. The letters Olivia told me about.' He laughed. 'I'm afraid no proof in the world will save Guy Kemp from the hangman tomorrow, Elaine. Nothing will.'

CHAPTER
FIFTEEN

THE PRISONERS were already on the quay. Mounted guards were menacing them with drawn swords as Elaine was brought out on deck when at last they reached Orford. As the tide rose, the ship had been warped against the quayside, and a gangplank had been run ashore. She was propelled, stumbling, along it to dry land. As soon as she reached the quay, she saw Kemp. Proud and cold, he stood aloof from the others, ignoring the drawn sword held at his back by one of the foot soldiers.

Without heeding the guards around them, she dragged herself towards him, forcing her aching legs to move, weighed down by the heavy shackles. No one stopped her. There was no movement on the quayside.

'Guy!' she whispered, but barely a sound came.

He looked down at her, slowly taking in the sight of her chains, and his gaze narrowed.

'Did you displease your husband again, Lady Brandon?' The mocking tone cut like a whip.

Fire sparked from her eyes. 'I displeased my husband, Guy,' she said boldly, 'by falling in love with the captain of *Black Witch*.'

She had not noticed Edward standing near them, holding back the guards with an upraised hand, nor the silent crew and their escort of soldiers. For her there was only one man on the quayside, and she clutched at his torn shirt. 'I did not betray you!' she cried. 'You must believe me.'

Slowly his hands came up to cover hers. His wrists were raw where the iron had chafed them, but he did not seem to notice. The blue of his eyes deepened as he bent to brush her lips with his own.

'I believe you.' His voice was husky. 'Would that I didn't, if it means that you will share my fate.'

She tried to cling to him. 'Guy, the King's pardon will come. It must!'

A shadow fell across them as Edward Brandon approached. 'There will be no pardon,' he said brusquely. His gaze swept over Elaine. 'And there will be no reprieve.' He swung away from them. 'Separate them!' he shouted at the staring guards.

Elaine did not scream or cry as a dozen hands dragged her from him. One minute her hands were held by his, warm and vital as they had always been, the next she was being dragged away up the track towards the castle. Slowly the whole procession of the captives and their escort made their way up to the towers and battlemented walls, across the bridge over the moat, and into the castle ward.

Her cell was small and damp, deep in the stone. One small window, too high for her to see out of, let in the air and enough light to show her only a heap of foul straw. The door grated shut behind her, and the bolt was shot home. Darkness came slowly, and with it intense cold. Slowly she paced up and down, unable to swing her arms to stop the violent shivering, as the watch called the hours from somewhere far away. Exhausted, she waited as the dark grew less intense and daylight came again, silent and stealthy. Swallowing her panic, she waited, facing the door, for the summons which would take her to her death. But none came. The light grew stronger, and with it a lessening of the cold, until it was full day. They brought her food, but that was all. She did not know if Kemp was alive or dead, and her prayers seemed to echo back to her from the thick stone of the walls.

At high noon on the second day the guard came for her. Her chains were struck off, leaving angry welts on her bruised limbs, and she was dragged up a long winding stair to a central chamber in the octagonal keep. Edward Brandon was standing there, looking out towards the sea.

As she was brought in, he looked at her with distaste. Then he snapped his fingers at an attendant who was waiting discreetly in the corner. 'Take Lady Brandon to the constable's chamber. She is to be made respectable,' he commanded.

Elaine said nothing. The sight of him filled her with loathing and fear as the guard propelled her back towards the spiral stair.

After a further long climb, she found two maids waiting for her with water and rough towels. They stripped off her filthy garments and bathed her aching body. They washed her hair in buckets of scented water, then carefully began to dress her. First a chemise of finest silk, heavily embroidered with gold thread; then a kirtle of deep blue velvet sewn with silver, and over it one of her own gowns, made as part of her trousseau, fifteen ells of rose-pink damask stitched with pearls. Her still-damp hair they combed out, tugging until the tears came to her eyes, before bundling it beneath a coif and silken veil. On her feet were shoes of midnight silk. Finally a heavy necklace of pearls and enamelled gold was clasped about her neck. Neither woman spoke to her as they went methodically about their tasks. Then the guard was summoned again, and she was led once more down the long spiral stair.

Within its stone walls, the huge chamber was cold in spite of the humid warmth of summer, and a driftwood fire smouldered in the draught of the chimney. Edward was standing before the fireplace. He, too, was dressed in rich brocade, a full-length fur-trimmed robe about his shoulders. Folding his arms, he leaned against the table at which he had been writing, and looked at her silently as the guards and servants withdrew. He gave a thin smile.

'Are you ready to die, my lady?' he asked softly.

Her mind blanked with fear, but she managed to control her expression. 'Quite ready,' she said in a low voice. It gave her a moment's satisfaction to see surprise and, perhaps, a little admiration in his face, both hastily hidden. Then he smiled, and all her revulsion returned.

'I have brought you here for several reasons. And I thought that as it was necessary to speak to you, I would at least make the experience pleasanter for myself by allowing you to look your most beautiful.' His eyes strayed across her body for a moment, before he reached out for a parchment lying on the table. 'This was among the ship's documents on *Black Witch*. It states, above your signature and your father's seal, that you are part owner.'

She raised her chin proudly. 'I am.'

'Then I think you should see her end, don't you?' He pushed himself away from the table and walked towards her. Catching her arm, he took her towards the window embrasure. It gave a view towards the short spit of shingle which marked the silver line of the sea. There, beneath the masses of thunder-cloud, two ships were heading out towards the open water.

Elaine at once recognised the graceful lines of *Black Witch* as the second one of the two. The vessels heeled before the wind, their sails set as they made good speed, racing before the strengthening westerly gale. For several minutes they sailed on, then of one accord they turned into the wind and lost way, sails shivering. Two small boats appeared at the stern of *Black Witch*, and the tiny figures of a dozen men swarmed down into them before they cast off their lines and began to row back towards the other vessel, which was almost at once under way again, setting course back down the coast.

She knew what was going to happen. Sick with misery, she saw the smoke drifting across the decks, as *Black Witch* yawed without a hand on her helm and red tongues of fire appeared, licking across the deck and drifting up the masts and along the rigging, seizing the sails with hungry suddenness.

She could feel the tears on her cheeks, but she was too proud to try to wipe them away, conscious that Edward was watching her closely. 'Is Guy dead?' she asked at last, her voice a whisper.

He smiled. 'Don't you remember? I promised that you would watch him hang. Did you think I had forgotten, and carried out the sentence without you? No. I wanted him to see his *Witch* burn first. Look.' He pointed to the curtain wall below them on the far side of the bailey.

Elaine caught her breath. A group of men were standing on the wall, staring out to sea, and even from that distance she could recognise the proud bearing and arrogant defiance of Kemp as he stood between his guards, watching his ship burn. She bit back a sob. She knew his heart must be breaking as he watched the fire racing up her masts and rigging, but he would never give them the satisfaction of showing it.

As though he could feel her eyes on him, he turned suddenly, gazing up at the keep, then he looked back out to sea.

'The next time you see him, he will be swinging on the gallows.' The quiet voice next to her was full of malice.

Elaine turned on Edward, her amber eyes blazing suddenly with fury. 'The King's pardon may still come!'

'No, Elaine. It won't come.' His tone was bored. 'If all this hope is based on my sister, give up. The first handsome courtier to cross her path in London will have carried her off, and her mission will have been forgotten. I know Jane a great deal better than you do. She starts something with enormous enthusiasm, then within a short time it is forgotten.' He smiled, reaching out to touch her cheek with a beringed finger. 'Your best hope, sweet Elaine, would be to try to cajole your husband.'

'Never!' She backed away. 'I belong to Guy. You have never been my husband! My place is with Guy, even on the gallows!'

'Oh no, my sweet!' He lunged forward. 'Not the gallows! You are not going to escape me as easily as that. If I hang you, I lose all your lovely inheritance.' He smiled. 'No, you are going to live with me, and love me, for the rest of your, no doubt, long and prosperous life.'

She paled, but he gripped her easily, his hand crushing her bruised wrist. 'Think, Elaine,' he went on in an undertone. 'Think. Supposing I were to spare Guy Kemp's life.'

She froze, her eyes meeting his suspiciously.

'That makes you pause,' he went on conversationally, his hold slackening slightly. 'I might consider it, if you were to persuade me. I think it is for you to say what happens to Master Kemp and his crew.' Smirking again, he released her.

Elaine was trembling. 'How do I know you're telling me the truth?'

'You don't. But surely it's worth a try?'

There was a tight knot of disgust in her stomach as he

moved his hands to her shoulders. 'As you rightly said, my dear, you are not yet my wife in anything but name,' he murmured. 'What more fitting than that we should spend our honeymoon here?' He brought his mouth down on hers slowly as he drew her into his arms.

Her body went rigid as she stood without resistance, allowing him to kiss her, and after a moment he drew back. 'You can do better than that, Elaine,' he said roughly. 'In fact you will have to do a great deal better if you wish me to change my mind about the hanging.'

He pulled her into his arms once more, and this time she reluctantly put her own about his neck.

Behind them, the door opened. There was a pause as the newcomer took in the scene, and Edward, releasing her from the kiss, slowly turned, his arms still round her. He let out a violent oath and pushed her away abruptly as Kemp stepped into the room, a naked sword in his hand.

Edward stood motionless before leaping for the table, dragging it between him and his opponent as he grabbed his own sword.

Elaine backed against the wall, incredulous hope sweeping through her. Moments before, she had seen Kemp on the curtain wall in chains, and now he was free!

She watched them circle each other, swords raised. They were of equal height, but Kemp's lithe form, dressed only in shirt and hose, moved as quickly as a cat. Edward, hampered by his fur robe and his heavier build, was sweating slightly as he read the murderous fury in Kemp's eyes.

The clash of swords jarred through Elaine's whole being while she watched, transfixed with terror, as she heard feet on the spiral staircase behind her, running up and up towards them. She turned in terror as Sam Fletcher arrived in the doorway, a dagger in his hand. He stood, panting slightly, seemingly content to watch his captain fight. Soon after faces appeared, crowding into the doorway, but no one entered the chamber.

'Help him,' she wanted to cry. 'Help him!' But no words came. Like them, she knew that this duel had to be fought alone.

Edward's breath was coming now in rasping gasps, and

sweat was pouring down his face as somehow he managed to rid himself of the robe, but he was tiring fast before the relentless fury of Kemp's attack.

The end, when it came, was sudden. One moment the two men were locked, their swords crossed below the hilt, their faces only inches from one another—then Kemp sprang back and lunged. For a second, Edward stood quite still, a look of astonishment on his face as the blade entered his body, then, his sword clattering to the flags, he lurched backwards and fell.

There was a long silence as Kemp stood looking at him, wiping the blade of his sword on Edward's robe. Then his men began to rush into the room.

'Hurry, captain!' Sam urged. 'We've got to get out of this place quickly. We can't hold the garrison for long. We're too outnumbered.'

Kemp turned. 'Out then, now. We'll go straight to the carrack by the quay. The last of the tide is with us if we hurry.' Then he looked at Elaine. His expression was cynical, and she was conscious suddenly of her fine gown, compared with his rags, and that when he entered the room she had been locked in what must have seemed a passionate embrace with her husband.

'No!' she whispered. 'How can I make you understand!'

'I understand perfectly,' he said quietly. 'You are, as ever, the mistress of duplicity. My consolations, my lady, on the death of your husband.' He turned away from her. 'Bring her!' he commanded. 'She'll still serve me as a hostage to her father.' Without looking back, he ran down the staircase towards the castle ward.

Elaine moved away uncertainly as two of his men approached her, but they seized her and led her down the stairs. At the bottom, they halted. Cautiously they peered into the lower chamber, which was normally alive with servants and soldiers, but at that moment it was deserted. With a grunt of satisfaction, one of them went to the outside door and the others followed, forcing her to run with them. The bailey was empty, the portcullis raised and the gates wide. No one seemed to be on guard.

A stitch was cutting like a knife into Elaine's side as she hurried with the men towards the quay. At first their way seemed clear, but as they fled, shouting people began to pour out of the township, waving bills and cudgels. From the castle, she heard the wild clanging of a bell. With one accord the men ran faster, dragging her with them, drawn swords in their hands.

It had been as dawn broke that Sam Fletcher had taken the three-masted carrack which lay by the quay, cutting the throats of the men who guarded her, and leaving ten of his own on board. His methodical plan to take the ship and infiltrate the castle had been formulated the moment he heard the news of Kemp's capture, and he and his men had travelled overland through the night, south towards Orford, desperate to reach their captain in time to save his life. For *Black Witch* they could do nothing—she was already out of the harbour as they crept into Orford. But while the garrison had crowded to the eastern walls to watch her burn, Sam and his men had slipped into the undefended bailey and taken the castle.

Kemp leaped to the helm of the captured ship, directing the crew, his eye on the sky. 'Hurry, men,' he cried. 'The wind is backing. We've only minutes to get out of here.'

A few spots of rain spattered across the deck as the ship began to drift from the quayside. Behind them the castle guard, free from wherever they had been imprisoned, came pouring down the track. A sudden spurt of flame and a crash from the high walls showed where the cannon were being trained on the harbour.

Kemp's face was tense as he watched his crew fend off the pursuers. Two feet from the quay, then five, then ten. The tide caught them, slowly moving towards the river mouth, but slick and deceptive shadows were catching the light. Kemp stared ahead, his helmsman straining for his every command. 'If we touch bottom, we're dead men.' His words cut the taut silence. At the mastheads, men hung in the rigging, while the sails flapped emptily.

Elaine held her breath too, her eyes on Kemp's face as they all waited for the keel to run into mud. Already the level of water had dropped several more inches. The river mouth was closer now, the beacon braziers on either side swinging slightly as the wind freshened and came round a point. Inch by inch they were gaining ground, past the windmill, on towards the open sea. Then the carrack gave a sudden shiver. Elaine gasped, and Kemp cursed softly. For a moment the ship hesitated as she sliced through the soft river bottom—then, with a shake, they were free. The coastline fell away on both sides and the ship was able to draw towards the south, heeling before the wind. Elaine murmured a prayer of thanks, but the men were still worried.

'We're too close in,' Sam muttered, and she saw Kemp nod curtly. The sea was dun-coloured, reflecting sand-bars close under the water, and the low sandy cliffs and marshes of the land were very close. The roar of the angry crowd was drowned by the rattle of the wind in the sails, but they all heard the reports as the cannon on the battlements opened fire one after another and saw the splashes as the balls hit the water ahead. Horsemen were following now, galloping parallel with them along the shore, and Elaine saw the muted gleam of armour. Every ounce of Kemp's skill was being brought to bear as he wrestled with the unfamiliar vessel, giving an inch and gaining two as the insistent north-easterly tried to nudge them back against the shore. Some time later, the motion of the ship changed. She had clawed her way out of the lee of the land and was sailing fast out towards the south.

'Lady Brandon?' The sailor at her elbow made her jump. 'Captain has ordered you inside, my lady.'

Kemp was standing in the rear cabin. He turned as she was brought in. 'The weather is turning foul,' he observed. 'I think you will be more comfortable in here.'

'Thank you.' She held her head high, her throat aching with the effort not to cry. She wanted to run to him, to feel his arms round her, to know that he still loved her as she loved him, but his eyes were cold.

'What are you going to do with me?'

Something like pain touched his face. 'I have not decided. First, we have to avoid our pursuers.'

She felt a new clutch of fear at her stomach. 'They've come after us?'

'Of course. Three ships.' He did not even glance out astern.

She shivered. There was no ship that she could see, but the thought of pursuers was frightening enough, hidden somewhere in the towering, toppling waves . . . Trying to concentrate on the sliding mass of water, distracted, she felt herself grow suddenly dizzy. The days of anguish, the hunger and lack of sleep, were catching up with her. She clutched at the bulkhead near her. He must not see her weakness. He must not . . .

'Are you ill?' His voice came from close by.

She shook her head slowly, feeling the blood draining from her head as the world began to spin. His arms were round her before she fell, and she knew she was being carried, her head resting against his chest, as, gently, he laid her on the bunk in the corner and sat beside her, holding her hands. But the blackness was sweeping over her, roaring in her ears. She felt his fingers warm on her cold forehead, and then she knew no more.

When she awoke, she was lying wrapped in a blanket. Kemp had vanished. The bunk was rocking violently, and in the distance, gunfire crashed again. With a little sob of fear, she staggered to her feet to find that her stiff heavy gown and kirtle had been removed. Beneath the blanket she wore only the embroidered chemise. Her hair had been loosened, and her face and neck were damp with rose-water.

Once more the guns thundered. She propped herself against the window and peered out. It was pitch dark. As a brilliant flash of lightning came, she realised that what she had heard was really thunder, not cannon.

'You're better.' The voice behind her took her by surprise, and she clutched the blanket round her tightly.

Kemp was standing in the doorway, a storm-lantern in his hand, his eyes alight with amusement.

'Why did you move my gown?' she asked breathlessly. 'You have no right . . .'

'I had every right.' He took a step nearer her. Her pulses

began to race as he contemplated her body. 'I have thrown a lot more overboard than an expensive gown, Elaine. I threw your lands and title, your inheritance, your wealth and your wedding ring.' His eyes gleamed as she held up her hand, where her finger was bare of its gold band. 'From now on, you are a pirate's woman.'

He caught the edge of her blanket, and drew her to him. 'Somehow I shall have to teach you to be loyal to me, Elaine,' he murmured as his lips found hers.

'I never betrayed you.' Her whisper was lost in the passion of his kiss. 'I swear it!' The blanket fell to the floor as he strained her against him. Her arms slipped round his neck and she clung to him, her body demanding his domination as he pulled her with him towards the bunk and began to rain kisses on her face and throat. Another crash of thunder echoed, but neither of them heard it. She was delirious with happiness.

'Kemp! You'd best come on deck. The wind's taking us back towards the shore!'

The man in the doorway was soaked to the skin, his greased leather jacket shedding water as he peered into the dark cabin.

For a moment Kemp did not move. His eyes held Elaine's, far away, piercing, sending a stab of desire through her whole body. Then he raised himself and stood up. 'I'll be back, sweetheart,' he whispered. He touched her lips with his finger, then he had gone.

She snuggled back into the warmth of her blanket, her body still trembling from his caresses, listening light-headed to the crash of thunder and the deafening roar of wind and water, and waited impatiently.

He did not return. Hours passed. She dozed. Then she woke, and it was still dark. The thunder was more distant now, but the wind seemed stronger. From somewhere aloft came a crash and shudder, and she felt the ship stagger as she slammed against the steepening waves.

Suddenly frightened, Elaine hauled herself upright, and dragged the door open, to look out. The decks were awash, and the two small sails that were still set were straining at the masts. Three men struggled to bring the nose of the ship round, and Kemp was with them, lending every ounce of his weight as he tried to make the ship answer their command. Even from where she stood, she could feel the fear among the crew: a fear she had never felt before in them, even when they faced battle and death. Following their gaze, she peered into the darkness . . . and then she gasped. Dead ahead lay the land. A beacon blazed in the distance, and near by she could make out some tiny lights.

A man was standing beside her suddenly, his hands raw from struggling with the ropes. He noticed her and grimaced. 'We're going in on a lee shore,' he shouted. 'Captain can't hold her. She sails like a barrel, not like *Black Witch*, God rest her wherever she lies . . .' His words were whipped away by the wind and he had gone to join the hands fighting to capture a flailing halyard. Elaine felt sick with fear. The ship, which earlier had seemed so solid and safe, bounced from wave to wave like a toy.

A particularly violent lurch dragged her grip free of the door-jamb to which she had been clinging, and she began to run across the deck. Kemp saw her and shot out his arm, catching her as she slid and stumbled. He pulled her to him, and his heartbeat was solidly slamming against her breast. Her blanket had gone, whipped away by the wind, leaving her clothed only in the thin chemise that clung to her in the soaking spray. For a second she felt Kemp's lips pressed against her hair. Then he grinned at her.

'So short a career as a pirate's lady!' he shouted, his words snatched by the storm. 'I'm sorry, my love.'

'Are we going to be wrecked?'

He nodded grimly. 'The bastard wind and the bitch sea turned on us finally,' he said. 'But for them, I'd have beaten Brandon's men. We'd have run for France or Scotland and made our fortunes there. But you still have a chance, love. Here.' He caught a rope passed to him by a sailor and he began to tie it round her waist. 'When we go, you'll be tied to these . . .' The man was pushing two empty water-casks towards her. 'They'll float you ashore as long as you don't struggle.' He held her face between his hands, staring at it, his eyes dark slits against the wind. Then his lips were on hers, warm and demanding. In spite of her fear, she felt a shiver of response.

The breakers were luminous on the shingle of the point, crashing in clouds of spray as the ship drove in. The crew were silent. They had ceased to fight the elements, lining the rail to watch the shore draw closer—and to see, beyond the spray, the crowd of armed men, some on horses, some on foot, and the dozens of villagers armed with sticks and bill-hooks, who waited for them by the light of the streaming beacon. One or two of them crossed themselves, and she saw their lips moving in prayer as another wave drove the vessel in closer.

Elaine hid her face against Kemp's shirt, clinging to him in despair, while with grinding fury the ship drove on to a shifting bank of sand and shingle. She capsized, before beginning the death-throes that would pound her into matchwood in the breakers.

CHAPTER
SIXTEEN

THE IMPACT tore Elaine out of Kemp's arms and across the deck, slamming her against the oak gunwales before a huge wave sucked her, spluttering and gasping, over the side. She clawed desperately for a hand-hold, but she was dragged and tossed away. The cold water closed over her head, suffocating her, as she reached up automatically towards the air. One hand found a rope, and she clutched it desperately; it held her, and she realised with frantic relief that it was attached to one of the empty water-barrels. Her head broke the surface for a second, long enough for her to snatch a choking gulp of air, before she was going down again into the milky greenness. A piece of wood bumped against her, knocking her half senseless, and her feet briefly touched the shingle, but another wave sucked her back into deep water and she felt herself begin to sink.

It was the last thing she knew. As the waves crashed round her, her body sank, pale in the clinging silk of the chemise, but the rope held, and one after another the empty casks bobbed to the surface, pounding towards the beach on the surf. The yells of the crew as they hit the water had turned to screams as they staggered out of the spray. The crowd waiting on the beach, encouraged by the shouts of the armed soldiers from Orford who had ridden down the coast as soon as the ship was spotted, had raised their weapons and attacked the half-drowned men ferociously as they staggered up the shingle.

Wreckage from the ship was being looted as soon as it came up on the beach, and one old man, his face alight with greed, saw the empty casks on the shingle. He pawed over them, and then noticed the near-naked girl. With a shout to his friends, he ran down and between them they turned her over, dragging her bruised body up the beach.

The movement revived her, and coughing and spluttering, she drew in an agonising gulp of air.

The man dropped her arm in surprise. Then he drew his knife. 'Pirate's whore!' he hissed. As he raised his arm, she opened her eyes. For a moment she lay dazed, then she screamed. But the agony did not come. With a surprised grunt the man doubled over, clubbed on the back of the head by a stone.

Kemp, soaked from head to foot, stood over him and snatched the knife. Then he whirled, astride Elaine's body, parrying the attack from the others. It was a swift battle and a bloody one. Kemp was an experienced fighter, the others slow-witted and afraid. One more body slumped beside that of the old man before the rest turned and fled.

Slicing through the cords that still bound her to the casks that had saved her life, Kemp picked her up. With a glance over his shoulder towards his men, he staggered with her towards the dunes. He put her down gently in a sandy depression among the marram grass and tenderly pushed her hair back from her face. 'Wait here, my love,' he whispered. 'I must do what I can to help my men.'

Elaine wept quietly, turning her head in the soft sand as she felt the rain cold on her face. It was a warm night, humid with the thunder, but the sudden squalls of wind were cold, and she was beginning to shiver. And now Kemp had gone back to the beach to die!

Slowly daylight was coming, and the beach was emptying as men staggered away from the sea, carrying what they had salvaged from the wreck. On the sand the murky light revealed piles of flotsam, and bodies lying among them, the sand still stained from the blood that had spilled and soaked away.

It was a long time before Kemp returned, and crouched by her. His face was grey with fatigue, his shirt hanging in shreds. 'Half the men are dead, and they hanged three from the beacon. But the rest have scattered inland. Come. We must move out of here. They'll be searching for survivors.' He slid his arm beneath her shoulders.

'I can walk.' Elaine struggled to stand, her body stiff and unnaturally cold.

'It'll be quicker if I carry you.' He gave her a ghost of a smile as he took her up. Stooping low, he began to move across the dunes. Gaunt Scots pine rose against the sky. Distant sheets of lightning still flickered as Kemp staggered on, not stopping to rest until they had found the comparative shelter of the trees. There he laid her down in the darkest shadows, and tried to coax some warmth back into her body.

'Are we safe now?' She could barely get the words out through chattering teeth as she clung to him, afraid that if she let him go for a second he would disappear again.

Somewhere a dog barked. He glanced round. Down to the left of them there was the dull gleam of the river, and he listened intently. The patter of dripping rain had lessened now, and a profound silence was settling on the countryside in the half light. He felt the shivering girl huddle against him, and he drew her close, nuzzling her wet hair. She smelt of salt and seaweed. He could never bring himself to tell her just how great their danger still was.

'We're safe now,' he murmured. 'They won't follow us up here, but even so'—reluctantly he began to get to his feet—'we can't risk stopping yet, and we must find somewhere warm and dry for you to rest.' Obediently she stood, too, swaying, and once again he picked her up.

They travelled for several hours, pausing frequently for rests and for him to chafe her freezing body, then just before midday they approached a lonely farmstead. Kemp laid her down on some hay in a lean-to shelter, and packed some of it round her in an attempt to keep her warm. The rain had stopped, and fitful sunshine was struggling through the heavy cloud.

'I'm going to see if it's safe for us to go to the house,' he whispered. 'I won't be long.'

She clutched at him. 'Don't leave me here!'

'I must.' He looked down at her. 'Try and sleep now. I'll be back very soon.' He piled more hay round her, and then he was gone.

Elaine was lost in a whirling land of mists; waves battered

her body, and she sank back into the cold waters that stifled her, tearing her limbs, bursting her lungs as she tried to scream.

Gentle hands bathed her burning body and anointed her bruised wrists and ankles; they gave her watered wine and herbal tinctures, then laid her back on soft pillows, but she did not know it. In the cool shadows of the room a succession of people came and went, tending her wants—but one was missing. Kemp never came, and when she fought her way back to consciousness and looked for him and he was not there, Elaine fell back, defeated, into the sea of fever.

It was a full week before she recovered enough to realise that Mab was sitting by her bed. The girl looked pale and strained, as she fumbled with her beads.

With an enormous effort Elaine stretched her hand out. 'Mab?' she whispered. 'Mab, is that you?'

Mab looked up, dropping her rosary with an incredulous cry. 'My lady? Oh, my Elaine, my little duck! You're better!' She smothered her with kisses. 'We thought you were going to die.'

Elaine managed to smile. 'It would take more than a silly fever to kill me,' she said slowly. 'Where are we? This isn't King's Brook.' She stared in puzzlement round the low-ceilinged room.

'We are with friends.' Mab stroked Elaine's hand. 'Do you remember what happened, my dear?' Her big eyes were soft with sympathy.

With an effort, Elaine gathered her scattered thoughts. 'I remember the wreck,' she said after a moment, and shivered violently. 'And then, lying on the beach in the waves . . . and the men waiting with knives and sticks . . . and the blood . . .' She bit her lip, fighting back the horror.

Mab squeezed her hand. 'Hush now! That's enough. You must rest.'

'No!' Elaine's eyes sought Mab's. 'Where is Guy?'

'He's safe, love.' Mab smiled at her reassuringly. 'Don't you fret about anything. Now, lie back and rest.'

'You're sure, Mab?' Elaine was trembling. 'I've had such bad dreams . . .'

'I'm sure.' Mab caught her other hand.

With an effort Elaine focused on her face. It was drawn, and there were shadowed rings beneath her eyes. She pulled herself together with a little grimace. 'Tell me what happened to you,' she said softly. 'How did you come here?'

Leaning forward, Mab laid a soothing hand on Elaine's forehead.

'After you went back to Aldebourne with Sir Edward, I didn't know what to do, so I stayed at King's Brook. Mistress Mary let me work for her. Then when Mistress Lockesley came back from Richmond, I went with her to find you. She went up to Southwold and then to Dunwich looking for Master Kemp, then Master Fletcher arrived with *Santa Anna*.' She grinned. 'Such celebrations there were when they arrived, with all those lovely things. Then only hours later we heard *Black Witch* had been taken. We thought you'd all been killed, but word came you'd escaped —then that you were prisoners. Master Fletcher gathered a rescue party, and they set off that same hour. He wouldn't let me come with him. He sent me to stay on the ship. The next thing I knew, there was a message from Master Kemp that you were here, and that I should come to you.'

Elaine managed another small smile. 'You didn't tell me where he is.'

'No one knows,' Mab blurted out. 'No one has heard from him since.'

Elaine closed her eyes. 'He said we were safe,' she murmured.

'And so you are, my duck! All you've got to do is get well and strong for him. He'll be back in his own good time.'

Suddenly bustling, the girl bent to pick up her rosary. She fastened it to her girdle and twitched the bed-covers straight. 'Now, no more talking till tomorrow. I'll go and fetch you some hot broth, then you must sleep,' she commanded. She dropped a kiss on Elaine's forehead.

Elaine was too tired to argue.

Her strength increased daily, under the combined minis-trations of Mab and her hostess Bet Kennedy, who was,

Elaine discovered, Sam Fletcher's sister. The stiff salt was washed out of her hair and her wasted body was bathed with almond milk and rose-water.

Sam Fletcher arrived as she rested in the sun. His face was solemn, but he smiled when he saw her. 'I misjudged you,' he said bluntly. 'I thought you were Brandon's plaything, but you didn't lie about those ships. Forgive me, my lady.'

Elaine felt her cheeks colour slightly. Until that moment, no one had mentioned Edward's name to her. With a shiver she recalled the vision of Edward falling to his knees, the sword still piercing his body.

'He really is dead?' she asked hesitantly.

Sam nodded.

She looked down at the grass. Bees were busy in the clover round her feet, and the air was loud with their humming. 'I'm glad.'

Sam pursed his lips. 'There are many would agree with you.'

'Please tell me where Guy is?' Her eyes were pleading.

He shrugged. 'We have both been scouring the countryside for the men. There were fifteen killed that night on the beach. Three drowned, and the rest beaten to death or hanged on the shore,' he said grimly. 'The others hid as best they could. He went back to find them. He won't rest until every man is accounted for.'

Elaine looked away. 'If it hadn't been for me, he would have stayed and helped them.'

'And likely been killed himself, my lady,' Sam said. 'It was Guy they were after, more than any of us. You saved each other.' He smiled. 'Don't fret. He'll turn up when he's ready. Meanwhile, I'm going back to Dunwich to supervise *Santa Anna* and take her to safety before anyone from Woodbridge starts nosing around the creeks and finds her.'

He left, and the days succeeded one another slowly, but still Guy did not come. And neither did Jane Lockesley. If she had told Sam anything of what had happened on her trip to London, he gave Elaine no information. Elaine fretted around the house, stronger now and almost herself again, the shining gold of her hair covered at Bet's insist-

ence by a widow's mourning veil. But still no word came.
The farm baked in the sun, and methodically the harvesting
began; men, women and children working from dawn to
dusk.

Then there was news. Mab heard it from a pedlar and
ran to find Elaine, who was in the still-room with Bet. She
turned eagerly as Mab burst in, but after one look at the
girl, the colour drained from her cheeks. 'What is it?
What's happened?'

Mab threw her arms round her and burst into sobs. 'The
countryside is alive with men. They are hunting for Master
Kemp, and for you!' Her blue eyes were blind with tears.
'My lady, you are being accused of Sir Edward's murder
at Orford. They say it was you that stabbed him with your
own hand! And that Master Kemp has fled to Scotland,'
she went on nervously.

'Who says that?' Elaine turned on her, her eyes blazing.
'He would not flee! If he had gone, Sam Fletcher would
have known and Bet would have told me.' She glanced at
the other woman.

For the first time, Bet spoke. She had been leaning on
the table, her gentle face heavy with concern. 'We'll send
for Sam. He must take you out of the country. Perhaps
you can go on this *Santa Anna* he is so proud of.'

Mab's face lit up. 'That's it! You must flee, my lady.
Master Kemp would want you safe above all else, wherever
he is. Can we send a message to Master Fletcher?' She
turned to Bet.

'I'll see that my brother is told quickly.' Bet turned
towards the door. 'Meanwhile we'll watch out for strangers,
and you'd best hide inside, my lady.'

A messenger was despatched within the hour. Elaine
and Mab watched him leave from the door of the farmhouse, then Elaine turned back inside. She climbed up to
the room she shared with Mab, and sat heavily on the bed.
If only the messenger could find Guy as well. If only Guy
would come for her! She longed for him so much.

Four days later, a carriage turned into the lane that led
to the farm, a dozen armed men riding behind it.

'Hide! For Our Lady's sake, hide!' Mab shrieked as she

ran in from the garden. 'They're here to look for you!' She
dragged Elaine towards the staircase. Her heart in her
mouth, Elaine followed her, heading for the smaller flight
that led up to the attic. There she squeezed into the dark
recess behind the chimneystack, her heart thumping so
loudly she felt sure it would be heard clear across the fields.
Her fingers to her lips, Mab disappeared down the stairs.
It seemed like hours, but it could have been only a few
minutes later that she reappeared. 'My lady,' she called.
'You can come out. I was watching from the windows. It's
Mistress Lockesley!'

Elaine got to her feet and crept out of her hiding-place.
'Jane?' she cried. 'Are you sure?'

She ran towards the stairs. On the first floor she paused
in the bedroom, untying her linen apron and flinging it on
the bed, her heart beating fast. Jane would know where
Guy was! Whatever the future held, whatever the news
from the King, nothing was as important to her as the
thought of seeing Guy again.

The main room of the farmhouse was empty. Puzzled,
Elaine stared round. Neither Bet nor her husband was
there, nor was their visitor, although the carriage was
standing in the yard. Behind it, the squadron of men stood
at ease beside their horses. Frowning uneasily, she was
turning back towards the stairs when the door from the
garden opened, and Jane appeared.

'Jane! I couldn't think where you were,' Elaine
exclaimed. 'Oh, I am happy to see you!' She ran towards
her sister-in-law, her hands outstretched. Then abruptly
she stopped.

Jane, dressed in severe black, had not moved from the
door. There was no answering smile on her face. Her eyes
were hard and cold. 'I was prepared to help you,' she said
slowly. 'I was prepared to do anything for you and Guy
and to see your marriage to Edward annulled. Why could
you not have waited? Why did you have to kill him?'

Elaine gasped. 'I didn't kill him! Edward was going to
hang Guy without trial. It was a fair fight . . .'

She backed away. There were, she now saw, four men
standing behind Jane, their faces impassive.

Jane's expression did not soften. Slowly she entered the room and stood aside to let the men in after her.

'There she is,' she cried clearly. 'This is Lady Brandon! You have the King's warrant for her arrest.'

Elaine stood motionless as the men stepped forward to surround her, her mind numb with disbelief. Jane had been her friend, her ally against Edward, her only hope for weeks as she prayed for Guy's pardon from the King. Now it was Jane who had brought not help, but betrayal!

There was no way of escape, and she moved obediently towards the door, not even glancing at Jane as she went out over the threshold towards the armed escort who would take her to her fate. The sun blinded her, and she did not glimpse the figure who had been waiting in the shelter of the stable.

Sam had remained carefully out of sight for several minutes as he watched the house and the dozen men who remained outside. He had followed them from Aldebourne, keeping to the shadows, reining back his horse to the pace of the stately carriage, almost certain he knew where Jane Lockesley was bound, pausing only to send a messenger towards the coast. Now he took a pace forward as Elaine appeared in the midst of her sombre escort, followed at a distance by Jane.

'I thought this was the way the wind blew, Mistress Lockesley,' he said grimly, his voice carrying in the silence of the yard, which was broken only by the stamping of the horses. He eyed the men at arms, who had stopped, their hands on the hilts of their swords, as he appeared, closing in more tightly on their prisoner.

'You do Lady Brandon a grave injustice if you think she killed her husband.'

Jane turned on him. 'What would you know, Sam Fletcher? You, a pirate and a murderer like your captain! And without the courage to stand and fight with him at the end.' Her eyes were bright with scorn.

Sam compressed his lips. 'Guy would not want me to let you take Lady Brandon.'

Two of Elaine's guards drew their swords. She caught her breath in terror—her eyes, like theirs, on Sam. He in

turn was watching Jane. 'What of the royal pardon you
told me his grace had been gracious enough to grant Guy?'
he went on swiftly.

'I burned it.' Jane looked defiant. 'The King would never
pardon the murderer of my brother.'

Elaine staggered. The King had granted the pardon—
and now it was gone! Her eyes were fixed in desperate hope
on Sam, when suddenly she caught sight of a movement in
the shadows behind him. Another man was standing there.
She saw the gleam of steel in his hand. Then there was
movement in the yard behind the carriage, and again on
the far side of the farmhouse itself. Every eye had been
fixed on Sam as he stood alone and unarmed in the bright
sunlight, but all around them men were appearing on silent
feet, armed with staves and cutlasses, creeping closer to
the escort who stood round her. She clenched her fists,
not letting herself move, concentrating on the exchange
between Sam and Jane.

Then she saw Guy. Sword in hand, he walked out into
the sunlight.

'Your brother was killed fairly, Jane.' His voice was
quiet, but in the silence his words rang clear. 'And it was
I alone who killed him. I fought him as an equal. Not as
his prisoner, but as a neighbour, who had fought a long
feud. He had a castle behind him, a hundred guards and a
trusted weapon in his hand, but God was on my side.' His
eyes blazed. 'And so, I hear, was the King. Don't think I
killed Ned lightly, Jane. He and I played together as boys.
Once he was my friend. It was his choice that it was no
longer so.'

For the first time, Guy looked at Elaine. He walked
towards her, ignoring her guards, who fell back, silently
watching Jane for orders. He pulled her to him, snatching
off her head-dress and veil.

'I claim Lady Brandon as mine,' he said softly. 'She was
never his wife in the eyes of God. And she was never his
murderer!' He swung back to Jane. 'You must be deranged
by Ned's death, or you of all people would never think
such a thing!'

He drew Elaine closer to him with one arm, the other

holding the sword before him. Then, slowly, he began to
move away, taking her with him as his men moved stealthily
out of the shadows, their cutlasses a protecting ring of
steel.

Jane did not stir. She seemed uncertain what to do,
and without her leadership, her men were obviously not
prepared to act. Elaine, glancing over her shoulder, saw
her watching as Guy led her away. The bleak terror that
had gripped her had gone, to be succeeded by stunned,
bewildered joy as she was lifted on to a horse and held in
the circle of Guy's arms. With a bow towards Jane, Sam
ordered the remaining men out of the yard, leaving her
standing, her face crumpling into tears.

Mab had not moved. For a moment she stood watching the scene, stunned, then with a cry of delight she picked
up her skirts and began to run after Elaine. One of Guy's
men stooped from his horse and scooped her up behind
him, then turned and galloped with her after his captain.

Elaine was conscious of nothing but the man who held
her so closely against his chest that they breathed and
moved and existed as one. Neither of them spoke. There
was no need.

The sun was low behind them when the horses crested a
rise and Elaine saw the broad Stour estuary laid out below.
A galleon lay at anchor out in the rippling tide. She closed
her eyes, trying to suppress a shiver as she looked down at
the ship. Guy felt it, as he had felt every breath and
every thought of the slim girl who lay in his arms, and he
understood. 'The sea is in gentle mood,' he whispered.
'She won't hurt us on this trip, my love.'

'Where are we going?' Elaine snuggled against him,
unwilling for their ride to end, not wanting him ever to
take his arms from around her body.

He smiled. 'France. The Low Countries. Scotland. Who
knows? As long as a man can be free.'

He sat in the stern of the longboat, his arm still round
her protectively as they were rowed out to *Santa Anna*,
then, once on deck, she was shown to the master cabin.
At the door, he bowed and blew her a kiss and left her

alone. The cabin was far bigger than that on the *Witch*, and richly furnished, the timbers ornately carved as befitted a merchant adventurer.

Mab followed her in, still giggling from her ride. 'Master Kemp says you're to change out of the black immediately, my lady. He says there is clothes in the chest by the bulkhead, whatever that is.'

Elaine smiled, and pointed to the vast brass-bound coffer, waiting while Mab dived in and extricated lengths of silks in the most exotic colours and covered in gold and silver embroidery. Some of them had been sewn into long flowing gowns, cut more like a chemise than the formal dresses Elaine was used to, and both girls exclaimed over their soft richness.

'But I can't wear these!' Elaine cried wistfully. She buried her face in the scented softness.

'Why not?' Guy had entered the cabin. 'The ship carries clothes which were fit for princesses of Arabia. They will serve my bride, surely?'

'Your bride?' Elaine lifted her face and stared at him, her heart thumping strangely.

He took her in his arms. 'It has been the tradition since ships first sailed the sea, my love, for a ship's captain, under certain circumstances, to perform the wedding rite. *Santa Anna* is Sam's ship now. He has agreed to marry us this very hour. It may not be a true wedding in the eyes of the church—I neither know nor care—but, to me, and my crew, and to my lady the sea, it will be true.' He smiled, his eyes devouring hers. 'Do you remember the first time I saw you, I thought you were a mermaid? Then, when you were pulled from the sea, you lay at my feet with your hair dark gold with brine and tangled with weed, and I knew I was right.' He raised her fingers to his lips. 'Mermaids do not wear black to their weddings, Elaine.' His eyes gleamed.

Elaine laughed. 'Then I shall change!' She stood on tiptoe and kissed his cheek. 'And you must go. You must not see me until I am ready!'

Mab pulled the heavy black gown and kirtle off her, and sponged her hot body with sea-water from a leather bucket.

Then she helped her into a long shift of transparent silk, the colour of clear aquamarine. Over it went a gown of pale blue and violet, laced with silver thread, and on her hair a veil of glittering gauze. Then a pair of strangely worked sandals with pointed toes was produced, and for her neck, filigree gold chains studded with enamelled flowers. Mab anointed her skin with some of the perfumed salves they found in another chest, and the bride was ready.

This wedding was so different from her first. On deck, beneath a crimson sunset as they rode at anchor on the tide, the entire ship's crew mustered to the pipe and in silence heard Sam repeat the words which would unite them, as Elaine put her hand in Guy's. He slipped a slim engraved gold ring on her finger, and then kissed her on the lips. A noisy cheer rang out, then one of the men produced a fiddle and began to play a dance-tune.

Long before the luminous summer dusk had turned to a brilliant starlit night, Guy had led her into the cabin and shut the door firmly as the jigging music went on on deck. Gently he unfastened the pins which held her veil, and tossed them away. Then he undid the ties of her gown, sliding the silk from her warm flesh so that it fell to the floor in diaphanous clouds. His face was inscrutable as he raised his hands and lightly touched her face. Slowly he ran his fingers down her throat to her shoulders, then he cupped her small breasts and dropped a lingering kiss on each rosy nipple. She closed her eyes with a little shudder of pleasure.

'No regrets, mermaid?' His eyes were slits of silver as he drew her close, his mouth against hers.

'No regrets,' she murmured. 'You are my master and my husband . . .'

He laid her on the bunk, then, stripping off his clothes, he paused to fill two silver goblets with wine before he sat down beside her. She pushed herself up on one elbow to take the goblet, her hair a silken cascade about her in the dusk, her eyes on his muscular tanned body as she felt once more the little ripples of excitement coursing through her veins. Softly he began to caress her once more, pushing her back against pillows scented with sandalwood and musk.

She felt his lips on her eyelids, whispering across her temples, nibbling her ear-lobes, before moving down possessively to her throat. Her hand involuntarily loosed its grip on the goblet and it slipped to the floor, but neither of them noticed. Of their own accord her fingers had moved feverishly up to clutch the wild tangle of his hair and then on to tease the sensitive nape of his neck. With an anguished groan he caught her wrists as his mouth roamed down over her breasts and he held her captive, as he made her his again and again, carrying her to the heights of passion with the almost savage frenzy of his love.

Outside the cabin, the music slowed a little beneath the starlight, and one by one the dancing feet hesitated and stopped, as exhausted and considerably the worse for wear for drink, the wedding guests slept.

Curled in the crook of her husband's arm, Elaine slept too, dreamlessly, her body warm and heavy with love, not even conscious of the slap of water against the ship's side near her head as the tide turned and the wind freshened with the dawn and the big galleon tugged impatiently at her moorings.

She did not feel Guy stir and slip naked from her, nor know that when he bent and kissed her lips she smiled in her sleep and gave a little moan of pleasure. She did not see him dress and tiptoe from the cabin to where Sam was waiting in silence. With a quick whispered word, Guy climbed over the side and began to row for the shore. A horse was waiting for him, grazing on the saltings.

For a long time he stood and watched as the sails of *Santa Anna* were unfurled and the anchor was hauled, dripping weed, from the estuary bed. Then, slowly, he mounted his horse. As the wind filled the sails and Sam Fletcher's ship heeled slightly to the helm, carrying Elaine out towards the open sea, Guy grimly turned his horse's head for London.

CHAPTER
SEVENTEEN

ELAINE WOKE slowly, secure in the warm, scented cocoon of furs, drifting up towards consciousness as she felt the fulfilled awareness of her body, satisfied, yet yearning for more. Gently she put out her hand, but Guy was not there. She sighed happily. He would be on deck, she knew, gazing at the horizon, his body swinging easily to the movement of the ship. Suddenly, unable to bear being out of his sight for another second, she sat up, throwing back the furs, and searched for something to put on. She had found the silk chemise and was slipping into a long shirt-like garment of deep crimson, embroidered with gold, when Mab came in with a tray.

'I've ale and bread and cakes, mistress,' she said with a smile. 'Breakfast for the captain's lady.' A slight shadow crossed her face.

Elaine paused as she was knotting a golden cord round her waist. 'What is it?' She knew Mab too well not to sense at once that something was wrong.

Mab forced her mouth into a smile again. 'Nothing!' She put down the tray and bent to pick up some of the scattered silks.

'Where are we going?' Elaine was still suspicious. Quickly she began to plait her hair.

'North, Sam Fletcher says. To Southwold, then perhaps as far as Scotland.' Mab looked down, her eyes filling with tears.

'But that's good!' Elaine caught her hand gently. 'We'll be safe in Scotland.'

'We'll be safe right enough, but not Master Kemp,' she whispered.

'What do you mean?' Elaine's voice was suddenly sharp with anxiety. 'Why won't he be safe?'

'He isn't coming with us, my duck. He's gone to London . . .' Mab broke off as Elaine pushed past her out through the cabin door.

Sam stood alone beside the helmsman, squinting into the sun, watching the crew clinging aloft as they set the topsails. There was no sign of Guy.

With anguish in her heart, Elaine ran to him. 'It's not true?' she whispered, clutching at his arm. 'Please tell me it's not true.'

Sam sadly shook his head. 'It is true he's ridden to London,' he said quietly. 'Be calm, mistress. Kemp knows what he's doing.' His sombre face softened a little as he looked at her. In the scarlet high-necked gown, so vivid and so strange a fashion with its eastern embroidery, with her hair half braided, blowing round her shoulders as she stared up at him from eyes as gold as the ring on her finger, she looked like some strange goddess. He resisted the temptation to cross himself, and smiled instead.

'It's for you he's gone,' he said softly. 'He wants you cleared of all blame for your husband's death. He said he could not live with himself, knowing you were wanted for any part of it.'

Elaine blenched. 'But he will be . . . arrested!' Her throat could hardly utter the word.

Sam gave a deep sigh. 'That is God's will,' he said after a minute. 'We can only leave it in His hands.'

For a moment, Elaine could not move or speak. Then she whirled back to the cabin, slamming the door behind her, sobs choking her as she held a kerchief to her mouth to stifle the sound. After all they'd been through! After all they had suffered: the misunderstandings, the terror—for her to lose him again seemed so bitterly unfair.

It was a long time before she calmed. Slowly she rose from the bunk where only a few short hours before his head had lain beside hers, and went to stare out at the sea.

She knew what she must do. She had to follow Guy to London, and stand at his side there as his wife. She did not want to live without him. If he had to die on the gallows, she would die with him.

Soberly she rebraided her hair, and tied a silk scarf over

it in as close an imitation of a coif as she could. When she caught sight of her ring, with an anguished clutch at her heart, she kissed it. It was in God's hands, Sam had said. And there would be plenty of time before they reached land for her to pray.

The low cliffs slipped by and drew closer as Sam felt his way in towards the harbour, and it was growing dusk as the ship was made fast and the crew began to disperse towards the taverns.

As though half anticipating her plan, Sam knocked on the cabin door. He looked at her closely. 'You will be safe here, Mistress Kemp. There are strong watchmen on the ship, and we've no reason to fear anyone in Southwold. We stay here for twenty-four hours, to take on water and supplies; then, with the right wind, we'll sail on north.' He smiled, the fatigue on his face making him look suddenly old. 'He'll be all right. You'll see. He has a way of winning his battles in the end, does our Kemp.'

Elaine managed to hold back her tears. 'I know.'

'You send your maid ashore tomorrow,' he went on, 'to get you some Christian clothes.' He sniffed disapprovingly. 'And get a good night's sleep now. God be with you, mistress.' He was gone.

She waited a long time before she tried the cabin door. It opened on to a deserted deck, but the lanterns of the watchmen shone out on the high forecastle.

'If you're going ashore, I'm going with you!' Mab's harsh whisper made her jump almost out of her skin. The girl had been waiting, half asleep, in the deep shadow of the cabin wall. 'You're going to follow him, aren't you? To the King.'

'I . . . I have to, Mab,' Elaine replied softly. 'But you needn't come.'

'Of course I need. Just how far do you think you'd get without me?' Mab grinned. She had a bundle at her feet, and hitching it to her girdle, she indicated the ladder up to the quay. 'You'll have to tuck your skirts up a bit to climb that,' she whispered with a giggle. 'Be thankful that it's dark!'

Quietly the two girls pulled themselves up the slippery

ladder, and after only a moment's hesitation, blinking in the flickering light of the brazier, they began to run towards the shadowed streets.

Mab led the way towards the crowded town centre, dodging into doorways if anyone stared too hard at the two unescorted women, one of whom was dressed in a gown of outlandish scarlet and gold.

After a while Mab pushed Elaine into an alley in the shelter of a twisted tree. 'Wait here,' she breathed. 'I must find something to cover that dress.' She had gone before Elaine could protest, down the street and out of sight.

Elaine waited, her heart thumping with fear, pressed back into the darkest shadows. It seemed an eternity before Mab returned, and already the streets were emptier as one by one the burgesses of Southwold made their way home.

Mab was astride a heavy-boned roan cob, her skirts hitched up to her knees as she guided it into the alley. Across the saddle in front of her lay a couple of black cloaks.

Grinning cheerfully, she slid from the horse's broad back. 'Meet Hercules!' She pulled one of the cloaks from the horse and wrapped it round Elaine. 'He may not move fast, but he's sound enough to get us well on our way, and he didn't cost a lot.' She tied the ribbons round Elaine's throat to fasten the cloak in place, and pulled the heavy hood up over the improvised coif. 'There! I defy anyone to recognise you under there,' she said with satisfaction. 'And if you're wondering where the money came from, Master Kemp gave it to me to buy you clothes. If we're stopped, we'll say we've been to the shrine of Our Lady at Walsingham as part of a penance!' She giggled.

In spite of herself Elaine smiled, cheered as always by Mab's unfailing good humour.

They travelled all night in the brilliant starlight, too afraid of being followed, once Sam had discovered they were missing, to stop, until at dawn they turned the horse loose in a small paddock, and nestling into a haystack, fell into an exhausted sleep.

As soon as they woke at midday, they rode on, keeping to well-trodden tracks, constantly alert for footpads. At

dusk they found a small inn, and Mab procured them a
bed with another coin from the supply she kept knotted in
her kerchief.

'How did you intend to live?' she asked indignantly, as
Elaine stared at the money.

'I was going to sell my wedding ring.' Elaine's voice was
barely more than a whisper as she looked at the bread and
cheese and ale the innkeeper's wife had brought.

'My duck! You wouldn't sell that!' Mab was horrified.
'Come on—eat and drink and sleep! We'll go quicker
tomorrow.'

However fast they rode, they were two days or more
behind Kemp. Elaine kept her thoughts only on the goal
of reaching London and finding the King. She would not
let herself think about what would happen then.

As they rode at last slowly and painfully into the narrow
streets of London, they were both tired, but Elaine felt a
strange elation. Soon—please let it be soon—she would
be with Guy.

The busy streets were noisy and crowded, but no one
they spoke to seemed to know or care about the whereabouts of the King. They were too much preoccupied with
the price of bread and vegetables to be concerned about
where the court was lodged. Whether it was at Westmins-
ter, Greenwich or Richmond, or perhaps further away,
still on its summer progress through the counties, they did
not care.

Elaine's eyes filled with tears of frustration. They had
ridden so far, yet she still seemed no closer to Guy than
when she had scrambled to the quay at Southwold.

'We're not asking the right people,' she sighed at last.
'We must find someone in authority.' The very people
they had been at such lengths to avoid on their journey
south!

Mab scowled. They were both covered in dust, their
clothes were torn and dirty, and the horse was exhausted.
'I warrant we'll be taken for vagrants if we approach a rich
man,' she said. 'We don't want to be thrown in gaol before
we ever get near the King.'

But Elaine would not be dissuaded, and within minutes

she was kicking the stumbling horse towards a group of velvet-clad young blades.

'Please, good sirs, can you tell me where the King holds his court?' she called.

They stopped and stared at her, and one or two began to jeer. Mab cowered back, and Elaine could feel the nervous clutch of the girl's hands round her waist, but she sat the horse erect, her cool eyes fixed on the young man who seemed to be their leader.

'God save you, mistress,' he said at last, pulling off his feathered cap. 'The King is at Greenwich, and we are going there ourselves. Perhaps we can escort you?'

She could see the puzzled glance he gave her gown, the scarlet skirt of which showed beneath her cloak. 'We have been on pilgrimage to Walsingham,' she said softly. 'Our journey is done, and we are seeking to rejoin my husband, who is with the King.'

He nodded, satisfied, riding beside her as he turned his horse south. 'You've had a long ride,' he said conversationally. He had seen her beautiful face, and caught sight of the gold of her hair as a random ray of sunshine strayed impertinently beneath her hood, but she was too tense to want to talk, and after a while he gave up, resigning himself to riding beside them in silence.

The young men rode confidently through the streets of London until they reached the Thames. There they dismounted, and leaving Hercules with their own horses at a livery, they commandeered a barge to take them downstream.

Greenwich Palace sprawled alongside the river, a maze of buildings old and new, lying sleepy in the country sun as the barge brought them ashore. The young man took Elaine's arm with a grin. 'You'd best give your name at the gate,' he said. 'Will your husband be near the King's grace?'

Elaine swallowed, growing more apprehensive now that they had arrived. She managed to smile at him, however. 'Thank you for helping us,' she said evasively. 'I shall find him easily, now that I'm here.'

The young men moved off, obviously reluctant to leave

them, but at last they were out of sight and the two girls were able to look about the crowded outer courtyard of the palace. 'What'll you do now?' Mab asked, awed by its size.

Elaine bit her lip. 'I have to find the King.' Some young men pushed past them with boisterous lewd comments, and she pulled her cloak round her defensively.

'They said to ask at the gatehouse,' Mab said uncertainly.

'I know.' Elaine glanced back. 'But they might turn us away.' Slowly she began to walk forward, following the direction taken by the young men towards the inner gateway.

Suddenly, behind, there was a commotion. People all around were bowing and curtsying, and Elaine turned, her heart beating fast. Was it the King? But the white horse that approached was being ridden by a woman.

''Tis the Queen,' Mab breathed. They stared at the tall, beautiful woman attired in silks and velvets. Her golden-brown hair was caught back beneath a head-dress of silver tissue, banded with scarlet silk, and her grey eyes were lively as she was followed by a noisy crowd of attendants. It was barely eighteen months since she had lost her last baby, but there was no sign of her deep sorrow as she looked around her, smiling.

Elaine, like those near her, curtsied low as the Queen passed by, then she straightened, meaning to follow in their wake. Behind Queen Katherine rode three beautifully gowned women, her ladies. Looking at them in some awe, Elaine found her eyes drawn to those of the woman at the rear, who was wearing the stark white wimple and heavy veil of full mourning, with the ebony train of her gown draped over the rump of her chestnut mare. It was the Lady Rosalind Berkeley.

For a moment Elaine's heart seemed to stop beating as Lady Rosalind abruptly reined in her horse and the eyes of the two women locked. Then Lady Rosalind turned away. She called out something sharply to the Queen's guard, and at once the pikemen broke formation and were running towards them. Elaine did not move. As the armed men surrounded her, she just stood looking up at her dead husband's mistress, wondering how so beautiful a woman could look so ugly.

She was lodged in a small room looking out over a grassed quadrangle. There was a guard at the end of the passage, but she had no heart to try and escape. Mab was allowed to attend her, and the food she was brought came, the girl said in awe, from the King's own kitchen. But, apart from Mab, she had contact with no one. Mab knew nothing. She had seen neither the Queen nor the Lady Rosalind again, and had no knowledge of the whereabouts of the King. She had not dared to ask about Kemp.

Two days passed, then another. Long days, when Elaine's nerves quivered with fear and frustration as she waited for news that never came. Then suddenly she had a visitor. The unfamiliar face in the doorway belonged to a young man of about twenty-eight, tall and handsome, but with his taut features softened by debauchery and a certain air of lassitude. He smiled at her mockingly, his eyes cutting, and she caught her breath. She knew those blue eyes. How often had she seen just that mocking challenge on the face of the man she loved . . .

Uncomfortably conscious of the bareness of the room and her position as a prisoner, even though there were no bars on the windows or locks on the doors, she rose, straightening out the skirt of her gown. Mab had failed in her attempts to obtain new clothes for her, even with her precious, but dwindling stock, of coins. It was as though orders had been given, somewhere, that Lady Brandon was to remain dressed as a princess of Arabia—a beautiful, exotic butterfly trapped in a cage out of reach of the sun.

With a barely sketched bow, her visitor came into the room and closed the door behind him. 'Lady Brandon?' he asked. His voice was thin and high, like a woman's, but there was an edge to it which made her shiver. 'It did not take you long, my lady, to revert to your title. Did you find plain Mistress Kemp beneath you?'

Elaine's cheeks blazed with sudden anger at the studied insolence of his words, but she controlled herself with an effort. 'It was as Lady Brandon, sir, that I was arrested,' she said softly. 'The King's warrant is in that name. But in my heart I am, and always shall be, Mistress Kemp.' Her eyes met his steadily.

'And, it appears, my sister-in-law!' He fingered his chin thoughtfully. 'It is only days since I found that my brother Guy still lives, and now I must meet my brother's wife as well.' His eyes took in every detail of her garb.

'Where is he?' Elaine moved towards him, her instinctive aversion to the man overwhelmed by her longing to see Guy again. 'Have you seen him? Please tell me!'

For a moment he did not answer. The eyes, so vital and so alive in his brother's face, were clouded in his blurred features, avoiding hers. 'He is here at Greenwich.'

'And can I see him? Oh please, my lord, can you arrange for me to see him?' Elaine clutched at his arm.

He took a step back, his face showing open distaste. 'My brother, madam, is a murderer, a pirate and a thief. Do you imagine he holds audiences, like the King?'

Elaine paled, her hope dying before it had a chance to take root in her heart. 'I am his wife! I have the right to be with him,' she said softly. She straightened, and he could not help looking into her face. Her cool gaze held his, and he was struck by her beauty. His eyes glinted, and he backed towards the door.

'It is for the King to decide whether or not you ever see him again,' he said slowly. There was an unnatural flush on his forehead. He groped for a kerchief and wiped his face with it. 'Perhaps he'll hang you together if you beg on your knees.' His voice was suddenly sharp with hatred, all his old jealousy of his brother welling up.

It was an hour before Mab reappeared. She had been exploring the vast palace as usual, trying to obtain news of Kemp, desperately attempting to find someone who would help her mistress. She walked by the two guards stationed in the passage that led to Elaine's room, and they let her pass with no more than a half-hearted leer, bored already by teasing the country girl from Suffolk with her broad vowels and her pink and white complexion. But they had on the whole, turned a blind eye to her comings and goings. When she came in, her face was alive with excitement. 'I think I've found a way to reach the King! There's a young man . . .' She blushed. 'I've talked to him quite often, and I've just found out that he's a gentleman of the bed-chamber!'

She had despaired of finding anyone who would help her, until at last she had smiled at Geoffrey Hastings. It took her two days to discover that he was so close to King Henry.

'He says you must write a letter,' she whispered. 'It's the only way.'

He had promised to see that the King received the letter. More than that he could not do . . . but it was something. Excitedly she produced pen and ink-horn and paper, and left Elaine alone while she went to collect her tray from the royal kitchens.

Elaine chewed the end of the quill in her anguish. How could she, in a few short lines, put down all she wanted to say? How could she persuade the King to see her; to allow her to see Guy; to honour his pardon? But as she dipped the pen into the ink, the words came.

Your grace.
It was I who killed my husband. I who owned more than half the pirate vessel Black Witch. It is I who should be blamed, not Guy Kemp. Please spare his life. He is a loyal and good subject. He would serve you faithfully until death. Please spare him, but let me see him once before I die . . .

The words poured out of her, pleading, desperate, squeezed on to the small single page, lines of narrow, frantic writing coming from her heart and soul. She stopped at last and threw down the pen miserably. Would the King bother even to glance at it? She doubted it very much indeed, but she had to try. She had to try anything at all.

When Mab returned, she left the tray of pigeon pie and quince jelly on the table, then tucked the folded letter into the neck of her gown, touched Elaine's hand, and went out.

Geoffrey was waiting for her by the river. Lost in the bustle of the palace—which seemed to her as large as a town—she had quickly made her way to the bank, watching the ships going up and down, and it had already become their favourite trysting-place. His face lit up and he put his arms round her eagerly, nuzzling her face, his hand fondling her breasts inside the low neck of her gown, but this time she pushed him away. 'I know what you're after, Geoffrey Hastings!' she giggled coyly, still flattered by the attentions of such a well-bred young man. 'And you'll not get it, not until you've done what you promised.' She brought out Elaine's letter and gave it to him. 'You see the King's grace gets this letter and reads it . . . . Then, we'll see.' She smiled at him archly.

'Oh, Mab!' He tucked the letter away and reached out for her again. 'There's no harm in us having a bit of a cuddle, surely?'

Mab dodged out of reach. 'When the King has read my lady's letter.'

'I said I could leave it where he'll see it,' he said crossly. 'I can't promise that he'll read it.'

'You'll have to make sure he does. Surely such an important gentleman as yourself can ask anything of the King?' She looked up at him, her eyes huge and bland, promising untold pleasures to them both if he would but comply.

It took her an hour, but he left her in the end, knowing he would get no further until Mab was satisfied that he had kept his side of their bargain. Jerking his doublet straight, his chin set in determination, he headed for the King's apartments.

The King sent for Elaine the next morning. He was surrounded by courtiers when her escort brought her, halting her some ten feet from him. Shaking with fear, she knelt, unable to look up. There was a long silence. Every eye was on her as slowly the King stepped forward. 'So, my Lady Brandon. It is not every day we entertain a lady pirate and a murderess at our court,' he said.

Elaine raised her eyes then. He was towering over her, hands on his hips, a tall, well-built man with tawny hair and beard and amused blue eyes. 'I confess, I have rarely seen so fearsome a rogue!' he went on over his shoulder, and there was a roar of laughter from the courtiers. He looked back down at her, extending his hand.

She kissed it miserably, but he went on to push back the hood of her cloak so that her hair tumbled about her shoulders.

His eyes lit up. He was a connoisseur of beautiful women. 'Lovely, indeed,' he said thoughtfully. 'Sir Edward must indeed have been a fool to alienate so desirable a wife. What is it, I wonder, that makes a woman ready to kill one husband, and yet ready to die to try to save another?'

She felt an icy shiver tiptoe down her spine at his words, but she held his gaze bravely. 'Love, your grace,' she said clearly.

'And love makes you claim the honour of having killed Sir Edward with your own hand?' He was looking at her thoughtfully.

'Sir Edward died in a fair fight, your grace. He was not murdered. But if anyone was to blame, it was I.'

'How can a fight with a woman be fair?'

The King's eyes were twinkling again, and he folded his arms. 'Your name, Lady Brandon—or should I perhaps address you as Mistress Kemp?—has been much mentioned to me lately in its various forms. I must confess I was very curious to meet you at last. Mistress Lockesley was, I remember, as passionate in your defence as she was later in your condemnation. Then came Lady Rosalind Berkeley, who appears to think you a vile criminal for whom the scaffold is too good. Henry Kemp tells me you are a witch who should be burned at the stake; his brother claims your absolute innocence . . . and now you say you are guilty!'

'He's here? Guy is here?' Elaine stared up at him in supplication. Out of all the King's words, one fact lodged in her brain, burning like a brand. The King must have spoken to Guy. 'Please, your grace, I beg you . . .' She was trying not to weep. 'Let me see him . . . before . . .' Her voice died away as she began to face the reality of the sentence which probably faced her. 'Before I die.'

'Such devotion,' he said gently. 'You will not have to

die, my lady. Guy Kemp is a lucky man. Would that I had such loyalty round me.' He smiled with sudden wistfulness as she raised her tearful eyes. Then he snapped his fingers.

'Ask Lord Kemp to join us,' he commanded. He stooped, and taking Elaine's hand, raised her to her feet. He looked her up and down solemnly. 'Court dress is obviously very different in Suffolk, madam?' he inquired.

She blushed. Beneath the homespun cloak, she was still wearing the diaphanous crimson silks she had found in the cabin of *Santa Anna*.

'I am sorry, sire. I had no way of changing,' she replied.

Behind them the door opened. She saw the King stare over her head at the newcomer.

'Ah,' he said. 'Lord Kemp. How is it you allow this lady to come to our presence quite so improperly attired?'

Elaine spun round, her hand still held fast in the King's great fist. It was not her visitor of the day before standing in the doorway, but Guy. And it was a Guy she had never seen. Dressed in elegant velvet doublet and slops of silk, he looked every inch a court gallant as he bowed to the King.

'My apologies, your grace,' he said with a chuckle. 'With your permission, I shall take her away at once and see she is attired more suitably.'

'Do so. And while you are setting your wife to rights, my lord, may I suggest that, from what you have told me, your marriage should be regularised before a priest.'

'It shall be done, sire.' Guy stepped forward, and took Elaine's hand with a grin. 'When I ask permission to present her next to your grace, I trust she will meet with your approval in every way.'

The King threw back his head and laughed. 'Indeed! I can tolerate such dangerous subjects in my kingdom only when they are impeccably dressed.' He planted a fat kiss on Elaine's cheek.

Curtsying to the ground, she allowed Guy to lead her out into the courtyard, where they stopped. His fingers tightened on her wrist, and he turned her to face him. 'What possessed you to come here and risk your life!' he said furiously. 'Was Sam out of his mind to let you do it?'

She stared at him, stunned by his sudden anger. 'I did not ask Sam! I came because I had to. My place was with you. Whatever happened!' She was hurt and confused. 'I thought you had come to take the blame, to save me . . . I thought I would find you on the gallows . . .'

'And you wanted to join me there? Oh, you silly, silly child!' Suddenly his arms went round her, his mouth lost in the golden haze of her hair. He cupped her face between his hands, gazing at her with eyes as unfathomable as the sea until she felt she was drowning, then at last his lips came down on hers. She gave a little moan, oblivious of the stares of the bustling men and women who came and went in the courtyard, and returned kiss for kiss.

'I was in no danger from the gallows after all,' he said softly when they had stopped for breath. 'Luckily for us, Jane Lockesley had done her work too well. She may have changed her mind about us when Edward died, but the King did not. He knew I had preyed only on those who had robbed me, and he had already heard what happened at Orford: he knew that it was a fair fight at the end. Your first husband, love, was not as high in the King's favour as he thought, for all his exotic relatives.' He laughed softly, caressing her shoulders until she shuddered with desire. 'His grace was pleased to tell me that he needed men like me to serve him. He admires seamanship above all else, and plans to build a great navy for England. I am to help him, by his special command. He has pardoned me for taking the law into my own hands. My men are pardoned with me, and Sam, too, shall have a place in the King's new ships.' His eyes were sparkling with enthusiasm.

'And your brother?' Elaine looked up, remembering her visit from Lord Kemp with a shudder.

His expression hardened. 'My brother was a fool,' he said slowly. 'But it is punishment enough for him to lose the title he coveted so much. His grace has banished him from court, and Kempsmere is once again mine. I plan to rebuild it, as I shall build another *Witch*. Can you bear to live again in Suffolk?' He looked down at her steadily, his eyes questioning as he scanned the pale, strained face, still so uncertain in its joy.

'I can live with you anywhere,' she said simply.

'Even with Olivia and Jane as neighbours?'

Taken aback, Elaine felt her face stiffen, but immediately she smiled again. 'Even with them.'

He grinned. 'Olivia, I think, will not be there. She is to go into a nunnery, I hear, where her talents for piety and penance can be used to the full. So only Jane is left to inherit Aldebourne—unless the grieving widow wants to claim the estate?' He looked at her quizzically.

Elaine shook her head. 'Let Jane keep it if she wants it. She deserves something after all her unhappiness.'

'And you won't hold against her her attempt to get you arrested?' Guy went on. 'I understand her grief at Ned's death. She and he never managed to agree, but he was all the family she had left, except for Olivia.'

Elaine's heart was touched. 'Jane and I are still sisters, as far as I'm concerned. But for Tom's sake, who loved her, not for Edward's.'

Guy grinned. 'Then you'll forgive her?'

'Of course.'

'So, finally, to the subject of your Papa.' Guy's eyes were suddenly dancing with humour. 'Even he is content with the way things have worked out, you'll be glad to hear. His daughter, after all, still has a title which I gather is important to him, and his new son-in-law, by some strange alchemy, has managed to return to him the booty so wickedly stolen by those pirates. Not all, admittedly —some was already dispersed among the villains'—he chortled unrepentantly. 'But enough to soothe his pride and his purse.'

Elaine flung her arms round Guy's neck. 'I never believed you were really all evil,' she murmured into his ear.

His grasp tightened. 'You didn't?'

She shook her head, laughing and breathless in his arms. 'Not in my heart of hearts. I am so pleased if Papa is happy again. I have prayed so often for him.'

'He is a selfish and miserly old man,' Guy said soberly. 'But, for your sake, I hope he prospers. And now'—he caught her wrists, gently disengaging himself from her embrace—'we have things to do. The King has commanded the presence of Lord and Lady Kemp at supper tonight in his private apartments. And before we obey that summons, we have to attend to your clothes.' The look he gave her made her catch her breath in suppressed excitement.

'What do you intend to do about my clothes?'

He grinned. 'Follow me to my chambers, and I'll show you. Eventually, I suppose, I must dress you in the latest and most expensive fashion to please the King and Queen, but in the meantime . . .'

'In the meantime, my lord?' she echoed. The gleam in his eyes left her in little doubt as to his intentions.

'In the meantime, I shall dispose of the clothes you have on,' he said softly, 'and remind my captive mermaid of her duties to her husband . . .'

Her secret from the past unlocked the door to her future.

In the Venice of 1819, the Contessa Allegra di Rienzi gave her love to the scandalous poet Lord Byron and left the legacy of a daughter he would never know.

Over 100 years later Allegra Brent discovered the secret of her ancestors and travelled to Venice in search of di Rienzi's heirs. There she met the bloodstirring Conte Renaldo di Rienzi and relived the passionate romance that started so long before.

W☺RLDWIDE

LEGACY OF PASSION.
Another longer romance for your enjoyment.

AVAILABLE FROM SEPTEMBER 1986. PRICE £2.95.